Honor Court
An Academic Thriller
Sid Stark

Want to keep in touch and hear about news and special offers first? Sign up for my mailing list and get your FREE novella by scanning the QR code below:

1

I HATE HOW HISTORY keeps coming back to haunt you, no matter how much you try to run away from it.

Right now, on the first day of classes for the 2016 spring semester, Chloe and I were catching up over an early lunch at Sullivan's, the nicest (and only) restaurant on campus, and trying to deal with a little of our own history.

Chloe and I had both started teaching at Crimson College the previous semester, me as a Visiting Assistant Professor of Russian, her as an Assistant Professor of Chinese. I was a "regular" hire. She was a "Special Diversity Hire." Crimson had brought her in as the college's first-ever African-American faculty member after a report had come out about the college's utter dearth of black faculty, and their overall unwelcoming atmosphere to black students. But as the college liked to remind us, thanks to a generous donation from Security Solutions, the private prison company that had given a pile of money to Crimson, they were able to hire Chloe, *and* to a tenure-track position.

We had both been incredibly grateful to have jobs, and ones that paid almost living wages. The sheen of our gratitude had dulled somewhat over the course of the fall semester, especially after one of my students had attempted to shoot one of Chloe's students during finals. I had tried to talk down Chris, my student, while Chloe had pulled Taylor, her student, to safety. Taylor, Chloe, and I had all escaped unscathed, at least physically. Mentally, we were maybe a little bit scarred. Especially, it seemed, Chloe.

Now she was pushing her Caesar salad around on her plate without looking at it. But she also couldn't bring herself to look at me. She had greeted me by saying that she *had* to talk to me, since no one else could understand what she was going through. Then she had chattered nervously about nothing for 20 minutes while failing to eat a bite of her salad. Judging by the weight she'd lost over winter break, she'd been failing to eat a lot.

"Taylor was in class this morning," she finally said, still not looking at me.

"How was that?" I asked.

"It was...it was weird. The whole thing was weird. I felt weird all break, and now that I'm back, I feel even weirder. It was so...it was so awful, what happened...Did you think you were going to die?"

"A bit," I said.

"I did. I could feel Death rising up to take me. As I lay there, my face pressed into the carpet, I could feel Death all around me, rising up out of the carpet to take me, filling the air all around me so that I was breathing it in with every breath, absorbing it with every pore. Death was coming for me, and there was nothing I could do about it."

"I know," I said.

"Yeah." Chloe shook her head, still not looking at me. "Yeah. And now it still feels like Death is with me every minute of every day. Especially when I was *there*. In my classroom. As soon as I stepped across the threshold, I felt Death rising up to take me once again."

"That's horrible," I said.

"And you know, I didn't *know* I was going to save Taylor until I did. Right up until the moment I grabbed her and pulled her into the classroom with me, I thought I was going to leave her there. I *wanted* to leave her there, with her blonde curls and all the men chasing after her. But then—it's funny how you can have so many thoughts at a moment like that—I realized that the way I felt about Taylor, and all those other blonde, pretty girls like her, the ones I kept hoping would have something bad happen to them, was like the way Celie felt at first about Sophia and Shug Avery in *The Color Purple*."

"Mmmmm," I said. Chloe did have a problem with other women. I had just never known how to point it out to her. Luckily, it was looking like I wouldn't have to.

"You know, I always hated Celie, especially at that moment, but here I was, thinking and acting just like her. Me hoping that men would come and teach all those pretty blonde girls a lesson was like Celie telling Harpo to beat up on Sophia because she wouldn't mind him. And I—I felt so ashamed of myself. And I knew that's not who I wanted to be. I didn't want to be the kind of woman who goes around telling men to beat up on other women."

"So you weren't," I said. "Just like Celie, in the end you stood up for yourself and other women."

"Yeah. Only...that was just the one time. What am I going to do the next time?"

"You'll do the right thing," I said. "I'm sure you will. And each time you do it, it will get easier."

"Maybe," said Chloe. "Anyway, since the...you know...the panic attacks I had all last fall have gotten really bad. I can't even set foot in Bedford Hall"—our classroom building was named Bedford Hall, quite possibly after the Confederate general Nathan Bedford Forrest— "without getting one. I don't know how I'm going to make it through the semester. And I've started seeing a therapist, and I've been really good about taking my meds and stuff, and none of it's helping. My therapist told me to go get a full physical work-up because I was freaking out about how maybe there was something really wrong with me, so that's what I spent winter break doing."

"What did the doctors tell you?" I asked.

"Well, first I went to see Doctor Blake, the same one who Mel"—Mel had joined the Crimson faculty at the same time we had, as a Visiting Assistant Professor of Arabic—"went to see last semester when she thought there was something wrong with her. You know, he wouldn't even do a proper physical exam? I know Mel said he was way too handsy for comfort, but with me he just sat on the other side of the examining room and told me I needed to see a psychiatrist. And maybe he's right, but it sure didn't make me feel any better about myself to have a known groper refuse to lay a finger on me. Like, am I really that ugly? I mean, Mel's a lesbian, and she's getting more action than me in that department. It's not right!"

"Um," I said. "Maybe. I mean, sure, being ignored by men is bad, but so is being groped and fondled in a gross creepy way."

"I guess. I'd like to have the chance to find out, though."

"Oh," I said. "Well, uh, so did you go see a psychiatrist?"

"Seems like I've seen dang near *everybody*. My dad—he's a surgeon—had to call in a bunch of favors to get them to see me so quickly, since normally you have to wait for weeks or months to get in to see a lot of these specialists. I don't know what happens if you're really sick. I guess you just die."

"I guess," I said. "So what did they say?"

She snorted, starting to loosen up now that she was angry instead of scared. "They all lectured me about losing weight and staying in shape and told me I have an 'aversive personality' and I'm just having a hard time adjusting to a 'real job.' They obviously thought I'm a total wimp who can't be trusted to get out of bed in the morning. I'm a black woman with a PhD from an Ivy League, Research 1 institution and a tenure-track job at a selective liberal arts college. What kind of person do they think I am? But they just told me to stop whining and lay off the fried chicken."

"I'm sorry. That's awful."

"I know. And then they kept going on and on about somatization disorder or some shit—did I just say that? I didn't mean to. It just kind of slipped out!"

"It's okay," I said. "I've heard worse."

"Yeah, I know you have, but I was still raised not to talk like that!"

"I won't tell if you won't tell."

"Deal. So, they kept going on and on about somatization disorder and did I have any episodes of childhood trauma and what was my difficult childhood like growing up in the 'hood. I told them I grew up in a loving nuclear family in a well-to-do suburb of Atlanta and I had about the least traumatic childhood a person could have, but they just shook their heads and muttered stuff about repressed memories and sent me to get more psychiatric counseling."

"Is it helping?" I asked.

She shrugged. "Maybe. I keep trying to tell myself that at least they didn't find anything really wrong with me, but I tell you what, there were times when I was hoping they *would*, just so that I could get them to take me seriously—is that girl trying to talk to us?"

A girl in a headscarf was edging towards us. *Gosh, she looks North Caucasian*, I thought.

"Professor Halley? The Russian professor?"

She sounds North Caucasian too. "Yes?" I said.

"I, um...I hoped I can talk to you," she said in a rush.

"Yes, of course."

"In Russian?" she asked hopefully.

"Of course," I said in Russian.

"Oh, thank God! I've been here for years but I still don't feel comfortable speaking English. My name's Aishat, by the way."

Boy, does she sound Chechen. The hairs on the back of my neck had risen at the sound of her distinctive Caucasian hard "n." Which was completely unfair. Probably she was a perfectly nice person who had nothing to do with the man who had held me at gunpoint in Moscow. But the visceral terror provoked by her accent remained.

"So is Russian your native language, then?" I asked.

"Well..." She looked down, twisting her toe on the floor. "Chechen," she mumbled, not catching my eye.

"I thought so," I said.

"Really?" Now she did look up. "Do you know many Chechens, then?"

"I've known some," I said. "Do you want to take Russian classes?" I couldn't think of any other reason for her to seek me out, although I was surprised that she would do that. There was not a lot of love lost between Chechens and Russians, as a general rule. But maybe it was the closest she could get here in small-town Georgia to reconnecting with her native culture.

"No." Now she was looking down at the ground again. "I, um...I might need your help. Over a question of honor."

2

OH GOD. "A question of honor" made me suspect we were dealing with a sexual assault issue. *Please let it be a cheating thing,* I prayed silently.

"Of course, I'll be glad to help you if I can," I said out loud. "What is it?"

"It's...well...did you have Owen Wu in your class?"

"Um, yes." Owen Wu was one of the Chinese students that Crimson had started admitting in large numbers. Families from mainland China were apparently thirsting to pay full sticker price to send their children to private colleges in the US. Most of them were keen students who spoke excellent English and brought a lively air of internationalism to the Crimson campus and Greenfields, Georgia (population 5,000).

I had had two such students in the second section of RUS 101 the previous semester. Jessica Chang and Owen Wu, to give them their Americanized names.

Jessica Chang combined two passions in life: Chinese nationalism and getting good grades. I could certainly sympathize with the latter, and I felt it was good for the American students to be exposed to the former, so I enjoyed having her in my class. She had gotten the top grade in RUS 101-002 last semester, signed up for RUS 102-002 this semester, and was already talking about doing an intensive study abroad over the summer. Jessica Chang was obviously going places, starting with the top of the Dean's List.

Owen Wu had been very different. Owen Wu had missed half his classes, shown up obviously hungover or high half the time when he did manage to drag himself into class, and failed to turn in 90% of his homework. As far as I could tell, the only thing he actually cared about was his frat and his sorority sister girlfriend. The only conversation of meaning we'd ever engaged in had been about her, when I'd said something about the Ukrainian gymnast Ganna Rizatdinova and Owen had said she reminded him of his girlfriend, Hannah Reiser. Then he'd disappeared for a week and flunked the next test. Since he had taken Russian before, he managed to scrape through the fall semester with a C-. There was no sign of him so far in either section of RUS 102, and I was hoping it would stay that way.

"What about Owen Wu?" I asked Aishat.

She rubbed the toe of her boot into the floor, and fiddled with the hem of her headscarf. "Can we talk about this somewhere alone?"

*Oh God. It's **definitely** something I don't want to get dragged into.* "Sure," I said out loud. "I have class from 12:00 to 1:00 today, but I'll be free after that. Can you come by my office at 1:00? It's Bedford 154."

"Uh, yeah. I can do that. Thank you." Aishat hovered for a moment indecisively, and then turned and walked hesitantly away.

"What was that all about?" asked Chloe. "What did she want?"

"To talk to me. Probably about testing into a Russian class." I highly doubted that was why Aishat wanted to talk to me, but that was the fiction I was going to go with for the moment.

"Oh God," said Chloe. "They can't leave us alone for a moment, can they?"

"Nope," I said. In fact, I didn't mind that my students often came to me for help or just attention. At least someone wanted me. But it was fashionable for faculty to complain about constant pestering by importunate students, so I pretended to go along with it. I had a strong tendency to rock the boat even without trying, so I made an effort not to make waves about things that were of secondary importance.

I checked my phone. 11:45. 15 minutes to pay up, double-time it across campus, and go teach my third class of the day. "I'd better go," I said. "But let's get together again soon, okay? Maybe Mel will be able to join us, too."

"Oh, right. You have class at 12:00. I guess..." Chloe looked down at her salad. "I guess I'll try to finish this off before teaching my one o'clock class. Although I don't like being here by myself. I always feel like everyone's looking at me."

"Maybe you can get a to-go box," I told her. As the only black faculty member, and one of the few black people on campus at all, Chloe tended to make heads turn wherever she went, and not in a flattering way. She didn't like to go places by herself because of it.

I left as she was negotiating the to-go box with the waitress. It was a more involved process than maybe it should have been, since Chloe was one of those people who always asked for very complicated things from wait staff. I made my escape as she was asking for two separate boxes so that she could split up the order into a serving for lunch and a serving for supper, with extra dressing on the side for both. Anyone who hadn't been looking at her before was certainly looking at her now.

I hustled through the dank January air across the front quad, around Lee Hall (the main administrative building, which may or may not have been named after Robert E. Lee), and onto the back quad. I was quick-stepping past Saunders Hall (home to English,

Classics, History, and half of Modern Languages; possibly named after a KKK leader) when, at 11:53, my phone *pinged*.

It was a text message from Alex. *Great news!* it said. *A Russian job has just opened up, practically right here in Monterey!*

3

REALLY? I wrote back. *What kind of a job?*

A VAP position at Carmel-by-the-Sea College. Just a few miles away from Monterey!

That's great, I texted. Alex, my boyfriend, taught Arabic at the Defense Language Institute in Monterey, California. It was a bit of a commute between there and Greenfields, Georgia. Since my VAP (Visiting Assistant Professor) position at Crimson College could be yanked away as soon as this semester, we had been talking quite a lot about me moving out to California to live with him.

We were both aware that it wasn't a great plan, since his position at the DLI wasn't much more secure than mine at Crimson. And there was the whole problem of him working with his ex-girlfriend. It was the still the best plan we'd managed to come up with. We'd assumed that I would have to quit teaching and leave academia in order to make it work, but now it looked like there might be a potential faculty job opening up nearby. Emphasis on the "potential." There would probably be somewhere between 50 and 150 other applicants for the position, and every one of them at least as qualified as I was.

I checked the time. 11:55. *I have to get to class*, I wrote. *I'll check in with you later, okay?*

No problem, he replied, as I sprinted into Bedford Hall at 11:58 and took the stairs two at a time to Bedford 218, where RUS/HUM 150, Introduction to Slavic Civilization, was waiting for me.

By the standards of Crimson College, RUS 150 was a big class, with sixteen students. There are a lot of downsides to tiny small-town colleges, but there are also upsides, and one of them is small class size.

RUS 150 had no prerequisites and fulfilled the Crosscultural Diversity general education requirement. It was filled with students who knew nothing about Slavic Civilization but were curious, or students who just had to fulfill their XD requirement and this was the only class that fit into their schedule. I spent the first part of the 50-minute class taking roll and trying to find the base level of knowledge about Eastern Europe. Once I had ascertained that half the students couldn't reliably find the former USSR on a map, I spent the rest of the class helping them learn the geographic location of the largest country in the world.

By 12:50 I had some confidence that most of the students knew where Russia was, and some of them even knew why that was important. A couple of them, most notably Alicia, an elfinly petite girl with a giant afro she'd died cotton candy pink and the only black student in the class, and Anthony, a tall, preppy-looking guy with an air of confidence that I hoped would be endearing rather than infuriating, even went so far as to make some astute observations about contemporary geopolitics and Eurasia.

Telling myself that this was an encouraging start, I dismissed class and set off at a brisk walk towards my office, on the first floor of Bedford Hall. If I was quick, I might even be able to check my email before Aishat showed up. My phone's notifications were telling me that I had already received a dozen messages about the start of the semester, all of them urgent.

When I came out of the stairwell, I saw Aishat waiting for me by the door to my office. But before I could go over to her, Karen, the Modern Languages department chair, came out of her office.

"Oh, Rowena, *there* you are," she said. "I've been looking for you all morning. We need to talk. You know this was supposed to be another probationary semester for you in any case, and after, well, *what happened*, it has been decided that your record must be examined *very carefully*. Come see me in my office right now, please."

"Um," I said. "I'm supposed to meet with a student..."

"Well, tell them to meet with you later! This is *important*. I want to see you taking your responsibilities as a Crimson faculty member seriously for once!"

"O-kay," I said. "I'll be right over."

Aishat was fidgeting nervously when I came up to her.

"I'm really sorry," I told her in Russian. "But my department chair wants to talk to me, and she says it has to be right now. Can we meet later? Maybe at 1:30 or 2:00?"

"My father will be coming to pick me up at 2:00. I'm not supposed to be out by myself after...What about tomorrow?"

"Tomorrow should work," I said. "Are you free at 11:00?"

"Yes," she said. "Tomorrow at 11:00. Thank you, professor."

"Of course," I told her. I watched her walk off, and then, steeling myself, I set off for my meeting with Karen.

4

KAREN HAD IMPRESSED me from our very first meeting with her bad temper and poor sense. Subsequent interactions had not improved my opinion of her. She had spent a good deal of the previous semester berating me for my incompetence and lack of school spirit, and suggesting that my contract was about to be terminated.

My contract had not been terminated, but she had told me that this semester was going to be another probationary semester. Since I was on a two-year contract, a probationary semester seemed like bullshit to me, but bullshit is the fertilizer for so much of what happens in large organizations.

After the shooting during finals week, I had given multiple statements to both campus and town police as well as the FBI, and undergone a lengthy interview with Jennifer from HR, who was heading up the internal investigation into the incident. No one had suggested that I was in any way at fault, or that my position at Crimson was in danger because of it. The repercussions of the shooting were likely to go rippling out for years, but I had been hoping that I had seen the end of the bureaucratic side of things. A vain hope, it seemed. Knowing Karen and her ilk, she had some particularly stupid yet refined torture lined up for me.

Don't blow your stack and do something you'll regret! I told myself as I walked with doom-laden footsteps up to her door. *She's not worth it! Just smile and go along with whatever she wants. It will all be over soon.*

"Oh, *there* you are," said Karen, when I knocked at her door. "What *took* you so long?"

"I had to explain things to my student."

"I *hope* you didn't tell her that you were on *probation*, under *investigation*," said Karen. "We don't want to do anything to harm student *morale*. It's already bad enough as it is!"

"I just told her you wanted to meet with me urgently," I said.

Karen pursed her mouth. She had a heavy, jowly face and a flabby, vaguely frog-like mouth that looked even worse when she made a face, which she did often.

I told myself that judging people by their physical appearance was shallow and immoral, and started clearing a pile of old papers and falling-apart textbooks off the guest chair. The desk was completely overflowing with homework, illegible notes, half-full coffee mugs growing mold, and cough drop wrappers, so I put the stack of papers and textbooks on the floor. Karen made another face at that, opened her mouth to say something, looked around, saw that there was nowhere else to put it, and made an unpleasant sniffing sound.

"So," she said, once I had seated myself gingerly in the chair. I started to cross my legs, and then stopped when I felt my trousers stick to something on the chair seat. I hoped it was just an old cough drop. I shifted cautiously. My trousers made a vaguely rude sound as I tore myself away from whatever it was. Good thing I had already taught all three of my classes today.

"Stop fidgeting," Karen told me severely. "Honestly, Rowena, you're like a student sometimes. I know you're young and inexperienced, but you're not *that* young."

"Thirty-five, in fact," I told her.

Karen looked startled, and then tried to conceal it. Most people mistook me for 5-10 years younger than my actual age. I knew many women envied me my youthful looks. In my chosen profession, however, visible signs of age were a marker of power and authority, so looking like I was still in my 20s was a disadvantage.

"*Anyway*," she said. "We need to make arrangements for you to have another teaching observation and performance review. After your rather *shaky* performance last semester, I want to make sure to get started on this early, in order to ensure that you are in fact teaching at a level appropriate for Crimson's *high standards.*"

She stopped and gave me what was supposed to be a stern look.

"Okay," I said. Why was it so hot in here? The heat must have just kicked on. Maybe that explained the sickening smell of mildew that was suddenly filling the room. "When would be good for you?"

"Well." She seemed taken aback at being put on the spot like that. "You see...we also have to arrange a time to hold the hearing about the, um...the *incident.*"

"There's going to be a hearing?" I asked.

"Of *course*. The senior administration is *very* concerned that such a, a *heinous* incident took place, right in our own classes. They are asking some *very* probing questions. I don't have to tell you how bad this makes us look. And I also don't—well, I *shouldn't*—have to tell you how disturbing it is that you *completely* failed to see any of the warning signs—or heed any of the *many* warnings I explicitly gave you that something like this might happen."

"Mmmmm," I said. Karen had pestered me repeatedly last semester about the fact that Miranda, one of my students, was a troublemaker. Only Miranda hadn't been involved in any of the troubles of last semester, except as a target. Chris and his semi-friend Nathan had been the troublemakers. And in my opinion, the true culprit was Nathan, who had been the leader of a Men's Rights group that put up blog posts blaming women for their unhappiness and fantasizing about rape and murder.

The actual members of the group hadn't had the wherewithal to carry out their fantasies, for which we should all be devoutly grateful, but Chris had sucked in their poison and decided to take revenge on the girls who had rejected him by coming into their final exams and...doing something bad. What exactly that bad thing was supposed to be was not clear to anyone, because Chris had ended up in a coma after getting shot himself and was still incoherent. But he'd shown up with an AR-15 and a .45 semi-automatic handgun, so we had to assume that mass murder had been on the agenda.

"This has caused me *so much* trouble," Karen was saying. "And will continue to cause a lot of trouble and inconvenience all semester, I'm sure. I want to hold your observation and evaluation as soon as possible, but I have been asked to find out your schedule and submit some possible dates for the hearing, and I want to make *sure* we do that first so that we don't have to reschedule the observation and make *even more* trouble."

"Okay," I said. "My teaching schedule is MTWF from nine to eleven, and twelve to one MWF. Any time other than that will probably work."

"Of *course,* for something as important as *this,* you may be called upon to cancel class. You should expect to adjust your schedule to theirs, rather than expect these *very* senior faculty and administrators to adjust their schedule to fit *your* convenience."

"No problem," I said.

"Well...well...I guess that's all for now, then. But be *sure* to be ready to attend the hearing whenever it's called!"

"Sure," I said, and, ripping myself free of the sticky chair, left.

5

IT WAS ONLY 1:15. AFTER picking off the remains of whatever sticky thing had stuck to the seat of my trousers, I hung around my office for a bit, hoping that maybe Aishat hadn't left yet and we could go ahead and talk about whatever difficult thing she wanted to talk about, but no such luck. Instead, I was forced to go through the emails that were stacking up in a holding pattern in my inbox.

I dealt with the least tedious of my emails first. It was a letter from Shaniqua, one of my students at UNC-Matthews, where I had taught as a one-semester adjunct the previous spring. Shaniqua's great-grandfather had gone over to the Soviet Union as part of the exodus of African-Americans fleeing Jim Crow. While it hadn't been the paradise of equality and freedom that they had hoped, Shaniqua's great-grandfather had survived the experience and come home with a Ukrainian bride. Shaniqua had started studying Russian as a way to find out more about that part of her family, and had gone on a study abroad program to Ukraine the previous summer. She'd sent me some updates about it while she'd been there, and now she was reaching out to me again.

Hi Rowena!

Hope you're having a great spring. Thanks so much again for writing that rec letter for me to go to Ukraine last year. I had a FABULOUS time and even got to visit the village where my great-grandmother came from. And I met a super-hot guy, just like you said I might :) Picture of me with Oliksiy is attached :) My family isn't super happy about it, but they say they understand—I must have gotten my taste for Ukrainians from my great-granddad ;)

I want to go back again this summer on the same program. It'll be my last chance before I graduate! Not sure what I'm going to do then :(Accounting doesn't seem so exciting anymore. Although maybe if I could do accounting in Ukraine...I'm not sure how friendly people would be to me there, though. I mean, I met lots of people who were very friendly to me, especially Oliksiy ;), but there were some pretty scary Nazi white supremacists too. Of course, we have them here too, but it was still kind of scary. I didn't have any trouble from them last summer, but Oliksiy has gotten some stuff from some of his friends that makes me worry. Though like I said, we've got lots of that bad stuff over here too, so...maybe I just need to follow my heart, huh? :)

Anyway, I'm hoping you'll be able to write another rec letter for me for the program and a scholarship that goes with it. I know it's been a year since I was your student, but I need two letters. I've already gotten one from Anna Ilinichna, my current Russian professor, but I was hoping you would give me one too. Of course, when I'm there I'll be studying Ukrainian, but I still thought rec letters from my Russian professors would be best. If you can't do it I understand, but I really hope you can!

Best,

Shaniqua

I wrote back that it would be no trouble for me to provide a letter of recommendation, and I would be happy to do so.

The neo-Nazi/white supremacist thing is concerning, I told her. *But I'm not sure there's anywhere you could go where you *wouldn't* encounter it right now. So I guess you might as well do what you want to do. Stay safe, and let me know how it goes!*

I spent a while staring at the picture of Shaniqua and Oliksiy. They had their arms around each other and were standing in front of a Ukrainian wooden house. Presumably far from the war zone. The war in Eastern Ukraine was still dragging on, although you wouldn't know it from their smiles. Love conquers all, and so on and so forth.

Well, enough of that, I told myself. Time to go through the rest of the emails.

But just then, as if conjured up out of my musings on love and war, or maybe my lack of desire to deal with my inbox, a message popped up on WhatsApp. From Dima.

6

ARE YOU BUSY RIGHT now?

No. What are you doing? Where are you?

I made three mistakes as I tried to type those lines, including in the word "No." From the fact that my hands were trembling, not because my Russian was so bad. I didn't know if that was comforting or not.

Dima and I had a history. We'd met back when I had been working for an NGO in Russia. I'd been collecting the stories of victims and eyewitnesses to various human rights abuses. Dima had come into my shabby, half-underground office and said that he'd been sent by a friend to tell his story.

"But maybe you don't want to hear it," he'd said. "After all, I'm not one of the good guys."

I'd said I listened to all stories without judgment. And I told myself that my willingness to listen to him had nothing to do with the way his shoulders strained against his shirt, or how his dark stubble emphasized the sharp lines of his Eurasian features, or how his eyes, so dark gray they were almost black, went from staring at the desk to staring at me as we spoke as if we shared some special secret.

The next day I met with him again. "To talk." About his former life in OMON, the Russian special forces riot police, and his current life as an investigative reporter. The next week he took me home to meet his mother. She had a story to tell too, about being the daughter and widow of war heroes. Eight months later we were engaged.

Eight years had passed since then. We'd never gotten married, or had kids, or done any of the things that we'd promised each other we were going to do. Instead, Dima had sent me away after I'd been kidnapped by men intent on stopping him from releasing his latest story. Then he'd left Moscow for the war in the Donbass, and not spoken to me for a year.

After both of us had ended up in life-or-death situations and decided we had to make peace with each other, we had come, very gingerly, back into contact. I had even thought last fall that Dima wanted to get back together. Then, after the shooting, he had told me he couldn't stand seeing me in danger anymore, and tried to cut off contact again.

That had lasted for all of three weeks before he'd texted me to wish me a happy New Year. He'd gone silent after that, but here he was, on January 11th, texting me again.

I was in the field, he wrote. *Working on a story. It's coming out tomorrow. Now I'm in Kiev. Talking to my new editor. He wants to fire me.*

Oh no! I replied. *Do you think you'll lose your job?* Dima was a war correspondent for *Nezavisimaya Pravda* (*Independent Truth*), an online opposition news source. It didn't pay well, but it did help Dima feed his conflict zone addiction.

Maybe, he wrote. *Might have to take up that job offer to do PR for the separatist battalion I was just embedded with)))*

Would you really do that? Dima, as a former OMON officer, had gotten several offers to join the Donbass separatists. So far he'd turned them all down. I knew he was drawn to the fighting, but I also knew that he believed both sides needed someone to criticize them, and that someone should be him.

Depends on how hungry and bored I am))))) Can you talk? On video?

My heart jumped. *Sure,* I texted back.

Thirty seconds later, his face was composing itself out of pixelated blobs on my screen. He had shaved off the beard he'd been wearing the last time I'd seen him in person. It was hard to tell through the grainy image, but I thought the scars on his jaw from when he'd been beaten up in the fall of 2013 were finally disappearing. He looked tired and worn, more like someone approaching middle age than the still-boyish young man he'd been when I'd first met him. But his features were still strikingly Eurasian, and his eyes still had that special something that marked him as intent, intelligent, and driven. Too bad it tended to drive him away from me.

"Thanks for agreeing to talk to me," he said, once the sound had connected.

"Of course. I'm always happy to talk to you."

"I have something I need to tell you, Inna. And I wanted to look you in the eyes as I said it."

"Okay." Sweat was trickling down my sides, and I felt sick, just as I had in Karen's office. Was he going to cut things off between us *again*? Or...tell me he'd met someone else and was planning to marry her? The very thought made me ill. I knew that was hypocritical of me in the extreme, since I was actively considering moving in with another man, but there it was. Dima had made it clear I should move on, and I was trying to, but I didn't think I could stand the thought of him moving on too.

"While I was in the field just now, I ran into a boy whom I saved in Chechnya."

"Oh. What was he doing in the Donbass?" Dima had done a couple of tours in the second Chechen war as part of his OMON service. The OMON had not exactly covered themselves with glory there. Dima had tried to make up for it a tiny amount by saving civilians, especially women and children, from the worst of his comrades' excesses.

The left side of Dima's mouth turned up in a non-smile. "Being a mercenary. It's a long story, one which will appear in detail in my forthcoming exposé article. But the point is that he believed he had a life debt before me, and he saved my life in order to repay it."

"Oh," I said. "Um. That's good."

"It is. And it made me realize..."

"Yes?" I said, when he didn't say anything for too many heartbeats.

"It made me realize that *I* have a life debt before *you*, Inna. You didn't stop a bullet for me or pull me out of a burning building, but you saved me just as surely as if you'd done those things, and now I have a life debt before you. I just don't know how to repay it."

"How do you want to repay it?" I asked.

He paused. "I don't know that either," he said. "I just know that I must."

"Is that a good thing or a bad thing?" I asked.

"I don't know that either. I'm afraid it's a bad thing. I'm afraid it will make me wreck your life once again."

"You never wrecked my life." I laughed, semi-tearfully. "You gave it a good try when you sent me away, but you never wrecked my life."

"Well, maybe this life debt is what will finally make me wreck it. But I'm selfish. I can't bear to go around with this unpaid debt hanging over me."

"So don't." I swallowed. It was so hard to say the words that might cut him off from me. "Do you want me to release you from your debt?"

"I don't think it works like that," he told me. "I think I can't be released, only redeemed. I just...is someone at the door?"

I turned around. Mel had poked her head in the half-open door.

"Sorry," she said. "I'll come back later."

But Dima had already hung up.

7

I WON'T BOTHER YOU anymore, Dima texted me after hanging up. *Goodbye, Inna. Go with God.*

Normally I was delighted to see Mel, but her interruption had been so inopportune, and Dima's response had been so unsatisfying, that I wanted to yell out something angry at both of them.

"No worries," I told Mel. "We were about done anyway. What's up?"

"You mean other than the usual first-day-of-class fuckups? I just got the last of the results back from all the tests and shit I had done over break."

"Anything interesting?" Mel had been having weird episodes all fall, culminating in a freaky seizure-y thing in my car the week of Thanksgiving. The cursory medical exams she'd gotten at the time had failed to turn anything up, so she'd thrown herself on the mercy of the VA and spent her break shuffling from doctor to doctor, getting poked and prodded and lectured about mental health and self-care.

"Nope. They've ruled out everything from leukemia to lupus to, what the fuck was it, myasthenia gravis. I'm the healthiest damn person they've ever seen."

"How do you feel?" I asked.

"Like shit. Like I still have the flu from hell that I just can't kick. I mean, I started getting the chills last night, and for a bit there I thought I was dying or some shit like that. I swear to God, that was the closest I've ever felt to death, even when I was Iraq. But when I woke up this morning, I was still alive."

"Still alive is good," I said.

"Yeah, but more days than not, I feel like shit. Like shittier than I thought it was humanly possible to feel."

"Including right now?" I asked.

She shrugged. "Now's not so great, I won't lie."

"Maybe you should go home," I suggested.

"Yeah, I probably should, but I've been feeling like shit since the beginning of last semester. If I went home every time it happened, I'd never be able to do anything at all. I already made it through my three classes, although I don't know how. Now I've got a meeting with Karen to discuss my performance and all that crap. Maybe that's what's making me feel so bad."

"I hope so," I said.

"Did she say anything to you? I know she was roaming the halls looking for you."

"Yeah," I said. "She told me I needed to set up another observation and performance evaluation pronto—and that there was going to be a hearing about the shooting. It didn't sound good. Like they're going to be putting us on trial. Have you heard anything about this?"

"No," said Mel. "But it sounds like just the kind of shit they'd pull. You know how universities love to hold their own extrajudicial trials. No doubt they'll find a way to blame us for almost getting shot."

"No doubt," I said.

8

THERE WAS STILL NO sign of Aishat after Mel left, so I concluded she had already gone home for the afternoon, and that I should do the same. I found my windowless closet of an office to be oppressively claustrophobic at the best of times. At the worst of times the very smell of it triggered nausea, migraines, and the peculiar sensation that my soul was becoming untethered from my body and floating somewhere slightly above me and to the left. I spent the absolute minimum there, and did all my real work at home.

Home for me was a 1-bedroom apartment at Peachtree Estates, a reasonably new and not too slummy apartment complex in a fairly slummy neighborhood about ten minutes from campus. It wasn't much, but it was the nicest place I'd ever lived in. Other than the teepee we'd lived in at that commune in rural Georgia when I'd been a small child. That had been awesome.

Alas, once my parents had left the commune, my living situation had never regained that former level of awesomeness. We'd lived in a series of crummy apartments and falling-down houses as they put themselves through grad school (my dad) and med school (my mom) while raising two children. Around the time my mother finished her residency and decided to take up a not-at-all-lucrative career at a clinic specializing in treating homeless drug addicts, I'd left home to go to school at the University of Georgia. Undergrad housing there was no worse than it was anywhere else in the 1990s, but it was a far cry from the kinds of swanky suites students at the better schools had now.

Then I'd graduated and moved to Moscow, where I'd lived in very unluxurious Soviet-style housing. After that I'd spent six years in grad school at Indiana University, experiencing all the delights of dealing with the petty slum lords there. Then I'd defended and graduated and gotten a real job, and my living situation had really gone downhill.

But now I not only had a real job, I had a real job paying $45,000/year. In a small Southern town that was enough to live in an okay-ish apartment, especially when your grandmother negotiated special rates for you. I could even shop in real grocery stores instead of dollar stores, and buy real food. My real food still mainly consisted of lentils and rice, but these days I frequently supplemented it with fresh vegetables.

I was still struggling to pay off the $5,000+ in credit card debt I'd racked up supporting my employment habit, though. I'd made some progress last semester, and then wiped most of it out by spending winter break visiting Alex in California and attending the annual AATSEEL (American Association of Teachers of Slavic and East European Languages) conference in Vancouver.

One of the perks of my current position was that I got $1,000 in travel expenses to attend conferences. Going to AATSEEL had cost $2,000, and I was still waiting to be reimbursed for the college's half of it, but seeing that $1,000 hit my bank account was an exciting thing to look forward to. I'd transfer it directly over to my credit card, and then I'd have a whole $1,452.37 left on my credit card limit. Enough to live off of for months if necessary. I'd still have $3,547.63 left on my balance, but it was only at 8.25% interest, which was practically nothing for a credit card, right? At least I didn't have any student loans, and my not-so-trusty fifteen-year-old Honda Civic was paid off. By contingent faculty standards, my financial situation was great. I'd never even had to go to a food pantry or apply for SNAP benefits, mainly because family members had stepped in and given me money when things had gotten really desperate.

And they might get desperate again if I lost this job. I'd applied for twenty jobs so far in this year's job market cycle. I'd gotten one first-round interview, for a visiting position in Ohio. The interview had been at AATSEEL, and had not, in my estimation, gone well. The interviewers had started off by asking if that shooting they'd read about had been at the same Crimson College I was currently working at. I'd had to say yes. Then they'd asked if I had been the Russian faculty member they'd read had been involved. I'd had to confess to that too. Then I'd been branded the professor whose student had tried to shoot her. It was hard to come back from that.

But maybe things would be different this spring. Maybe this job Alex had told me about would turn into something. Telling myself that reassuring thought, I texted him as soon as I got home, asking him what was up and if he had any more information about the job.

Hey, he texted back. *I'm 110 minutes into a 90-minute meeting that's still going strong. So, you know, the usual fun and good times. But I can send you a link to the job description and you can check it out.*

Thanks! I wrote. The link came through a minute later, and I clicked on it, full of entirely unwarranted optimism that I was clicking on my shiny new future.

9

THE JOB DESCRIPTION, when I clicked on it, was for a Visiting Assistant Professor of Russian at Carmel-by-the-Sea College. Carmel-by-the-Sea was a small town on the California coast, heavily populated by artists. Presumably well-healed artists. It had a small private arts/liberal arts college that had a tiny Russian program sandwiched in between its Pottery Arts and Creative Textiles programs. I wondered how many of the students had dreads and wore hand-dyed shirts. Probably a lot of them. Probably I would fit in there way better than I would like to admit.

Unfortunately, I wouldn't fit in there quite as well as the college would like. The job description specifically encouraged instructors with experience in arts or handicrafts to apply. Despite the best efforts of the adults around me at the commune I'd lived in as a child, I had zero skills in macrame-knotting, wood crafting, or carding, spinning, and knitting my own woolen garments. The only real skill I had in life was speaking fluent Russian. Maybe if I made it through to the final interview round, I could learn to make Orenburg lace shawls. Maybe that could be a side hustle for me so that I could afford the outrageous California housing prices.

Thinking those thoughts almost convinced me that it wasn't even worth applying. Probably there were dozens of eager candidates with native or near-native fluency in Russian, excellent pedagogical technique, an impressive research profile, *and* the ability to hand-carve and paint *khokhloma* wooden dishes.

Plus, the application required a separate teaching statement that specifically addressed the applicant's ability to teach in a small liberal arts/fine arts college environment, along with the usual cover letter, CV, research statement, writing sample, course evaluations, sample syllabi, and letters of recommendation.

I had all of that gathered together already, but the thought of rewriting my teaching statement, tweaking my cover letter, reformatting everything to meet this particular online portal's formatting requirements, paying to have my confidential letters of recommendation securely forwarded to the committee, and then sitting back and waiting anxiously to see if I was one of the lucky ones to get a first-round interview, was so disheartening that I wanted to go crawl under the covers and never come out.

Fevronia, the tan long-haired rescue cat I'd adopted as a way to distract myself from the original breaking-up-with-Dima fiasco, suddenly appeared from wherever she had been hiding and gave me a firm headbutt in the calf. When that failed to provoke an adequate response, she stood on her hind paws and started clawing at my trousers.

"You're so right," I told her, as I tried to gently disengage her before blood was shed or my one decent pair of trousers was irretrievably ruined. Fevronia believed in taking a firm stance with the humans around her, and making sure they didn't ignore her.

"I have to have a job, or how else am I going to be able to buy cat food?" I asked her.

She swatted at my hand, claws unsheathed, by way of response.

10

BY SUPPERTIME THAT night, I'd rewritten and reformatted all my application materials for the Carmel-by-the-Sea position. Bitter experience had taught me not to send out applications or other important documents at the end of a long, frazzling day, so I just saved them for a final review and send-out the next day.

On Tuesdays Mel and I both had classes from 9:00 to 11:00, so we'd agreed to carpool to campus together. In my car. After all of Mel's weird health problems, I was leery of letting her drive me around, even though she swore she was fine to be behind the wheel.

"I've got a meeting with a student at 11:00," I warned her. "I won't be able to leave right away after class."

"That's okay," she said. "I've got job apps to work on. And if that gets boring, I can prepare for the hearing, or something."

"Has it been scheduled already?" I asked.

She made a vague noise that could have been a sign of assent or a moan of distress. "I haven't heard anything yet."

"I wonder when they'll let us know," I said.

"No doubt Karen's waiting to spring it on us at a bad moment," said Mel. "I tell you, I've dealt with some pretty fucking shitty supervisors in my time, but Karen has to be right there near the top. I think she might be even worse than my language program director in grad school, and she was so bad that all the grad students took to creating two separate syllabi for each class. We'd make one that we'd submit to her, and one that we'd actually use. It was the only way to keep her bullshit off our backs." She looked sideways at me. "I don't think I've ever told that to anyone before. Most people would be horrified. Even other academics would be horrified."

"That's okay," I said. "I never had to go to quite that extreme in grad school, but I won't say I wasn't tempted. And I used to live in Russia. That sounds like perfectly rational behavior to me."

"Yeah. Any luck with any other jobs yet?"

I told her about the train wreck of an interview for the Ohio job, and the California job that had just popped up.

"California would be nice," she said. "Carmel-by-the-Sea's nice, in its own weirdo way." Mel had studied Arabic at the DLI as part of her Air Force career.

"I just applied for a job in California too," she said. She was looking out the window as she said it. "But in LA."

"Oh?"

"Yeah. Where I was adjuncting before. But this is a VAP position. So I might even be able to afford to take it."

"Would you want to move back to LA?" I asked.

"I don't know." She was still looking out the window. "There were some great things about it—but they were mostly about being with Jewel." Jewel was Mel's ex-girlfriend. "And there were some terrible things about it—and they were mostly about being with Jewel too. And Jewel is still there."

"Are you still in touch?" I asked.

She shrugged, moving like it cost her effort. "Sort of. Not really. And LA's a big town. It's not like we'd ever have to interact, or even run into each other. But we *could*."

"Yeah," I said. "Well, maybe see what happens with the application before you worry about anything else."

"Yeah," said Mel. She shook herself all over. At least, I hoped she was shaking herself, and not convulsing. She looked back over at me, her smile extra-wide from being forced. "And first we've got to get through this hearing, right?"

"Oh joy," I said.

Karen did not accost me in the hallway with portentous news about the hearing, as I'd feared. Instead, I was left to teach my two classes in peace. They went about as expected.

Most of the students from the first section were quiet and timid, obviously still shocked by what had happened last semester. Even Miranda, the most outspoken of the students in that section, kept her head down and hardly said anything.

She'd shed her goth-rocker eye shadow over winter break, and had transformed the edgy undercut hairstyle she'd had last semester, with its harsh black dye job, dramatic pointed slice over her left eye, and highlights of bright purple and robins-egg blue, into a simple bob. Most of the highlights had been chopped off or covered up, and what I assumed was her natural dark auburn was growing in. I was willing to bet that by the end of the semester the transformation I had foreseen for her, from goth rebel to wholesome do-gooder, would be complete.

I just hoped she would hold up psychologically in the meantime. She'd volunteered to go out and face a shooter, and that could leave a long-term scar. Worse than that, the shooter had been her friend, and had blamed her for his actions. She must be wondering how many other people felt the same way, and whether there was some truth to that accusation.

The students in the second section, who had not been present for the shooting, were their normal student selves. Most of them had forgotten most of their Russian over break. Only Jessica Chang had spent the break pre-studying the material for this semester, as she made sure to inform everyone.

After class I extracted myself from Jessica's clutches—she grabbed me and demanded to know what was going to be on the first vocab quiz of the semester, and whether there would be review exercises posted before the first test—and quickstepped over to my office for my meeting with Aishat.

I had been half-hoping that Aishat wouldn't show. I wanted to help her, and I was curious about what her problem was, but I was also afraid of getting sucked into a horrible sexual assault case.

Sexual assault cases were terrible enough in general, but American colleges, in their infinite wisdom, had in their attempts to stop the problem done some things that made it worse. For example, any member of the college faculty or staff who found out about a sexual assault was required to report it. In principle this was supposed to ensure that sexual assault cases were not swept under the rug, as was the norm.

In practice, in meant that victims had no one to turn to. Since reporting a sexual assault normally meant an excruciating ordeal for the victim, and precious little chance of getting any kind of justice or satisfaction, most people were understandably reluctant to report their assaults. And they couldn't speak unofficially with a sympathetic resident advisor, faculty member, counselor, or anyone else who might help them out and advise them. As with so much of the legal system when it came to women, the laws designed ostensibly to protect them from abuse and injustice just recreated that abuse and injustice.

I hated it. I just didn't think I was going to be able to change it singlehandedly, and so, like a coward, I wanted to stay well away from it. Plus, I already had enough bad juju attached to me with the shooting. I needed to clear my name of all the bad vibes associated with that before I got involved in anything else controversial.

All those good intensions melted away when I found Aishat waiting for me at the door to my office. She looked so much like so many of the women I had listened to when I had been investigating human rights abuses in Russia. She was dressed in a below-the-knee skirt and modest blouse, with Caucasian (as in, from the Caucasus) prominent cheekbones and strong chin, and just the right amount of dark hair peeking out from her headscarf. Having just the right amount of hair exposed was of life-or-death importance. Going around with your hair uncovered in the wrong neighborhood could get you hassled, arrested, or killed for not being sufficiently modest and following Sharia law. Arranging your headscarf too modestly and covering too much of your hair and forehead could get you labeled a Wahhabite and killed for extremism. The perfect example of the fine line women had to walk everywhere.

Aishat responded to my greeting with a silent nod, and remained silent as she followed me into my office. When I shut the door she relaxed a little, but refused my offer of a seat with a wordless shake of her head.

"Well," I said, when the silence had been going on for longer than I could stand. "Why don't you tell me how I can help you."

Aishat rubbed one booted foot anxiously with the other. "Well," she said. She crossed her arms, then uncrossed them self-consciously, and started rubbing the other foot. "I don't know how to tell you..." she began, and then stopped.

"Is it about Owen Wu?" I asked.

Relief filled her face at this way into the conversation. She really was quite pretty, in a strong-featured, dark-complexioned fashion. I wondered how long she had been in the US. Everything about her, from her clothes to her posture to her facial expressions, screamed "foreigner." That must be difficult in small-town Georgia.

"Did Owen Wu hurt you in some way?" I asked.

"Well," she said. She fidgeted from foot to foot for a moment, and then, gripping the back of the chair I had offered her and visibly steeling herself, said, "That's the thing. I think so. But I don't know. But my father and my brothers want to avenge my honor even so."

11

OH FUCK, I thought. "I'm very sorry you're having to deal with this problem," I said out loud. "How can I help you?"

"Well..." She squirmed some more, still clutching the back of the chair with both hands. Since she was standing, I didn't feel like I could sit down either. But after teaching two classes back-to-back my feet ached, and there was a dull pain in my left knee where it had been injured in an unfortunate move-in-day incident the previous semester. I compromised by propping one hip on the corner of my desk.

"The thing is..." she said, not looking at me.

"The thing is what?" I asked after a while, I hoped not too curtly. I felt sorry for her, I really did. And I'd interviewed enough rape and torture victims to know that pressuring her and backing her into a corner was the worst thing I could do. But I also had lots to do and lots of problems of my own, and I wanted to cut to the chase and find out how, exactly, she was hoping I could help her.

"My family is quite old-fashioned," she said, looking down at where her hands gripped the back of the chair. Her knuckles and the tips of her fingers were turning white from the pressure she was exerting.

"Mmmm-hmmm," I said.

"They were strict and old-fashioned back home in Urus-Martan"—Urus-Martan was a small town in Chechnya— "and when we came here, they became even stricter. Especially with me. The boys, well...they're boys. Although they cause more trouble than I do. But still. They're boys. There's a different law for them."

"Mmmm-hmmm," I said again, when Aishat fell silent.

"My parents didn't want me to go to college," she said after a while. "But I convinced them that I wanted to become a nurse, and they said that would be okay. Frankly speaking, we need the money. Somehow my father got a job as an IT technician here, but both his parents live with us and they're invalids. Healthcare is so expensive here...so my parents agreed that I could go to college and then become a nurse. I got a scholarship to study here because my father works here. But I don't fit in at all. None of us do, but it's where we are."

"Mmmm-hmmmm," I said for a third time. Nodding and smiling and saying "Mmmm-hmmmm" sympathetically was almost always the right response in situations such as this.

"I met Owen Wu my first year here—I'm a sophomore—and we became friends. He wanted to practice his Russian with someone. I thought because he was Chinese he would be safe. The Chinese are supposed to be very studious, aren't they?"

"Normally," I said.

"But he wasn't. He got involved in one of those 'fraternities'"—she struggled with the difficult English word, before switching back into Russian—"and he kept inviting me to go to parties with him."

"Mmmm," I said.

"At first I said no. But he kept asking me, and then Jibril from the Muslim Students' Union said it would be good outreach. We're very small and no one cares about us at all. There was a party that sounded good. Pi Chi and Rho Beta Delta were co-hosting a costume party. It was supposed to be fun and safe, and with everyone in costumes, we thought I wouldn't stand out so much in my headscarf, and people would accept me better. And they promised no alcohol. So I spoke with my parents about it, and they said: 'What's the harm? These are all nice boys from good families, right?' So I went."

"Mmmmmmmm," I said.

"So I went. And...and..." Her voice climbed higher and higher, before cracking and rendering her speechless for a moment.

"And," she said, when she could talk again, "they gave me a drink. They swore there was no alcohol in it—I don't drink, of course; it's against my religion—but there must have been something in it, because...because I don't remember the rest of the evening. I don't remember it, but Owen told me they have a video of me, and if I don't do what they want, they'll post it on YouTube and then I'll never be able to hold my head up or live a normal life again."

12

"OKAY," I SAID, WHEN it became apparent that Aishat wasn't going to say anything more. "Do you know what's on the video?"

She shook her head. "Just that it's something terrible."

"Or so they tell you," I said.

"I think..." She squirmed some more. "I think they're telling the truth. When I woke up...I had all my clothes on, but they felt...strange. Like someone else had dressed me, someone who didn't know what they were doing. And my hair was damp, like it had been washed, and I smelled like strange soap. And I was...in pain. You know. *There*."

"That does sound bad," I agreed. "Did you tell anyone? Officially?"

"Well...Eventually. Once Owen started blackmailing me. Before that I was ashamed, and I was afraid the same thing would happen to me that had happened to Brittany. You know, Brittany Gutierrez. The cheerleader. That was at the same party."

"I thought that was last year," I said.

"It was. It was the end of the spring semester last year."

"But nothing came of it, right?" I asked.

"Brittany got expelled," said Aishat. "When I tried to tell my story, they told me that the same would happen to me if I didn't keep quiet."

"Mmmmm," I said. There had been a few whispers about the case, but the college had done a good job of hushing it up. From what I had heard, Brittany Gutierrez, captain of the college cheerleading squad, had accused Jamal Warner, quarterback of the college football team, of sexual assault at a frat party.

Brittany's accusations had put the college in a nasty quandary. Like many colleges, Crimson was trying to grapple with the fact that it had a sexual assault rate similar to that of the less desirable kind of prison. Also like many colleges, especially colleges in the South, it was trying to grapple with its unfortunate history of slavery and its current dearth of black faculty and students. Hence, for example, Chloe's hire as a Special Diversity faculty member.

The college's public relations coup in hiring a rising star with an Ivy League degree and a blindingly brilliant publication record was rather dampened by sexual assault allegations being leveled against its most high-profile (of three, I guessed uncharitably) black students. Plus, Jamal had been largely responsible for the Crimson Chargers' unusually win-heavy season last year. Any sort of criminal charges, or, God forbid, expulsion, were totally out of the question.

Luckily for the college, at that crucial moment someone had whispered into their ear the happy thought that (white) women were known for lying about sexual assault in order to cause trouble for (black) men. This heartwarming narrative, of dishonest women conniving to bring down decent men through fake accusations of sexual assault, aligned so perfectly with what most people wanted to believe, that it was being greeted with open arms by uber-woke liberals who otherwise might have to face up to the reality of rape and other unpleasant forms of sexual coercion and violence.

I myself had originally been very sympathetic to the plight of non-white men accused of sexual harassment or assault, despite my own many, many experiences of sexual harassment by non-white men. However, now that the progressive wing of the anti-racism movement appeared ever more determined to ride the misogyny train to victory, I was becoming ever less sympathetic.

Or rather, I was still sympathetic towards the largely working-class men who got the book thrown at them for minor offenses, although I was sure that most of them were, in fact, guilty as charged. But I was full of ever-growing outrage against my fellow liberal intellectual elites who were, consciously or not, co-opting the struggle against racism to assert class privilege and patriarchal oppression. The fact that a lot of the people doing this were women just added to the amusing irony. But then again, back when I'd been gathering stories of human rights abuses, the most vociferous denials of prison and barracks rape had come from its victims. People were funny like that.

In Brittany's case, though, there hadn't been a lot to laugh about. Although technically she was the lone Hispanic member of the student body, she was cute and blonde, which was more than reason enough to accuse her of dishonesty, narcissism, attention-seeking behavior, white woman privilege, and every other heinous sin the college could think of.

Rather than holding a police investigation and criminal trial, the college had held an "honor court" hearing, where it had expelled Brittany and exonerated Jamal, thus slaying the twin demons of racism and sexual assault in one fell swoop. Brittany had been labeled the Girl Who Lied, and according to the article I had read about it last summer, had received so many rape and death threats that she'd changed her name and gone into hiding. Rape itself might ruin a person's life and leave them traumatized and suicidal. Speaking out against rape almost certainly would.

"So, let me get this straight," I said. "You were at the same party as Brittany Gutierrez?"

Aishat nodded. "She was a member of Rho Beta Delta, and one of the organizers of the party. I saw her there. With Jamal and the other football players. They were just in their sports uniforms, so they were easy to recognize."

"And then something bad happened at the party, and now they're telling you they have a video of it?"

Aishat nodded again.

"Do you know if Brittany is also on the video?"

Aishat shrugged. "I don't know. And like I said, I don't remember most of the evening. But I kind of 'came to' in the middle of the night, on a couch in a back room. And when I did, Brittany was on the couch next to me."

"Ooooookaaaaayyy," I said. "Have you told anyone about this video?"

She nodded. "I told the woman who was in charge of the committee that held the 'honor court' hearing for the case. I guess she is the, what do you call it, 'Title IX officer.' Why do they call it 'Title IX'? And why do they call it 'honor court'? There doesn't seem to be much honor in it."

"They just do," I said. "When did you tell her?"

"As soon as I found out about the video. The end of last semester. Owen came up to me during the last week of class and said I had to help him get an A in Russian. I said I would study with him. He said that wasn't enough. I would have to write his final essay and final project for him, and help him cheat on the final to get an A."

"And did you?" I asked.

"No! I told him I wouldn't write his final essay or final project for him, and I didn't know how to help him cheat on the exam. Besides, my grades have...not been so good. I knew something terrible had happened to me at that party, even if I couldn't remember it, and I...I hardly got through my finals, and then I spent all summer hiding in my room. I was supposed to work at the hospital, and we really needed the money, but I—I let my family down! First I was dishonored, and then I compounded dishonor with dishonor by hiding in my room all summer and crying! But I could not face the world. I did not feel I deserved to be amongst decent people. And now...I came back, but...the shame still clings to me. It's all I can think about. I cannot clear myself of this shame, but perhaps I can clear my family of it. And my grades have been poor since I came back, adding to my shame."

"That's understandable," I said. "I'm glad you didn't help Owen cheat, at least." I almost told her that Owen's final project, essay, and exam, like everything else he had submitted over the semester, had been a disgrace, so I was glad to hear she hadn't been involved in them. Probably that was a FERPA (Family Educational Rights and Privacy Act) violation.

"So what did he do then?" I asked instead.

"That's when he told me he had a video of me at that party, and if I didn't do what he wanted, he'd put it on YouTube, and my life would be ruined!"

"So what did you do then?"

"I went to that 'Title IX officer,' the woman who is supposed to handle these things, and told her all about it! But she told me I needed to stop lying and making racist accusations, or I'd get expelled like Brittany."

"Who was the woman you talked to?" I asked.

"That dean," said Aishat. "The dean of, how do you say it"—she switched to English, and stumbled over the difficult word—"'di-ver-si-ty and in-clu-si-on.' What's her name? Do-ro-thy Talbot."

13

"AH," I SAID. "I KNOW Dorothy."

That was all too unfortunately true. I had first encountered Dorothy during the mandatory Diversity and Inclusivity training at the beginning of last semester. I had found her saccharinely insincere to the point of nausea. She had promptly marked me as a Bad Apple. Nothing that had happened since then had changed our opinions of each other.

I hadn't imagined her capable of actively suppressing a sexual assault investigation, though. Mainly because I hadn't believed she had the gumption for it. I was horrified to discover she was the college's Title IX officer, responsible for handling allegations of sexual harassment and assault, but not surprised. No doubt she was the best they had at providing CYA spin while mouthing the popular political shibboleths of the moment.

"Did you report it to the police?" I asked Aishat.

She shook her head vigorously. "Not after what Dean Talbot told me. I was sick with worry all during exams, sure that Owen was going to post the video."

"But he didn't?" I was still trying to wrap my head around the idea of Owen Wu as the mastermind behind a rape and revenge-porn scheme. It was easy to imagine him guilty of some petty mischief. Sexual assault seemed beyond him. Although many men could surprise you in that way.

"I didn't hear anything about it all December," she said. "But then, last week, he emailed me and said I *had* to help him this semester, or he'd release the video to the world."

"Help him with Russian?"

She shrugged. "I think with everything. I was a good student. Owen is not."

"Mmmmm," I said. "So then what happened?"

"Then my mother asked me why I was so upset and sick—again. Finally she made me tell her. Then she told my father. Now my father wants to do something terrible to Owen Wu."

"Do you think he will?" I asked.

She squirmed her shoulders. "Maybe," she said, in a tiny voice. Then she raised her eyes to mine. I could see a transformation taking place. I just wasn't sure it was a good transformation. Back home, women in Aishat's position had become *shakhidki*, female suicide bombers, as the only way to redeem their honor and rid themselves of their pain. I could understand where they were coming from. Being raped, especially for a woman in a culture that prized female virginity highly, would be such a terrible violation that killing yourself and everyone around you probably seemed like the best way out.

But I could also remember being on the Moscow metro during both of the 2004 attacks carried out by North Caucasian suicide bombers, and the terror and helplessness we had all felt, trapped in the train in the middle of that tunnel deep underground. That had also been the kind of trauma that many people never recover from. So I couldn't condone that kind of thing either, no matter how justified.

"We have to stop Owen before my father does something!" Aishat was saying. "I can't lose my father. My family has been through so much. So many of my aunts and uncles and cousins were killed during the wars. We can't lose my father as well! Before I was sad and ashamed. But now I could kill Owen for what he has done! And if anything happens to my father, I will!"

"Okay," I said. "Let's see what we can do to prevent that."

14

AISHAT LEFT SHORTLY after that, showering me with profuse thanks and looking relieved. I was touched by her faith in my ability to help her out. I was also profoundly uneasy about it. My instinctive response was to say that I had zero training or capability to handle a situation like this. True, I was naturally curious—some might even say snoopy—and I had extensive training in research and critical thinking. But my training was all in textual analysis.

Well, that wasn't quite true. I'd done lots of interviewing and information-gathering in my job back in Moscow. But I'd never *done* anything with that information other than pass it on to others who then collated it into worthy-sounding reports that no one read. What Aishat was asking for seemed a lot more like vigilante justice. Vigilante justice made me nervous. Plus it might get me fired.

I needed to talk to someone about it. Not someone from Crimson, at least not at first. Mel would be a good person to bounce ideas off of, but I didn't want her to get drawn into this until I was sure it was a good idea. I needed an outside perspective.

My first thought was to ask Alex, but I quickly nixed that. I already knew how Alex would react. He would be angry with me for getting involved in something that was likely to be messy and maybe dangerous, and he would tell me to report it to the proper authorities and then butt out. Extrajudicial actions were not something Alex was fond of. For all his I-don't-give-a-shit exterior, at heart he was an officer and a gentleman, and preferred to walk on the legal side of the law.

The person I really needed to talk to was Dima. Dima was different. Dima would understand. He might not be any happier about it, but he'd understand why it seemed like a good idea in a way most Americans wouldn't.

Feeling like an addict about to sneak her first fix of the day, I opened up WhatsApp and sent Dima a text.

Are you free right now? I need some advice.

I expected no answer. Dima was frequently out of cell phone range, and he didn't always answer my texts even when he was in range. But two minutes later I got a response.

I'm always free for you))))) What do you need advice about?

I got a request from a student. A complicated request.

I laid out Aishat's problem as succinctly as possible. Dima replied immediately.

Get those motherfucking bastards.

That was the response I expected from him. Instead of making me feel validated, though, it caused all my original doubts to return.

I'm supposed to report this to the authorities, I wrote. *I'm definitely not supposed to get directly involved.*

Didn't she *already* report it to the authorities? Dima wrote back. *And they told her to go to hell?*

Well...yes.

I'd say that gives you carte blanche to do whatever the hell you want, then.

The university might disagree, I told him.

So, what'll they do? Arrest you?

No, just fire me. I'm already in big trouble with them for not stopping the shooting last semester.

Are you afraid of getting fired? he asked.

Very. I'm a coward))))

I'm no coward, but I'm scared!))))))

)))))) I wrote back. That was a famous line from the Soviet comedy film *The Diamond Arm*. Dima must have been in a good mood to be citing it.

No fooling, I wrote. *What should I do? It seems to me that if I don't do anything about this, then nothing will be done. But I don't know if I should get involved. What if I make things worse?*

I think that's the excuse of petty-bourgeois cowards everywhere, and as we know, Inna, you are neither petty bourgeois nor a coward.

So you think I should get involved? I asked.

It's necessary, Fedya, necessary))))) That was also a line from a classic Soviet comedy film. I wondered if Dima was drinking.

Are you sober? I asked.

Not entirely. We got an early start on celebrating Old New Year. The Russian Orthodox calendar was two weeks behind the regular Western calendar. "Old New Year" was a holiday some people embraced with enthusiasm.

What's on a sober man's mind is on a drunk man's tongue! I wrote back. *But speaking seriously: what would you do in my place?*

You know what I'd do in your place, Innochka. I'd track down every single one of those gutless bastards and nail them to the wall. Metaphorically speaking. But maybe that isn't the right thing for you to do. To tell the truth, I don't like the idea of you mixing with rapists. Maybe you *should* turn this over to the authorities. Is there a police officer you trust?

Maybe, I wrote back. *It's a place to start, anyway. Thanks for your advice, and Happy Old New Year!*

Happy Old New Year, Innochka. And this hasn't discharged my life debt. I still need to find a way to repay you.

You have no debt before me, I wrote. *Just keep yourself alive.*

You too, he wrote back. Which did not fill me with courage and confidence for what I was about to do. But maybe a little fear was what I needed.

15

AFTER A LITTLE HEMMING and hawing, I decided to take Dima's explicit advice, and the implicit advice I knew Alex would give me without even asking him, and go talk to Brian Michaels, chief of campus police.

I had grave doubts overall about anyone in a position of power helping me out with the Aishat issue. From what I had heard from others and witnessed firsthand, getting anyone to even consider the possibility of sexual assault was an uphill battle. If I had been the victim, I probably would have given up without even trying.

But it did seem faintly possible that Aishat might have more luck, at least at an ostensibly liberal, "safe space" place like Crimson College. Brittany Gutierrez had gotten drummed out of town in disgrace. But perhaps Aishat, who spoke with an accent and covered her head to show she was under authority, 1 Corinthians-style, had a chance of playing on the college's constant hunger for good PR. A very slim chance, but it seemed worth a shot as an opening gambit. And maybe Brian Michaels could give me some good tips.

When I showed up at the campus police station, which was just two rooms in a back corner of the basement of Lee Hall, I found Brian Michaels about to leave for lunch. When I said I wanted to talk to him, off the record, he suggested we go get lunch together. So within ten minutes I found myself ordering at Sullivan's for the second time in two days.

Once again I went for the fried chocolate-and-PB sandwich, with a side of fries. If I kept this up, I was going to regain all that dissertation weight I'd lost last year while living on literally starvation wages. Oh well. Right now a little weight gain hardly seemed like the worst thing that could happen to me.

"So what's up?" asked Brian, once the waitress had taken our orders. "Is it your brother? How's he doing, by the way? Be sure to tell him I said hi."

Brian Michaels's hellraising son had served with my brother John in the Marines, including a tour of Iraq together. John had kept him on the straight and narrow, and saved his life in some way that neither Brian nor I quite understood. But Brian had said he'd do whatever he could to help me out. Normally I preferred to build my own good karma, but in this case I was happy enough to ride on the coattails of John's good deeds. I was even happier to think that John was capable of building good karma at all. Acting like a respectable member of society was not one of his better skills.

"It's..." The waitress came back with glasses of ice water. I sat there in silence while she flirted with Brian Michaels. Brian was in his mid-fifties, with buzzcut blond hair going to gray, skin that put the "red" in "redneck," and the beginnings of a middle-aged paunch and jowls. In other settings he might not have been a babe magnet. But his Southern charm was strong, and his steady paycheck made him a prize catch for every single woman in Greenfields.

I was under the impression that he was divorced and wasn't averse to a little love action with any woman who was willing. I was also under the impression that my status as Lieutenant Colonel John Halley's kid sister made me off-limits as a romantic target. As a feminist scholar I decried the need to seek protection as the possession of a high-status male. As a woman who got tired of fending off unwanted attention, I was grateful for the break it provided.

"Oh, have you heard?" the waitress said, after she and Brian had gotten the first round of flirting out of the way. "Chris—you know, that boy, the one who—anyway, he's been released from the hospital. My cousin's a nurse at Grady Hospital in Atlanta, where he was kept, you know, and she said he's been released to a secure rehab facility. She said he still doesn't know his own name half the time. They're saying he'll probably never be fit to stand trial. I know I shouldn't say this, but poor thing! He came in here a time or two, you know; I recognized his picture and I darn near screamed out loud when I saw it. I guess you never know, do you? He always seemed like such a nice kid. Did either of you ever meet him? I mean, before, obviously."

"Um," I said. "He was, um...my student. It was my final that he came to stop."

The waitress's eyes and mouth went round into almost perfect Os. "Aw, sugar!" she said. "Bless your little heart! You poor thing. You poor, poor thing! Wait"—she looked back and forth between me and Brian—"is that why you're here?"

"Sort of," I said.

She relaxed tension I hadn't realized she'd been holding. She must have thought me a rival for Brian's affections. Probably she'd been jealous, sure that my glamorous status as a professor was going to beat out her waitressing job.

"Well, I'll leave you two to it, then," she said. "If you need anything, you just give me a call, okay?"

"You know I will," said Brian, which earned him a smile and a promise of extra fries.

"I was going to tell you," Brian said once she'd gone. "About Chris getting transferred out of Grady to a rehab clinic. But like Mandy said, he can hardly tell you his own name, and it don't look like he's gonna get better any time soon."

"I guess I'm sorry to hear that," I said. "Although I don't want him to go to jail, either, even though he did almost shoot me."

"I know. I don't think any o' us want anything bad to happen to him, despite what he did. And our buddy Nathan Willoughby is in rehab now too. Still in a wheelchair, and likely to remain that way for a good long time. I heard about this—this is just between us, okay?—'cause his parents were askin' about him coming back to school here, and the Dean's Office wanted to know, off the record, you know, what I thought o' that."

"Gosh," I said. "Do you think he will? Come back to school here? If it were me, I wouldn't want to. And I kind of feel like Nathan should be charged with something, even if he wasn't the one who tried to carry out the shooting."

"That's what Chris's parents are arguin', but so far it don't look like Nathan's gonna get charged with anything."

"It's all so awful," I said. "They're so young, and so stupid, and they ruined their own and other people's lives so thoroughly."

"Yeah," said Brian. "You know, sometimes I think this is what we get for what we're doin'. My second cousin has a hog farm, and sometimes I think what we're doin' here ain't that different from he's doin'. We're factory farmin' our own kids. Maybe this is the result."

"Yeah," I said. Brian Michaels might be a redneck and a good ol' boy, but he wasn't stupid.

"And Nathan's parents raised a real ruckus over break, threatenin' to sue the school, and maybe you and me too, for harassment an' endangerment, but I get the feelin' that's blown over. Maybe they came to their senses and realized we were doin' everythin' we could to protect Nathan from his own fool self. Too bad he was hellbent on not takin' our help."

"Yeah," I said. "I should probably be more worried about that than I am. I just can't believe that anyone would think it made sense to sue me for harassment."

"Some folks ain't got no sense at all, an' you know that. Now, what was it you wanted to ask me about?"

"Well," I said. "This is strictly off the record, okay? And I'm trying to figure out a way to ask you about it without putting you in an impossible bind."

A line appeared between Brian's eyebrows. "I don't like the sound o' that at all."

"Yeah, neither do I. So, okay. A student came to me recently with allegations of possible sexual assault."

"You know you gotta turn that shit in right now," said Brian. Most of his good ol' boy exterior had been shed, and someone a lot harder was staring out at me.

"I know. But the thing is, this student has already reported the issue, and been dismissed. Only new, um, evidence, I guess you'd say, has potentially come to light."

Brian leaned back in his chair. "This student come report this alleged assault to me? Or the new evidence?"

"The student reported it to the Dean's Office. To the Title IX officer."

"Goddamn Dorothy Talbot. They shoulda come straight to me with it. When was this?"

"Um, well...this is all kind of in confidence, but since the student *did* report this to the Dean's Office at the time...end of last semester."

"That was a busy time for all o' us," said Brian. "I guess it coulda got lost in the shuffle. Although I'd hate to think we'd lose somethin' like a possible rape."

I resisted the urge to point out that police forces across the country managed to avoid investigating and prosecuting rape cases on an astonishingly regular basis. Instead I said, "According to the student, the report to the Dean's Office about the possible new evidence was met with accusations of lying and threats of expulsion. You see...um, well, the student is being blackmailed with a video that supposedly exists from the party at which Brittany Gutierrez said she was assaulted."

I thought Brian was going to explode into outraged outbursts of foul language that would have done John proud, but instead he went completely still. "Brittany on that video?" he asked softly.

"The student doesn't know. They've never actually seen the video. But the student says they were at that party, and passed out, and woke up next to Brittany, and their clothing was disarranged and they were in pain. Unfortunately, they didn't report it or get examined at the time, but they also think they were washed off while they were unconscious, so there may not have been any evidence to find."

"What do you think?" Brian asked, still speaking softly. "You think the student is lyin' like the Dean's Office says?"

I shook my head. "If I thought they were lying, I wouldn't be here. I'm as sure as I can be on the word of someone I don't know very well that the student passed out at that party, and now is being blackmailed with a video showing something that the student is sure would ruin their life. Her life. I guess I might as well share this bit too. It's much worse for this student than it would be for most students. I mean, having a video of some kind of awful assault being circulated would be bad enough for anyone. But this student is from a conservative Muslim family, from a culture that still believes in things like honor killings. So it really is a matter of life and death. But at the same time, any kind of public report and trial is probably out of the question."

"I get that," Brian said. "My little sister has two teenage girls, and when I think about what it'd actually be like if somethin' like that were to happen to 'em, well...I get it. But I also gotta say the official line is very definitely to report it."

"I know," I said.

"And if there really is a video out there that could shed some light on what happened to Brittany...you know, I've always felt kinda sick about that case. I interviewed her three times, and I was as sure as I could be that somethin' awful had happened to her. She couldn't stop cryin', and there was, you know, uh, physical evidence that some, uh, rough sex had taken place. But 'rough sex' ain't the same as rape. You know, the difference between my neighbor takin' my ol' car off my hands and usin' its parts for his fixer-upper project, and him committin' grand theft auto and sellin' it to a chop shop, is just whether or not I said he could take it. But somehow that's easier for us to see with cars than with sex.

"And Brittany'd been drinkin' and she couldn't remember what'd happened, and there was no solid DNA evidence or nothin' like that—she said she thought she'd been washed off before she woke up too, 'cause her hair was wet—and she didn't get a tox screen until the next day and it came back inconclusive, and so..." He spread out his hands. "I don't know that what she said happened, happened, but *somethin'* bad happened that night at that party. And if we could get some video evidence of it, it'd make me feel a whole lot better. But what'd you want to ask me, specifically?"

"What I should do, I guess," I said. "Given that this student has approached me off the record, and asked specifically for my help."

"Tell her to come talk to me," said Brian promptly. "And for the love o' God, if that video surfaces, tell her to get it to me ASAP. It ain't just about her, you know?"

"I know," I said. "I'll tell her."

"You do that," said Brian. "You do everythin' you can to get her to come in and give me a statement—me and no one else—and in the meantime, I'm gonna write up a report sayin' Doctor Rowena Halley came to me with information that could be potentially related to the Brittany Gutierrez case. If the shit hits the fan with this, which I think it might, maybe that'll cover your ass enough to keep you safe from the blowback."

"Thanks," I said. "Hopefully it won't come to that, but thanks."

"Thank me when I actually help you," said Brian.

16

I HAD BEEN HOPING THAT a huge weight would be lifted from my shoulders when I told Brian about the video and Aishat's allegations, but instead another weight came crashing down on me. To wit: should I also tell him about Owen Wu's potential involvement in the case? I didn't want to withhold essential evidence or cover up anything that needed to be uncovered, and I certainly didn't want to protect a rapist from justice.

But I also didn't want to go around spreading damaging rumors. I tended to be pretty unsympathetic to all the people who were constantly bemoaning the destructive nature of sexual assault allegations and how they could ruin innocent people's lives. It was vastly more likely that rapists were getting away scot free in large numbers, and it was their victims' lives that were being ruined.

But it was also true that one of the reasons I felt that way was because I was careful not to go around making unfounded accusations, regardless of the crime committed. What I needed to do was to convince Aishat to make a formal statement to the police. Let them deal with Owen and his complicity in whatever had happened at that party.

I taught my first two Wednesday classes on autopilot while I wrestled with that moral and practical quandary. I had just settled it with myself that I would get in touch with Aishat and suggest that she and I go over together to talk to Brian, when I came out of my second class and found Chloe slumped on one of the benches that lined the hall outside our classrooms.

"Panic attack?" I asked her.

"Mmmm-hmmm." She was massaging tiny circles in her temples, around the scars she had there from too much hair straightening, while staring at the ground and shivering slightly.

"Let's get out of here," I said.

"I can't let this beat me!" She tried to say it fiercely, but the effect was spoiled by her shivering and her chattering teeth.

"I know. We're not going to let it beat you. We're going to outsmart it. So let's get the heck out of here. You don't have class for another couple of hours, right?"

"Uh-huh," she said, still staring at the floor while massaging her temples.

"Let's go get some fresh air. We'll both feel better. And we can grab some lunch if you want."

"I feel sick. I feel like I'm coming down with something."

"Maybe you should go home then."

"I...canNOT...let...this...BEAT ME!" she said through clenched teeth.

"Let's go get some fresh air, then."

After a couple more rounds of this, I cajoled her into getting up and walking with me over to Brew's Up, the campus coffee shop.

"Wow, I do feel a lot better," said Chloe, once we were in Brew's Up. She was no longer shivering, and her speech was almost normal. "Good enough to...I don't know, what do you think? Should I go crazy and order a muffin or something? My dad has been telling me maybe it's just blood sugar. Maybe I'm just having hypoglycemic attacks because of this diet I'm on."

"That could very well be it," I said. "In any case, if you think a muffin would make you feel better, go crazy. I'll get one too. It'll be fun."

Five minutes later Chloe was sipping chamomile tea and nibbling at an orange and cranberry scone. I had gone for a cappuccino and a chocolate muffin. I knew that neither my bank balance nor my waistline could maintain this kind of splurging, but after all the deprivations of the previous year, somehow I couldn't stop myself. And I was being a good friend, right? Chloe looked like she needed my moral support, and this was part of offering her that moral support.

"Anyway," said Chloe, once she'd eaten half her scone. "My dad wants me to go get a full metabolic panel, in case I'm developing, you know, diabetes."

I made an involuntary face. Diabetes didn't sound so bad until it was happening to you or someone you cared about. "Do you think that might be it?"

"I don't know. I hope not. It's something I've been scared of my whole life. Half my family has it, and I've always thought it's just a matter of time before I have it too. Then I'll be doomed to a life of measuring every bite I eat and sticking myself with needles four times a day." She shuddered. "I'm phobic about needles. My dad's a surgeon, and I can't even look when I get a blood draw. So I'm afraid my dad's right, and I'm a pre-diabetic and getting weird blood sugar swings and that's why I'm having these panic attacks, but I keep hoping for something else. My aunt keeps telling me I'm experiencing ascension symptoms and I should welcome it."

"Ascension...like the Rapture?" I asked. "Or like in *Stargate: Atlantis*?"

She shook her head. "No...I think your physical body stays on this plane. But you ascend to a higher spiritual level or something."

"Um...okay."

"And I hate that I'm almost considering it!" she burst out. "I *know* it's BS, but I want answers, and this is an answer I want to hear. I don't want to be diagnosed with a horrible illness, and I also don't want to be horribly sick and not have a diagnosis. Telling me it's 'ascension symptoms' is kind of like telling me it's 'just stress,' but it makes it sound better. Like it's serving a higher purpose, or something, instead of blaming me for it. Now I know how people get suckered into these alternative medicine scams."

"Not all of them are scams," I said.

"I know, and that's the worst part! *Some* of them aren't scams, but some of them are, and I don't know whom I can trust. It seems like everyone is trying to gaslight me and pull the wool over my eyes, and my own doctors are as least as bad as those quacks on the internet. It's up to me, just when I'm least in a position to take care of myself."

"Yeah," I said. "That sucks."

"And it also seems like it really is stress, or something about the job, because it's always worst when I'm teaching or in my office. My mom says it's probably because I'm working at a place where all the buildings are literally named after slave owners. And I think she may have a point, because it always feels like the air there is literally poison to me. But I also feel like I shouldn't complain. Both because I'm lucky to have any job at all, and because if someone hears me, they'll deny me tenure for sure. But...I miss New York." Chloe had done her PhD at Columbia University.

"Small-town Georgia must be a quite a change, even if you did grow up in Atlanta," I said.

"For sure. And I miss not being the only black person except for the women who clean the toilets. I was just thinking about my first month in New York and going to the public library on 125th St, in Central Harlem, just north of campus. I remember walking down the street and noticing everyone else walking by me was black too. And then I went into the library and all the librarians and all the other patrons were also black. And I picked some random books off the shelf and they were all by black authors, about black characters.

I flipped through them and saw that most of them were terrible, but then I was like, 'But at least they're trying. And what do you expect? The language they're writing in wasn't designed for them to tell their stories. Now they're doing the best they can with it. And look at all these people enjoying themselves here.'

"And I checked out a couple of books and I kept on walking down 125th St., past the Apollo Theater and the African market and all these people who looked like me. I almost decided"—she fingered the scars on her temples—"to grow out my natural hair. But then I went back onto campus and into my class and looked at everyone else's shiny straight hair, and I lost my nerve."

"You could still do it," I said. "I think it would look nice."

"Then I wouldn't get tenure for sure," said Chloe. "I just wish...I just wish I didn't have to teach! Oh shoot. Did anyone hear that?"

We both looked around, searching for moles from the Dean's Office. But if any of the chattering undergrads flirting and goofing off at the corner tables were spying on us, they were doing it so skillfully we couldn't tell.

"I just wish I could just write all the time," she said. "I know most people don't feel that way, but I wish I could just write articles all day, every day. Especially since when people read something by 'Chloe Taylor, PhD,' they don't know I'm black. They treat me just like anyone else. But when I'm standing in front of the classroom, I feel like everyone's staring at me and thinking how much I don't belong there. That's why they won't talk, not even when I call on them."

"Some of them probably are," I agreed. "Most of them probably aren't, though. Most of them are probably so intimidated by you that they're too afraid to say anything."

"See, that's not how I feel at all! And I don't want to intimidate them. I just wish they'd respect me a little more."

"I know," I said. Chloe had the trifecta of student disrespect going against her: she was young, female, and black. Also overweight. And her desperation to get respect was the final nail in the coffin.

"Do you tell jokes in class?" I asked. "Especially about the material, or yourself?"

"No. I know you've said that's what works for you, but I just don't think it'd work for me. And I've never been good at telling jokes anyway."

"It can be a challenge," I said. "But humor can be a tool of the strong. The right kind of humor, that is."

"I know. It's just so much pressure! I have to figure out how to be funny and self-deprecating while teaching and planning lessons and grading and submitting for publication—*and* I've been drafted into a committee! Did I tell you about that? A second committee! I was drafted into the Committee of Diversity and Inclusion as soon as I started here. Now I've been pulled into the committee that's looking at the reorganization of the language programs. I'll never get my book published if this keeps up!"

"Yeah," I said. "Do the committees keep you pretty busy?"

"Not the Diversity and Inclusion one—surprise surprise, we hardly do anything—but I think the language program reorganization one could be a nightmare. We've already met twice, and everyone wants my opinion, but no one wants to listen to what I have to say. So I end up saying a lot and not getting listened to at all. And I think it's going to drag on for years and never accomplish anything at all."

"Seems very likely," I agreed. Crimson College was looking at reorganizing its language programs into several smaller departments instead of just Spanish, Classics, and Modern Languages, which was an unwieldy umbrella department for everything that wasn't

Spanish, Latin, or Greek. In theory it was a good idea. In practice it was turning into a lot of meetings and not a lot of accomplishment.

"Maybe you should make a point of prioritizing your book," I said to Chloe. "Let the people with tenure worry about the committees."

"Yeah. I guess." Chloe sighed and nibbled at the last piece of her scone, her shoulders slumping at the thought of books, committees, tenure, and everything else. I thought about asking her for her advice on what to do about the Owen situation. Then I decided against it. She already had enough on her plate without that. It would just stress her out and not help me in any material way.

"Work on the book," I said firmly. "That, at least, will be a worthwhile accomplishment."

"Yeah," said Chloe. Her shoulders straightened. Infinitesimally, but they still straightened. "That'll be something, won't it? To see a book with my name on it?"

"That will definitely be something," I said. "A very big something."

17

ON THURSDAY I HAD NO class. My plan was to spend the morning putting in an application for a two-year visiting position in Illinois. According to the job Wiki, invitations for second-round interviews had already gone out for the Ohio job, and I hadn't gotten one. So I'd struck out there, but my Midwest credentials were strong—I'd gotten my PhD from Indiana University—so my interview invitation rate for Midwestern schools was four times what it was for schools in other regions. I'd sent off the application for the job at Carmel-by-the-Sea Tuesday evening, but I really wasn't holding my breath for that one. Best to press my Midwest advantage as much as I could instead.

Then in the afternoon I'd get to work on my book proposal. I really, really would. Like most recent PhDs in the humanities, I was planning to turn my dissertation into a book, and try to get it published. Technically, it already was published, since dissertations were considered published once they had been defended and deposited. But it wasn't the same as turning it into a "real" book and having it published by a "real" publisher. Especially in the eyes of a hiring or tenure committee.

Talking to Chloe the day before had fired up my low-simmering enthusiasm for the project. During the previous semester I'd managed to put together both a brief (two paragraphs) and a full (two pages) description of my project, along with a chapter-by-chapter detailed outline. That should have been easy, since I already had the completed dissertation to work from, but it had been remarkably difficult and time-consuming, especially since it had entailed rewriting large sections of my dissertation in order to bring it into line with what I wanted the actual book to be.

I knew that if I were serious about sending out the book proposal, I wouldn't let myself stray into the sucking quicksand of rewrites. But, if I were perfectly honest with myself, not only did I find the process of putting together the book proposal to be tedious to the point of nausea and collapse, I was also just plain scared. I'd already had to face so much personal and professional rejection in the past couple of years. In theory that should have hardened me to it, and in some ways it had, but it had also made me strongly averse to starting up another, difficult and time-consuming, project that was guaranteed to lead to dozens of rejection letters. If I was lucky. I assumed that a lot of publishers were the same as job search committees, and didn't even bother to reject you.

But that kind of small-souledness, as we called it in Russian, never led to success. Over winter break I'd written a template cover letter and updated my CV. Now I needed to do the part that seemed most difficult to me: write up something on the market and competition for the book. I was finding this particularly heavy going. It was not something I'd ever been asked to consider before, and I wasn't even sure how to go about finding the information. And it seemed like that was the kind of thing the publisher should be concerning themselves with. What was the point of them if they weren't the ones with the expert knowledge on current market conditions?

I was staring at my computer screen, fruitlessly searching for hints on how to find out what the market and comp titles would be for books about Silver Age (early 20th century) Russian poetry, when I got a text from Mel.

I just had a big social media fight with two different sets of people instead of doing my real work. Now I need to go blow off some steam. Want to go running?

Heck yeah, I texted back. *Meet you by the front gate in 10?*

10 minutes later, Mel and I were setting off at a slow jog from the front gate of Peachtree Estates. It was at the end of Peachtree Road, a private road that separated it from the pawn-and-smoke-shop main strip of this side of town. If you ran past the pawn shops, smoke shops, and run-down fast food joints, you'd end up in the drug dealer neighborhood, where junk cars filled the lots and Rottweilers and pit bulls strained at their tenuous chains and snarled as you ran by. It was not the greatest place to go running. But since neither Mel nor I had been in great shape since the beginning of last semester, we'd only managed to make it all the way to the pit-bulls-and-junkers part of town twice. Most of the time we crashed by the time we made it to LeRoy's Fine Pawn Shop, less than a mile away.

"You gotta keep me from hurting myself," Mel told me as we set off. "I'm so fuckin' mad, I'm afraid I'll wreck my knees for good."

"Just stay level with me," I told her. "My left knee is still unhappy, so a light jog is all I'm going to be good for today. But you're welcome to vent while you run if that would make you feel better."

"Okay. Although it's my own damn fault. I got drawn into a political argument on Facebook like the fuckin' moron I am."

"Ah." Election primaries were heating up, with all the ickiness that entailed. I had taken to spending less and less time on social media in order not to be forced to break off all ties with most of my friends and family.

"Yeah," said Mel. "So of course a lot of my family have been spouting a lot of conspiracy theory shit and all kinds of BS about how the libtards are coming to take their guns and kill their babies. And then my liberal intellectual friends have been pulling classic Nice Guy Syndrome shit and telling me I have to march in lockstep with them because they're the only ones on my side. I already done enough marching in lockstep while I was in the military. Plus, I don't appreciate being lectured to and bullied into submission. Got plenty of that in the military too, and I never could get off on that kind of thing like a man or a sub would." She glanced at me sideways. "You didn't hear me say that, if it freaks you out."

"No worries," I said. "I feel exactly the same way."

That made her grin a faintly feral grin. "Thought you might. Anyway, conservatives might feel entitled to my body, but progressives seem to feel entitled to my vote, and frankly I don't know which is more offensive. I just wanna say fuck all y'all and storm off into the sunset."

"Yeah," I said. "Sometimes I think I might be right there with you."

"And then I got two different people telling me my problems are my own damn fault for choosing to go into academia. Everyone's so quick to judge me for going into this dead-end career, and they're so proud to look down on me for wasting my time learning something difficult to a high level, but they sure are happy to send their kids to college. Not sure what they think college is all about, and I can't tell if it's insanity, stupidity, or complete self-absorption driving 'em to shit all over me for choosing to go into a career educating *their* kids. They've got some kind of disconnect there, and for all my fancy education, I can't fix it for them."

"Maybe you should spend less time on Facebook," I said.

"Yeah. I keep thinking that too. Only that's the only way I can keep in touch with most of my friends and family. And they make me mad, but they're the only friends and family I got, you know what I mean? Especially since I keep moving all the damn time."

"I know what you mean," I told her. "In that case, do you want me to tell you about my problems? They're at least as enraging, but they might take your mind off things."

"Hell yeah," said Mel.

I outlined the Aishat situation, leaving out her name but emphasizing the fact that there might be a video out there that might shed some light on what had happened to Brittany Gutierrez, and that Dorothy in the Dean's Office had already tried to shut Aishat down when she'd come forward about it.

"Oh fuck," said Mel when I was done. "Now I'm really fuckin' mad."

"I know," I said.

"You think this student of yours is telling the truth?"

"I'm as sure as I can be. And it sure is sounding like something really bad happened to Brittany Gutierrez, just like she said. And the college is going to hush it all up as best they can, and claim it's in the name of fairness and equality and making the world a better place. Only, surprise surprise, while they're so busy saving the world, they're turning into just another patsy of the patriarchy."

"Fuck yeah," said Mel. "Thinking that you're on the side of the angels is the surest path to destruction I know of."

"Yep," I said. "Case in point: lots of good talk about how enlightened and progressive you are, while silencing women and taking money from, say, a private prison company like Security Solutions."

"I don't think you understand how it works, Rowena. Taking money from private prison companies is fine. It's us women who are the real ones to blame, the way we seduce men with our sinful bodies and then lie about it."

"Yep," I said. "They've turned all these progressive social movements into witch-hunting for liberals. You find the conservative, working-class, or Southern woman who represents everything you hate in society, and then you drive her out and destroy her."

"Yeah," said Mel. "And like all witch hunts, you never know what you're gonna do that'll cause them to come after you with pitchforks."

"I know. But I still feel like I have to stand up against human rights violations and horrendous animal abuse and the destruction of our planet, even if it means standing with people I don't like."

"That's 'cause you're a better person than me," said Mel. "I'm this close"—she held up her thumb and forefinger a quarter of an inch apart—"from running off and joining the militia group I think my uncle is forming. At least that way I could pretend to have some kind of focus for my rage. Plus they'd probably give me a gun."

"How about you help me out with finding some rapists and bringing them to justice instead," I said. "You can always go join a private militia group once they fire us."

"Sounds like a plan," said Mel.

18

I HAD HOPED TO HAVE a heart-to-heart with Aishat on Friday and convince her to go tell everything to Brian Michaels. I completely understood her reluctance to come forward and make any kind of official statement, especially after what Dorothy had done. But self-interest made me uneasy about the position she had put me in, and a desire for justice made me want to unearth this video that Owen supposedly had.

But she was nowhere to be found on campus all day, and I didn't have her contact information. She had not given me any way of reaching her, or even told me what her last name was. Confusion from the emotional stress of telling me her story, an attempt to protect herself and her family, or part of her cunning plan to deceive me for reasons known only to her? I had been so sure she had been telling me the truth. Not giving me her contact information could be a confirmation of that—or a sign that she was not to be trusted. Three days out from meeting her and hearing her story, I was starting to feel the doubts creep in.

So when she didn't come to me, I went searching for her after my third class. The Crimson campus was not that big. The chances of running into a student during a random stroll were high. For example, during my fifteen-minute search for Aishat, I ran into Miranda, Camden, Amber, Isobel, and Jessica from my language classes, and Caitlyn, Emma, Alicia and Anthony from my Intro to Slavic Civ class. But there was no sign of Aishat.

I stopped and said hi to all my students, and asked if they knew Aishat and had seen her around today.

"Oh, yeah," Alicia told me, just when I was wondering if Aishat even went to school here at all. I mentally congratulated myself. I had almost not stopped to talk to Alicia and Anthony, who were in what looked like a very cozy, flirtatious conversation, half-hidden away under a big magnolia tree. "She was in my Diffy Q class last semester. She was really good at it. She helped me study for the tests—otherwise I never would have passed. Math isn't really my thing. Hope the rest of this engineering major doesn't kick my butt like Diffy Q did."

"Hopefully not," I said. Diffy Q, AKA Differential Equations, was one of the "washout courses" used to gently, or sometimes not so gently, direct students to a different major. "So have you happened to see her today?"

"No, I haven't seen her this week at all. Too bad. I was hoping to talk to her more about Islam, you know? I'm really interested in it. Not in, like, a Nation of Islam way, just a way of connecting with my heritage. We did DNA testing last year and discovered that part of our family is from the Sudan." She made a face. "So I started learning about the region, and, well, it was, like...pretty awful, actually. Like, they, like, still have crucifixion, stoning women to death, and stuff like that. But, like...it's my heritage. And there's a lot that's good, too, right? Like, you know, what you were saying about Russia today in class. Anyway, so then I, like, got, like interested in Islam, and started asking Aishat about it."

"There's a lot of interesting—and good—things about Islam," I said. Since Alicia was one of the three black students on campus, I could see Aishat gravitating to her, as two inherent and obvious outsiders in an extremely conformist culture.

"Yeah, right? Only I'm not sure about the dress code, especially the hijab and stuff."

"Yeah," I said. "That would be a problem for me too."

"I know! But they can be very empowering," Alicia told me earnestly. "It's an important part of their culture, you know."

The words "Heritage, not hate" rose up to my lips. Fortunately I was able to bite them back before they came out. Pointing out how many of the arguments in favor of hijabs, burkas, etc. could also be used to justify the wearing and flying of Confederate flags probably wouldn't win me many converts—or friends. Especially not with my non-white students and colleagues. I also wrestled for a moment with the urge to point out the problematic nature of the phrase "their culture," which was only a half-step away from "you people."

Luckily, I was able to maintain my self-control, and, instead of picking an argument, asked Alicia if she had Aishat's email or phone number.

Alicia made a sad face. "My phone totally crashed over break, and a bunch of contacts got lost when I switched everything over to my new phone! But you should be able to find her through Crimsonmail. There can't be that many Aishats. And her last name...it was something funny...Asel...Ashal...no, that's not it...I know! It had 'Aslan' in it. You know, like the lion in Narnia?"

"I know," I said. "And thanks a lot. See you on Monday!"

Alicia gave me a double thumbs-up and went back to giggling at everything Anthony said. She really did sound like an elf. Sitting next to Anthony, who was at least a foot taller than her, underlined how much she looked like one, too. And while Alicia's skin tone was more Mediterranean than sub-Saharan, next to Anthony's English rose complexion, it seemed strikingly dark. They looked well on their way to be one of those cute "opposites attract" couples. I waved at them and continued my sweep of campus.

After failing to find Aishat on either the upper or lower quads, I went back to my office, opened up an email in my Crimsonmail, and typed in "Aishat Aslan" in the "To" field. To my intense gratification, it automatically populated with "Aishat Aslanbekova." I composed a short email in Russian, suggesting that she go ahead and make an official report to the police, and offering to help her with this. Then, feeling like I had done what I could, I shut my computer down and headed home.

I spent about a nanosecond contemplating the idea of contacting Owen directly and asking him about the video. Then I promptly rejected it. Not only did I have grave doubts about the legality of such an action, I was afraid it would scare him into deleting the video. And I really, really wanted that video to come to light.

I was hopeful that Aishat would write back to me immediately, but there was nothing when I got home, so I was forced to work on my book proposal some more.

By suppertime there was still nothing. The doubts were starting to creep back.

After some hemming and hawing, I started to compose a text to Alex to ask him what he thought I should do. I was aware that maybe I should have told him about this earlier. Especially since I'd told Dima about it right away. I had never had the slightest inclination to cheat, or done anything that could remotely be called cheating. One of the good/bad things about me was that I had always been the painfully faithful kind. The very thought of infidelity made me feel ill. And there was nothing going on between me and Dima that could possibly be classified as infidelity. But I could see how, from Alex's point of view, it might be jealousy-inducing.

More than that, I was feeling a bit icky about it in the pit of my stomach. I never had until recently. But our interactions over winter break, when he'd wished me a happy New Year and I'd finally poured out all the things I'd wanted to tell him for years, all the reasons why

I wished he'd take more care of himself and have less of a death wish, had crossed some kind of a line. Texting him instead of Alex when I'd wanted advice on what to do about Aishat felt like it had crossed another line.

So my guilty conscience made me put off texting Alex, and when I finally made myself do it after supper, my guilty conscience made me jump like I'd been stuck with a pin when my phone rang as I was halfway through composing the text. I jumped again when I saw the call was from Alex.

19

"HEY," I SAID, I HOPED with just the right amount of goodwill and innocent nonchalance. "I was just in the middle of texting you."

"Great minds think alike. I feel like I've been neglecting you all week. So finally I was like, 'Fuck it, better call Rowena before she tells me to go to hell.'"

"I wasn't going to tell you to go to hell," I said. "I've been super-busy, actually, and I was feeling bad about neglecting you. It's just been a crazy week."

"Yeah, for me too. What's been going on with you?"

For a moment I almost said, "Nothing really, just start of the semester stuff." I was pretty damn sure Alex wasn't going to be happy when I told him about the Aishat situation.

Stop being such a coward! "Actually, I've gotten pulled into something pretty weird," I said out loud.

Alex's sigh was so heartfelt, it seemed like I probably could have heard it come all the way over from California, even without the aid of a telephone connection.

"What is it this time?" he asked.

"It turns out there's a student from Chechnya here at Crimson," I began.

Alex sighed again. "Why am I not liking the way this is going?"

"You're going to like it even less in a minute. So this Chechen student came to me earlier this week, and says she thinks she might have been sexually assaulted. One of those things where she passed out at a frat party and when she woke up, something wasn't right. Another girl also made allegations of sexual assault against someone at the same party, and that girl was expelled. So my student was afraid to come forward. But then she started getting blackmailed by someone claiming to have a video of her from the party that would ruin her life if it were to be made public. She's from a conservative Chechen family. Her father and brothers found out recently, and have sworn to avenge her honor, that kind of thing. She's hoping I can take care of it somehow, since the student doing the threatening used to be in my class."

"Take that shit to the police," Alex said promptly. "Do not pass go, do not collect $200, take that shit directly to the police. If you don't think the campus police will do anything about it, take it to the city police."

"I already did," I said. "Sort of. I explained the broad outlines of the situation to the chief of campus police, and asked what he thought I should do."

"Well, thank fuck for that. What did he say?"

"He told me to try to get the student to come make an official statement. See, she already went to the Title IX officer, who's also a dean, who threatened to expel her like the other girl was expelled if she didn't keep quiet about it."

"God damn, sometimes I fucking hate academia," said Alex. "Not that anywhere else is much better. But yeah, you've got to get that student to go to the police, whatever that dick from the Dean's Office says. And whatever you do, you CANNOT get any more involved in this than you already are."

"I know," I said. "I'll try to get her to go to the police. I definitely won't go all vigilante."

Alex emitted a third sigh, this time of relief. "Thank God. I was worried there for a moment. Which is in itself worrying. I wish I didn't have to worry about you going all vigilante as a general thing."

"When have I ever gone all vigilante?" I asked.

"I guess when you put it like that, you never really have, but there's always the feeling that you're about to. That you're always on the edge of doing whatever you think needs to be done, and fuck the consequences."

"Huh," I said. "Because in my own mind I'm a weak-willed, conformist coward who can be bullied into submission with one hint of unemployment."

Alex laughed, not very mirthfully. "What you must think of the rest of us, then."

"I try not to think badly of others. I don't always succeed, but that is my intent."

"I know it is, Rowena, which almost makes it more annoying. Shit! I didn't just say that. I didn't call you up to say shitty things to you. And I meant that as a compliment, anyway. I called you up to complain about what a shitty week I've been having. Which maybe isn't any better."

"It's fine," I said. "I'm happy to listen to you tell me about your shitty week."

"Yeah...it's just...I started having doubts about the wisdom of getting a PhD and going into this career path. A little late for that, you might say, and you'd be right, but I started to think this week about how I kind of got, I don't want to say tricked, but sort of cornered into doing it. Or at least that's how it felt to me."

"I know you said it was what your father wanted for you," I said.

"I know, so of course I spent years saying I was never going to do it, no fucking way. But after I got out of active duty...I hated the way that everywhere I went, it seemed like I had the words 'Iraq vet' tattooed on my forehead. I hated being defined by six months of my life I didn't even choose. So I figured I'd do something else to overlay that, so that people would stop seeing that 'Iraq vet' tattoo when they looked at me and start seeing 'PhD' instead. So here I am. Now people think *both* 'Iraq vet' *and* 'PhD' when they see me. I've gotten two labels instead of one."

"Yeah," I said. "That must suck."

"And then...that's not the real thing that's bothering me. I mean, it's part of it, but it's not the real thing. Some buddies...some of the ones I told you about earlier, the ones who wanted to get together last fall...they were back in town, and they wanted to get together again, so of course being a stupid dick, I agreed, and then I was stuck with them all evening, listening to their stupid macho bullshit stories."

"Ouch," I said.

"Yeah, and of course they all did much more macho things than I did. So I had to sit there all evening listening to them talk about firefights and shit. Then of course they wanted to hear some of *my* stories, and I had to be like, 'Well, nothing like that, man, but I did once watch someone I knew get beheaded on a livestream broadcast, while I sat back in my closet doing nothing.'"

"Oh my God," I said.

"It was a pretty sucky day," said Alex. "Although much suckier for him than for me."

"Yeah, but that's still a terrible thing to have to witness."

There was a long pause at the other end of the line. "Yeah," he said eventually. "And you know what the worst thing was? I mean, for me personally?"

"What?"

"What I did afterwards."

"Lots of people get sick or go crazy for a bit when they witness something like that," I said.

"Yeah, I know. And that would have been okay. But, see, the thing is, I didn't. I could have lived with myself a little better if I'd burst into tears, puked my guts out, smashed up some of our super-expensive equipment in a fit of uncontrollable rage—all things that other people there did, I might add. But I just sat there calmly, analyzing the situation. And then I wrote up a report about it."

"That may have been the most helpful response," I said.

"Yeah. I mean, that report I wrote was instrumental in catching the guys who did it. Or so they told me. I figured out where they were located and reported it, and they found them two days later. But no one looked at me quite the same after that. Fuck, *I* didn't look at me quite the same after that. It really fucking freaked me out, Rowena. And it freaked me out even more when...you know what, I'd better not tell you."

"Now you *have* to tell me," I said.

"Yeah, but...you know, like..."

"Was it interrogation?" I asked, as gently as I could.

Alex swallowed audibly through our fuzzy connection. "How did you know?"

"You speak Arabic. You were in intelligence. It was a logical guess."

"Yeah, well...yeah. It was. Not for long, thank fuck. And, you know, I never...I never did any of the really bad things. No waterboarding or Jerusalem chair or any of that shit. Mostly just more paperwork, to be honest. But I was still one of them, you know what I'm saying? I was still one of the torturers."

"I'm really sorry," I said.

"You're really sorr—Jesus Christ, Rowena, why? Why are *you* sorry?"

"Because you had to go through that. And carry it with you."

"Nothing I don't deserve."

"I'm still sorry," I said.

Alex sighed. Again. Maybe he needed to be used to generate wind-powered energy or something. I probably shouldn't be thinking thoughts like that right now. "Rowena, I'm going to hang up now. Not because I'm mad at you or anything. Because I'm fucking mad at myself, and you don't need to deal with that shit."

"I don't mind."

"Well, I do. The only thing that makes me sicker than knowing I was caught up in that, is knowing that it's touching you, even a little tiny bit. You shouldn't have to have anything to do with that shit."

"I'm not a porcelain doll," I said. "I used to interview torture victims for a living, remember?"

"Yeah. Which makes me one of the bad guys, no question, in your world. I'm one of the monsters."

"All of us have a little bit of monster inside. And I don't think you're bad."

"Well, maybe you fucking should, Rowena." Alex's voice was sharp, with a note of anger he'd never used towards me before. "I'm sorry," he said quickly. "No, don't you go jumping in and apologizing! Let me be the one to apologize for what a fucked-up piece of shit I am. And...fuck. I really need to hang up before I say something I'll regret even more than I regret what I've already said."

"I don't want you to hang up when you're angry," I said.

"Fuck! I'm not angry with *you*, Rowena. Mainly I'm angry with myself. And the world."

"I know. But you're angry, and upset, and you shouldn't be alone right now."

"Yeah. I really wish you were with me right now."

"I wish that too," I said. "But maybe we can be together again in the flesh pretty soon. You probably don't have spring break, right?"

"Nope," said Alex. "No spring break for the DLI."

"Well...maybe I could come out and visit you again."

"That'd be great. Can you afford it?"

"No," I said. "But that's what credit cards are for, right?"

"I think I'm getting angry again," said Alex. "But I also think you should come out and visit me if you can. And have you applied for that job in Carmel yet?"

"Sent off the app on Tuesday, got the confirmation."

"Well, maybe something will pan out with that. Maybe six months from now you'll be a California girl. Maybe with the buying power of both our salaries together, we'll be able to rent a decent place to live. Maybe even get some decent furniture. How do you feel about interior decorating?"

"I've always thought I would hate it, but since I've never had a place that could be decorated, or money to pay for decoration, I don't know," I said. "Maybe we'll discover it's my secret passion."

"I like the sound of that," said Alex. The sharpness was still there in his voice, but it was being overlaid with warmth. "We just have to make it through the next few months, and then maybe we'll be together full time."

"Yeah," I said. "That would be great."

20

I SPENT THE WEEKEND perfecting my book proposal to the best of my ability. By Sunday evening I'd gone over it three times, including in hard copy with enlarged font; had Mel, Chloe, and Alex all proofread it; considered and discarded most of their conflicting suggestions for improvement; cleaned my apartment, done my hapkido forms and my yoga asanas; and planned all my lessons for Monday. There was nothing I could do to put off the inevitable any longer.

So at 7:00pm EST I pulled the trigger and emailed all 20 carefully polished pages to the most appropriate-sounding acquisitions editor at the first academic press on my multi-page list of prospects.

I woke up three times during the night racked with terror that I'd accidentally emailed it to the wrong person, or misspelled Marina Tsvetaeva (the subject of my book), or failed to fix all the errors in numeration and pagination that autoformat seemed determined to insert in all my documents. I tried to console myself with the thought that even if everything were absolutely perfect, chances were excellent that I still wouldn't get accepted. That thought was not as comforting as I had hoped it would be.

The result was that I was in a rare mood when I showed up on campus Monday morning. I tried to conceal it from Mel as we carpooled in together. Judging by the sideways looks she kept giving me as we left the pawn-and-smoke-shops district behind and drove into the faux-antique-boutiques district outside of campus, my performance left a lot to be desired.

"Is it that time of the month or something?" she finally demanded, as we rolled through the front entrance of campus and started down the front drive, with its sweeping view of the front quad and its neocolonial brick buildings.

"No."

"Hey, no judgment if it is. Sometimes I just want to punch someone in the face if it's the wrong day of the month."

"I know. But it's just my book proposal. I sent it off, and now I'm freaking out about it."

"Your proposal was great!"

"Thanks. But I'm feeling...I guess I'm freaking out because I really care about this project, and I really, really want to get this book published, and I know it's going to be awful and there will be lots of rejections, and then if it *does* get accepted, there will be soul-sucking revisions, maybe several of them, and there's a good chance that by the time the book sees the light of day, it won't be the book I wanted to write, and it's quite possible that I'll hate it and never want to have anything to do with it, and..."

"I think you need to stop thinking about this," said Mel. "And I think you're scared because you've finally decided to go after something you really want, and now you might not get it—or you might get it, and that's even scarier."

"You may be right," I said.

"I mean, what else have you gone after that you really wanted in life?"

"I really wanted to get married to Dima," I said. "And look how that turned out."

"Just 'cause that turned to shit don't mean this has to...what the hell are those kids doing?"

We had just turned down the lane that led to the faculty parking lot behind the football stadium. On our right was a small wooded copse. Supposedly there was a kind of forest glade in the center of it, where students went to hang out, make out, and pass out from too much alcohol and other drugs. This was known as The Hollow.

Despite the fact that it was 39 degrees outside, with the promise of a bone-chilling rain in the air, a line of boys dressed in nothing but boxer shorts and some kind of occult-looking sigils painted onto their chests were filing out of the woods. Most of them had paint on their faces as well, in patterns that looked like sloppy copies of a mixture of Native American, Maori, and African tribal markings. They must have undergone some kind of ritual at The Hollow. They were joining a group of students gathered around a display made of balloons, banners, and folding tables on the other side of the road, by the beach volleyball courts.

"Oh God," I said. "It's the Frat Dash. It has to be. The frats hold a race every January. They run around campus in nothing but boxers and 'war paint.' I'm astonished they haven't been cited and banned for cultural appropriation."

"They're frats," said Mel. "They can get away with stuff the rest of us can't. Hey, is that Jamal Warner?"

I craned my neck around as we drove past the tables, which had large banners reading "Frat Dash 2016: Registration" on the front. I was pretty sure it said "Sponsored by Security Solutions" below that. A handsome, extremely fit-looking boy, the only black student in the entire group, was writing something down at the table, while other students gathered around him and slapped his back.

"Has to be," I said. "Oh look: the others are marking his chest with blood. They all sign their names with blood when they enter the event, and mark each other's chests with their blood before they set off. They're supposed to become blood brothers. It was a thing back in my mother's day, and I guess it's still a thing today."

"Men," said Mel. "Well, I guess it's nice that they're breaking down racial barriers and forging the bonds of brotherhood, or some shit like that."

"Yeah," I said.

"Whaddya think?" asked Mel. "Does he look like a rapist to you?"

"Not really," I said. "He just looks like an unusually athletic college student."

"Yeah," said Mel. "I read an interview with him in the *Crimson Champion* last semester. He seemed like a nice kid there. A heartwarming hard-luck tale of growing up in a bad part of Atlanta, finding a coach who supported him in high school, getting a life-changing scholarship to college—the usual story. I mean, if he really did hurt Brittany, then justice should be done, but I'd sure hate for something bad to happen to him unless he really deserved it."

"Yeah," I said. "Somehow my thirst for vengeance and justice always dries up in the face of the actual people my zeal would be destroying. Oh look, it's Anthony next to him. Anthony Wainwright III," I explained. "He's in my Intro to Slavic Civ class. I guess I should go watch the race. No one's going to come to class anyway. We might as well have a field trip to watch the race and pretend that we held class."

"That sounds appropriately educational," said Mel. "Certainly worth the $50,000 a year the students are paying in tuition."

"I'm pretty sure a major part of what they're paying for is not to learn the Arabic writing system or Russian verbal aspect, but the chance to go to silly events on the quad," I said.

"Too fucking right," said Mel. "Okay, you've convinced me." She wheeled her Jeep Grand Cherokee, which had seen better decades but was still chugging along more days than not, into a spot on the edge of the faculty parking lot. "How's the knee?" she asked. "Do you need the walking stick?" Mel had been loaning me her walking stick on and off since my knee injury last semester.

"It's okay today," I said. "How about you?"

"Today I feel almost normal. Maybe it'll continue."

"Let's hope so. See you at the race, I guess."

"Oh boy," said Mel.

21

AS PREDICTED, FEWER than half my students were present when I showed up for my first class. The three who had shown up jumped to their feet with alacrity when I asked them if they wanted to go on a field trip to watch the race instead of staying in class. Camden was already out the door before I finished asking the question, with Isobel hard on his heels.

"Jeez, everyone's really keen to watch this race," said Miranda, as we squeezed past the too-large table and broken chairs in order to escape from the classroom. It was the same table we'd used to barricade the door last semester when Chris had come for us, now rather worse for the wear. I was surprised the college hadn't replaced all the furniture in the room on a matter of principle. Surely some of the students found it upsetting to be reminded four days a week in such a tangible way of how one of their classmates had nearly mown them down with a semi-automatic rifle. I knew I did. I'd like to think that's why I always got a headache whenever I went into this classroom, but it had started happening months before Chris had had his murderous outburst.

"Surely the *Champion* is covering it," I said. The *Crimson Champion* was the campus paper. Miranda had been a journalist and photographer for it last semester. "I'm surprised you're not out there photographing it."

She shrugged a small shrug. "I asked for some time off. I couldn't...it was weird, you know? Being a story instead of covering a story. And everyone was weird to me, too. They didn't mean to be, but...I'm sure a lot of them think it's my fault. What happened. And..." She trailed off.

"It's not your fault," I said.

"It feels like it is," she said.

"I know. It feels like it's my fault too. I'm sure all of us who had anything to do with Chris feel like it's our fault. And we *are* our brother's keepers, and our sister's too. That's part of choosing not to be Cain. But you weren't the one who dripped poison about women into Chris's ear every day all semester. You weren't the one who raised him in a household full of guns, and you weren't the one who made it easy for him to get his hands on an AR-15 and a .45 semi-automatic. But you *were* the one who stood up and shouted at him not to shoot people. You *were* the one who wanted to go out and talk to him so that he wouldn't shoot anyone else. That has to count for a lot."

"Yeah. Maybe." We were waiting at the back of the crowd that was trying to push its way out of Bedford Hall. A group of girls in Alpha Delta Pi shirts were discussing the chances of the Kappa Alpha Order team versus the Pi Chi team. Their chatter covered up our conversation, and their ADPi blue shirts gave us something to fix our eyes on. Maybe that was why Miranda was suddenly talking.

"I was so scared," she said. "And I was so sure I was going to wimp out and be a coward."

"Yeah," I said. "Me too. And so was Professor Taylor. And I'll bet Professor Wilson felt the same way too."

"None of you acted like it, though," she said. "And yeah, I did stand up and say I was going to come out and talk to Chris, but you wouldn't let me. You made me stay in the room...and I stayed. I *didn't* go out and confront him."

"You did the right thing," I told her. "If I had thought that you coming out would have made things better, I would have told you to come out."

That almost made Miranda smile. "Jeez," she said. "Way to protect your students, Professor H."

"If I had thought that you coming out there and talking to Chris would have saved all the other students, I would have told you to come out. But I didn't think that. Staying with the others and helping them stay calm and brave was the best thing you could have done. We were all scared, but all of us did the right thing in the end, and none of us are to blame for what Chris did, not really. Like I said, we are our brother's keeper, but our brother is also our keeper too. Taking on more guilt than we deserve to carry won't change anything or fix anything, and none of us can bear that burden, anyway."

"I guess," said Miranda, like I hadn't really convinced her. She was looking down at her shoes, her hair falling forward to reveal the nape of her neck where her undercut was still growing out. Her neck looked much too vulnerable and fragile. I was willing to bet she'd lost ten pounds over break, and she hadn't been heavy to begin with. I thought about nagging her about it. I decided it would be more helpful to change the subject.

"So," I said. "Any hot tips for the winner? Who should I go put my money on?"

Miranda started to smile. A tiny, tremulous smile, but still a smile. She was also looking up now to where a group of Tri Sigmas were greeting the knot of ADPis in front of us with ecstatic cries of joy, as if they'd been journeying across the barren Sahara for a month during sandstorm season to find each other, not across the quad for five minutes.

"Jamal Warner, obviously," said Miranda. "It was a big deal when he got accepted into Pi Chi. He was the first black member of a Greek organization here at Crimson. We did a big write up about it at the *Champion*. Plus, Anthony Wainwright was his Big Brother, and anything the Wainwrights do is big news here."

"Really?" I knew that Anthony Wainwright had that "III" after his name, which suggested old money, but old money kids of middling intelligence were a dime a dozen here at Crimson. Anthony was tall and good-looking and well-mannered in a preppy way, and seemed more ambitious and intellectually curious than your average Crimson student, but he didn't jump out at you as an obvious misfit the way Miranda or Aishat did. Anthony seemed like someone in his element, who had spent all his previous life in his element and was expecting to spend the rest of his life in his element too.

"Yeah. They were one of the founders of Crimson, and are still big donors. You know, as in 'Wainwright Health'?"

"The health center is named after them?" I asked.

"Yeah. The original central classroom building was too, but it got merged into a wing of the library when they expanded it, and then they donated money for a health center. Like I said, major benefactors of the college. And I think they really are trying to do some good. Like with the health center, or how Anthony sponsored Jamal for his frat."

"That's cool," I said. "Oh look, here they come."

About fifty boys, all dressed in nothing but boxers and culturally appropriated "war paint," came dashing down our side of the quad. Some of them, led by Jamal and Anthony, appeared to be running in a semi-serious manner. Anthony looked to be keeping up with Jamal pretty handily. I wished I weren't looking at one of my students in the semi-buff. Anthony did have a good body, in a rangy, racquetball-and-lacrosse-playing kind of way, but the knowledge that he was my student made me feel nothing but a faint queasiness when I looked at his fit arms and chiseled abs.

"Anthony Wainwright is *so hot*," sighed one of the Tri Sigs in front of me.

"He's *fire*," agreed the ADPi next to her, also sighing. "*Fire*, Ashlyn, *fire*!"

"He asked me to dance at a formal last year," said Ashlyn the Tri Sig. "I thought maybe he'd ask me out, but then I heard he was going out with some RBD girl." She heaved another heavy sigh, while the other girls said unkind things about the promiscuity of Rho Beta Delta girls.

They broke off discussing the sluttiness of girls in other sororities in order to emit ear-splitting shrieks of excitement as Anthony, Jamal, and the other frontrunners sprinted past. Anthony shouted something incoherent about ADPi and Tri Sig. Jamal blew a kiss in our general direction, causing the shrieking to rise to a near bat-sonar pitch, before putting his head down and surging ahead.

A feverish discussion broke out over whether he were aiming that kiss at someone specific, or at the group in general. None of the sorority girls could claim the honor of being the object of his admiration, although several of them wanted it very much.

"It's not you, is it?" Ashlyn the Tri Sig asked Miranda, making it clear with every fiber of her being that it should be impossible for someone like Miranda to attract the attention of someone like Jamal.

"Nuh-uh," said Miranda.

"Oh. Is it *you*?" asked Ashlyn, in my general direction.

I looked behind me. No one else was there. Ashlyn was looking expectantly, and rather superciliously, at me. It was clear she thought it even more impossible for someone like me to attract the attention of someone like Jamal, but I was the only other female in the group. Wow. I guess I really did look young.

"No," I said.

"Why are you laughing like that?" demanded Ashlyn. "Are you one of those girls who'd never date a black guy, or something like that? 'Cause that's gross."

"I'm laughing because Jamal must be half my age," I said. "The chances of either of us being interested in each other are vanishingly slim. I'm a professor."

Ashlyn & Co. all gave me a horrified look, and edged away from me. For a moment my professorial presence acted as an oppressive weight on them, but then Jamal pulled decisively to the front of the pack as he dashed up the stairs outside Lee Hall and around to the front quad, and they started shrieking in appreciation again.

The frontrunners were followed by, well, the non-frontrunners. Many of them had chosen boxers with extremely garish, and in some places highly obscene, designs on them, and accessorized them with a variety of Hawaiian flower leis, feather boas, extremely long multi-strand pearl necklaces, and the kind of hat that women traditionally wore to weddings or the Kentucky Derby. Many of them were in high heels. Some of them appeared to be three, or possibly four, sheets to the wind. Their progress down the course was, consequently, not swift.

"This is bullshit," muttered Miranda. "I can't believe the college still lets this happen."

"Me too," I said. "I know it's a time-honored tradition and all, but it's not what I'd call appropriate on multiple levels."

"They were talking about shutting it down," Miranda told me. "Because of all the drinking and stuff that goes on around it. But Security Solutions stepped in and said they'd sponsor it. The college agreed when Security Solutions said they'd sponsor some stuff about preventing binge drinking as well. And I think they've been sponsoring some stuff for the frats about hazing too. Anthony Wainwright was organizing that last semester."

"Good for him, I guess," I said. I had rather uncharitable views of fraternities, but anything that could be done to reduce the drinking, hazing, and sexual assault that always seemed to happen around them had to be a good thing.

The last runner in the race stumbled past us in bright pink boxers with a kind of dildo—at least I hoped it was a dildo—sticking out the front, red patent-leather spike heels, and a hat that would have been appallingly garish even at the Royal Enclosure at Ascot. The crowd greeted his passage with ecstatic cheers and rapturous applause. To be fair, anyone who could remain upright at all, let alone run, in spike heels that high, with a blood alcohol level that was obviously even higher, deserved applause. I wondered where he had gotten his hat. There must be a shop in town that catered just to this event.

As I was contemplating the economics of running a hat shop dependent on the fraternity fancy dress trade, the cheering rose to even more ear-splitting heights. Jamal, now so far out in front that the other runners weren't even visible, had rounded the far corner of Lee Hall and was making his way in strides that were so smooth and even that he didn't even appear to be making an effort to the finish line on the far side of the back quad.

"Jamal! JAMAL!" shrieked the girls in front of me. I would have been worried about hearing loss, except that their pitch quickly got above the range of human hearing anyway.

"CHAMP-I-ON! CHAMP-I-ON!" The chant started on the other side of the quad, where Jamal was still the only runner visible on the course, and then spread around all four sides until it reached us. I looked over at Miranda. She was mouthing it too, her face alight with happiness for the first time since Chris had come looking for her with a loaded AR-15 in his hands.

22

JAMAL BURST THROUGH the finish line just as the rest of the frontrunners, with Anthony at their head, came around Lee Hall and started down the home stretch. The cheering was so intense I was a little afraid that some of the students were going to burst the air vesicles in their lungs.

"That was great!" said Miranda. She was smiling ear-to-ear for the first time I'd ever seen. "Really great! And you know what? I should go interview him. For the paper. I know someone else is covering it, but I could go over too. What do you think?"

I looked down at her. Already her smile was starting to fade. "I think you should do it," I said.

"Yeah...wish I'd brought my recorder and my good camera..."

"Come on," I said. "Let's go over now. You could tell him you'd like to make an appointment to do an in-depth interview later. A human-interest piece on what it's like to spearhead racial integration of Crimson's Greek culture, or something like that."

Miranda's face lit up again. "That's a great idea! I'm sure the editor will love it. Um...will you come with me? It's just...I feel kind of weird doing stuff by myself since, well..."

"Sure," I said. "Let's go."

We pushed our way through the thronging hordes to the finish line, where the other students were finishing the race. I was afraid we wouldn't be able to get to Jamal because everyone else on campus would be trying to do the same thing, but when we got there, we discovered that Security Solutions had set up a winner's circle and were keeping everyone back from it.

Jamal was standing by himself in the middle of the circle, looking both pleased and awkwardly alone. Despite his muscular physique, he looked younger than his nineteen years. As he had crossed the finish line, there had been a childlike purity and innocence to his striving and his joy. Now, standing in the winner's circle, there was something about his stance that made me think that this was what a young Count Vronsky must have looked like: full of confidence, self-assurance, and the conviction that he was God's gift to everyone around him. But there was also a hint of Count Vronsky's future loneliness, too, in the occasional glance Jamal would throw at the Security Solutions guards and the screaming fans and the empty space all around him.

"Press!" Miranda was trying to shout over the din, as she fought her way to the tape marking the winner's circle. "Press! *Crimson Champion!*"

The guard closest to her stepped up and said, "I'm sorry, ma'am, but no one is allowed through."

"I'm from the *Champion*! I want to interview Jamal for the paper!"

"Do you have any ID, ma'am?"

Miranda patted at her jacket pocket, disconcerted. "No, I...I left it in my dorm..."

I stepped forward. "Hi, Carl," I said. "I can vouch for her, if that helps."

Something that on a less impassive man might have been a smile crossed Carl's face. We had met last semester when he had been assigned as the security detail for Miriam Chen, the guest speaker I had brought to campus. Carl was a short, bald, incredibly fit-looking black man who avoided emoting whenever possible. We'd only encountered each other briefly, but I was pretty sure he'd gotten a huge kick out of telling Dean Talbot, AKA Dorothy the Dread, that my name was not Regina but Doctor Rowena Halley. I was hoping that would count for something now.

"Doctor Halley, right?" said Carl. "You say this girl really is from the paper?"

"The college newspaper, yes," I said. "She's also my student, so I can vouch both for her job and her character."

Another ghost of a smile crossed Carl's face. "Wait here," he said.

A moment later he had brought Jamal over to us. Up close the impression of an adolescent Vronsky was even stronger. An adolescent Vronsky who was trying to hide his adolescent insecurities behind a mask of cocky bravado. It would take another half a decade or so for the mask to turn into the real person.

I eyed him critically while Miranda arranged an interview with him that afternoon. High cheekbones, very dark skin, big smile, large, lively eyes, sponge twists with frosted tips that bounced energetically every time he turned his head. It was a face that would look great on any team roster or endorsing a whole range of sports equipment. Was it also the face of someone who had drugged and raped Brittany Gutierrez and/or Aishat? I didn't want to think so, but men really, really could surprise you that way.

Miranda finished setting up the interview appointment as Anthony and a half-dozen other boys in Pi Chi gear came over to scream, shout, and chant their congratulations to Jamal. The loudest was the boy in the red patent-leather spike heels and Ascot-style fascinator hat. Somehow he had managed to get even drunker during the course of the race, and instead of slapping Jamal on the back, he ended up swaying, tripping on his spike heels, and falling right into Carl's arms. Still with the same impassive expression, Carl laid him out full length on the grass, where he continued to wallow back and forth like a beached whale while bellowing something about "Pi!

Pi! Chi! Chi!" mixed in with drunken salutes to Jamal's running prowess.

'Thanks, man," Anthony said to Carl. "Coming through for us as usual." He went over to the drunk boy. "Come on, man," Anthony told him, trying to pull him to his feet. "Stop acting like an asshole, okay? This isn't just about Pi Chi winning the Frat Dash. This is about healing the wounds of racial injustice and shit like that. We've got press here and everything. Act like a real Pi Chi gentleman."

"Pi CHIIIIII!" bellowed the other boy, before sitting halfway up and barfing all over Anthony's shoes.

"Shall we go?" I asked Miranda.

"Yeah, I guess." Miranda's normally milk-pale skin was flushed with what looked like excitement and attraction, and she turned and looked back at Jamal three times as we fought our way back across the quad to Bedford Hall.

23

"OH ROWENA, *there* you are! *Why* weren't you in class?!?"

Karen, looking even more like she'd been sucking on an unripe persimmon, or possibly a stick of antiperspirant, came barreling down the hallway towards me.

"We were watching the Frat Dash," I told her. "Like everyone else on campus."

Karen sniffed. "Stupid waste of time, if you ask me. And the frats are *nothing* but trouble."

Under other circumstances I would have heartily agreed, but since it was Karen saying it, I felt compelled to say, "The students like it. And it builds school spirit."

"And *alcoholism*," said Karen. "Half those students were falling-down drunk, and it's not even ten in the morning!"

This was an incontrovertibly true fact, but since hell would freeze over before I gave Karen the satisfaction of agreeing with her, I said, "Were you looking for me?"

"Oh, *yes*. I *was* looking for you, Rowena, especially after I *failed* to find you in your classroom during your appointed class time! That is a *serious* breach of Crimson protocol, I must inform you!"

"Mmmmm," I said. Pointing out that it was a breach of protocol committed by every single class on campus was unlikely to help my cause. "Did you need to meet with me about something?" I asked instead.

Karen looked like she wanted to say "No" just to avoid giving *me* the satisfaction of appearing to agree with me, but she swallowed down her displeasure, her saggy throat gulping like a bullfrog's (I thought uncharitably), and said, "Yes, I was! I wanted to inform you—as a *courtesy*, since you'll be getting the official email soon—that the hearing about the, well, the *incident* that *your student* was involved in will be held next month. 3:00pm, Tuesday, February 16th, Saunders 385. The big conference room in Saunders Hall where we hold our department meetings," she added, seeing my blank expression.

"Oh," I said. "Well, thanks for telling me. I appreciate it. Do you know what the procedure will be?"

"I *expect* they'll be questioning everyone they think might be at fault for, well, the *incident*."

"The police have already questioned me. Extensively. Both campus and town police. Even the FBI gave me a call."

"The FBI!" Karen's expression of horror at the mention of the FBI would have been more appropriate on the face of the head of a gang of money launderers, not the head of a department that had had a school shooting.

"They like to keep an eye on incidents of mass violence," I said.

"We did *not* have an incident of mass violence! We didn't have a single death!"

"No, but we could have," I said. "Law enforcement gets twitchy these days when teenagers stroll into school buildings carrying loaded semi-automatic weapons. It's a thing. The FBI does a lot of training of local law enforcement for active shooter situations, and stuff like that. So someone from the Atlanta office called me and asked me to walk him through what happened."

"Even the *FBI* is investigating you!" said Karen, looking even more horrified.

"The FBI isn't *investigating* me," I said. "They were looking into the shooting, that's all."

"Why didn't you *tell* me, Rowena? We *need* to know if one of our instructors is bringing the college into ill repute!"

I opened my mouth to scream, "Cooperating with the FBI isn't bringing the college into ill repute!" Then I shut it and breathed in slowly through my nose. "So who else will be at the hearing?" I asked when I could speak calmly again.

"Dorothy Talbot from the Dean's Office is chairing it," said Karen. "And Theresa will be there, of course." Theresa Mayfield was the Dean of the College of Arts and Sciences. She was also the former chair of the Modern Languages department, and the person who had hired me for this position. I regretted pretty much every day that she had been promoted. From everything I'd seen of her, Theresa was okay. Karen, not so much. And the less said about Dorothy, the better. Having her as chair of the hearing did not bode well

"And I *suppose* Brian Michaels—*you* know, the chief of campus police—will have to be there as well."

"I know Brian," I said. "We worked together on the security for the Miriam Chen talk last semester."

"Oh, yes." Karen's saggy mouth pursed up into a vaguely obscene-looking line, like something in a low-budget alien horror flick that would suddenly disgorge a disgusting, penis-like tongue and suck you into its vagina-esque maw. Karen was afraid of Brian, for reasons unclear to me. Maybe she was just afraid of everyone who was even the tiniest bit competent at their job.

"And all the, uh, people *involved* in the *incident*. All of...what was his name? That student. All of his instructors, plus Melissa Wilson and Chloe Taylor, since they were directly involved as well. I don't have to *tell* you, Rowena, that the college is taking this *very* seriously. We do *not* want a repeat of this incident—and, of course, we *certainly* don't want a faculty member who fails to uphold their responsibilities to guide and protect their students."

"Mmmmm," I said, and fled to teach my second class.

24

BETWEEN SUBMITTING my book proposal and getting sucked into the Frat Dash, I'd only spent about every third minute of the past few days fretting over the fact that Aishat hadn't gotten back to me. But during the 33% of my fretting time that I was spending on her, I seesawed back and forth between worry and aggravation. Had something dreadful happened to her? Had her family decided to solve the problem with a good old-fashioned honor killing? Or had she just lost her nerve or blown me off in the time-honored manner of students everywhere?

Tuesday morning I thought I caught a glimpse of her out of the corner of my eye as I was heading to my first class, but before I could go over to her, I ran into Miranda, who grabbed me and thanked me for making her go over and ask Jamal for an interview.

"So you got the interview?" I asked.

"Yeah, and it was *great*! We talked for like, almost two hours yesterday, and I got all kinds of great stuff! I'm sure it'll be a great article! And he seemed like, a really cool guy, too. Not at all like I was expecting. I thought he'd be, like, totes full of himself, or a complete moron, since he's, like, a football player, but he's actually a really smart, thoughtful guy."

"That's great," I said. Miranda's face had picked up a healthy glow, and her whole being seemed animated and alive for the first time since she'd come back from break. Excitement about having a good story and, I suspected, excitement about Jamal himself. They must have really hit it off. Surely he wouldn't have spent half the afternoon with her if he didn't like her back.

Please don't let him be a rapist. I closed my eyes and sent a silent prayer out to St. Fevronia and anyone else who was listening. *Let him heal Miranda of all the pain and guilt she needs healing from. Let him be worthy.*

When I opened my eyes, Aishat was hovering at the end of the hall, rocking back and forth like she couldn't decide to come over to me, or hide. I waved at her. She promptly disappeared around the corner.

Oh well, I thought, and went to teach class.

When I came out of my second class, she was hovering at the end of the hall again. This time when I waved at her, she came over to me, walking like a nervous horse about to bolt off for the horizon.

"I got your email," she said.

"Okay, good," I said.

"I...I..." Her throat spasmed shut.

"Let's go into my office and talk," I suggested.

She followed me silently into my office. This time she did sit down instead of standing over the chair and holding onto it with a death grip, but she couldn't seem to bring herself to speak at all.

"Brian Michaels, the chief of police here, is a friend of the family," I told her, when it became apparent she wasn't going to start. "I trust him as much as I trust anyone about this. I told him a bit about what you told me, but I didn't give him your name. He would really, really like to talk to you. Both because he wants to help you, and because he wants to find out what happened to Brittany. He's sure that something bad happened to Brittany, but he doesn't know what that is. If there's been some terrible injustice, we want to find out about it and fix it. But we need your help to do that."

"I..." Her throat spasmed again. "I...my family..."

"I know," I said. "I know. I used to work with refugees from Chechnya. Believe me, I've heard lots of stories just like yours, and worse. And they're all terrible. I really want to help you, Aishat. If you want, I can go with you to talk to Brian Michaels together, so you won't have to go alone. Or your mother could accompany you. Or both of us."

"I just..." She was twisting the hem of her headscarf in both hands, causing it to slip to one side. "I just...I want it to go away. I want it to have never happened."

"Of course. That's natural."

"Can't you..." Her lips were trembling. "Can't you make Owen delete the video, and make it all go away? My father..."

"We don't want Owen to delete the video," I said, as gently as possible. "We want him to give us the video, so that we have evidence of what happened. Otherwise it will be very hard to achieve any kind of justice."

"Justice..." she repeated. She gave her headscarf an extra-hard twist, and jerked it off her head. "Oi!" she cried. "Oi, I'm such a clumsy, stupid idiot! I can't do anything right!"

"You're not an idiot," I told her.

"Maybe..." said Aishat, once she had fixed her headscarf with shaking hands. "Maybe...maybe I was mistaken."

"Mistaken about what?" I asked.

"Mistaken about what happened. At the party."

"You seemed pretty sure the last time we talked about it. And there must be something, if Owen has a video he can use for blackmail."

"He hasn't tried to blackmail me recently," said Aishat. "Maybe he was bluffing."

"Maybe."

"I think...I think I don't want to do anything about it," said Aishat. "I think...maybe it won't be such a big problem. My father is so angry about it, and my brothers are even angrier. I think if I do anything more, it will only make things worse. Whatever happened can't be undone, and maybe nothing that bad happened anyway."

"You said you were in a lot of pain when you woke up, and you thought you'd been washed," I pointed out. "That sounds like something really bad."

"Maybe it was just...you know...that time of the month. I think maybe I'll just forget about it. Maybe I was mistaken anyway. Maybe nothing bad happened at all."

"Maybe," I said again. "But that doesn't seem very likely."

Aishat gave me a wan smile by way of a response, and fled before I could say anything more.

25

AFTER THAT WE WERE at a bit of an impasse. I ran into Aishat a couple more times over the next few weeks, but the first time she told me that it had all been a big mistake and I should forget everything she had told me, and the second time she turned and ran at the sight of me.

I told Brian Michaels what had happened when he ran into me on a cold Friday afternoon at the end of January and asked me if I wanted to go grab a coffee and warm up.

"So how's it goin'?" he asked once we were seated in a back corner of Brew's Up, each holding a warm cup of coffee and inhaling the steam. The temperature this time of year was normally in the 60s. At the moment it was 41 degrees and rainy. As far as I could tell, I was the only person on campus who had the wardrobe for sub-60-degree weather. Brian had a zip-up synthetic jacket as part of his uniform, but no hat, scarf, or gloves. At least he was wearing long pants. Half the students were dashing from class to class in shorts, exposing their gooseflesh-covered legs to the damp, chill air. Any Russian grandmother worth her salt would have pulled them over and given them an earful for endangering themselves that way. I was half tempted to do it myself.

"Okay," I told him. "Busy, and I just got my first rejection for the book proposal."

"Screw 'em," Brian told me. "You're too good for 'em. And don't you worry," he added, seeing the doubt on my face. "You'll get your book published, I'm sure of it."

"Thanks," I said. "That's what John said, too."

"'Course he did. How's he doin'?"

I shrugged. "The usual. Struggling to keep it together, and only sort of managing." John had a lot of problems, and they only seemed to be getting worse as he approached 40. Spending his entire adult life in a rigidly hierarchical society that worshipped violence had not been helpful, although I thought that John's fundamental problems were not because he was a Marine. John was a Marine because of his fundamental problems.

"Yeah," said Brian. "His twenty years must be almost up, right? He got any plans for once he gets out? Or is he gonna try and stay in and make General or somethin'?"

"I think he's planning to leave when his twenty years are up," I said. "John loves the Marines—sort of. And he's sort of sick of it, and I think he wants to do something else with the rest of his life."

"Yeah," said Brian. "You tell him if he wants to know more about law enforcement, he should come talk to me, okay?"

"Okay," I said. "Although I think he might have a similar problem to me: he'll have a very specific skill set, be ridiculously overqualified for most entry-level positions, and be completely unqualified for most non-entry-level jobs out in the 'real world.' And he'll be much more hardheaded about it, too."

"Yeah," said Brian. "You tell him to come talk to me if he needs to, okay?"

"Sure," I said. "Although you don't know what you're getting yourself into by making that offer."

"I know I'm offering to help the man who straightened out my son and maybe saved his life, too. I reckon I can put up with a bit o' bad behavior from him if I have to."

"I appreciate it," I said. "John might not, but I do."

"Yeah." He stirred his coffee. "Speakin' o' bad behavior, you heard anythin' more from that student o' yours? The one who said she was assaulted at the same party as Brittany Gutierrez? She gonna come in and give a statement?"

I told Brian about Aishat's change of heart.

"That's how it is more often than not," he said. "Can't say I'm surprised. I went ahead and dug a bit around on YouTube in case there's a video up on there." He made a face. "I found a lot of sick shit, but nothin' that had any Crimson students that I recognized. Nothin' with Brittany for sure."

"If the video exists, it probably hasn't been released yet," I pointed out. "Since it's being used for blackmail."

"Yeah. This student ever say anything about who the blackmailer might be?"

Brian was looking at me out of the corner of his eye as he asked it, like I was a wild bird that might fly away if he looked at me directly.

"Well..." I resisted the urge to scuff my boots over each other like Aishat. "Yeah, actually, she did. I was just hoping she would tell you directly, so I wouldn't have to go tattling to you."

"Reportin' a crime ain't tattlin'."

"I know. I just don't feel good about passing on second-hand information like this, especially when it's something that could mess up someone's life if I got it wrong."

"You let me worry about whether it's right or wrong," Brian told me. "You're tellin' me what this student told you, right?"

"Yeah. So, well...one of the reasons she came to me was because the student she said is blackmailing her was one of my students. She wants me to intervene with him directly."

"Don't do it," Brian said immediately. "It ain't your place, and you might scare him off, or even get yourself into danger."

"That thought also occurred to me. So...the student she said was blackmailing her is Owen Wu."

Brian made a disgusted noise in the back of his throat. "That one of those Chinese students the college is bringin' in 'cause they can charge 'em a hundred thousand bucks a year or somethin'?"

"Yep," I said.

Brian made another disgusted noise in the back of his throat. "That sure as hell complicates things. The only thing the college'll hate even more than bringing' up their star football player and poster boy for diversity and inclusion on rape charges will be if we do it to one of their foreign cash cows as well."

"This thought has also occurred to me," I said.

"So whaddya think? Could this Owen kid have done it?"

"Just between you, me, and the wall, he's a lousy student and a pain in the ass to deal with. I could see him cheating on an exam. I have a harder time seeing him as a rapist. But blackmail? Maybe."

"Tell you what," said Brian. "I'll say I got an anonymous tip about new evidence in the Brittany Gutierrez case. Maybe I can get my hands on Owen's computer. If it's college-issued then I can confiscate and search it without a warrant—if the college agrees. If the college don't agree, the situation's a bit stickier. And o' course, he might not have the video on his computer. It might be on his phone, or another computer, or somethin' like that. And if we start searching for it, it might tip him off, make him delete the video before we can find it. Best if I can get warrants for all his devices at once."

"Yeah," I said.

Brian grinned a hard grin. "The college ain't gonna like this one bit. We could be lookin' at a whole storm o' shit comin' our way. But like I said, I'm sure as sure can be that something real bad happened to Brittany Gutierrez, and I ain't gonna spend the rest o' my life wonderin' what that was and if a rapist is walkin' around free on my watch if I can help it. And if you hear anythin' more, or you can get that student o' yours to come forward, you do that, okay?"

"Will do," I promised.

26

NOT AT ALL TO MY SURPRISE, the next time I ran into Brian, he told me that he hadn't been able to get permission to confiscate and search Owen Wu's college-issued laptop, or get a warrant for any of his devices. As far as the college was concerned, the issue of any sexual assaults at that ill-starred frat party had already been settled. Any digging into it would "only reopen painful wounds and delay the critical process of healing." All the local judges were of the same opinion, although they couched it in terms of probable cause or the lack thereof. Apparently twice-told tales don't stand up well in court.

"I'm still gonna keep my eyes open," Brian told me. "And you try again to get that student to come forward, okay?"

"Okay," I promised, although my confidence in my ability to do so was limited. It was now the middle of February and I hadn't seen Aishat once all month, which was quite a feat on a campus this small. I had to assume she was continuing to avoid me deliberately.

I wanted to help Brian—and Aishat, if I could—out as much as possible, but right now their problems were being crowded out by my own. My book proposal had been rejected, and with insulting promptness, by a second publisher, so I needed to redo it and send it out to the next publisher on my list. I had planned to spend the weekend doing so, but Friday afternoon I got an email from the search committee for the job at Carmel-by-the-Sea College. They were very interested in me as a candidate, and would I be available for an interview by Skype. Say, Monday afternoon?

I wrote back promptly to say that I would be *delighted* to have a Skype interview with them Monday afternoon. Then I texted Alex with the good/nerve-racking news. He spent Friday evening trying to convince me, with only limited success, that I should take it easy over the weekend and just prep for the interview rather than trying to prep for the interview *and* rewrite and submit the book proposal. He even offered to be my video sex slave all weekend if that would take my mind off things and keep me from working myself into a state of nervous prostration.

Tempting, I wrote back, *very tempting. But I thought you didn't like video sex.*

For you I am willing to sacrifice myself :) :) Besides, I'll bet you'll make it worth my while.

That I would :) :) Well, maybe just one quick session. I really *do* have a lot to do this weekend.

As long as that includes doing me :) :)

Needless to say, I got nothing productive done Friday evening. Saturday morning I got up still feeling glowy and cheerful, did all the forms and asanas I could do with my still-twingey knee, and set off for an early-morning grocery run. I could hit the store before the big weekend rush started, and be back and ready to start my interview prep by nine. Interview prep was a drag and I normally would have preferred a lengthy dental procedure over anything interview-related, but the thought that *this* interview could lead to a job in the same county as Alex, with everything that entailed, only increased my general level of glowiness.

My glowiness took a sharp hit when I went out into the parking lot and noticed a patch of oil beneath my elderly Honda Civic. I was not at all mechanically savvy, but I knew that leaking oil couldn't be good.

So instead of going grocery shopping, I did a quick search for mechanics and called around until I found one who could fit me in on a Saturday morning. The closest Honda dealer with a service department was in Macon, more than half an hour away. I didn't want to spend the time driving out there and back, and I didn't want to risk a breakdown on the way there in case there was something really seriously wrong with the car, so I settled for Bubba's Car Repairs, just down the street from LeRoy's Fine Pawn Shop.

The car started up when I turned the key, which I thought was a hopeful sign. But the Check Engine light stayed ominously lit as I pulled out of the lot and headed towards the front gate of the apartment complex.

I held my breath as I went through the gate and started down Peachtree Avenue. The car was rolling along just fine, right? Oh wait, what was that sound? That ticking sound? Probably it was just the radio, right?

I switched off the radio, cutting off Death Cab for Cutie telling me that sorrow was dripping into my heart and my love was going to drown. The percussion for that song had a kind of clicking quality to it. Probably that was it...

The clicking noise only seemed louder with the radio off. Oh dammit. I didn't know what it heralded, but I was willing to bet it was nothing good. I started making mental calculations of how much I had left on my credit card limit.

I coasted into Bubba's Car Repairs with all the care of someone driving on black ice. I had been by Bubba's pretty much every day since I'd moved here, but never truly appreciated it for what it was. A rusted, peeling sign stood outside a garage I was convinced was leaning slightly to the left. The cars parked outside it made my Honda look like a luxury vehicle. I couldn't actually see any duct tape or baling twine, but I sensed its presence.

A man in greasy overalls that had "Bubba" stitched on the left breast came out of the garage, wiping his hands on a rag. He had the ruddy skin of a born-and-bred redneck, a little-brick-shithouse build, and a beard that came down to the bib of his overalls.

"You the lady that called me 'bout the oil leak?" he asked.

I confirmed that I was, and told him about the clicking sound. He sucked on his teeth.

"Could be the timing belt," he said.

I didn't know what that was, but it sounded expensive. "Is it serious?" I asked.

He laughed. How nice that someone was getting some amusement out of this. "You could say that," he said. "Give me the keys and I'll check 'er out."

I handed over my keys and went into the waiting room. It was an alcove off the side of the garage, with a counter for the cash register, and two elderly chairs with ripped plastic seats and a wobbly plastic table that struggled to hold up a pile of two-year-old issues of *Field and Stream* and *People*. Good thing there was nothing there that interested me, since I thought touching the magazines would require an immediate tetanus shot.

I got out my phone and started reading about Carmel-by-the-Sea College. Ugh, I wasn't feeling so good. I wasn't sure if it was stress or the smell of motor oil and old cigarette smoke that was making me feel sick. I put down my phone and tried to do some relaxing deep breathing while focusing on the water stain on the wall in front of me. Deep breathing was a bad idea. Along with motor oil and old cigarette smoke, the air was redolent with the reek of mold. I went back to shallow breathing and tried to distract myself by reading about Carmel's commitment to critical enquiry and artistic expression.

After fifteen minutes of that, an overweight black woman with shoulder-length braids, two small children, and an expression even more harried than mine came in, talking loudly on the phone and to her children simultaneously.

"So he said it'll be at least a thousand dollars"—I thought she might be about to cry at those words, a sentiment I could heartily sympathize with—"Yeah, that's what I said, a thousand dollars! You deaf or somethin'? Sit down! Sit dow—Taye! *Taye!* Did I tell you you could do that? Jayla! Stop messin' around with those magazines and make your brother sit down! Sorry 'bout that," she added to me. "Jayla! Taye! Both of you get in that chair together and stop actin' like fools! Yeah, a thousand dollars, that's what I said! Where am *I* gonna get the money? Where are *you* gonna get the money, that's the question? It's your damn car!"

I got up. "Why don't you take this seat," I whispered to her.

"Oh no honey, you don't have to—Taye! *TAYE CRAWFORD! YOU SIT DOWN AND STOP MESSIN' AROUND AFORE I WHUP YOUR ASS RIGHT HERE IN THE WAITIN' ROOM!*"

I got up. "I'll just go check on my car," I said, and fled.

Mid-February meant that spring was already well on its way in Georgia, and at nine in the morning the weather was already a pleasant 55 degrees. On campus the daffodils were in full bloom. On the poor people's strip out here on this side of town, though, there were no daffodils. I leaned against the outside of the waiting room, and went back to perusing my phone.

Half an hour later I had discovered that Carmel-by-the-Sea College had an undergraduate population of 1,573 students, most of whom studied some form of art or craft along with more traditional academic disciplines. I also discovered that they had a small language program, but one that they were committed to developing, and that language students had the benefit of being near the DLI and the Institute of International Studies, with their intensive language programs. I had also reaffirmed a discovery I'd made many times before, which was that 55 degrees was warm for February, but it was still cold for standing around doing nothing in. Also, leaning against a dirty wall was unpleasant and tiring. My bad knee was twinging, my arms hurt from holding up my phone, and when I looked up, pain went stabbing through my left temple.

"Agh!"

"You okay?" Bubba had come out of the garage and was making his way purposefully towards me.

"Just a headache."

"Yeah. I get those too sometimes. Welp, I got good news for you, an' I got bad news for you."

"Uh-huh?" I asked, when he paused, obviously wanting to draw out the suspense.

"It's your timin' belt, just like I thought," he told me. "The good news is you got it to me afore it snapped entirely. So you don't need a total engine rebuild, just a timing belt replacement. But your gear box is all shot to hell. You should really get that replaced while you're at it."

"How much for just the timing belt replacement?" I asked.

He sucked on his teeth some more. "$350," he told me. "But you really need to replace your oil pump as well, and that'll be another $1,000. Plus that transmission rebuild."

I'd looked into transmission rebuilds in the past, and concluded that it would be more cost effective to replace the entire car. "Can I get away with just the timing belt?" I asked.

Bubba shook his head. "Maybe for another hundred miles or so, but then you'll be right back here lookin' for that oil pump replacement—if you ain't stuck by the side of the road waitin' for a tow truck."

I wondered if $1,350 was really the right price for the work. Would John have gotten a better deal? I suspected yes. But I knew that I didn't have any negotiating power here. "I guess let's do the timing belt and oil pump replacement, then," I said.

"It'll take me a couple days to get all the parts in," he told me. "Won't be till Tuesday at the earliest."

"Okay." I said it with surprising calmness. Numb resignation was already setting in. I put down the thousand dollars that Bubba required up front, and called Mel for a ride.

27

MEL'S ELDERLY JEEP Grand Cherokee, with its dented rear quarter panel and peeling paint that had once been white, fit right in at Bubba's. I skirted around a group of very short men holding an urgent conversation in Spanish by the hood of a tan Ford Ranger that looked to be of approximately the same vintage as myself—namely, 1980—and, after a short struggle with the malfunctioning passenger-side door, climbed in.

"What's the damage?" she asked once I was inside.

"Replace the timing belt and oil pump. $1,350," I told her.

Mel inhaled through her teeth as if I've just stuck my thumb into an open wound. "You got that kind of money?"

"I have just enough on my credit card limit. I'd made some real progress on paying it off, but I'd just bought tickets to go out to California to see Alex—and now this. Right back into debt and being one bad decision at the grocery store away from going into the red."

"Yeah. I hate that. Let me know if I can help, okay?"

"Thanks," I said. "But you don't have to do that. I know you've got plenty of problems of your own, including medical bills."

She waved her hand. "The VA's taking care of most of it."

"Any more news on that front?" After a couple of months of back-and-forthing, Mel had finally gotten an MRI of her brain the previous week. The weird twitching and seizure-y events that had started last semester kept recurring, and her doctor at the VA was concerned that they had something to do with the concussion she'd gotten when her convoy had hit an IED in Iraq.

"Got the MRI results back yesterday afternoon. Everything's clean, they say. 'Course, they just did a 1.5T MRI without contrast, so..." She shrugged.

One of the many pieces of random information I now possessed that I wished I didn't was that MRI strengths were measured in Teslas. 1.5T was on the low end. I'd done my own rounds with MRIs back when my migraines had first become a big problem in undergrad, and now I was getting to hear all about Mel and Chloe's MRI adventures too.

"Still good that they didn't find anything obviously wrong," I said.

She shrugged again. "I guess. I just...I just have this really bad feeling, you know? Like there's a monster lurking inside of me, just waiting to come out and fuckin' devour me. I know they haven't found anything yet, but I'm almost starting to hope that they do, just so I can have something to hang a name on."

"Yeah," I said. "Do they still think it's 'just stress'?"

"And fuckin' PTSD. They're talking about enrolling me in mandatory counseling if I don't get it together soon."

"You *do* have a lot to be stressed out about," I pointed out.

"Yeah, I know. Speaking of which, did I tell you I got an interview invite? To that job in LA."

"Oh wow!" I said. "Congratulations! When is it?"

She wrinkled up her nose. She had a long thin nose over a wide thin mouth, both of which were mobile and expressive. The extensive freckling and lines from sun damage only added to the expressiveness. "Friday," she said. "What a fuckin' week, huh? Hey—you'll probably need me to drive you to campus next week, right?"

"If it's not a problem," I said.

"Of course it's not a problem. Oh—you wanna go running today?"

I considered. "I've got a ton to do and I'm going to have to walk to the grocery store if I want to have anything to eat tonight. Besides, are you feeling up to running?"

"I'll drive you to the store. I gotta go myself. And I feel like shit, but if I didn't do stuff just 'cause I felt like shit, I'd never do anything at all. That's my new mantra for the semester. Sittin' around ain't gonna get me anywhere. Sittin' around ain't even gonna get me healthy, as far as I can tell. Might as well run. 'Specially since we got the Lamb Chop Trot next month to train for."

"Oh God. Do we have to?"

Mel grinned one-sidedly at me. "You're cute when you complain. You hardly ever do it, which makes it even cuter."

"Gee, thanks. But seriously: do we have to? Didn't we humiliate ourselves enough last semester?"

The Frat Dash was not Crimson College's only race/spectacle. Sadly, the others all involved faculty. The fall had the Pre-Turkey Trot on the weekend before Thanksgiving, when faculty raced each other around campus for the honor of wearing turkey costumes to class. Due to a series of circumstances out of our control, Mel and I had ended up winning it last semester. Now everyone was expecting us to run in the Lamb Chop Trot, the pre-Easter faculty race in the spring.

"There's never enough humiliation," said Mel. "Surely you've figured that out by now. So whaddya say: grocery run followed by training run?"

I sighed. "You've talked me into it. I'm too upset about the car thing to do any good interview prep anyway."

"Hey." Mel reached over and squeezed my knee. "It'll be all right, okay? It'll all turn out like it's supposed to."

"Sure," I said.

28

MEL SPENT THE RUN TRYING to talk me down from my plan of prepping for the interview *and* rewriting and submitting my book proposal over the weekend. Then I listened to her agonize over what it would mean to move back to LA, financially and romantically. At least it took our mind off the pain in our knees and the heaviness in our legs.

I texted Alex about the car issue when I got back from the run. He then spent a good portion of the afternoon texting me sexy messages to cheer me up and distract me from my very ill-advised, in his opinion, intention to work on the book proposal as well as the interview prep.

Damn, I wish I were there, he texted at one point. *Because then I could drag you into the bedroom and go down on you until you forgot all about work. You're going to hurt yourself, you know?*

Hurt myself worse than unemployment would?

If you burn yourself out, you'll end up unemployed and unemployable anyway. Take a fucking break, Rowena. What the fuck do I have to do convince you?

Describe in detail your plans for going down on me!

You asked for it ;) ;) ;)

Alex's efforts were valiant, and even involved video at one point. But it wasn't until Chloe emailed on Sunday morning and suggested we get together for a writing session next Thursday that I agreed I could put off the book proposal until after the other events of the looming Hell Week were over.

I was therefore convinced that I was as rested, refreshed, and ready as a person with no working car and thousands of dollars of credit card debt could be when I left my apartment Monday morning to meet Mel. We were going to carpool into campus together, teach our classes, and then come home in plenty of time for my 4:00pm interview with Carmel.

This plan took a sharp turn as soon as I climbed into Mel's Jeep and saw that she was shivering uncontrollably. Since the temperature was already almost 60, it seemed unlikely that cold weather was the cause.

"Are you okay?" I asked.

She rubbed her forehead. "Feel like I'm coming down with something," she said. "*Again*. I feel all feverish and icky, and I hurt all over, and I've had two of those weird twitchy episodes already."

"Do you want me to take you to the doctor?"

She shook her head. "What's a doctor gonna tell me? I already got a clean bill of health from every doctor in the Southeast."

"Maybe you should go home and lie down," I said. "Maybe it's just that flu that's going around."

"I thought I already got that flu last week."

"Maybe it was a different one. You know how campuses are: there's normally at least three strains of crud circulating at any given moment. It's a good year when you only get Influenza A and norovirus and manage to skip out on the pinkeye."

"Yeah. I've already cancelled class twice this semester 'cause I was sick, and it's only February. Plus, I gotta drive you to campus."

That was a serious consideration. Before I could force myself to tell her that it was all right, I could cancel class too, she said, "Tell you what: why don't I loan you the Jeep?"

Which was how I found myself ten minutes later driving as fast as I dared in a vehicle with the maneuverability and cornering capacity of a medium-sized boat. The rumbling of the V8 engine coming up through the gas pedal should have given me a sense of power. But the acceleration and braking were so slow that mainly what I felt was terror. And perched up as high as I was above the road, I was convinced I would accidentally run over a dog, child, or Crimson's entire track team without noticing.

If I caused any accidents, I was unaware of it. I maneuvered the Jeep into a parking spot in the far corner of the lot behind the football stadium, hoping that no one would park next to me. Well, they couldn't even if they wanted to: the Jeep was spilling out over the lines on either side. This parking lot had been built in a previous, more compact era.

I slung my bags over each shoulder and set off at the briskest trot I could manage across the parking lot, around the football stadium, past the athletics center and the entrance to The Hollow, through the beach volleyball courts and the winding paths between the dorms, and across the back quad. I burst into Bedford Hall at 8:58, almost knocking over Chloe, who was stumbling out the front entrance just as I was trying to race in.

"Panic attack?" I asked as I ran past her.

"Uh-huh."

"You okay? You need anything?"

"I'm fine! You get to class!"

I felt bad about leaving Chloe, but not bad enough to be late for class. I sprinted across the foyer and down the corridor to Bedford 132.

"Agh!"

"What is it, professor?!?" Miranda, who had just been taking a seat by the door when I came bounding in, jumped to her feet.

"It's just a headache." Clutching at my temple with my left hand, I edged around the too-big table and installed myself in front of the board. The stabbing pain in my left eye was already gone, replaced by a blurry dot in the center of my vision.

The blurry dot developed shimmering edges and turned into a weird castle-y thing as we went through dates and numbers. By the time 9:50 rolled around and I was able to stop trying to convince the students that yes, they really did have to learn the ordinal forms of the numbers *and* put them in the correct cases in order to express dates in a comprehensible fashion, the weird castle-y thing had turned into a jagged shimmer all around the edges of my field of vision.

The jagged shimmer was replaced with nausea and pain during my second class, when I got to go through the whole song and dance about dates again. Jessica was the only student willing to accept that yes, you really did have to use the genitive case of the ordinal form of the number when expressing that something had happened on an exact date. The others didn't appear even to understand what that meant. This was par for the course, and normally I would make jokes and jolly them along into some kind of acceptance or at least submission to the inevitable. Today it took all my effort not to scream at them in frustration. At least I wasn't being observed.

"Oh, Rowena, *there* you are."

Oh fuck! Karen was waiting for me as I stepped out the classroom door.

"I've been *looking* for you," she said. "Now that we know when the hearing is, we *need* to set up a time for your teaching observation and performance review."

Karen always sounded a bit like Debbie Downer on *SNL*. But today her voice had a gleeful undertone that made it even more sickening. Or maybe I was just feeling sick.

"Okay," I said. "When would be good for you?"

"Let's see...I'm *so* busy, with my teaching obligations *on top of* my obligations as chair..." I had started walking down the hall towards my office, and Karen was panting slightly as she tried to keep up.

"How about next Tuesday?" I said.

"Well...I suppose...*when* do you have class on Tuesday?"

"Nine and ten. Both sections of RUS 102."

"I would really like to see you teach a *culture* course. I observed you teach a language class last semester."

"RUS 150 is MWF, 12:00-12:50," I said.

"Oh, no, I couldn't do that...that's my lunch hour...I suppose I *could* skip it for something *important* like this, though...Next Friday, then. Make a note of it, Rowena. Next Friday."

"Sounds great," I said. "Looking forward to it." I accelerated down the hall, leaving Karen behind.

I gave into temptation once I got into my office and laid my head down on my desk. Then I jerked it up when Anthony Wainwright appeared suddenly in my door.

"Oh, hey, prof," he said. "You got a moment? It's about that girl, the one you were asking about, what's-her-name, Aishat."

29

"WHAT ABOUT AISHAT?" I asked.

"See, the thing is...can I have a seat?"

"Sure," I said. Anthony sat down comfortably. Everything he did looked comfortable and confident. Probably lots of girls found that attractive. Probably I found him annoying right now only because of my stress-induced migraine.

"So, I know you were asking Alicia about her."

"Uh-huh," I said. "I was trying to find her for something."

"How'd that go?" Anthony sounded interested and sympathetic, like a superior talking to a nervous and only marginally competent employee.

"I found her," I said.

"Good, good. Alicia—Alicia and I have been kind of seeing each other, you know?—Alicia pointed her out to me the other day."

"Uh-huh," I said.

"I know they were friends and all last year. But now Alicia says she's been acting weird. And I think..."—he smiled with self-deprecating charm—"I know this sounds crazy, or at least crazy self-involved, but I think she's been following me."

"Oh," I said. I had not been expecting that.

"And Alicia said that Aishat's Russian or something, and *you're* Russian, or close enough, and you're friends with her, so I was hoping you could, like, ask her to back off and leave me alone."

"Has she done anything to bother you?" I asked.

He wriggled his shoulders in a kind of indeterminate shrugging motion. "Nothing you could, like, call the police on—*yet*. But it's weird, you know? Like I've never seen this girl before in my life, and now everywhere I turn she's behind me."

"Maybe she just has a similar schedule this semester," I said.

"Yeah, but I never see her in class. I just see her in, like, weird places. Like outside the frat house and stuff like that. And Alicia thinks she's been following *her*, too. Frankly, it's really kinda freaking Alicia out. And she's got enough on her plate, you know what I mean? I've been doing what I can, but she's having a hard time assimilating here and stuff like that. So the last thing she needs is some girl Single White Femaling her."

I thought about asking Anthony if he even knew what that referred to. *Single White Female* had come out years before he was born. Then I felt incredibly old and curmudgeonly.

"Maybe Alicia should talk to her about it," I said. "Since they're kind of friends. It's probably all a simple misunderstanding."

"Alicia's pretty freaked out about it," Anthony repeated. "And like I said—she's got a lot on her plate already. Someone wrote—well, I won't repeat what they wrote, but it had the N-word in it—on her dorm room door this weekend."

"Does she think it was Aishat?" I asked.

"She doesn't think so since Aishat doesn't live in her dorm, but it makes you wonder, doesn't it?"

"Um," I said. "I guess."

"Yeah, so anyway, I'd really appreciate you helping out with this, professor."

"Okay," I said. "I should probably check in with Aishat anyway."

30

I SPENT THE REST OF my office hours convincing myself that laying my head down on the desk and crying wouldn't accomplish anything. At 11:55 I dragged myself down the hall and up the stairs to Bedford 218, where RUS/HUM 150 was held.

150 passed in a haze. Fortunately the nausea and pain from the migraine never progressed from "annoying" to "debilitating," but I felt unfocused and out of it nonetheless. When Alicia came up to talk to me after class, it felt as if the words coming out of my mouth belonged to someone else, and I was hearing them from a long way off.

"I did that reading you suggested," she said. "What's-her-name, Politkovskaya." She said each syllable of the name carefully, and still mangled it.

"That's nice," I said. Since this was Introduction to Slavic Civilization, we had started with the Scythians and were now talking about the rise of Muscovy. Some of the students had asked about current events and contemporary writers, and I had thrown out the name Anna Politkovskaya. Alicia, it seemed, had paid attention.

"Only I didn't like it nearly as much as I thought I would," she said, following me out of the classroom. "It was full of names and stuff I didn't understand, and, honestly, it made me kind of, like, you know, mad."

"Well, you know how it is," I told her. "A really good book is like a really good love—sparks have to fly. So at first you might feel a little burnt." I felt as I walked down the hall as if "I" were floating along above my left shoulder, a wraith encased in deep water or thick glass. Maybe that was why I was able to say such smart things.

"Oh." She contemplated that for a moment. "I don't know that I like really good books, then. Or really good loves. Sparks flying sounds more fun than it is."

"It depends on the sparks," I said.

"So is that why you read Politkovskaya?" she asked. "Because she makes your sparks fly?"

"No," I said. "I read Politkovskaya because it makes me feel better about the world."

She made a face. "I don't know *how*. It's the saddest sh—stuff I've ever read!"

"Because reading Politkovskaya lets me know that there are real heroes in the world," I told her. "Real monsters, yeah, too, but you can't have real heroes without real monsters. And Politkovskaya's books are full of both. And since the world is full of real monsters, it makes me feel better knowing there are real heroes out there fighting them. It makes me feel like *I* could be a real hero."

"Oh. That's like...Oh, hey, Anthony."

Anthony came running down the stairs after us, the sound of his shoes on the industrial rubber flooring causing my head to clang like a bell. "I thought you were going to wait for me," he told Alicia.

Alicia gave him a shy smile and ducked her head, making her cotton-candy pink hair bounce wildly. "Yeah, but then I saw my chance to talk to Professor Halley on my own, so I took it."

Anthony took her hand in his. "So did you talk to her about Aishat? We thought it might help if you heard about it from Alicia," he said, turning to face me, his hand still on Alicia's. His face and voice were the picture of sincerity. Alicia cuddled up close to him as they walked, his height acting as a shield to her elfin petiteness.

"I've got an appointment soon, but we can talk for a moment," I said.

"Tell her, Alicia," Anthony commanded.

We were now on the first-floor corridor. It was teeming with students. Not really ideal for this conversation. I thought about inviting Alicia to come to my office so we could speak in private. A wave of lassitude and I-don't-give-a-shit washed over me. "Sure, tell me," I said.

Alicia, still letting Anthony pull her along as she trotted behind him, peeked around his side. "I guess Anthony already told you about the situation?"

"He gave me the basic outlines," I said. "I don't really see what I can do about it, though, to be honest. Have you tried to talk to Aishat?"

"I tried once," said Alicia. "Anthony and I were having lunch on Friday when I saw her and we went over to talk to her, but she turned around and ran away! Like straight-up turned and ran when she saw us! That's when I started getting really suspicious. And then...did Anthony tell you what happened at my dorm this weekend?"

"About someone writing something nasty on your door?"

"Yeah, that! I've got a cute little whiteboard on my door, my friends like to leave little messages and stuff on it, and then...*that*."

"Yeah," I said. "Did you report it?"

"I told my RA. She cleaned it off for me so that I wouldn't have to touch it, and then she wrote a real sweet little poem on it for me."

"That's nice," I said. "Did you take any pictures of it? Did you tell the police?"

She shook her head. "No, I...it was just so awful...I thought my dorm mates were my friends...and then to find *that*...I just wanted it gone."

"Understandable," I said. "But if it happens again, take a picture of it and tell campus police, okay? I don't know if they'll do anything about it, but it's good to have a record of stuff like that."

"Okay," said Alicia, in a way that made me think she wasn't actually going to do it. I could understand her reluctance. What were the chances of the all-white, distinctly redneck campus police force taking much of an interest in racist graffiti? And realistically, even if they did care, what could they do about it?

"It's good to have a record of it," I repeated. "And the campus administration is really making an effort to combat this kind of thing. They will want to know so that they can issue a statement."

"Yeah. I guess. But...what if it's Aishat?"

"Do you really think it could be her?" I asked. We'd reached my office. I unlocked it and let us in. I took my seat on my side of the desk. Since the office wasn't very big, the desk was arranged kitty-corner across it, which meant my chair was pressed back against the corner. Alicia and Anthony took the two stained chairs on the other side of the desk. Anthony was big enough that he blocked out most of the view out the door. I could feel my claustrophobia rearing its head, fighting to get free. I wanted to vault over the desk, leap past Anthony and Alicia, and run screaming out the building.

Instead I took a deep breath. That was a mistake. It triggered a sneezing fit that morphed into a nasty coughing spasm.

"You okay, professor?" Alicia's eyes were wide with alarm. "You have asthma or something? You got your inhaler with you?"

I tried to take deep but shallow breaths in order to calm the spasm that my entire upper body had gone into. The migraine pain lanced through my skull and down my neck. Screaming or crying in front of students would be terrible, so I didn't.

"I don't have asthma," I said, once I could speak again. "It must just be dust."

"Yeah. Or that flu that's going around."

"I hope not," I said. "So do you really think it could be Aishat?"

Alicia shrugged uneasily. "I don't want to think so. I thought we were friends, you know? Like, she helped me a lot with Diffy Q, and told me a lot of great info about Islam and stuff. But she's *definitely* been following Anthony around for the past week, and she looked *so weird* on Friday, so...can you talk to her, Professor? See what's going on with her, make her back off?"

I gnawed on my lip. Talking to Aishat about this seemed entirely inappropriate. But what was the alternative? Bringing in the police, when we didn't know if she'd done anything wrong? That would just be more trauma for a girl who'd already had a life full of it. Counseling and Campus Wellness? I suspected that would be a complete fiasco too. They might be well-intentioned, but they existed primarily as CYA insurance for the college. There was no one who would be on both Alicia and Aishat's sides. Except me.

"I'll reach out to Aishat," I said. "But it might take a little while. I really do have an important appointment this afternoon, and another one tomorrow. But I'll see what I can do."

31

A LOT OF THE CLAUSTROPHOBIA, nausea, and the weird tightness in my chest eased when I finally, *finally* escaped from my office and Bedford Hall. Blue lights were still flashing around the edges of my vision, but the cool damp wind that lifted my hair away from my face also blew away a lot of that strange out-of-body feeling as I walked across campus to the parking lot.

The Jeep was still there, although it took me a couple of tries to find it. Newer, younger, more ginormously bloated SUVs, each straddling two parking spaces, had been parked on either side of it, hiding it completely. I wondered what it would be like to drive something that huge. Like driving a tank or a cruise ship.

The Jeep coughed and sputtered, but, just as I was starting to go into contingency planning for what I would do if it wouldn't start, leaving me stranded on campus before a major interview, it roared to life. I maneuvered it with extreme caution out of the parking lot, through campus, and onto College Drive.

I made it home unscathed shortly before 2:00pm. I parked the Jeep in front of Mel's building and sent her a quick text telling her that we had made it home in one piece and asking her how she was doing.

A little better, she wrote back. *Slept all morning and now I'm experimenting with sitting upright. You got your interview this afternoon?*

Yep.

Good luck!

Thanks, I wrote. I couldn't say that I was feeling good, but the walk across the apartment complex to my building was blowing away more of the sickness of the morning.

Just a stress-induced migraine, I told myself. *I just have to get through this afternoon and tomorrow, and the worst of Hell Week will be over.*

Fevronia came running up to me when I stepped into the apartment. I reached down to pet her. She swiped at me and ran off to hide under the bed. So she seemed to be doing well, at least.

I set my alarm for 3:30 and lay down on the bed. Resting, I told myself firmly, would be the best thing I could do before the interview.

By 2:45 I was back up, having achieved absolutely zero rest. I went through my interview notes. 2:55. I went through the job description and the department website. 3:04. I tried to do my lesson planning for the next day, which I really needed to do if I wanted to finish my workday at a decent hour. The topic was the genitive plural. That should be more than enough to fill anyone's mind. Right?

3:07. Hard-stem nouns ending in vowels in the nominative singular take a zero ending. 3:10. Nouns ending in *-ia* in the nominative singular take a soft sign. 3:11. Nouns ending in hushers or soft sign in the nominative singular take *-ei*. 3:13. Nouns ending in hard consonants in the nominative singular take *-ov*. 3:16. Caveat: stem-stressed nouns ending in *-ts* or *-y* take *-ev*. 3:17. Nouns ending in *-ets* or *-ok* in the nominative singular *may* lose a fill vowel when the ending is added. 3:20. Nouns ending in a consonant followed by *-ka* in the nominative singular will gain a fill vowel. 3:22...

My phone *pinged*. My body broke out into a sweat before my mind registered that it was an email from the Carmel search committee.

Dear Rowena—We find ourselves at loose ends at the moment. Please don't feel obliged if you're busy, but if you're available now, we can start the interview early.

My brain screamed *No! I'm not ready yet!* I reminded it that I'd been desperate for the interview to be over for the past half an hour. *Sure*, I wrote back. *Ready whenever you are!*

By 3:25 the Carmel search committee was shuffling into position on my laptop screen. They were sitting with their backs to a sunny window, so all I could see was the black outlines of their heads, and blinding sunlight flooding the rest of the screen. Even virtually, the bright sunlight was making my eyes do funny things.

"Thank you so for much for agreeing to meet with us—and earlier than planned, too," said an older, comfortably plump woman with what I was pretty sure was flyaway graying hair, a shapeless dress, and a fringed shawl hanging haphazardly from her shoulders. I felt better already. Women like that were legion in the halls of academia, especially Russian academia. Normally they were okay.

"My pleasure," I said.

"How nice," said the older woman. "So, I'm Cornelia, from French. And this is Brad, from Classics." Brad was, as best I could make out through the blinding glare, a slender man with short salt-and-pepper hair and a neatly trimmed salt-and-pepper goatee above a shabby brown suit. "And the third member of our committee is Zaria, who teaches ceramics." Zaria was a young woman with blonde dreadlocks, a tie-dyed shirt, and a chunky necklace that looked like it was made out of handmolded clay.

Pleasantries were exchanged. The committee got excited when I said I'd already spent time in Monterey. They got even more excited when I revealed that my boyfriend taught at the DLI.

"Does he also teach Russian?" asked Cornelia.

"Arabic," I said.

"Oh. Well, that's a good combination too. Is he from the Middle East—I'm sorry, I probably shouldn't be asking these kinds of questions. Don't feel like you have to answer. I'm just curious about how people end up teaching things like Russian or Arabic."

"It's okay," I said. "He's American, like me. But in his case, he learned Arabic in the Navy. He's a civilian now, but he teaches at the DLI."

"His Arabic must be excellent," said Cornelia. "To teach there when he's not a native speaker...but I apologize; that's not the subject of this conversation. Do tell me more about yourself, Rowena. How did *you* end up teaching Russian?"

"It's no problem," I said. "And I took Russian in undergrad on a whim, I guess. My first-year advisor said something to me about how I needed to fulfill the language requirement and of course I'd want to take Spanish, not something difficult and obscure like Russian. So I signed up for Russian. Four years later I had a Russian degree and a job in Moscow for a human rights NGO. After a while I decided to go to grad school." I skipped neatly over the part about Dima. Bringing up a current boyfriend who lived and worked in the area was borderline acceptable, since it suggested I'd be keen to move there and stay there. Bringing up a troublesome ex in another country would be an interview-killer on so many levels. I murmured something about my commitment to multiculturalism instead. Well, that was true. I'd been very keen on creating a multicultural marriage and a multicultural family. Oh well.

"That's all very interesting," said Cornelia. "So now let me tell you about our situation. We've been offering Russian on and off when Zaria or Leona—Leona is a weaving professor who dabbles in Russian on the side—can fit it into their schedules. Now we've received a very generous donation to enable the teaching of Russian here at Carmel on a full-time basis. The initial donation would enable a two-year appointment, but if the subject takes off, there's a strong possibility we could make the position permanent. The Russian community here in California is growing by leaps and bounds, and we're getting a lot of interest in Russian from students from Russian families. So while we can't make any long-term commitments at the moment, there is a very good chance that the position will be here to stay. But we're getting ahead of ourselves. As you must know, we're a very art-focused school, so we'd be interested in hearing your ideas on how to reach out to art students and make Russian relevant and interdisciplinary for our art programs."

The bright light from the screen was making another blob grow in the center of my vision. This one had a purple tinge to its grayness. When I started talking about Russian arts and crafts, the words seemed to be coming out of a mouth that was slightly to the right of mine.

The words that didn't feel like mine must have been sensible enough, because Cornelia and Brad nodded along with what looked like genuine enthusiasm. Zaria looked bored and contemptuous.

We moved on to town-and-gown outreach. My whole face felt numb. How long had we been talking? It felt like an impossible eternity, even though a check of my computer's clock showed it had barely been ten minutes. Oh God. We had at least another twenty minutes to get through before we could legitimately call it a day.

They moved on to asking about what I would do for Carmel's First Year Experience, in which students took themed blocks of courses designed to introduce them to the college experience and prepare them for rigorous upper-division classes. I said something about teaming up with art teachers to create a block on Russian art that involved both theoretical and experiential learning.

"Or, since a big part of my focus is contemporary culture and current events, I could do something about that," I suggested. "I've already got some of the students in my Intro to Slavic Civ course reading Politkovskaya on the side."

"Po-lit-kov-ska-ya," Cornelia repeated carefully. "Who's he?"

Zaria, who had been shifting restlessly in the background during this entire conversation, straightened up. "She," she said.

"I'm sorry?" said Cornelia.

"She," repeated Zaria. "Anna Politkovskaya was a woman. A journalist. Something you would know about. Is it true that you were in a relationship with Dmitry Kuznetsov?

32

"THAT'S *hardly* a fit topic for an interview!" Cornelia exclaimed. "I apologize, Rowena: of course you shouldn't feel obliged to answer that." Her words said the legally appropriate thing to say. Her face said she was consumed with confusion and curiosity.

From a legal standpoint I probably shouldn't answer the question. But if I didn't, I was sure Cornelia would run to Google the moment the interview was over. I didn't know what Google had to say about me and Dima, but whatever it was, I was sure that I needed to answer the question and control the messaging about me if I had any hope of getting this job.

"It's true," I said. "I'm surprised you've heard of him, though. It's not like he's a household name, especially in the US. He's also a journalist," I explained to Cornelia and Brad, who were still looking lost. "For the online opposition paper *Nezavisimaya Pravda*, which means *Independent Truth*. So yes, I do have a strong interest and a direct connection to current events in Russia."

"One of my cousins is also cousins with Rinat Mustafaev, and is over there with him right now," said Zaria.

My blank look of confusion was not feigned.

"Rinat Mustafaev is an observer for the OSCE," Zaria told us. Her mouth was twisting in delight at knowing more than I did about something I should be an expert on. "He's currently in Eastern Ukraine. He's friends with Dmitry. He introduced him to my cousin, who's in Kiev. She told me all about him." Zaria's mouth twisted in even more delight. "I think she's pretty taken with him. He's quite the hero, isn't he?"

"Um," I said. "Well, I mean...I suppose so..."

"So what kind of a connection do you have with him now?" asked Zaria. "It's relevant to the interview," she added to Cornelia, who was opening her mouth to object to this line of questioning. "I mean, what if she could bring him over as a guest speaker?"

"Well..." I said. "I could ask, I suppose."

Zaria smirked. What was with her? What was going on that I didn't know about? What was going on with *Dima* that I didn't know about? Had he gotten involved with this cousin of Zaria's, and was now badmouthing me to her, and she was sharing everything he said with Zaria? No. Dima had a lot of irritating qualities, but I couldn't believe he'd complain about me to another woman. I knew that was the kind of thing people did when they were moving on from their exes, but...but I just couldn't believe that Dima was moving on. I *couldn't*. And if he did, he'd do it in a gentlemanly fashion.

I swallowed back the fresh wave of pain and nausea that this conversation was causing. Of all the bad luck. The world of academia was small, the world of professional Slavists even smaller, and the number of well-known Russian journalists could be counted on one hand, so it wasn't that surprising for me to encounter another Russian-speaking academic who had some kind of distant connection to Dima. But still, why did it have to happen now?

Zaria was watching me with mean-spirited glee. Cornelia was watching me with sympathy. Brad looked like he wished he were somewhere else, somewhere where he wasn't in danger of getting sued just for being in the wrong place at the wrong time.

"I would be happy to ask him, if that's something the college would be interested in sponsoring," I said. "And I'd be happy to invite any of my other journalist contacts, if that's something the college would like to do. But you wouldn't be hiring me for my ability to use my personal contacts to put together a one-time event. You'd be hiring me to create a long-running program that would be more than a flashy poster. So yes, I was in a relationship with Dima Kuznetsov. I'm not ashamed of it at all. And from your perspective, what that means is that my grasp of contemporary vernacular Russian is, if you'll excuse the expression, shit-hot."

Oh shit! The migraine must be really getting to me! Why did I say that? Sweat was trickling down my sides, and I suddenly felt like I was back in my body.

Brad was smiling. "Shit-hot Russian sounds like just the kind of thing Carmel needs," he said.

Cornelia was smiling too. "Indeed. I like your spark, Rowena. Well, and I think it's time to move on. Do you have any questions for us?"

I said something that appeared to be semi-coherent about study abroad, and five minutes later, the interview was over.

33

AFTER THE INTERVIEW I felt so horribly drained that I just texted Alex about it and called it a day. I had only half-planned tomorrow's lessons, but whatever. The genitive plural was the toughest thing that first years faced, but it was something I'd taught at least twice a year for the past five years running. I could wing it.

The next day Mel came to pick me up in the Jeep at 8:30am. She looked pale and haggard, but she wasn't shivering uncontrollably like she had been the day before.

"I guess it wasn't the flu," she said. "Although I would have sworn it was. Or maybe it was the world's shortest flu. Maybe I'm just so damn healthy that when I get the flu, I kick its ass in under 24 hours."

"Is that what it feels like?" I asked.

"No. It feels like the monster is creeping out from under the bed. Only it's invisible. I've been poked and prodded and bloodlet and scanned within an inch of my life, and they can't find a damn thing. Maybe it really *is* just fucking PTSD."

"Maybe it's Gulf War Syndrome," I said.

"Different war," said Mel.

"Maybe you could have it anyway," I said.

Mel made a face. "I don't want to have some shit like that," she said. "I want something with a proper name—and a proper treatment. Or better yet, I don't want to have anything at all. Except that would mean feeling this shitty is normal, and I don't want that to be true either."

"Understandable," I said. I stopped pursuing the topic, but I made a mental note to get in touch with John and ask him what he thought. Were any of his Marines experiencing anything similar? Were we about to see a big wave of Gulf War Syndrome amongst OEF/OIF vets? Or was it just your usual wave of "war heart" or "shell shock" or whatever you wanted to call it? And since when had war heart caused the flu?

That was much too big a question to spring on someone at 8:35 on a Tuesday morning, especially since we had the delight of an official hearing about our involvement in Chris's shooting in the afternoon.

I was afraid that another migraine would whack me as soon as I stepped into Bedford. The only thing that hit me, though, was that sense that I was floating along somewhere slightly above and to the left of my body. It persisted through both my classes, and grew even stronger when I went into my office.

I looked at my phone. 10:53. More than four hours until the hearing, and I was stuck here, in this claustrophobic office I hated. Mel taught at nine and eleven on Tuesdays this semester. We'd arranged to meet with Chloe for lunch at noon. That would kill at least an hour, or two if we stretched it out. I could do it. I could survive until then.

I considered trying to find Aishat and asking her what was going on with her and Alicia. That seemed way too fraught for my current state. I considered reaching out to John and asking him about Mel and the possibility of her having Gulf War Syndrome. That also seemed way too fraught, for me and for him. Better to do it on a weekend when I would be less frazzled and he would be mellowed by about six pints of Guinness.

This meant I only had one option: lesson planning for tomorrow. I pulled out a piece of scrap paper and started jotting down notes about tomorrow's topic for RUS 102, which was counting adjectives.

I was just finishing up writing out what I wanted to say about 2, 3, 4 + the nominative plural for adjectives modifying feminine nouns and 2, 3, 4 + the genitive plural for adjectives modifying masculine and neuter nouns, when Chloe poked her head in my office.

"You ready to head over to Sullivan's?" she asked.

I glanced up. Rather than looking like she was about to pass out or burst into tears, like I was expecting, Chloe was alight with happiness.

I checked my phone. 11:45. "Let's give it five more minutes so that Mel can walk over with us," I said. "How's it going?"

"Great!" Chloe gave me a rare full-on smile. Normally she looked anxious and vaguely oppressed. But now she was glowing. "Guess what!" she said. "I just got a request from a publisher! For the full manuscript!"

"Fantastic!"

"Yeah! You know I got invited to submit a proposal at a conference over break. So I did, and then I didn't hear anything from them for like, more than a month. I figured they weren't even going to respond. But I just got an email from the acquisitions editor for a series on *China: Past and Future*, and she said she was very excited about my project and since I already had a draft of the completed manuscript, could I send it to her! If she likes it, she'll send it out for review!"

"That's great. Is it a good publisher?"

"Yeah! My top choice, actually. So it'll be crushing if they reject me, but this has to be a good sign, right?"

"Right," I said. "A great sign, surely."

"That's what I'm telling myself! And it's great that it came today. I was soooo stressed out about this hearing this afternoon that I couldn't eat last night or this morning. Which is bad, 'cause I think my dad is right and maybe I've got, like, a pre-diabetes thing going on or something like that. Something's up with my blood sugar, anyway. So I've been super stressed about that on top of everything else. I was afraid I was going to pass out or something at the hearing. But now I feel like there's nothing they can do to hurt me! I guess that's not true, huh? I mean, I guess they could fire me, and then probably the publisher wouldn't want my book anymore..."

"That's not going to happen," I said firmly, before Chloe could work herself into a state of panic. "They can't fire you. You were a hero. If anything, they should give you a commendation or something."

"Yeah, but...you know how they are."

"Yeah," I said. "I do. But I really don't think you're in any danger of losing your job. And this request from your top-choice publisher for the full manuscript is fabulous. Maybe it's a sign that the rest of the day is going to go equally well."

34

ALAS, THAT WAS NOT the case. Chloe's news, which was a once-in-a-lifetime piece of good fortune, was definitely the high point of the day.

We focused on that as much as possible during our lunch get-together at Sullivan's. By the end of it, we'd made a plan for our meeting on Thursday at Chloe's house for a writing session. Mel would get started on her book proposal, I would rewrite mine for the next publisher on my list, and Chloe would tackle the revisions for an article that had been hanging over her head for the past month.

"I just couldn't face it," she said. "I knew I needed to do it, but I couldn't even make myself open up the files. But now I feel like I could do anything!"

"Yeah!" Mel and I said together. "You can!"

I really should have left the lunch in time to write my lesson plan for Wednesday's 150 class on the rise of the Romanovs, but I felt like I could only maintain my good mood, or even my basic sanity, as long as I stayed with Mel and Chloe and talked about positive things. So that's what I did. And it was work, right? We were making plans for publishing our research, which was the primary thing we were supposed to be doing. We just let the day-to-day low-level urgency of teaching get in the way most of the time. So sitting around talking about where and how we could get published was the best thing we could be doing.

By 2:30, though, we couldn't put off getting ready for the hearing any longer. We paid up and walked to Bedford, ran to the bathroom and did a quick email check, and then headed over to Saunders.

"Is it true that it's named after someone who was a KKK leader?" Chloe whispered as we approached it.

"Don't think about it," Mel said.

"So it probably is," said Chloe.

"Yeah," Mel admitted. "Just like pretty much every other building on campus. Don't think about it right now. Don't let it distract you."

"At least there's Wainwright," said Chloe. "*That's* not named after someone from the KKK."

"Yeah," said Mel. "But none of that matters now. Stay sharp, stay focused. We're going in."

We stepped into Saunders, which stood next to Bedford and was its neoclassical twin. It housed Spanish and the German and Japanese wings of the Modern Languages department, along with English, Classics, and History. Its conference room was often used for department meetings and, apparently, college hearings.

"I don't feel so good," said Chloe.

"It's just fuckin' nerves," said Mel. "I don't feel so good either. Push through it and keep going. It'll be over soon."

We started down the hall towards the conference room. Chloe was rubbing the scars on her temples. Mel was wavering slightly as she walked, and falling behind me even though dread was making me walk at half my usual speed, as if I were approaching the lair of a particularly horrifying ogre.

It was silly that I was so scared. What could they do to me, really? Oh, yeah, fire me, make it impossible for me to ever get a job in the field I'd spent a very laborious decade becoming qualified for, and leave me in bitter emotional and financial devastation. But whatever. You're not supposed to let other people get to you, right?

"Hey," I said to Mel. "You okay?"

"Yeah. This shit happens to me sometimes when I'm super stressed out. I get all lightheaded and walk weird. 'Specially since the concussion. Hypoxia from stress or some shit like that. It'll be better once it's over."

"Okay." Blue lights were flashing on the edges of my vision. Was I about to vomit? Or was I just about to scream? Either way, I wished I'd eaten less lunch.

"Oh, *there* you are. I was about to come looking for you! I was afraid you were going to be *late*."

Karen was bearing down on us. I checked my phone. 2:50. Nowhere near to being late.

"Here we are," I said.

"*Finally*. It doesn't look good for you to *almost* be late! Oh, *hello*, Dorothy. You three know Dorothy—Dean Talbot—don't you?"

"We do," I said. "Nice to see you." I said it because I could tell it was up to me to observe the social proprieties. Chloe looked like she was on the edge of a panic attack, and Mel looked like she could barely stand. I tamped down the wild burst of fear that thought engendered. Mel had always been the toughest of us, and certainly the strongest physically. I'd seen her sick before—a lot—but this was somehow scarier and more sinister. I reminded myself that she'd said this was something that happened to her. And I promised myself I'd ask John ASAP if he'd ever seen anything like this from PTSD.

Fortunately, no one else seemed to notice. Karen and Dorothy were too busy in a mutual round of flattery and congratulations to pay any attention to us as we trailed after them into the conference room.

Brian, Theresa Mayfield from the Dean's Office, and Tanika Scott, Dorothy's assistant, were already there. Over the next ten minutes a dozen more people trickled in, all of them Chris's other instructors and the chairs from those departments. Most of them looked as sick and stressed out as we felt.

Theresa opened the meeting with a brief statement about the official report Brian had submitted. He had placed a lot of the blame squarely on the Men's Protection Alliance and its frequent incitements to violent outbursts against women.

"I value the First Amendment as much as any American," he said, when Theresa was done summing it up. "But y'all kept asking me to go after the Gang of Six, when the real problem was the MPA."

"Christopher Atherstone was a member of the Gang of Six!" Dorothy, who had remained smugly silent until then, snapped out. "They *were* the real problem!"

"Yeah, but if you'd read my report, you'd see that Chris specifically named Nathan Willoughby as his 'inspiration,' for want of a better word, for what he did. I'm no fan o' the Gang o' Six, but blamin' them for what Chris did is like blamin' his professors and his friends and everyone else who knew him. A lot of us didn't see what was goin' on, but Chris said straight out it was Nathan and the other MPA boys who made him decide to do what he did."

"I thought Chris wasn't talking!" Dorothy said. "*How* can you know his motivations then?"

"He talked while he was doin' the shootin'," said Brian. "We got eyewitnesses here, don't we?"

"Yes," said Theresa, taking back control of the hearing. "So perhaps we should hear from them now. Chloe Taylor and Melissa Wilson were both eyewitnesses to the incident, while not having any other connection to Christopher. Chloe, would you care to speak first? Just tell us what you saw. We'd be particularly interested in hearing about anything that Christopher said that might shed light on his motivation for the attack."

Chloe swallowed and started talking. She looked nervous, and sounded even more nervous, but enough of the morning's glow was still with her to allow her to speak up loudly enough for everyone to hear as she described how Chris had come shouting for Taylor, demanding that she come out of Chloe's class.

"I didn't know what to do," Chloe said, looking down at her hands, her voice wavering but still audible. "I didn't know whether to send her out there in order to save the other students, or keep her in with us and hope that we could save her. So...so I thought I'd go out with her. We'd both go out and maybe that would placate him and he wouldn't kill the rest of the class."

"A very difficult decision," said Theresa sympathetically. "Did Christopher say what his plans were once he had Taylor?"

Chloe shook her head. "I don't know what he had planned. I don't think *he* knew what he had planned. I was hoping that maybe if we came out quietly, he wouldn't hurt us or anyone else. So I got Taylor and we started to go out. Only then Mel distracted him and...I thought he might shoot us, and I also thought maybe this was our chance, and I *couldn't* send a student out to him like a lamb to the slaughter. So I pulled Taylor back inside and...we hid."

"You should have tried to protect her, not hide behind her!" said Dorothy. "Protecting your students is your duty!"

"She did!"

Mel had jumped to her feet. She no longer looked feeble and sick. Fury was having a marvelous healing effect on her.

"When Chloe says, 'we hid,' what she means is that she pulled her student back inside the classroom and covered her with her own body." Mel's voice wasn't quite a shout, but it wasn't quite not a shout, either. "I knew people who got decorated for valor for that kind of thing. So we should treat Chloe with a little respect."

"Indeed," said Theresa. She gave Dorothy a sideways look that was as close to hateful as was possible in a civilized meeting of pacifist intellectuals. "I think there's no question that Chloe acted with a high degree of courage at a very difficult moment. One final question, Chloe: did you hear Christopher say anything about his motivations?"

Chloe shook her head. "I hardly heard him say anything at all. Just shouting for Taylor. I could hear him talking a little after that, but once I closed the classroom door, it was all muffled. I couldn't make out actual words. Just...just the gunshots."

"Thank you, Chloe," said Theresa. "And once again, allow me to extend my thanks and my admiration for your courageous behavior under very difficult circumstances. Melissa, would you care to describe what you witnessed?"

Mel's story started off the same as Chloe's, with hearing Chris come down the hall shouting for Taylor. But she was able to confirm that Chris had then turned on Nathan, saying that he was the real problem.

"Do you remember what he said exactly?" Theresa asked.

"Pretty sure he said something like, 'You kept blaming everything on the girls, but the real snake in the grass was always you!'" said Mel.

Theresa looked over at me. "Rowena?" she asked. "Did you also witness this?"

"That's exactly how I remember it too," I said. "Chris started off coming for Taylor and Miranda, but then he said that Nathan was also to blame for ruining things, and that he was the real snake in the grass."

Theresa frowned. "That *could* be indicative of Nathan being the instigator—or it could be indicative of Christopher putting the blame on others instead of accepting responsibility himself."

"I don't think there's any question that our boy Chris is guilty," said Brian. "But what I'm sayin' is that it was hangin' around with Nathan and the other MPA boys that put all these bad ideas in his head. I don't want to step on anyone's toes or take away anyone's rights, but as long as we've got stuff like this goin' on on campus, we ain't gonna be safe. I'm recommendin' we do somethin' about hate groups like that. I ain't heard much about the MPA so far this semester, but now I'm gettin' rumblins' that there's someone goin' around leavin' racist graffiti on campus. I don't know what y'all want to do about that. But I'm recommendin' we do *somethin',* and we do somethin' soon."

"Indeed," said Theresa. "Thank you for your report, Chief Michaels. We will definitely take it under advisement. Now, I believe we wanted to ask Christopher's instructors if they had noticed anything that in retrospect seemed troubling. I want to emphasize that the point of this is not to assign blame, but to develop a better set of protocols in order to prevent tragedies like this in the future. Now, let's see..."

"I believe we agreed I would conduct this portion of the hearing," Dorothy interrupted her. "Since *my* office will be in charge of creating and implementing the protocols for these situations. I'm sure if we all *think hard* we can come up with a list of *clear* warning signs that, had they been properly heeded, would have allowed us to give Christopher the *help* he so *clearly* needed in a timely fashion. So let's begin. Who had Christopher in their classes last semester?"

His math instructor said that Chris had always been a quiet and reasonably competent student who had never shown any sign of doing anything exceptional in any way. His history instructor said the same thing. Crimson was small enough that professors normally knew all their students, and so everyone knew Chris and could say something about his academic aptitude, but no one could say that they'd noticed anything alarming about him. Except me.

"I knew he was hanging out with Nathan Willoughby," I said. "And that bothered me, but I couldn't really prevent it. And I knew he had a crush on two other students, and had a big fight with both of them on the last Friday of class. But it never occurred to me that he'd do something like that."

"It sounds to me like you should have paid a little *closer* attention to your students, Regi—uh, Rowena," said Dorothy. "I know you're new here, so perhaps you don't *understand* Crimson culture, but we expect our faculty to form close, personal bonds with our students. That what sets us apart from so many other schools."

"Yes, but..."

"As a Crimson faculty member, it's your *duty* to take an interest in your students, Regi—Rowena," Dorothy told me sternly. "Frankly, I find it concerning that it never even *occurred* to you to hold some kind of intervention. Instead you kept harassing Nathan Willoughby, who was a victim in this *terrible* tragedy. Incidentally, his parents are still considering suing the school—and you. That's not *at all* the kind of conduct we expect from Crimson faculty. You neglected an at-risk student and harassed an innocent victim."

I opened my mouth to say something. I closed it. What would I say? Dorothy was smiling smugly. Karen was smiling smugly too. A sharp stab of pain went through my temple. Or was it hate? It released me, releasing whatever had been holding back my tongue as well.

"Look, what do you want me to say?" I demanded. "That I lie awake every night, wondering what I could have done differently? Because I do. And I hope you do too. I hope we all do. But when it comes right down to it, we all did everything we could think of to do, and it just wasn't enough. And it wasn't enough not through any fault of ours, but because Chris was able to get his hands on an AR-15 and a .45."

"I think it's more *complicated* than that," said Dorothy. "We have to approach these things with a little more *nuance* than that. Mental health..."

"Is not the problem," I interrupted her. The dragon of don't-fuck-with-me was once again rising in my chest and coming out of my mouth. I was probably going to lose this job anyway, so why should I stay silent? If I even could, which apparently I couldn't. "The world is full of unhappy, fucked-up people," I said. "Lots of them fantasize about destroying everyone around them in sick revenge, and many of them try to bring that fantasy to fruition. But most of them don't have easy access to weapons of mass destruction. So yeah, they make others miserable and spread around their low-grade evil, but they don't walk into public spaces and start killing people at a rate of one per second."

"Toxic *masculinity*..." began Dorothy.

"Is a scourge, but the world is full of shitty men who want to hurt people," I said. "If we went around arresting all of them, we'd have to arrest half the world. The truth is that any one of those boys who had anything to do with the MPA could have done something like this—as could most of the other boys on campus, and maybe a couple of the girls as well. It was just our bad luck—and his, frankly—that Chris was able to get his hands on a couple of horrific killing machines right when he was having a really, really bad day."

"You should have known!" Dorothy's face had gone red, and her treacle-y exterior had slipped, showing the fundamentally unkind person underneath. "You should have known, and stopped him!"

"Yeah," I said. "I should have. So should all his other teachers, the police, the Dean's Office who saw all that poison the MPA was spreading, his friends, and his parents, *but we didn't*. Because really, Chris was just another adolescent boy, just another college freshman. Boys were being boys, until one of them went too far and changed from an unhappy young man into a monster. But it could have been any of them."

"That's why we have to watch over them!" Dorothy snapped. "That's why we have to monitor them!"

"And what?" I demanded. "Engage in 24/7 mind control? Because that's what it will take. As long as angry young men can get their hands on dangerous weapons, the only way to stop them from doing something terrible is the kind of surveillance that would make totalitarian dictatorships green with envy. Is that what we want? Gun control, or mind control: those are our choices. So far we seem to be moving in the direction of mind control. But it hasn't been working out very well for us."

"You should have done something," Dorothy repeated, her mouth in a mean line.

"I did," I said. "I talked to Nathan, the main trouble-maker, on multiple occasions, as did Chief Michaels. For which we are now in danger of being sued. So when I *did* try to reach out to an at-risk student, that only got me into trouble.

"So you know what? I *do* feel guilty. I *do* wish I had done something more. But I did everything I thought I could do, including going out into that hallway and talking him down while he pointed a loaded gun at my face. So I'm not going to be your scapegoat. I'm not going to bear your guilt for you. That's a burden you're going to have to carry yourself."

There was a moment of stunned silence, long enough for me to feel the sweat of rage and fear trickling down my sides. At least, I tried to tell myself, when I got terminated I could walk out of here with the knowledge that I'd gone out guns blazing. Bad choice of words. Whatever.

"Hell yeah," Brian Michaels said. "What Rowena just said. Y'all are so desperate not to have to take any responsibility for this, you're tryin' to pin it on anyone who can't fight back. So I'm standin' by the report I submitted to you. It coulda been any one o' those boys, or none o' them. We knew somethin' bad might happen, but no one wanted to shut campus down and search everyone, so what happened, happened."

"I'm afraid you're right." Theresa, who had remained silent during my tirade, suddenly spoke. "Of course we all bear guilt for this—but we all did what seemed like the right thing at the time.

I confess I don't like the idea that any one of my students could do what Chris did, under the right circumstances—but I fear that's all too true. Put deadly weapons in people's hands, and some of them are going to use them." She rose from the head of the table. "I think we've spent enough time deliberating what should be perfectly obvious to all of us, which is that our faculty are not at fault here, and should not be punished for showing initiative and exemplary bravery. The Dean's Office will take what was said here and Chief Michaels's report under consideration, and begin drafting a set of recommendations for dealing with at-risk students."

Dorothy's mouth went into an even meaner line. Karen's mouth sagged in a disappointed frown. But neither of them said anything as we filed out of the room.

I wondered what plans for revenge their silence was hiding.

35

AFTER THAT MEL AND I went to Bubba's Repairs, where the Honda was waiting for me. I forked over the rest of the money, holding my breath until the credit card ran through and accepted the charges, and got my keys back and drove home.

When we got back I asked Mel if she wanted to go running, but she said she felt too shitty, so I went for a short jog on my own, made the simplest supper I could come up with, and collapsed into bed. I had a lengthy mental list of things I should be doing, but the migraine that had been threatening to descend all day finally swooped down and claimed me, and my vision was too messed up for me to able to read anything. I ended up lying there with my eyes closed while Alex told me about his day and his plans for what we would do when I came to California next month.

The next day I still felt hazy and drained, but I managed to pull it together enough to send Aishat an email that morning telling her I wanted to check in with her and see how she was doing.

By the evening there was no answer. I contemplated various strategies for tracking her down, and rejected them all. They all smacked of stalking, and I didn't want to start stalking students, especially with the possibility of a lawsuit from Nathan's parents for stalking and harassment hanging over me. I knew the accusations were bullshit, and I was pretty sure that any reasonable judge would think so too, but not all judges are reasonable, and grieving parents have a powerful emotional appeal. There were a lot of people, including people in positions of power, who were going to be on their side. What I needed was someone powerful on *my* side...I called my grandmother.

We went through a few rounds of pleasantries, and I promised to come visit her in Macon that weekend, and then I got down to the real business of the call.

"I was wondering if you'd give me Irene Collins's contact information," I said.

"Oh, of course, darling, I'm sure she'd be thrilled to hear from you—is this more Crimson business?"

"It is." Irene Collins was a close friend of my grandmother's. She was also a former lawyer, married to a judge. And she was on the Crimson Board of Directors. The "Big Board," as my grandmother liked to call it, the one that actually called the shots, as opposed to the alumni board that my mother and grandmother belonged to, which wielded only ceremonial power.

"Is it still about those bad boys you got mixed up with last semester?"

"Some of it is. Some of it is about new bad boys."

"My, my, darling, there sure are a lot of bad boys in the world, aren't there? This sounds like more than a phone call. Tell you what: why don't I invite Irene and Alan"—Alan was Irene's husband—"over for dinner on Saturday. That way you can talk to both of them about your old and your new bad boys in person. And I'm hoping John will be there too. He's talking about taking a couple of days off and coming down to help your grandfather with that fencing project."

My grandparents had a white picket fence that they had been talking about replacing for the past five years. Perhaps this was going to be the year it finally happened.

"Sounds good," I said. That way I could visit with my grandparents, talk to Irene, and talk to John all in one fell swoop.

That settled, I went off to Chloe's on Thursday afternoon with a clear conscience. My lessons were planned, my job applications were submitted, my extracurricular student counseling obligations were pushed back to the weekend, and I could focus 100% on rewriting my book proposal according to the specs of publisher #3.

Chloe's house was on the other side of Greenfields. Greenfields wasn't very big, but in the course of the fifteen-minute drive I left behind the pawn shops, smoke shops, dollar stores, run-down fast food joints, cash-for-gold and payday loan places, low budget barber shops and hair salons that catered to a largely non-white clientele, and all the other trappings of the poor side of town.

Chloe's neighborhood, by contrast, was so upscale it didn't even have a gas station. If you wanted to get gas, groceries, or something more sinful, you had to literally drive across the tracks to the low-class places with non-residential zoning.

"Nice," said Mel when we pulled up outside Chloe's house. "Might be worth trying to get a tenure-track job just to live in a place like this."

"Yeah," I said. Chloe's house was not, in fact, that fancy. It was a plain Cape Cod that was probably less than 1,000 square feet, on a lot that was maybe a tenth of an acre. But it was a detached house in safe-looking neighborhood. The sidewalks didn't even have any chicken bones or fast food wrappers on them.

"Nice place," Mel said when Chloe came out to greet us. "What's the rent like compared with an apartment, if you don't mind me asking?"

"Oh, well..." Chloe looked away and rubbed the scars on her temples in embarrassment. "Actually, I, um...own it. Well, not really. Mostly the bank owns it. But I bought it. And the mortgage is, well...it's not that bad at all. A little over $600 a month, actually."

Mel and I stared at her. She was paying less for her whole house—*that she owned*—than we were for our apartments.

"Yeah, housing prices are really affordable here," Chloe was saying. "It's crazy, actually. I never thought I'd be able to buy my own home, and...here I am." She wrinkled up her nose. "Of course, I'm the only black person in the whole neighborhood. I always get the feeling that people are looking at me out of the corner of their eyes when I go past. But they've been pretty nice to my face, at least."

"Wow," said Mel, when she could speak again. She cleared her throat. "Did it take much of a down payment?"

Chloe shook her head. "I mean, not really, not for a house. Just 10%. 20%'s better, of course, and my parents were hoping they'd be able to help me out more so I could do 20% down, but my aunt had some health problems—she had to have her insulin pump replaced—and my cousin totaled his car, and then my other cousin got in trouble with the law—he's from *that* side of the family—and needed a lawyer, so...my dad's the one pretty much everyone in the whole family goes to for help. I mean, he's a surgeon, so it only makes sense, but...well, of course he had to help them out, and it was great that he was able to help me out too. I'm paying him back now. He didn't want me to, but *I* wanted to, and I know, like I said, how much everyone depends on him, and, I mean, he makes good money, but he's basically supporting, like, a dozen people on it, which means he's never been able to save for retirement or anything, so..."

"That's awesome that you were able to buy your own place—and that you're paying your dad back," I said.

"Yeah, and it's been much more fun than I thought it would be. More stressful, too—I thought I was going to faint or something when I handed over the check for the down payment, and the first night I spent here I was sure the place was going to burn down around me or something. It was like my baby and I felt like I had to watch it every minute, you know? But decorating and stuff has been way more fun than I thought it would be. I guess I felt like...nesting or something."

"Yeah," I said. I had never felt the slightest desire to nest, but right now I could see the attraction. "Can you show us around?"

The inside of the house was straightforward. Living room on the right, dining room on the left. Kitchen behind the dining room. Bedroom and bathroom tucked away behind the living room. Furniture was sparse, and there were still unpacked cardboard boxes in every room. Even so, it was stunning to think of one of my peers actually owning a house. I knew that people did that kind of thing, even people my age—or younger. Chloe was only 28. There was a time in America when it was normal for 28-year-olds to own their own homes. But for an academic it was amazing. I was starting to think that this contingent-faculty thing I'd been doing was even shittier than I'd known. I'd been so focused on the daily struggle to afford food that I hadn't thought about the housing thing. But jeez, owning my own home suddenly seemed like a worthy goal in and of itself.

We settled down around the dining room table, opened up our laptops, and got to work. For the first fifteen minutes that work was mainly listening to Chloe shriek in justified outrage over what the reviewers had said about her article. Then the next fifteen minutes were taken up with convincing Mel that she really did want to write a book proposal, and she should start it right now instead of engaging in more prep for her interview tomorrow.

"You've already prepped for it, right?" I asked.

"Yeah. I spent all morning on it. Plus it's a school I used to adjunct at, so I already know more about it than I'd like to. I just feel weird doing something so fuckin' long-term like working on a book proposal when I've got three classes and an interview tomorrow. Seems...wrong somehow. Sinful, or some shit like that."

"Isn't this a tenure-track job? Don't they want evidence of research and stuff like that?" I asked. "You'll want to say you're working on your book if it comes up."

"Yeah...I just...I'm just looking for a fucking excuse not to do this. And I'm freaking out about not getting the job, and I'm freaking out even more about getting it and ending up in the same city as Jewel."

"I get it," I said. "But working on your book proposal is an investment in *you*. And hopefully a significant contribution to scholarship as well. You should take an hour or two every now and then to do it."

"Yeah. Well, I'm going in. Cover me."

I said I would, and we all settled in for a solid half an hour of work before taking a spontaneous break. Half an hour was a long time in academic writing. Already I could feel my brain hollowing out and my ideas running dry.

We made ourselves some tea and settled back down for some more writing. Chloe's phone suddenly *pinged*, making us all jump.

"Oh jeez," she said. "It's Alicia. I wonder what that poor girl wants this time?"

36

"IS THIS THE SAME ALICIA who's in my class?" I asked. "Alicia McTighe?"

Chloe sighed. "Yes, that's her. I swear, that girl is so needy...I'm not advising anyone this year, but somehow I ended up with some 'mentees'—well, you know how it is. Every black student on campus, it seems like, is now my 'mentee.' And I get it, I really do. They're lonely and out of place and kind of scared and looking for someone who knows what they're going through. I know because I went through the same thing. But I spend hours every week dealing with their emotional dramas."

She read the notification on her phone screen. "Some of them have no filter, either. Alicia's asking me about advice for dating white men. Like I know! I mean, I'm only really interested in dating white guys, but it's not like I've got men all over me or something. Most of them won't even look at me. But now apparently I'm supposed to be teaching students about the intricacies of interracial dating along with pitch tones, Chinese calligraphy, and the Ming dynasty. None of which are actually my areas of expertise, I should add."

She opened up her email and sighed again. "Yep, dating white men. Not something I actually know about. Not something I'm an acknowledged expert in. Dating white men, where I'm a complete failure. Maybe you two could help her out better than me."

"Not me," said Mel. "I can do 'white,' but the 'men' part gets me every time. I'd just tell her to run screaming."

Both of them looked at me expectantly. "I'm not really an expert," I said. "More of a huge failure, really."

"Yeah, but you actually have a boyfriend," said Mel. "And he's white, right? You sound extremely qualified."

Now it was my turn to sigh. "This is probably a violation of FERPA or something." We were always getting lectured about not violating FERPA, or the Family Education Rights and Privacy Act.

"Nah, FERPA's for grades," said Mel.

"Because discussing a student's love life is so much better," I said.

"She *did* specifically request help," said Chloe. "In writing. And we're allowed to share information with a colleague if it's necessary. I'm going to say this is necessary. Especially since I can't take another day of this foolishness. So I'm turning it over to you."

Mel and I both straightened up in our chairs and put our listening ears on. Mel looked avid to hear all the dirt. I still had misgivings, but I couldn't deny that I was curious.

"So, it seems that Alicia met this guy called Anthony this semester. Actually, I think it was in your class, Rowena."

"If it's the Anthony I'm thinking of, then yes," I said.

"Oh good," said Chloe. "Then you'll definitely know better than the rest of us. Anyway, Alicia's in her second year here at Crimson, but she keeps thinking about transferring. She really doesn't feel like she fits in here, and she's gotten this thing about connecting with her roots."

"Yeah, she mentioned that to me," I said.

"She did a genetic test that shows she's part Sudanese, so she's become obsessed with her Sudanese heritage recently. I pointed out to her once that with a name like McTighe, her main heritage is really Irish. Especially since, I mean, she's practically what my grandmother would call 'high yeller.' Practically white."

"Uh-huh," I said.

"Plus, she's decided she'll only date white guys. Which I totally get. Like I said, I only date white guys too. Black guys just have waaaaayyyyy too much drama. But then she's all about her African heritage. She keeps talking about converting to Islam. I pointed out to her that Islam is also a foreign religion that was imposed by a bunch of white dudes, or close enough, and if she wanted to get in touch with her African roots, she needed to start studying Yoruban gods or something, but she said that was completely the wrong side of Africa and I didn't know what I was talking about, which was kind of true.

"So anyway, she's yakking up a storm about converting to Islam one moment, and talking my ear off about how she feels about dating Anthony the next. I tell you, that girl is exhausting me. And she has *no* boundaries. So now she wants to know if it's normal for white guys to be all protective and stuff. I mean, it's what she thought she wanted, but now that it's happening, she's not sure about it. Anthony's constantly doing stuff for her, romantic stuff, and also helping her out all the time, and she's wondering if it's normal."

Mel and Chloe both looked at me.

"Um," I said. "It depends on the stuff, and the guy. I *think*—I wouldn't know firsthand—that there's a certain aspect of rich white men treating their girlfriends like a princess or, more accurately, like a doll and a trophy, although I suspect that's more about the 'rich' part and less about the 'white' part. But lots of guys of all ethnicities and socioeconomic backgrounds can disguise creepy controlling behavior with a facade of romanticism."

"See," said Mel, "this is why I don't do men. Well, one of about a thousand reasons."

"Yeah," I said. "So, um, I guess I'd say that my impression of Anthony is that he's got the protective alpha male thing both through genetics and upbringing. I'm sure he'd treat any girlfriend of his like a pretty doll to bring out and show off to his friends—although maybe don't tell Alicia that. And maybe I'm wrong about him. Anyway, I guess I'd tell her that he'll probably want to 'take care of her' by buying her stuff and making romantic gestures, so it all depends on how she feels about it. Is it fun, or is creepy and stifling? Is he doing it to show his genuine appreciation, or as a form of control and dominance?"

Chloe snorted. "I'm guessing the latter, but I think Alicia really sent me this email to brag about her rich white boyfriend and how he's spending money on her."

"It's a nice fantasy," I said. "I'm sure we all fantasize about some strong man coming along and sweeping us off our feet, or at least sweeping away all our problems."

"Speak for your own damn self," said Mel. "'Sides"—she looked at me out of the corner of her eye—"I got the impression that wasn't really what you're into."

"Not the sweeping off the feet part," I said. "I prefer to keep my feet planted firmly on the ground. But a man with plenty of money that he wanted to use to make your life easier sounds pretty attractive sometimes."

"Yeah," said Chloe. "Well, I'll tell Alicia he's probably just being nice, but if she gets any bad vibes from him, she should break it off. She's just bragging, though, she really is."

"Probably," I said.

37

MEL'S INTERVIEW ON Friday went "Okay, if not great," she said, and then Hell Week was over for both of us. Well, sort of. I had my visit on Saturday to my grandparents. I didn't normally consider visiting my grandparents to be hellish, but at the moment all I wanted was to crawl into bed and never get out.

I got there around four, in plenty of time to help with dinner before Irene and Alan got there at six. John pulled into the drive right behind me.

"Ro!" he shouted as he got out of the car. "You made it!"

"So did you, and from a lot farther away," I said. John was stationed at Camp Lejeune, in North Carolina.

"Eight fucking hours on the road. This better be a pretty damn good fence Grandpa wants help with." His grin, which filled his face and made his eyes crinkle up at the corners, belied his words. He appeared to be in a good mood for once, even though he was sober. Good thing I was the only woman receiving the full wattage of that smile.

John was tall and fit and had Black Irish looks, just like me, although he was solid where I was willowy. He looked sort of like a younger Alec Baldwin if Alec Baldwin had gone into the military rather than acting. Women threw themselves at him left, right, and center, even when he wasn't in uniform. When he was, he probably needed a protective detail to keep from being overwhelmed by the crush of female lust. Too bad he was a fucked-up drama queen who specialized in one-night stands with cheap blondes and married women.

"I'm sure with your help it will be the best fence that ever was," I told him.

"For fucking sure. How's Miller? Has he finally gotten his act together and stopped dicking around and doing the long-distance thing with you?"

John always asked after Alex. Although it would never have been obvious to the casual observer, John actually liked Alex a lot. Also, he was very keen for me to get married and start a family, and he saw Alex as my best chance. Sometimes I suggested to him that his desire for me to get married and start a family was an expression of his own repressed longings. That never went down well. The truth rarely does.

"Alex is fine," I said. "I've got tickets to go see him in Monterey over spring break."

"No shit? That's great!" John gave me another genuinely happy grin.

"It is. What's up with you?" I wanted to ask if his good mood was because he was seeing someone special, but I knew better.

"Same ol', same ol'. Hanging in there. Unlike Jase—did I tell you about him?"

"You said he'd totaled his truck when he hit a deer last year." Jase and John had gone through basic training together, and been inseparable ever since. The rest of us found it encouraging that John was able to retain at least one true friend.

"Yeah. So, he wasn't hurt too bad from that—we thought. But he hurt his knee and his chest in the accident, and it would *not* fucking heal. Three months later he was still limping around and saying he couldn't do pushups. Then he started having fucking seizures and shit. I saw one—he screamed and jerked all over like he'd been tazed.

And then one side of his face started getting paralyzed at weird times."

"Oh my God," I said. "Did he have a brain injury from the accident?"

"Weirder than that. Turns out he had fucking *Lyme* disease. Probably had it for months or years before the accident. It'd just been lying in wait for something like that. His doctor told him it likes to snack on damaged collagen, so it'll lie low and wait until you get sick or hurt or something, and then take over."

"Wow," I said. "How's he doing now?"

John grimaced, losing a lot of his good mood. "He's been on doxycycline for the past month. Like we didn't get enough of that shit in Afghanistan. He said it made him sick as fuck for the first few weeks, 'cause that's what it does when you have Lyme—make you sicker before it makes you better. He says the weird seizures and face paralysis is starting to get better now, but they're telling him he might have to be on antibiotics for months, maybe years."

"My God," I said. "That sounds miserable."

"Yeah, like he hasn't been through enough already." That was John's way of referring to the fact that Jase had vomited every morning for 373 days straight after he'd gotten back from his first deployment in Afghanistan. The military, in its infinite wisdom, or maybe desperation, had sent him back twice more.

"Yeah," I said. "I hope he starts seeing some real improvement soon."

"Yeah. I guess it's one of those shitty tricks the universe plays. They say he probably picked it up around here. The man made it through three deployments, and he might end up an invalid from a bug bite back here in Georgia. He's staying with family outside of Atlanta, so I'm going to check on him while I'm here." John shook his shoulders, physically shaking off his scary thoughts. "Looks like Grandma and Grandpa are coming our way, so smile, sis."

"Weena! Vannie!" Our grandparents were practically skipping down the porch steps in their eagerness to get to us.

"When the fuck do you think I'll be able to train 'em to stop calling me Vannie?" John said *sotto voce*, before plastering on a giant smile.

"Never," I *sotto voce*'d back. Our parents had named us Rowena Arwen and Ivanhoe Elladan. John had legally taken "John" as his first name when he turned 18. But our grandparents still called us Weena and Vannie, as they had when we'd been three and six.

Hugs were distributed all around. Traffic on the drive down was inquired after. We moved into the house, and John headed off to drop his backpack in the guest bedroom. I followed, intending to make use of the guest bathroom.

"You better let me do a sweep first," John told me. "Fuck knows what shit Grandpa has planted this time."

"Okay." Our grandfather was a notorious practical joker. He'd mostly given up on me, since I'd never found his jokes funny in the slightest and had in fact threatened to stop visiting unless he stopped playing them. John, as the only person who would put up with them, got the brunt of them.

"God damn it to fucking hell!"

I poked my head into the bathroom. John was backed up against the far wall, staring at a snake that was hanging out of the top drawer of the vanity. His eyes were dilated like he'd just snorted a double line of coke, and I could see the pulse beating in his neck.

"It's okay," I said gently. "It's a toy snake."

"I know." John swallowed. "It's one of those fucking jack-in-the-box thingies. It exploded out at me when I opened the drawer. Stupid." He laughed a mirthless laugh. "I'm not even afraid of snakes."

"I don't think it's the snake that's the problem," I said. It hadn't occurred to our grandfather that a surprise explosion, even of the jack-in-the-box variety, might not be the best thing to spring on John. "Why don't I finish the sweep?" I suggested.

"I'm not gonna wimp out over a little toy snake," said John. "'Sides, you're not even trained for it."

"I've had plenty of training in dealing with Grandpa's surprises." I slipped past John into the bathroom and removed the snake from the drawer, before continuing the sweep.

The next drawer down held a variety of rather alarming sex toys with a note inviting people to help themselves, and a stern PS addressed directly to John, telling him not to hurt himself.

"I don't even wanna fucking think about Grandpa ordering this shit," said John. "Where'd he even find it? And what the fuck is this?" He picked up a kind of starfish-shaped thing and hefted it cautiously.

"I think it's a vibrator."

"Oh shit yeah, it's started vibrating! How the fuck do you make it stop?!?"

I took it away from John and, after some fumbling, managed to turn it off.

"I don't want to fucking know how you know what that is, let alone how to use it," he said.

"I got stuck in a waiting room with poor cell reception and only old copies of *Cosmo* to read," I said. "It was extremely eye-opening. Let's put the sex toys away and keep going with the sweep."

With me taking point and John covering my back, we discovered that the toilet had been clingfilmed, the bed had been short-sheeted, and there was another jack-in-the-box in the closet, this one with a terrifying clown that freaked both of us out way more than the snake.

"I need a fucking drink," John declared when we were done. "My nerves can't take this shit much longer. You want anything?"

"Just to go pee," I said. "I've been desperate since I hit the Macon city limits, and that was the better part of an hour ago."

"'Kay. I'll clear out and let you take care of business then. And Ro?"

"Yeah?"

"Thanks," he said. "For, like...helping me out. And for, like...not laughing at me. I know I was kind of a pussy back there. I just can't..."

"It's okay," I said, when John couldn't finish explaining what he couldn't do. "And remember: balls are wimpy and weak, but a pussy can really take a pounding."

I was rewarded by the sound of John laughing to himself all the way to the whiskey bottle.

38

WHEN I CAME OUT OF the bathroom, John and our grandfather were examining the fence and gesturing at it animatedly with their tumblers of whiskey. Whatever made them happy. I considered approaching Grandpa and having a quiet word in his ear about not planting explosive devices in John's room. Then I considered how John would react if he found out. He'd probably prefer the panic attacks he was currently having to the embarrassment of having his fear exposed. I decided to keep my mouth shut.

"They sure do look happy, don't they?" My grandmother had come up behind me as I'd been watching them out the window. "Even Vannie. Wonder what's up with that boy? Does he seem happier to you than he has in a while? I know he's only been here a few minutes, but he's got a different aura, don't you think?"

"Actually, yeah," I said.

"Maybe he's *met* someone, darling, what do you think? Wouldn't that be wonderful? I know he was seeing someone when he was in, well, Afghanistan, but I guess that ended when he left."

"Tammy," I said. "A private contractor. I think he was more broke up about it than he let on, but I also think we should all be grateful that it didn't go any further. From the hints he dropped, she was a gold digger who would have made a terrible long-term prospect."

"No doubt, darling, but I sure wish he'd find someone who *would* make a good long-term prospect—and maybe he has."

"Maybe," I said. "He hasn't said anything to me about it, though."

"Well, keep your ears open, darling. And how are things going with Alex?"

I filled my grandmother in on my plans to go visit Alex over spring break, and our speculations on the Carmel job. I hadn't heard anything back from the committee either way, but it was early days yet. I wouldn't expect to hear anything until next month at the earliest.

Irene and Alan showed up a little before six, and there was an hour of drinks and hors d'oeuvres and happy chatter. It wasn't until we sat down at the table that the real business came up.

"So, Rowena honey, how *is* dear old Crimson doing this semester?" Irene asked me. "I haven't forgotten what I said last semester: I *do* think I should be more involved. I'm just still thinking of ways to do that. Of course I'm still *that mad* about them taking all the money from Security Solutions. For-profit prisons! You know I'm not exactly what you'd call a raging liberal, sweetie, but for-profit prisons are just a bridge too far! That money is just, well, it's just *dirty*, when you come right down to it. And they're whitewashing it through Crimson College!"

"Mmmm," I said. I personally considered for-profit prisons to be a scourge and a loathsome cancer. But aside from my hesitance to criticize my one and only employer to a member of the board, I wasn't entirely sure what kind of a reaction any mention of the racial issues around for-profit prisons would provoke. Irene Collins might say she wasn't a raging liberal, but in her own way she was a rebel and a fighter for justice. And despite what my Yankee friends and colleagues seemed determined to believe, not everyone in the South, even small-town white folks, were die-hard racists.

That being said, Irene was from a generation that considered it perfectly okay to make casual comments that would cause woke Millennials to choke in outrage. I was pretty sure I could control myself. I was less sure about John. He might delight in teasing our father and enraging any woke liberals he happened to encounter, but he'd spent his whole adult life relying on his largely black and Hispanic comrades to literally pull him out of the fire when necessary. Comments about "shiftless," "lazy," or "irresponsible" minorities were likely to provoke explosive outbursts.

Plus, the whole conversation was guaranteed to be a downer. So I contented myself with nodding and making supportive mouth noises.

"Now, now," Alan was saying. "Don't you get yourself all het up, Irene! It's her latest hobby-horse," he told the rest of us. "Only it's been going on for a good year now at least. I keep telling her it's a done deal, but you know how she is once she gets her teeth in something: like a pit bull."

"You're dang right I am!" said Irene. "Of course, I knew there was nothing we could do about it, not once that *darn* Anthony Wainwright realized he could launder his dirty money through *our* college, but still! I had to make my opinion known!"

"Anthony Wainwright?" I repeated. "What does he have to do with it? He's just a student."

"Oh...I suppose his son's college-age now. No, I meant Anthony Wainwright, Junior. Our chairman of the board. His family acquired controlling shares in Security Solutions a couple of years back. They've got to have their fingers in every single pie that has so much as a dollar in it, and the prison industry has millions and millions of dollars in it, especially in Georgia. And Security Solutions started off running detention facilities overseas. You know, so they could torture people without contravening US law.

"Then they started making money hand over fist by imprisoning our poorest citizens right here in the US of A. It's *blood* money, that's what it is, but when I tell people that, they don't want to hear it! Especially because it's our beloved Wainwrights doing it. They're the college's founding family, so everything they do has to be perfect. But they went from making money off their plantations to making money off their prisons. Just like King Solomon says, there's nothing new under the sun."

"Um, yeah," I said.

"And of course if you go back into anyone's family history, there's going to be dirt. I don't blame the Wainwrights for what their ancestors did. But they didn't have to take that money and use it to buy up *prisons*."

"Now, now, Reenie," said Alan. "I'm sure our hosts don't need to hear all of this—again."

Irene took a deep breath. Bright splotches of color had bloomed on both her cheeks. "You're right," she said. "And there's nothing we can do about it, anyway. But I still want to be a thorn in their sides as much as I can. So, Rowena darling, if there's anything you need help with that might let me *stick it* to them, you just let me know."

"Well," I said. "I don't know if there's anything you can do about this or not, but I'll tell you anyway." I told her about Nathan Willoughby's family's threats to sue me.

"Well, hon, that sounds like pure bull honkey to me—but if they start causing you any trouble, you give me a call, okay? I'll give you all the free legal advice you need, and find you someone who's still practicing to defend you if it comes to trial."

"Thanks," I said. "Although I'm really hoping it doesn't come to that."

"Me too, hon, but it's best to be prepared. So what else is the college up to? Edith said something about there being more bad boys up to no good this semester."

"Yeah." I outlined the Aishat/Owen Wu situation, leaving out all the names. I finished with the fact that the college had refused to allow the police to search Owen Wu's college-issued laptop, and because so far all he had was hearsay, Brian hadn't been able to show probable cause and get a warrant.

"And you say this video might shed some light on what happened to that Brittany Gutierrez girl?" Irene asked when I was done.

"That's the hope," I said.

"Well, hon, I'll think about what I might be able to do. You know, what happened to that girl was a crying shame. She was the best cheerleader we'd had for ages. I'd go to games as much to watch her as to watch the players. I met her once too, and she seemed like a real sweetheart. When I heard she'd done made it all up, I was brokenhearted. I sure would like to know the truth of what really happened."

"Yeah," I said. "I think we all would." *Except for the rapist.* But I didn't say that out loud.

39

IRENE TOLD ME TO PUT her in touch with Brian Michaels, so I did. She also said that she'd feel out the rest of the board about pushing to reopen the investigation into the Brittany Gutierrez case.

"And of course, if you could get this girl to come forward and make a statement, that would help us out a lot," she told me.

I agreed that it would help a lot. Unfortunately, with Aishat avoiding me, there wasn't much I could do about it. Instead, I fretted about my upcoming teaching observation.

Fretting that turned out to be wasted, because Monday morning Karen was hoarse and congested. She spent a couple of hours standing around in the hallway ostentatiously coughing and sneezing, before declaring that she was much too sick to spend the rest of the day on campus, or come onto campus at all tomorrow. She interrupted my second class to tell me that Friday's observation would be cancelled "Until I get over this—I take *so long* to recover from colds," and then exited with a final disruptive sneeze.

Having the observation cancelled was a wonderful temporary reprieve, and if it had been anyone else I would have felt compassion for their illness, as well as gratitude at them for staying away and not infecting the rest of us. But since Karen had made so many remarks about Mel calling in sick all the time, I couldn't help but feel that her canceling because of a cold was the height of hypocrisy.

She was out for the rest of the week. I made no move to remind her about the observation when she returned the following week. No doubt she'd remember all too soon.

I also made no move to follow up with Aishat. I'd expressed my willingness to help her several times—and made it clear what my help would involve. If she was in a difficult situation, nagging and stalking her seemed counterproductive. When I didn't hear from her, I figured she'd decided not to pursue it any further.

Instead, I made plans for my summer. Normally I'd teach an intensive class at Indiana's Summer Workshop. But this year I wanted to try to get a job at the Summer Intensive Language Program at Monterey, so I could spend the summer with Alex. So I turned my attention from Aishat to interviewing for a position there.

But then, on March 1st, two weeks after I had emailed her, Aishat suddenly showed up in my office after my last class.

"Oh, hello," I said. "Come on in. How have you been?"

She moved her shoulders in a motion that could have been a shrug and could have been a wriggle of discomfort. She stepped tentatively into my office, like a nervous gazelle approaching a watering hole known for concealing crocodiles and possibly lions, but she couldn't make herself take a seat.

"I was thinking..." she said softly.

"Mmmm-hmmm?" I said, when she failed to say anything more.

"My parents were thinking...we wanted to invite you...would you come to our house? Tonight?"

"Um," I said. "Okay. Sure. That's very kind of you. I'd love to come over for a visit. What time?"

"Um...I have a meeting this afternoon. For our Muslim Students' Union. There are only four of us. Well, there were five of us, but then Alicia stopped coming, I don't know why. So now there are only four of us. But we meet every month anyway. The meeting will end at six. So...after that?"

"Sure," I said. "Can I give you a ride? That way you can give me directions."

This engendered some more hesitant wriggling, but eventually Aishat agreed that yes, I could give her a ride. She slipped out of the office before I could ask her why she had been following Alicia and Anthony.

I had carpooled over to campus with Mel that morning, so I found her after her last class and asked if she could give me a ride home so that I could reorganize myself and pick up my own car in time to go pick up Aishat.

"Sure," said Mel. "Only...could you maybe do the driving?"

"Sure," I said. We had come in Mel's Jeep. She had been quiet and withdrawn on the drive over. When I'd asked her how she felt, she'd said, "Like I'm shutting down. Like I'm too tired to talk. Even to complain about how tired I am." Then she'd been silent for the rest of the ride to campus and the walk over from the parking lot to Bedford Hall.

Now she seemed marginally more animated, but..."What's wrong with your face?" I demanded.

"It feels all weak," she said. "And my jaw hurts, and I've got a nasty headache." Or at least that's what I thought she said. Her speech was slurred, and one side of her face was sagging.

For a split second I stood there frozen, considering my options. Call 911? It would take 10-15 minutes for campus paramedics to arrive. Then they would call for an ambulance. The nearest real hospital was in Macon, over half an hour away. Even in the best case it would be at least an hour and a half before Mel would even be admitted.

"Give me your keys," I said. "Sit down right here and don't move. Try to relax. I'll be back in a second."

I walked calmly out of Bedford Hall. As soon as I was out of sight of the bench where Mel was sitting, I broke into a dead run.

I sprinted across the lower quad. Miranda, Jackson, Alicia, Jessica, and Isobel all saw me and shouted something as I went past, but I was moving too quickly to respond. I darted between the dorms and out onto the beach volleyball courts. My left knee buckled when I hit the sand, but I got my other leg under me in time to keep from going down, and I shot forward with a renewed burst of speed.

My lungs felt like they were filled with fire by the time I reached the stadium. I kept going, past the copse and the entrance to The Hollow, all the way around the football stadium, and across the parking lot, where we'd parked this morning, all the way in the back.

I dry-heaved a little as I unlocked the Jeep, but I managed not to puke as I climbed in and started it up. I backed it out of the parking spot at a speed I would have found terrifying under any other circumstances, and set off towards Bedford Hall with a screech of tires.

There was a small access alley behind Bedford for deliveries. I pulled into it, the Jeep rocking wildly from the speed of my turn, and drove right through it and onto the back quad. Students scattered like pigeons as I drove across the manicured grass right up to the front entrance to Bedford.

I jumped out, leaving the engine running and the door open. Hayley Kiyoko serenaded the entire back quad about girls liking girls like boys do as I sprinted up to the entrance to Bedford and then walked, slowly and calmly, inside.

"Let's go," I told Mel. She was still sitting there. Still upright and conscious. Thank God. "I've got the Jeep parked right in front of the front door."

"Why?" she asked. Her face was sagging even more than it had been when I'd left her just a few minutes ago. No one else appeared to notice at all.

"Because," I said, speaking softly and very calmly as I pulled her to her feet and directed her towards the front door, "I'm a little bit worried that you might be having a stroke."

"Rowena! Melissa! *There* you are! I wanted to talk to you about your teaching observations and performance reviews...*Where* are you going? *What* is that *Jeep* doing right in front of the door?!?"

"I'm taking Mel to the ER," I told Karen. She opened her mouth like a bullfrog about to burst into a mating croak, but I was past her and out the door before I could hear what she had to say.

Mel climbed into the Jeep on her own, which made me feel a little bit better. I steered it back towards the back alley—where Brian Michaels was standing, blocking my access.

As soon as he saw it was me, he made rolling-down motions with his hand. I rolled down my window, stuck my head out, and said, "I have to take Mel to the ER right now!"

"Okay," he said. "Put your hazards on then. The closest decent ER is at Macon Presbyterian. She gonna make it that far?"

I looked over at Mel. She was still conscious and upright. "I hope so," I said.

"I'll make a call to the highway patrol to let them know not to stop you. And I'll call Presbyterian to let them know to expect you. What do you think it is?"

"Maybe a stroke," I said.

He stepped back. "You get goin'. I'll make those calls."

I pulled past him with another screech of rubber on pavement and headed for the main entrance at twice the recommended speed.

"I've got directions to Presbyterian," said Mel. She held up her phone, showing me the map function she'd pulled up.

"Thanks," I said. "How do you feel?"

"I feel like shit. Also pretty damn scared now that you've put the idea of a stroke in my mind. But not like I'm going crazy or dying. Do I seem normal?"

"You're a little hard to understand," I told her. "But you're coherent. Just...try to relax, okay? Keep your blood pressure down."

"Okay." Mel closed her eyes and, as far as I could tell, sang along softly with Hayley Kiyoko. I hoped it helped.

We zoomed through Greenfields at a speed that made my palms sweat, and got onto the Macon-Greenfields Highway. It was a four-lane road that was only sort of a highway. Praying that no animals, small children, or day drinkers chose this moment to get too close to the road, I put my foot down on the accelerator. The Jeep's engine gave a happy roar, delighted to be able to finally put its V8 power to good use.

Once the needle on the speedometer crept up towards 80, the wheel started giving a little shimmy in my sweaty palms. I eased back to 75 and glanced at Mel's phone screen. Our estimated trip time was 25 minutes. I glanced over at Mel. She was still singing along softly with Hayley Kiyoko. I told myself this was a good sign.

About five miles out of Macon, a highway patrol car pulled out from a side road and fell in behind us, lights flashing and siren blaring. I wondered what would happen if they were trying to pull us over and I ignored them. They probably didn't have roof-mounted RPGs or anything that could blow us off the road while we were driving, right? US police forces were scarily militarized, but ordinary state troopers didn't have the firepower to shoot down a Jeep Grand Cherokee, right? Right?

The state trooper pulled in front of us, stuck his arm out the window, and made a waving gesture before pointing ahead down the road.

"I think he's our escort," I said out loud.

Mel opened her eyes. "Cool," she said. "Police escort." Her speech was now so slurred that she couldn't pronounce "l" and "r" sounds at all.

We screamed through the outskirts of Macon, scattering other cars like chickens. A beautiful, beautiful blue hospital sign with a right turn arrow appeared. The state trooper made a hard right. The Jeep's shocks creaked in protest as I followed. An even more beautiful "Emergency Room" sign appeared. We made a hard left and pulled into the hospital complex. Cars pulled aside as we made another right and then a left and pulled up in front of the entrance to the ER.

Two paramedics came running up to meet us. "This the one we got the call about?" the older one asked me. "Young woman, possible stroke in progress?"

I nodded and pointed at Mel. The paramedics looked at her face. "We're gonna get you in there real quick, hon," said the older paramedic. "Don't you worry."

They got her out of the Jeep and loaded her onto a gurney. She wasn't thrilled about being strapped onto the gurney, but after a fierce argument she let them do it.

"That's a good sign," said the state trooper, who had come over to stand by my door. "That she's still got that much sass."

"Yeah," I said. "Yeah...I just...I just..."

"Aw, hon," said the state trooper. "After something like that? It's okay to cry."

40

MY POST-ADRENALINE-rush crying jags had always been a source of embarrassment. This time was no different. I cried the whole way as I drove the Jeep to the parking deck. By the time I parked, the crying had morphed into full-body shakes. I had to spend several minutes waiting for things to calm down before I could clean my face and leave the Jeep. I knew it was a natural reaction to the massive rush of hormones that had flooded through me at the crisis moment, giving me the superhuman strength and crazy courage to do whatever needed to be done for immediate survival. That didn't make it any less unpleasant and embarrassing.

The trek from the parking deck was long enough that I had plenty of time to pull myself together. I also had plenty of time to consider the inconvenient logistics of the situation. It was—I checked my phone—2:45. It seemed very unlikely that I would be able to make it back to meet with Aishat this evening, even if I wanted to leave Mel by herself in the hospital, which I didn't. If Aishat had a cell phone number, I didn't know it, so I was going to have to hope that she checked her email this afternoon.

Then there was Mel's family. Someone should probably notify them. I didn't even know their names, let alone have any contact information for them. All I knew about them was that Mel was on strained terms with them, although she still went to South Carolina to visit them at least once a month.

I'll worry about that later. First I have to find her.

Macon Presbyterian was not large by hospital standards. But by any other building standards it was still huge. It took me the better part of ten minutes just to make it back to the Emergency wing entrance. I asked about Mel at the Reception/Direction desk near the door. I was a little afraid they would deny me access since I wasn't family, like you see all the time on TV, but actually the receptionist gave me a sympathetic smile before telling me that Mel was being examined right now and sending me off to the ER waiting room.

The ER waiting room held the usual cross-section of desperate humanity. It was a little less desperate at 3:00pm on a Tuesday than it would have been on a Saturday night, but I was still wedged between a softly crying young black woman whose nephew had had a scary asthma attack, and an anxious elderly white man whose wife had fallen and hurt her hip. The row of chairs opposite us held what looked like three-quarters of a lawn crew. From the few words of Spanish I managed to pick up, I guessed that the fourth member had been hurt when his mower had flipped over on top of him.

I emailed Aishat that there had been an emergency and I wouldn't be able to meet with her tonight. I talked a little bit with the woman sitting next to me, whose name was Jazmine and who was taking care of her nephew with her mother now that her brother was in jail. I heard some amusing stories about the elderly man's wife. I traded three ones and a handful of loose change with the lawn crew for a five-dollar bill reeking of gasoline and cut grass so that they could go get something from the vending machine.

By 4:00pm Jazmine, the elderly man, and the lawn crew had been led away to pick up their patients. They were quickly replaced by a heavyset rednecky-looking mother-daughter pair whose son/grandson had overdosed on opioids, a black woman about my age whose diabetic mother had collapsed from a hypoglycemia attack, and a couple of preppy college-age white boys whose friend had been in a car accident.

By 5:00pm they had all been replaced by a fresh wave of friends and family of disasters. I texted Alex to let him know what was going on. Since it was 2:00pm in California, he was teaching, but he texted me quickly back to ask if I was okay.

I'm fine, I wrote. *I'll let you know how it goes.*

I'll call you as soon as I'm free, he texted back. *Take care of yourself, okay? Have you had anything to eat?*

I should do that, I wrote. That was more to reassure Alex than a definite plan of action. I'd given all my ones and my change to the lawn crew, which meant that the vending machine was useless. There was probably a cafeteria somewhere, but I was afraid to go off in search of it and miss being called back to see Mel. Good thing I was used to fasting. This would just be a good chance for me to burn off a few of those restaurant lunches I was suspecting were starting to build up on my hips and thighs.

By 5:30 I was feeling the harbingers of a migraine building in my temples and flashing on the edges of my vision. Maybe I needed to risk a trip to the cafeteria.

I went over to the reception desk, where a different receptionist told me after some computer searching and phone calls that Mel was "in Radiology," and gave me one of those flying-saucer-like beepers that restaurants hand out so that I could be paged anywhere in the hospital.

Feeling relieved, I headed off in what I was told was the direction of the cafeteria. Three long corridors, two elevator rides, and a trek across a leaky skywalk later, I could smell food. My mouth watered instinctively. I deserved fries, right? Who cared about expanding hips and thighs under these circumstances, right?

I had just gotten into the line for Chik-Fil-A when my pocket *pinged* at me. I jumped, and then, remembering the beeper, patted myself down until I found it and pulled it out. Nothing. My pocket *pinged* again. I pulled out my phone.

Darling Inna, I read. *Are you free now?*

41

I'M FREE, I texted. I could feel my pulse jump in my throat. Dima and I had texted a few times since our interrupted video call in January, but we'd never finished that conversation. And he hadn't called me "darling" since he'd broken off the engagement. Something, I could tell, was up. Something important was about to happen.

Can you talk on video?

Maybe, I wrote. *I'm actually waiting for a friend in the hospital. I'll have to go outside, and see how the connection is there.*

In the hospital? Is your friend OK?

I don't know. I'm afraid she might have had a stroke.

"Whatcha want, hon?"

It was the lady at the Chik-Fil-A serving station. I was holding up the line.

"Fries, please." I paid for my fries with my dirty five-dollar bill, went over to a table as my phone *pinged* insistently, and—feeling like it probably wasn't enough after handling that bill—sanitized my hands. They still smelled of gasoline, now overlaid with the scent of alcohol and artificial fragrance.

Let's just text. I don't want to distract you when you're waiting to hear about your friend. Besides, sometimes it's easier to converse in written rather than spoken form.

Very true, I wrote back. *How are you?*

You know me))))

I do. Are you still on the front?

I'm in Kiev, would you believe it? And looking into going back to Moscow. Mama's not feeling well.

Her diabetes? Galina Ivanovna, Dima's mother, was a Type 1 diabetic. She was a doctor, and had managed her diabetes with scrupulous attention, but she was also in her sixties, and had spent most of her life in very stressful circumstances, including weathering multiple death threats aimed at herself and her only son.

She got the flu this winter. Then it turned into pneumonia. Now she's having problems with her kidneys. The doctors say it might be just too much strain for the organism and her kidneys are shutting down.

My God, I wrote. *What can be done?*

That's what I want to find out. Plus I've got my own business in Moscow. And maybe Petersburg as well.

Is it safe? I asked.

They've been sending hired killers for me here in Ukraine—and then there are the regular dangers of a war zone))))) I've decided I might as well go back home. At least for a bit. But that's not what I wanted to tell you.

What did you want to tell me? I wrote.

How are things with you and your American?

Why?

The thing is, he wrote, *my friend Rinat—have I told you about Rinat?*

You've mentioned the name. After my conversation with Zaria, I had delicately inquired about who this Rinat Mustafaev she seemed to think I should know was. *He's the Canadian, right?*

Right. The Daghestani Canadian who's acting as an international observer in the war zone. The thing is

The text cut off abruptly.

Yes? I texted.

Sorry. This is somehow very hard for me to write. The thing is, he's trying to marry me to his cousin.

42

IN CANADA OR DAGHESTAN? It was a stupid question. But it was the only response I could come up with.

She's currently in Kiev. But she has Canadian citizenship. I think she lives in Ottawa. Is that the right name? Something like that, anyway.

Ottawa is the capital of Canada, I wrote. *So it's very possible.*

Have you ever been there? Is it nice? Was that where you were this winter?

No, I wrote back. *I've never been to Ottawa. I've only ever been to Vancouver, to the conference this winter. That's on completely the opposite side of the country.* Then, feeling like my fingers were disconnected from the rest of me and were asking the awful question on their own, I wrote, *Is she nice? Do you like her?*

She's nice enough. Rinat has a plan to marry me to her and get me and mama Canadian citizenship. She'd probably be a good wife.

"Hey hon, you okay?"

It was the woman from the Chik-Fil-A stand. No one was in line, and she was now cleaning the nearby tables.

"Thanks," I said. "I'm okay. It's just been a tough day, and it doesn't look to be getting any easier."

"Mmmm-hmmm. I know how that goes." She was about my mother's age, black, with the face and hands and body of someone who'd done menial labor her whole life, and the eyes of a person who'd had more than her fair share of hard days. "Sometimes the Lord sends you these hard days," she said. "'Specially in hospitals. Every day I see people havin' the toughest day of their lives in here. And I've had a few of my own. But I just pray to Jesus, and he sees me through. You want, I can pray to Jesus for you too, hon."

"Thanks," I said. "That's very kind of you. And anything that might help is worth trying."

"You got that right, hon. I'm praying for you real hard right now."

"Thanks," I said again. "And, um, likewise."

"Thank you, hon, thank you. And oh lordie, here come a whole bunch o' folk, lookin' for food. I better get back to my station."

"Good luck," I said. "And thanks again."

I looked back at my phone. That last text was still there, staring me in the face, requiring an answer.

Do you want to marry her? I wrote.

I want to provide a good, safe life for mama. Maybe marrying this cousin of Rinat's and moving to Canada will do that. Canada is supposed to be very safe, right?

Very safe, I confirmed. *But will you be happy if you do this?*

I'm not very happy now, Inna. Maybe I'll be happier if I do this and make mama happy.

You know that you don't have to marry this cousin of Rinat's in order to move to the West, right? I wrote. *You know I'll do whatever it takes to make things alright for you and your mother, right?*

I know you've promised this many times, Inna. And I know you'd do it, too. But I can't let you do this.

There's no "let" about it. This is my offer, freely given.

I know. But I still can't let you do it. I have a life debt before you, remember? Maybe I have to discharge it by not letting you throw your life away on me.

IT WOULDN'T BE THROWING MY LIFE AWAY!!!!!!!!

I want to pay back my life debt to you by making sure you have a good life, Inna. I'm just not sure how to do that yet. But I *am* sure that it can't be by letting you throw away this good life in America and this American man you have in order to fall back into my darkness and danger.

YOU DON'T GET TO DECIDE HOW I LIVE MY LIFE!!!!! YOU DON'T GET TO DECIDE HOW I SPEND IT!!!!!!

Yes, Inna, I do. Life debt, remember? So let's agree that your life belongs to me now, and it's my duty to make sure you don't waste it.

THAT'S NOT HOW A LIFE DEBT WORKS!!!!! *YOUR* LIFE BELONGS TO *ME* NOW!!!!!!

No, Inna. Or rather, yes, I guess so. But my most important duty is to make sure that you don't throw your precious life away. Even if it hurts me.

All caps didn't seem to be having an effect. Since they made me feel like an overwrought idiot, I switched them off. *Anything you do that hurts you will hurt me more*, I wrote. *If you say you have a life debt before me, then repay it by listening to me and doing as I ask.*

And what do you ask, Inna?

I wished I weren't having this conversation on the fly in a hospital cafeteria. I wished I had been given some warning that it was going to happen, like with an interview or a job offer, so that I could prepare a list of questions and points for negotiation. Because things had gotten so complicated that I didn't actually know what I wanted from Dima. Other than that I didn't want him to enter into a marriage of convenience with some woman he barely knew.

I ask that you not rush into anything with this woman, I finally wrote. *I ask that you not waste *your* life on a bad marriage out of a misguided sense of duty.*

Thank you, Inna.

For what?

For always trying to watch over me, little as I deserve it. I'll think about what you said. Promise me you'll think about what I said.

My pocket suddenly started beeping and vibrating like mad. A text popped up at the same time on my phone. From Mel. *You still there? They're going to discharge me in a few.*

I'm still here, I wrote to Mel. *I promise,* I wrote to Dima. *If you promise the same.*

There was, as usual, no reply.

43

I MET UP WITH MEL ON the sidewalk outside the ER main entrance. She was leaning against the hospital wall when I came out, checking her phone.

"So you're okay...your face is still messed up," I said when I saw her.

She grimaced. With just the left side of her face. The right side was even more droopy and paralyzed than before.

"Yeah," she said. "So, after what no doubt will be hundreds if not thousands of dollars of MRIs and shit, turns out I have Bell's Palsy. The nerves to one side of your face get inflamed and paralyzed. Normally temporarily, they told me. They said I'd probably get over it on my own in a few weeks or months."

"Well, that's good," I said. "Do they know what caused it?"

She shrugged. "They said it's often caused by an infection, especially upper respiratory infections and stuff like that. They asked me if I'd had the flu recently. I said the better question was when I *hadn't* had the flu."

"Did you tell them about being sick a lot?" I asked. "Did you tell them about the weird twitching and seizures?"

"I did. I told them about all of that. And you'll be glad to know that I *totally* called it. They told me getting sick all the time was what you get for going into education, and the other stuff was probably stress. And suggested counseling for PTSD."

"Oh," I said. "I think you might need to talk to my brother's friend Jase."

As we walked over to the Jeep—Mel said she wanted to stretch her legs after spending several hours trapped in a hospital bed—I told her about Jase and how it had turned out he had Lyme disease.

"I asked about that," said Mel. "'Cause half my dad's dogs have come down with it, so I started to wonder about it. And they told me we don't have Lyme disease in Georgia."

"Aren't your dad's dogs in South Carolina?"

"Yep. And it has not escaped my attention that South Carolina is right the fuck next to Georgia. I don't think insects and infectious diseases are very considerate about respecting political boundaries. Also, I haven't lived my whole life in Georgia."

"I think you should talk to Jase," I repeated. "Maybe he can give you some pointers."

"Yeah. And thanks, by the way." We'd reached the Jeep and were climbing into it. I automatically went to the driver's side. Mel seemed pretty calm and pretty functional, all things considered, but I didn't feel good about letting her get behind the wheel.

"No problem," I said.

"Yeah, well, thanks anyway. Especially for driving me yourself instead of calling an ambulance. Those motherfuckers cost a grand, easy, maybe two, and I don't have a spare two grand on me. And you got me here faster than they would have, anyway. If I *had* been having a stroke, you probably would have saved my life."

"I knew it could take hours to get you to the ER if I called 911," I said. "And I knew no one would run faster to save you than I would."

"Yeah." She reached over and squeezed my knee. "I know. And thanks again. I don't know anyone else who woulda done that for me. Maybe my dad—when he's not drunk off his ass. Jewel sure as shit wouldn't have. Not even when she was telling me I was the love of her life and she'd do anything for me. But you did."

"Of course." Her hand was still on my knee. It didn't feel creepy or unpleasant. But it did make me worry about hurting her in some way I really didn't want to.

She seemed to realize the same thing. She pulled her hand away and folded it in her lap. "Whaddya think?" she asked. "Am I too scary-looking to go into a restaurant? I'm starving."

"Me too," I said. "It's up to you. I don't mind going into a restaurant if you don't. But if you just want to go home, I can pick something up for you."

She considered it. "I don't mind the stares, but I'd probably make a big mess of myself," she said. "They warned me that eating and drinking might be difficult, and I think they're gonna be right. And they said I might have problems with spontaneous drooling."

"Oh boy," I said. "Do you think you'll be able to teach?"

She shrugged. "It's not like I've got a fucking choice," she said. "There's no one to fill in for me, and I need that paycheck if I'm ever gonna pay off this little visit. So I guess I'm gonna teach, or die trying."

"Yeah," I said. "Why don't I get you home."

44

EATING DID, IT TURNED out, pose a rather difficult challenge. By the time we got home it was after seven and we were both starving. After a brief debate over what would be the quickest and easiest thing to get, I dropped Mel off at her apartment, took the Jeep down the road to the hole-in-the-wall takeout Chinese place that I'd never had the nerve to try before, and got a couple orders of vegetable lo mein and vegetable fried rice. I was a little nervous about the vegetables, but I was hoping that Mel could slurp up a few noodles at least.

A little experimentation proved that the stir-fried broccoli and baby corn were indeed too challenging, but that Mel could handle the noodles and rice reasonably safely.

"God, I hope this heals really fucking fast," she said. "Otherwise I'm either gonna waste away, or blow up like a pig from eating nothing but simple carbs." Her speech was still slurred, but I was getting better at deciphering it. A catastrophic problem for a language instructor to have, though. There were many disabilities that wouldn't cause too many problems for someone in our profession. Speaking or hearing difficulties, however, were disastrous.

"Yeah," I said. "You want me to spend the night? Or come spend the night at my place? I don't want to leave you alone if you don't feel safe."

There was a long pause. Mel looked at me, her good eye measuring. Measuring what, I wasn't sure.

"I reckon I'll be alright," she said eventually. Her voice was low and rough. She cleared her throat. "They kept telling me it's not dangerous and I'll be fine. We'll both probably sleep better in our own beds."

"Okay," I said. "I'll leave my phone on. Don't hesitate to call if you need something or think something's wrong."

"Ten-four," she said. "And Rowena? Thanks again."

"Any time," I said.

"I fucking hope not."

We both laughed. I went back to my own apartment, where I was faced with a rather peeved Fevronia—her food dish was three-quarters empty!—and an avalanche of emails.

Aishat wrote that she had gotten my email and we could reschedule our meeting for another day. She didn't specify when that day might be. Karen had sent me a series of increasingly peeved emails about her teaching observation, which HAD to be scheduled THIS WEEK, since next week was spring break and she didn't want to delay it ANYMORE, after it had already been put off TWICE. She didn't know WHY I wasn't responding to her emails, but it was very unprofessional. and she expected BETTER from me.

I wrote back to say that I had spent the afternoon with Mel in the ER, but, barring further complications, I would be coming in to teach as regularly scheduled on Wednesday and Friday and she was welcome to come observe any or all of my classes on those days. She responded almost immediately, which made me feel a mixture of scorn and a tiny amount of pity that her life appeared to revolve around unimportant and mean-spirited work emails, to say that it was VERY INCONVENIENT to have to do all this at the last minute, but that she would come observe my 150 class on Friday afternoon. She complained that she hadn't heard from Mel all day and she didn't know WHAT she was going to do about that. I told her that Mel had spent the afternoon in the ER with some serious health issues and she needed to talk to Mel directly about her situation.

This is SO inconvenient! she wrote. *As I have told Melissa REPEATEDLY, there is no one else to fill in for her. The program cannot AFFORD to have someone in her position who can't be relied upon. We expect more professional conduct from our faculty members.*

I thought of a lot of responses to that. In the end, I used none of them, and shut down my computer and went to bed without replying.

45

THERE WERE NO EMERGENCY texts from Mel in the middle of the night. When I checked on her the next morning, she said she felt crappy, but not crappy enough to stay home, and could she hitch a ride with me to campus.

"The kiddos will be in for a fun surprise when they see me," she said as she got into the car with me. "How do I look?"

"Like one side of your face is paralyzed," I told her.

"Awesome. That's what I thought. How do I sound?"

"A little slurred, but mainly comprehensible."

"Double awesome. I can tell already that this is gonna be a fabulously character-building experience."

"Maybe you should take the day off," I said.

"And do what? Sit around feeling sorry for myself? 'Sides, Karen has already sent me about thirty thousand emails about how I didn't respond to her first thirty thousand emails in a timely fashion, and how they need someone completely reliable, blahdeefuckinblahblah."

"That doesn't mean you should do something that might hurt you."

"I think I've already gotten hurt. One side of my face is paralyzed, remember?" Mel laughed. I tried to laugh along with her.

She was still in good spirits when I took her home that afternoon. All the students, she said, had been very sympathetic and only a little bit ghoulishly fascinated with her situation. The other faculty, on the other hand, had been unable to meet her eye when they passed her in the hallway. Karen had even turned and rushed off in the other direction at the first sight of her.

"And if it gets Karen off my back, it might be worth it," said Mel. "She hasn't even brought up my teaching observation. Major fuckin' win, that's what I say."

"Yeah," I said.

I had my doubts about the value of that trade-off. At least until Friday. Then I started to think that maybe a little facial paralysis might be a worthwhile sacrifice to avoid having Karen observe another one of my classes.

She was late, just as she had been the previous semester. This was a good thing, since Alicia and Anthony cornered me as soon as I came into the classroom.

"Hey, Professor," said Anthony, coming over to me with his loping, confident walk. As usual, he had a smile that suggested good manners and better intentions. "Can we talk a minute?"

"Sure." I looked up into his handsome face, and then down at Alicia, who was hovering just a little bit behind him, as if using him for a shield. I spent a moment imagining what their children would look like. I wondered if the Wainwrights knew about Alicia, and what they thought about her. I ran a mental scenario of them getting married and having a brood of mixed-race children who inherited all that ill-gotten plantation and prison money. Justice, or a perpetuation of the cycle of injustice, now with the original victims becoming the victimizers?

Anthony was talking and looking at me with half-concealed reproach, like he knew I wasn't really paying attention to him.

"I'm afraid I haven't heard from Aishat for several days," I told him. Natural talent and years of training had made me a good listener, even when half my mind was miles away. "We were supposed to meet on Tuesday, but something came up and we had to put off our meeting. Now I guess it'll have to be after spring break."

"Yeah. See, the thing is, professor, I think something really needs to be done about her. She's really going off the deep end."

"How so?" I asked. "Have there been any more threats or attacks aimed at you?" I looked directly at Alicia as I said that, hoping to draw her into a conversation that was supposed to be for her benefit.

"A few." She giggled, from nerves, I thought, not because it was funny. "There've been more, like, hateful messages left on my whiteboard."

"Have you reported them?" I asked.

She shrugged in the way people do when they don't want to answer a question. "My RA did, I think."

"Well, that's something," I said. "Has anyone actually seen Aishat in your dorm?"

She shook her head. "But she could have come in during the night or something."

"Are the messages there when you get up in the morning?"

She shook her head again. "No, when I come back from class."

"It seems very unlikely that she's sneaking in during the night, hiding out all day, and then leaving the messages while you're in class," I said. "It really sounds more like something someone in your hall might be doing."

"I don't want to think it would be any of my hallmates!" said Alicia, sounding almost tearful. "They're not just my hallmates, they're my Rho Beta Delta sisters, too!"

"Yeah," I said. "That would be a pretty shitty thing to do. But..."

"Aishat's really losing it, Professor," Anthony interrupted me. "She's really getting dangerous. You know Jamal Warner?"

I nodded.

"So, he and I are Pi Chi brothers, and he's started getting ugly messages too."

"On his dorm room door?" I asked.

Anthony shook his head. "By email. About...well...you know the story about, like, well, Brittany Gutierrez?" Anthony flushed bright red as he said it, as if the very mention of it was so embarrassing and enraging that he couldn't stand even the taste of the words in his mouth.

"Uh-huh," I said.

"So, he's started getting, like, messages saying, like, they're gonna get him for what he did. He's going to pay for what he did, and honor will be returned to the ones he took it from; sick, scary shit like that."

"And he thinks these messages are from Aishat?" I asked.

Anthony shook his head. "Nuh-uh, Professor. He thinks they're from her family. He thinks they're planning to do, like, an *honor killing* or some shit like that."

"Of Aishat?"

For a moment Anthony's normal expression of smooth confidence was replaced with confusion.

"Honor killings are normally of the woman," I said. "If her family are planning an honor killing, that means that the person in danger is her."

Anthony was already recovering from his confusion. "Jamal thinks he's the target," he said. "So you could please, Professor, go talk to Aishat?"

"I can talk to her," I said. "But Jamal really, really needs to take this to the police."

Out of the corner of my eye I saw Karen come bustling down the hall towards the classroom door, and the clock above the door, which read 12:03. Oh shit.

"So," I said loudly, making all the chattering students look up and pull themselves into class-taking shape. "What does everyone know about Tolstoy?"

46

THE DISRUPTION CAUSED by Karen's ostentatious entrance covered up the scramble to get class started, which was convenient. The rest was less convenient.

Like last time, she occupied two spaces. Since this classroom had chairs with little individual desks rather than a big seminar table, she dislodged the student in the chair next to hers, an unassuming boy named Kyle, so that she could have his chair for her pile of stuff. Most of which she promptly dropped on the ground. She spent the first several minutes of the class on her hands and knees gathering up loose papers, pencils, and pens. One of her pens rolled under Kyle's new chair and she crawled around for a horrifyingly long time looking for it before Kyle realized where it was and handed it to her. She treated him with a poisonous glare before retreating huffily to her chair and shuffling her pile of papers loudly.

I wanted to feel sorry for her. I *did* feel sorry for her. She was constantly embarrassing herself and turning people against her. But she was just so damn mean. Dostoevsky would have had a lot to say about her.

Since we were supposed to cover the entire sweep of Slavic civilization in one semester, I had chosen to have the students watch key movies instead of reading key texts. Sometimes, like this time, we stooped so low as to watch English-language adaptations with

Western actors. For our section on Tolstoy we had watched *The Last Station* and the 2012 version of *Anna Karenina*.

Now I was trying to foster some discussion of Tolstoy, *Anna Karenina*, and the "woman question" with the few students who had shown up for a class on the Friday afternoon before spring break. The two pairs at the front of the classroom, far away from Karen, were engaging in a lively if painfully superficial and misinformed discussion of Anna and divorce. As usual, modern American students were horrified by infidelity, didn't understand why the characters didn't just get a divorce, and felt that Anna was a selfish slut. The two pairs in the back of the room were completely silent.

I tried mixing up the pairs. Same result. I tried doing a "write-pair-share" exercise. Even worse. Karen's flabby mouth was pursed in a mean little quasi-smile. I could see unemployment looming.

Might as well shake things up a little.

"For the last fifteen minutes, let's do a thought experiment," I said loudly. "Take a few minutes to come up with arguments defending the social arrangements of Anna's time: semi-arranged marriages between very young partners and much older partners; no divorce; children automatically belong to the more powerful partner; one partner has total control over the family's money. Only in this case, the disadvantaged partner will be the man. Come up with arguments for why men should not be allowed to have money or property, not be allowed to have custody over their own children, should be married off as teenagers to women in their thirties and forties or beyond, and should not be allowed to divorce their spouses. Come up with arguments in support of that system. And ask yourself: what would Tolstoy say about that? What would his wife say about that?"

The students burst out into nervous laughter. I waited for it to die down before assigning them to new groups. I arranged for all the pairs to be at the front of the room. Soon they were all giggling and laughing—nervously—and arguing over what it would be like to live in a society that was "like, totes run by cougars."

Karen watched this for a few minutes, her mean little smile morphing into something that boded even less well for me. At 12:45 she stood up, gathered up all her papers, pencils, and pens with a lot of ostentatious bustle, said loudly, "Rowena, please come see me in my office *immediately* after class," and left.

Her departure was followed by another round of nervous giggles. Then several students made some genuinely insightful comments, so class hadn't been completely wasted. And then it was 12:50 and we were all free to go and engage in whatever debauchery we had planned for spring break. There was another outburst of nervous giggles when I said that, and then the few students who had bothered to show up disappeared into the half-empty hallway, and there was nothing to delay me going to see Karen.

Half the faculty had already left for spring break too, so I saw no one else on my way to her office. Bedford Hall had an eerie, deserted feel to it.

Karen was sitting slumped down in her chair when I showed up, looking like someone in the throes of despair. She jerked up when I knocked, and then broke into a racking fit of coughing.

"Are you okay?" I asked, wondering if I was going to have to make a second run to the ER in one week.

"I'm fine," she wheezed. She coughed up a cough drop, which slithered through her fingers and onto her keyboard, where it stuck. "I have this *constant* tickle in my throat," she explained, looking guilty about that and also confused as to what she should do with the cough drop. When it looked like she was just going to leave it there on the keyboard, I fished a piece of tissue out of my purse and gave it to her. She eyed it with distaste, as if she suspected it of being covered with boogers rather than just removed from its packet, before taking it and dabbing ineffectually at the cough drop for what felt like several minutes.

"Allergies are *such* a trial," she said, once she'd finally gotten the cough drop corralled and dropped into the trash. "I've been a complete *martyr* to them since I moved here. And it seems like they get *worse* every year. They say it's because of global warming. Although I find the HVAC system here is what *really* gets me."

"Me too," I said, leaping at this opportunity to bond over mutual misery. "I think it's one of my migraine triggers."

Karen's mouth pinched shut, closing off all possibility of bonding. When she reopened it, she said, "Really, Rowena, I hope *you're* not going to start missing class all the time for *health reasons* too. Dealing with Melissa's constant absences is enough of a problem. The *last* thing I need is for *another* one of my instructors to become unreliable. As I have to keep reminding her, this *isn't* why we hired her—or you."

"Mmmmmm," I said.

"Anyway, I have to say I was *very* disappointed with the way you *failed* to implement any of my suggestions from your *last* teaching observation."

"Mmmmm," I said again. "Like what?"

Karen looked flustered. "Like...like...I have to say I was *very* disappointed at the *striking* lack of student engagement in your class. And attendance seemed low—*what* is the total enrollment for that class?"

"Sixteen," I said. "Although only eight students showed up today. It is the afternoon before spring break, though. 50% attendance is the norm for the Friday before spring break in my experience."

"We have to do *better* than that, Rowena! We have to *inspire* our students to want to come to *every* class session! And I *must* say, your students did *not* seem very inspired today. And neither, frankly, did you. To be honest, the whole class seemed rather dozy." She stopped to yawn, and then broke out into another racking coughing fit.

"This *cold*," she panted when she was able, sort of, to speak again. "It just *won't* go away. I think it's developing into bronchitis." She put her hand to her forehead, which was flushed and sweaty. "I even feel a bit *feverish*, if you can imagine."

"Maybe you should go home," I said.

"We really *must* finish this performance review..." She broke into another coughing fit that made my chest hurt just to hear it.

"Maybe you're right," she gasped between coughs. "Maybe we've talked enough today. I will be sending you a *full* written report, of course."

"Sure," I said. I stood up. "Have a nice spring break. I hope you feel better soon."

Karen tried to purse her mouth in response, but that only caused more coughing. The sound of it followed me down the hall and all the way out the building.

47

I HAD, BACK IN SOME insanely optimistic moment in the past, booked a flight leaving Atlanta at 5:43pm. I needed to leave Greenfields by 2:00pm to make it on time. That had seemed very doable. Then Karen had wanted to observe my last class on Friday. That had thrown a wrench into my plans, but I hadn't been able to change my flight without paying ridiculously high rebooking fees. I had taken my backpack with me to campus and prepared myself to get up and walk out of the meeting without permission if necessary. But now, unexpectedly, I had been given a reprieve. Karen had barely held me for fifteen minutes, and I was going to be able to run home, check on Fevronia, and still leave for the airport on time.

Fevronia gave me a very jaundiced look when I told her to guard the apartment with extreme ferocity. I had hired a brave pet sitter to come in and check on her once a day—more money I couldn't afford to spend—and hoped that it wouldn't be too terribly traumatic. I couldn't tell if she treated my absences as periods of desperate loneliness, or a welcome break from my annoying presence. I suspected the latter.

The drive to the airport was as much fun as one might expect from a drive to a major airport on the Friday before spring break for most of the colleges in a three-state area. But I made it in time, so that was a win.

The packed flight to O'Hare was almost as much fun as the drive to the airport, and the equally packed flight to San Francisco was even more delightful. I was in the middle seat, and the people on both sides of me coughed continuously from when the doors closed at O'Hare to when we deplaned in San Francisco. Looked like I was going to be joining Karen in coughing my head off when I got back.

It was 10:30pm Pacific Time when I got off the plane. So 1:30am back in Georgia. I did not feel I was at my best. Alex still vaulted over some luggage and pulled me into a dramatic embrace when he found me at baggage claim.

"Two months is too long," he said into my ear. "Way too fucking long. We've got to get you out here permanently."

"Yeah," I said.

"Have you heard back about the summer job here yet?"

"Nope," I said. "Still waiting."

"What about Carmel? Any word from them?"

"Not yet. But according to the wiki, they haven't made an offer to anyone else yet, either."

He pulled away from me. "I guess this isn't the sexiest conversation to be having at a time like this. We've gotta stop talking about jobs for at least five minutes."

"It's okay," I said. "But I'd appreciate it if we could move on to the next leg of this trek across a vast continent. How long a drive is it from here to Monterey?"

"Hour and forty-five minutes at least."

I suppressed a groan and reminded myself to be brave.

"I won't be offended if you sleep in the car," Alex told me.

"I don't normally sleep on transport. But I can try."

"My car is a piece of shit, as you know," said Alex. "But you're probably safe enough to sleep in it. Or anyway, you're in just as much danger awake as asleep."

"I know." We were making our way out the airport, weaving around all the other late-night arrivals. I realized I had one hand on Alex's arm, like a child reaching for reassurance—or maybe like a cat placing a paw on you to demonstrate possession and affection. I preferred the latter interpretation. "I just don't sleep well on transport. And I don't want to waste even a minute of being here with you." I was following behind him through the crowd the way Alicia seemed to follow Anthony around campus, always half a step behind, always in his shadow. It was giving me a sense of wrongness, but the airport was too crowded for us to walk side-by-side.

"I don't want to waste a minute of you being here either." We pushed through the crowd by the entrance and stepped out onto the sidewalk. Still crowded, but at least we could walk side-by-side. I stepped up level with Alex. Something in me relaxed.

"Good," I said. "So maybe we can use this time to catch up, and I can vent about work. Then I'll get it all out of my system, and by tomorrow I'll be ready to do relaxing, touristy things."

"Works for me," said Alex. "And I've got plans to help you relax, too."

"Do tell," I said.

48

ON THE DRIVE TO MONTEREY I outlined the latest developments in the Aishat situation to Alex, including Anthony's allegations that her family was sending threats to Jamal.

"That *really* sounds like something for the police," said Alex.

"That's what I told him. Although I may have to get involved anyway, as an interpreter."

"Yeah." Alex sighed. "I don't like the thought of that. But you may be right. But don't go riding off on some vigilante quest on your own, okay? People bent on honor killings are *not* someone you want to fuck with."

"I know," I said. "This isn't my first honor killing rodeo, after all."

"Really?" Alex looked away from the road for a second to glance at me, his face half in shadow, half in the yellow light of the midnight highway. I couldn't see much of anything beyond the safety barrier, but I could sense that I was in a different place, on a different coast, one foreign and alien to me. Not in a bad way, but still foreign and alien. I was a stranger in a strange land here. It was a sensation I was used to, and I could feel it filling me with strength and resolution, preparing me to make my mark and assert myself amongst these strangers if necessary.

"Yeah," I said. "A big part of my work with the NGO in Moscow was taking down the stories of refugees from the North Caucasus. Some of them were running away from their families because they were afraid of being murdered in an honor killing. And some of them were running away because they'd committed one."

"Fuck. No shit? You actually talked to people who'd committed honor killings?"

"Not a lot. But a couple."

"How'd you do it?" Alex asked. "How'd you do it without snapping and attacking them? I'd have a hard time with it, and seems like it'd be way more painful for you."

"It was painful," I said. "It was hard not to hate them. But the ones who came to me were just kids themselves, who'd been caught up in something terrible and did terrible things as a result. They were both boys still—one was sixteen, one was fifteen. Their families had been destroyed by the war. Their sisters turned to prostitution with Russian soldiers to survive. Hardcore nationalists and Wahhabite fundamentalists offered these boys a substitute for the families they'd lost, the pride that'd been destroyed, and a path forward to becoming a man. All they had to do was murder their sisters. So they did. One of them cried and cried as he told me about it. He maybe still had a chance at redemption. I told him I'd keep his secret, and helped him apply for political asylum. The other shouted and raged about the evils of women and the West and stormed out of the room when I asked him if he wanted to apply for asylum. I think he was going to try to go to a jihadist training camp in Pakistan or Afghanistan. I have no idea if he made it."

"Jesus fucking Christ," said Alex. He gave me another sideways glance, patches of dark and light flashing over his face as we drove.

"Sometimes I forget," he added slowly.

"Forget what?"

"That you were part of it too. All this...badness that's the War on Terror. I think of you as pure and untouched by all that evil. But you were there talking to wannabe jihadists and fucking honor killers."

"Does that make me seem contaminated to you?" I asked.

He shook his head. Slowly. "No," he said. "One of the things that drew me to you originally—other than how fucking hot you were compared with everyone else in that department—was that I could tell that you and I shared something that none of the rest of them did. We'd seen stuff, we'd walked on the dark side. Once you've done that, it's awfully hard to connect to someone who hasn't—or even take them seriously. But you still seem somehow...pure to me. Undefiled."

"Hmmm," I said.

"And I don't mean I was under the impression that you'd never been with any other man before me, or some shit like that. That's not what I'm talking about at all. First of all, I don't think that sex is dirty and degrading and doing it defiles you."

"It depends," I said.

"Well," said Alex. Patches of darkness and light were still passing over his face, but I could catch glimpses of the smile that was starting to break out. "Not the way you do it, for sure. That's sort of...shit, I feel like I'm spouting all kinds of crap, but here we go. That sort of feels like that's part of your purity. Like...this is probably some kind of horrible metaphor that will get me in trouble with the PC police if they hear about it or something, but like being with you is like some kind of, I don't know, ritual bath or something."

"I'm flattered," I said. "I think. No one's ever compared me to a mikveh before. At the very least it has the attraction of novelty."

"Haha, yeah. Not exactly my smoothest speech. But I guess I wanted you to know how I feel about you."

"Hmmm," I said again.

"Okay, that was also not the smoothest. But I meant it as a compliment."

"I can accept that," I said.

"And so I hate the thought of any of that ugliness touching you. I think of you as completely separate from it, even though you seem to understand it. Which I guess is one of the reasons I hate the thought of you getting mixed up with this business with Aishat and the frat. It's dangerous, and it's just...ugly. Every bit of it is ugly, and I don't want any of that touching you."

"I know," I said. "But darkness and danger have already touched my life, and will continue to touch it. No one can escape it completely, and if you want to help people, which I do, you have to get down in the dirt and the mud where the problems are. You don't have to become dirty, but you do have to have a passing acquaintance with dirt."

"I know," said Alex. He put his hand on my leg, high up on my thigh. "Is it weird that this conversation is turning me on?"

"I don't know," I said. "Is it?"

49

IT WAS A VERY LATE night, especially for me. Double especially since Alex couldn't keep his hands off me the rest of the drive to Monterey, and the walk into his apartment, and once we were inside his apartment. And when I woke up on East Coast time the next morning, he quickly woke up too—and said we needed to get serious about not wasting a single moment of my time there.

All that was delightful, but left me feeling pretty droopy with exhaustion by the time Saturday morning was actually starting to get going, California time. Alex said he would be totally okay with spending the rest of the day in bed if I wanted to.

"No," I told him. My head was resting on his chest, and my eyes were closed, but I was determined to stay awake. "I'll have the rest of the week to hang out doing nothing at the apartment while you're at work." The DLI didn't have spring break like regular colleges did, so Alex would be teaching every day during the work week. "Let's go out and do something touristy and couple-y," I said.

"Okay," said Alex. "And that way I can show you off to the world, too. How about we stroll down Cannery Row and stop off at Tidal Coffee for some breakfast? If you'll consent to eat pastries for breakfast, of course."

"I probably will," I said. I pulled myself off of him and got, slowly and sleepily, out of bed and started searching for my clothes.

"Although not too much. I think I'm starting to gain weight. Too much restaurant food and not enough running."

He reached over and squeezed my hip. "Nah," he said. "You're still plenty slender. And besides, any weight gain just means there's more of you to love."

"Oh please," I said. "But I'm taking that as permission to eat as much as I want while I'm here."

"I like a woman with appetite," said Alex, squeezing my other hip.

"Good, because I'm starving. It's almost midday as far as I'm concerned."

"I suppose this is a hint for me to feed you." He got up and started gathering up his clothes too. "Just give me a minute to get ready. Will you hate it if I don't shave?"

"Stubble is sexy," I told him.

"I thought you liked me clean-shaven."

"I do." When I'd met him, Alex had had a stubbly beard. He'd shaved it off after discovering a gray patch and also impelled, he later confessed, by some ghost of his previous military training, which made him feel like he couldn't look scruffy at the DLI. "Stubble, in appropriate quantities, is still sexy," I told him.

"Glad to hear it." He kissed the back of my neck and disappeared into the bathroom.

Fifteen minutes later we were dressed and somewhat presentable as we headed off to Cannery Row, Monterey's tourist strip. I'd visited it both times I'd been there before, but it was still fun and the restaurants were still good.

It was a bright spring morning and the wind off the coast tasted of salt. We held hands as we walked down the street. Every now and then Alex would give my hand a squeeze and smile at me as if he were thinking of something secret and wonderful between us.

We stepped into Tidal Coffee. Like many places in Monterey, it was light and clean and open and felt decidedly coastal, although no coast that I was used to. I could feel myself relaxing and becoming a tourist, shedding a big part of that jangling ball of ambition and nerves that I normally carried around with me.

Alex dropped my hand. "Hello, Erin," he said.

50

A COUPLE WAS COMING out the door just as we were coming in. The woman was slender and petite, with an oval face, dark wavy hair, and big, slightly cat-like, blue eyes. She looked like she should be playing a beautiful village girl in some BBC drama set in Scotland or Ireland. She looked eerily like me, only six inches shorter and fine-boned instead of athletic and rangy.

"Hello." She had dropped the hand of the man she was with, too. "How, uh, nice to see you, Alex."

"Yeah," said Alex.

There was an awkward pause. I felt like I should say something, break the ice. But my jet-lagged brain seemed to be made of cotton wool.

"I don't think we've met," the other man said to me. He was big and tall, with a florid complexion and thinning red hair. He still oozed alpha male magnetism. It was easy to picture him as a vigorous clan chieftain, directing cattle raids in a well-worn kilt, casually hefting his claymore with one hand as he shouted orders at his warriors. "Frank McAvoy."

My mouth finally kicked into gear. "Nice to meet you. Rowena Halley."

Erin shifted, like she wanted to disown her connection with Frank and also hide behind him.

"I've heard a lot about you," she said. "Really great to finally meet you." Her face and her voice were both tight with pain, and I could feel in my own face how much it cost her to say those words.

"Yeah," I said. "Really great to meet you too." I tried to smile warmly. Then I felt like that would only increase her pain.

"Well," said Frank. "We were just on our way out, so we'll let you folks get on with your morning, but we should get together for dinner or something. If you're the Rowena Erin's been telling me about, then you're only here for a few days, right?"

"Right," I said. I wondered what Erin had been telling him about me. I wondered what *Alex* had been telling Erin about me.

"And you teach Russian, is that right?"

"Right," I said again.

"Well," said Frank. "Qualified Russianists are always in high demand. We should definitely keep in touch."

"Absolutely," I said.

"Great," said Frank. "Enjoy your morning, folks, and we'll talk soon." He went out the door, certain that Erin would follow him without question. Which she did. I thought she wanted to look back as she went through the door, but she kept her eyes fixed firmly ahead.

"Fuck," said Alex once they were gone. A family with two small children were coming in behind us. The children giggled. The parents fixed us with stern glances. Alex didn't appear to notice. "I'm sorry about that."

"It was bound to happen," I said. "Don't worry about it. You ready for some coffee?"

"Fu—" Alex saw the children and stopped. "Heck yeah. Only...can we get it to go? Let's go out onto the trail. I feel like I should explain, and I don't want to do that here."

"Okay."

Alex was quiet and withdrawn as we waited in line, ordered, and headed off to the Monterey Bay Coastal Recreation Trail, an 18-mile, two-lane trail that ran along the coast, including right by Monterey. We'd gone walking there before when I'd visited. This time we made our way to our favorite bench, which overlooked the sailboat marina, without speaking.

It was a beautiful sunny morning, the blue sky only slightly obscured by the Northern California haze. The temperature was a cool 53 degrees, with a salty wind coming off the bay. I pulled my jacket more tightly around me and sipped at my coffee. Pleasantly warming. I took a bite of the salted caramel chocolate croissant I'd bought in defiance of my own fear of blimping out and not being able to pull on my jeans. Whatever. I needed the calories, both to keep warm and to keep up my strength for what I sensed was going to be a difficult conversation.

Alex stared at the bay in silence. I went through and discarded half-a-dozen conversation openers, before settling on, "Who's Frank?"

Alex twitched. "Oh, him. He's some kind of former Special Forces asshole—you didn't fucking hear me say that—who's with the FBI now. So he really might be able to hook you up with a good job.
"

"Huh," I said. "I guess the FBI probably has a big presence in San Francisco."

"Probably," said Alex. He was still looking off at the bay without seeing it.

"Well," I said. "We've been talking about possible career paths for me that would enable me to move out here. I guess that could be one, if this thing with Carmel doesn't work out."

"I don't want you working with the fucking FBI," said Alex, not looking at me. "I don't want you working with *Frank*."

"Okaaaay," I said.

"Frank doesn't remember me," said Alex. "But I fucking remember him. We crossed paths in Iraq. He was always hot for Erin, even then."

"Uh-huh," I said.

"And I think he was the one..."

"Uh-huh?" I said, when Alex stopped talking.

"I think he was the one who recruited her for his fucking black site torture program. And me."

51

I DIDN'T SAY ANYTHING. Sometimes, when you're extracting a particularly painful story from someone, silence is best.

"It was so fucked up," said Alex eventually. "We were so fucking young, and we had absolutely no idea what the fuck we were doing. And we were the officers."

"Mmm-hmmm," I said.

Alex contemplated his coffee. He tore off a small piece of croissant—plain—looked at it in disgust, and threw it at the seabirds that were inching closer to us in hopes of just such an eventuality.

"Now I understand the whole 'I was just following orders' defense," he said, over the sound of squabbling seabirds. "Because I *was* just following fucking orders. I didn't even know what most of those orders were about. At least not at first. And then when I figured it out, I still kept following them. There were always good reasons not to raise hell about it, so I didn't. And now I..." He took a deep breath and blew it out. "Now I have to live for the rest of my life with the knowledge that I'm *not* a hero. I'm a fucking coward who processed the paperwork for government-sponsored torture. I mean, that's not all I did. But it kinda feels like doing that cancels out all the other stuff I did, the stuff that might have actually saved lives. Because maybe I saved half-a-dozen lives, but I processed the paperwork authorizing dozens of people being tortured.

"So afterwards, and even now, whenever someone says, 'Thank you for your service,' I want to vomit. I want to shoot someone in the face and throw up. Because people shouldn't be thanking me for my service. They should be condemning me. Throwing stone after stone."

"I'm sorry," I said.

Now Alex did look at me. "Didn't you hear a word I just fucking said, Rowena? I'm a shit person and a bad, fucked-up mess. I might even be evil. And not just any sort of evil, but the evil you personally are committed to fighting. Didn't you say you used to work interviewing torture victims?"

"Yes," I said. "But..."

"But nothing! Can't you get it through your head that I'm everything you hate? I mean, I'm everything *I* hate too, but I can't escape myself. While you seem determined to stick with me. Even inviting me into your fucking bed, for fuck's sake!"

I took a deep breath. Then another one. "I know this must be a very difficult thing for you," I said. "And I'm sorry you're having to deal with that. You were put in a bad situation with no good options, and you tried to do the best you could."

"My best wasn't good enough!"

"Sometimes that's how it is," I said. "And yes. I abhor torture, and specifically dedicated myself to exposing and fighting it. The fact that America had a state-sanctioned torture program is something that we'll spend a long time recovering from. But it's hardly the worst thing that we as a nation have done. And just like I told John last spring, I really do believe that everyone deserves a shot at redemption. I mean, you say you've done bad things, and I believe you, but Dima was in *OMON*, for God's sake. In Chechnya! And that's something he thinks he'll have to spend the rest of his life seeking absolution for, but it can be done. And if he can find absolution, I'm sure you can too."

"Maybe I don't deserve absolution."

"It's not a question of deserving."

"Then what is it a question of?"

"I don't know," I said. "Seeking, maybe."

"But I haven't even tried to seek it out!"

"Well, maybe you should," I said. "I'm not saying that as a nag. I'm saying you seem very unhappy about this, so maybe you should try to seek some kind of redemption or absolution or expiation or whatever you want for it."

"That seems really fucking selfish, doesn't it? Worrying about *my* feelings about this shit? I wasn't even the one who was tortured!"

"But you're being tortured by it now."

"Not fucking enough."

"Even if you spend the next fifty years torturing yourself over it day and night, it won't undo one iota of the suffering that's already been caused," I said. "Even if you die from it, that won't change the past one jot. The only thing that will make it better will be if you do something to make things better going forward."

"Like what?" demanded Alex. He was staring off at the bay once again. "What the fuck could I possibly do that would make things better?"

"Make the world a better place because you're in it," I said.

He laughed the least mirthful laugh I'd ever heard. "I think the world is very definitely a worse place because I'm in it."

"My world is a better place because you're in it," I said.

Alex put his face in his hands. I put my arms around his shoulders and kissed the back of his neck. I could feel him shaking under me, racked by dry sobs, his skin sweaty from intense emotion in the cool coastal breeze.

"You'll think of something," I said. "You're a good man, Alex Miller. I knew it from the moment I met you. You'll find your shot at your redemption, I'm sure of it, and when you do, you'll take it."

52

EVENTUALLY ALEX'S SOBS, those dry, super-painful sobs that strike men particularly hard, stilled, and we walked home. In silence. With him walking a little bit behind me, like he couldn't stand to be beside me.

When we got back to his apartment, I put my arms around him and tried to hold him, but he pushed me away and said he wanted to go for a run, and I should get some rest. Which I took as him saying he wanted to be alone.

"Sure," I said. "Sounds good. Have a good run."

I took a shower. He wasn't back when I was done. I lay down on the still-unmade bed and closed my eyes. I would just doze for a second or two while I waited for him.

When I woke up, it was two in the afternoon. There was still no sign of Alex. My paranoia, honed to a fine edge during my years with Dima, immediately started feeding me images of disaster, starting with a car accident, moving on to suicide, and ending with some kind of super-secret black ops team, headed by the dastardly Frank, swooping in and kidnapping Alex off the street for spilling state secrets to me.

He's probably just hiding from me. Ooops, let's call it something more flattering. He probably just needs his space. Lots of people, especially of the male persuasion, go into deep hiding after sharing a confidence. This was not my first go-round, and I knew not to take it personally. Well, in theory. In practice it was pretty damn hurtful. Also worrying, since you could never be 100% certain that the other person wouldn't go do something supremely self-destructive. Also, dammit, I'd spent a ton of money I didn't have to fly out here in order to be with Alex, and here he was avoiding me.

I considered going for a run myself. I flexed my left knee. The plane ride had not been kind to it. Also, I didn't have a key. I searched around a bit to see if I could find a spare. I didn't find an extra key, but I did find Alex's phone, which he'd left in the pocket of his jacket hanging by the door. No wonder he hadn't texted me. I squashed the trickle of worry that tried to worm its way into my brain, and told myself everything would be fine and I'd just have to wait till Alex got back to go out.

By 4:00pm I'd cleaned out all my inboxes and checked the AATSEEL, MLA, Higher Education Recruitment Consortium, and Russian and Slavic Academic Job Wiki for any new job postings. Nothing good. I wondered if Frank really could get me a job. If it was for something benign, like, I didn't know, translating wire taps, maybe it wouldn't matter that he had once been a torturer. The *FBI* didn't really go in for torture, right? That was just the CIA, right? Maybe Frank was a reformed man, and he could help me out, and I could move out to Northern California and work some kind of meaningful *and* remunerative job, and Alex and I would get married, and Frank and Erin would get married, and we would all live happily ever after as colleagues and friends.

The door unlocked. Alex came in. "Sorry," he said. "I forgot my phone. What time is it?"

I checked my phone. "4:23."

He winced. He was sweaty and windblown and scraped up. "Shit. You're probably starving."

"A bit. Did you go rock climbing?"

"Yeah. Bouldering. I wanted to clear my head. I didn't realize it was so late. I really am fucking sorry."

"It's okay. I'm glad you were able to go do some climbing. Do you feel better?"

"I will once I get in the shower." He strode past me without touching me and disappeared into the bathroom.

53

ALEX REMAINED QUIET and withdrawn for the rest of the evening. He spent the night as far away from me as was humanly possible to be on his double bed—until he moved onto the couch sometime in the middle of the night.

The next day was more of the same. At my insistence, we went for a hike. He didn't speak the entire three hours we were out hiking. And when I asked him if he wanted to join me in the shower afterwards, he said he had work to do.

I could feel a scream building up in me. I knew he wasn't doing this to hurt me—or at least, that was not his primary motivation. People in pain do all kinds of stupid stuff. I knew he had a lot he needed to think over, and solitude would be better for that. I knew he probably felt like he needed to protect me from himself. I also knew how much I'd spent—of both money and time—to come out here, and how little time I'd get with him before having to say goodbye for two months, and how I had made it clear I wanted to be there for him, and how I was also going through a difficult time, and all the reasons why he was being a selfish, inconsiderate, pigheaded ass. I also knew that grabbing him by the shoulders and shaking him while screaming ultimatums at him was unlikely to turn out well. Like I said, this was not my first rodeo with this shit.

I told myself that patience was the crown jewel of princesses and anyone who had to deal with trauma victims. I'd done a fair amount of reading on trauma, and also witnessed its effects firsthand on a lot of people, including people I cared about, and one of its more irritating effects was turning its victims into self-centered, self-pitying, grandiose *assholes* who couldn't see beyond their own suffering to consider for a second how their behavior affected those around them...I decided to go for a run.

I ran too far and too fast for my still-fragile knee, and was limping by the time I got back. But it was also late enough by then that we could legitimately go out to dinner, which was a way to avoid spending any more time in the one-bedroom apartment together, with all the intimacy that implied and all the promised closeness we had planned on.

Alex's departure for work Monday morning was a relief. Unlike regular college instructors, he was expected to work more or less regular office hours on campus, which meant he'd be gone for most of the day during the work week. He'd told me when he'd first started the job that it had taken a while to get reaccustomed to going into an office and hanging out there for most of the day every day, instead of directing his own time. It was sort of a pain, but on the other hand, there was less expectation to work evenings and weekends. His evenings and weekends, he'd promised when I'd made the reservations to come out here, would be reserved solely for me. I did some deep breathing when I had that thought, and reminded myself once again not to scream at him.

Knowing that he'd be gone during the day, and also that I would go stark raving mad even under the best of circumstances if I didn't have something to do other than sit around and moon over my man, I had plenty of work saved up to do in his absence. So when he left Monday morning, I went for a very slow, careful walk/jog along the waterfront, and then settled down in front of my laptop.

I started off with my lesson planning for next Monday. Once that was knocked out, I started reading the submission requirements for a journal I was thinking of submitting to. My book proposal was still languishing with the latest acquisitions editor I'd sent it to, so in the meantime I really, really needed to start work on another article. The article I'd gotten accepted last year was supposed to come out this spring, but I couldn't rest on those laurels for long. Time to start the slow, painful process all over again.

I'd just finished jotting down the formatting requirements for submissions, and was contemplating the joy of changing all my citations from MLA format to Chicago style, and how that would be just the kind of time-consuming and mind-numbing activity that would distract me from my woes, when I got an email. From the search committee at Carmel-by-the-Sea.

54

DEAR DOCTOR HALLEY,

Greetings from Carmel-by-the-Sea! We hope you are enjoying your spring break, if this week is spring break for you.

We are writing to ascertain your interest in proceeding further with the search process for our Visiting Assistant Professor of Russian position. We were very impressed by your first interview, and we would like to invite you to a second interview, this time with our tenure approval committee to discuss your research. Although the position is a visiting one, there is the possibility of it becoming a tenure-track position, and therefore we would like to vet our top candidates' research as the next step in the process.

We assume you are not in California, and so would like to extend the possibility of conducting this second-round interview virtually, rather than the usual campus interview. We know this is not ideal, but it is a good deal more convenient :)

Please let us know your interest at your earliest convenience.

Sincerely,

Cornelia Debenham, PhD

Professor of French

Carmel-by-the-Sea College

Well, at least something was going right for me. Maybe I wouldn't have to take Frank up on his offer to find a job of dubious morality for me. Of course, right now moving to California seemed a lot less desirable, or even possible, but I should press on. I wrote back:

Dear Doctor Debenham,

Thank you very much for your email. I am still very interested in the position and would be delighted to move forward with the interview process.

I am actually in Monterey at the moment for spring break. I would be happy to meet with the committee in person this week, or, if it would be better, I would be happy to set up a virtual interview at your convenience.

Sincerely,

Rowena Halley, PhD

Visiting Assistant Professor of Russian

Crimson College

I wasn't sure what to expect from that. I'd made the offer to show up in person mainly out of a strong desire to get out of this claustrophobic apartment and take a break from Alex's silent treatment. As soon as I sent it, I started to worry that it made me seem desperate. Besides, everyone would be off on spring break and wouldn't want to meet with me this week. And how would I even get there?

Half an hour later I got a reply:

Dear Rowena,

That is wonderful! And how delightful that you are currently just down the road in Monterey.

If, and only if, it will not be too much of a crimp on your spring break plans, we would love to meet with you in person while you are here. I am sure you did not come prepared to give a job talk, but this will be much less formal than that—just a simple discussion amongst colleagues about your current research and future plans.

Would Thursday afternoon suit you? We are fairly flexible at the moment, so if that time is not convenient for you, we can arrange another one.

All the best,

Cornelia.

I wrote back that Thursday afternoon would suit me perfectly. By the time Alex got home, it had been arranged that I would meet with the Carmel search committee and tenure review committee to discuss my research at 2:00pm on Thursday.

55

WHEN I TOLD ALEX ABOUT the upcoming interview, he responded with a noncommittal sound that may have been "good."

I then offered to make supper, so that he wouldn't have to go out after a long day at work. He did genuinely look exhausted, with his face drawn and dark circles under his eyes. He'd tried to shave that morning, but missed patches and nicked himself in the process, which added to his general air of dishevelment and misery. He looked like he needed some kind woman to take care of him. Maybe a home-cooked meal would thaw him out and make him fit to be around again.

"No," he said to my proposal. "You didn't come here to cook for me, Rowena, especially when I'm being such a shit to you."

"You're not being a shit to me," I lied.

He gave me a pained look.

"Okay," I said. "You're being a complete shit to me. But I'm still happy to cook supper if you'd rather stay in."

"The least I can do is fucking take you out to dinner," he said.

Unfortunately, that was the high point of our interaction. He made a stab at talking over dinner, but everything he said had such an acid edge of anger to it that I quickly decided silence was preferable.

He was moodily silent on the walk home, and remained moodily silent for the rest of the evening, speaking only to inform me that he was going to spend the night on the couch. I protested that the couch was too short and he should stop being an idiot and sleep in the bed.

"I promise I won't molest you," I told him. "Your honor is safe with me."

He didn't even crack a smile, but just dug an extra blanket out from the closet and disappeared into the living room, closing the bedroom door behind him so that I was effectively locked away from him. I contemplated storming out of there and giving him a piece of my mind, and possibly a good clip round the ear. Then I reminded myself that I didn't believe in violence, and also that bitter experience had taught me that men in the throes of a PTSD-and-guilt-inspired sulking session do not respond well to being given a piece of my mind. I settled for hoping that the couch really bothered his back.

Tuesday and Wednesday continued in the same vein. About the best that could be said for them was that Alex didn't actually kick me out onto the street, or insist that I move into a hotel. He did suggest, in one of his rare moments of lucidity, that I might want to check into a B&B and do some traveling up and down the coast.

"When I check into a romantic B&B on the coast, it's going to be with you," I said. I meant to sound compassionate and full of strength, like I was standing by my man, ready to jump into action as soon as he was ready to accept my support and comfort. What I really sounded like was a woman on the brink of bursting into a world-class nagging spree. I could feel my lips pinching into the same thin line my grandmother's did when boys spray-painted rude words on the lawn in front of her church—a regular occurrence—or John was being particularly pigheaded.

Alex gave me another pained look—the only look he seemed capable of giving me at the moment—and retreated to the couch. The fact that he had taken the couch meant that he had also taken over the living/dining room area, leaving me trapped in the tiny, windowless bedroom. That was probably the reason why I'd had a dull headache that flared up regularly into a low-grade migraine since Saturday. Well, one of the reasons.

I offered to rent a car or take an Uber to Carmel-by-the-Sea, which was less than four miles from Monterey, but Alex, in a misguided attempt to be helpful, insisted that I take his car. So Thursday afternoon saw me cautiously driving his piece-of-shit—his words—elderly Nissan Sentra down Cabrillo Highway towards Carmel-by-the-Sea College.

Carmel-by-the-Sea was located on the same blobby peninsula as Monterey, but on the south side rather than the north. The downtown was full of fairy-tale style houses that I wanted to hate for being fake and tacky, but that I secretly found myself loving.

The college was exactly the kind of Spanish Mission-style architecture you'd expect. If Crimson College looked like a movie set of an East Coast liberal arts college, Carmel-by-the-Sea College looked like a movie set of a West Coast arts college. It was located on Carmel Point, just south of the town proper, with a campus that opened out onto the bay. According to the website, tuition alone was a cool $53,000 a year, with another $20,000 for room and board. In this part of California, that seemed cheap. Still, dropping the better part of $300,000 for a college degree struck me as a questionable life choice. Of course, my students at Crimson were doing the same thing, and they were in small-town Georgia, not coastal California, so I should keep my lips zipped on that subject.

The campus was mostly empty for spring break. I found parking with no difficulty and set off through the cool Northern California air in search of Emerson 241.

Emerson Hall turned out to be one of four Mission-style buildings surrounding the main quad. I went in through the front entrance, and, after a mere ten minutes roaming through the History, English, and Philosophy departments, found Emerson 241, a classroom next to the Modern Languages department.

It was 1:50. No one was there. I double-checked my instructions. Emerson 241, Thursday at 2:00pm. I checked for any emails or messages that had come in. Nothing. I went back over to the Modern Languages department. No one was in the admin office, the chair's office, or any of the other offices. I wandered back to 241. Still no one.

At 2:01, when I was running through all my options and not liking any of them, a heavy-set older woman came hurrying down the hall.

"Rowena?" she called at the sight of me. "Rowena Halley? Oh, thank goodness! Cornelia Debenham. I'm afraid we're all running a bit late—you know how it is on spring break. Did you have any problem finding the place?"

"No trouble at all," I said.

"Oh good—and here comes Brad."

The man with the goatee and salt-and-pepper hair I recognized from the first interview came down the hall. He was soon followed by a white-haired man named Harry, and a very thin woman with flyaway gray hair named Orna. Cornelia explained they were members of the tenure review committee, and added, "But of course this is a very informal chat, not a job talk at all."

We all moved into the classroom. There was no sign of Zaria. Cornelia said she'd make us all some herbal tea while we waited, to make things seem more relaxed. She headed off in the direction of the office, leaving me with Brad, Harry, and Orna.

"Having a nice spring break?" asked Brad.

"Very nice," I said.

There was a heavy pause, which no one else seemed willing or able to break.

"This is my third visit to Monterey, but my first visit to Carmel," I said eventually. "It's very pretty."

"Do you have family in the area?" asked Orna. "Oh wait, are we supposed to ask that?"

"It's fine," I said. "And my boyfriend teaches at the DLI. I've been coming out to visit him. And I might be working at the Summer Intensive Language Program here this summer."

"How nice," said Orna.

There was another heavy pause. I cast about for more topics of conversation.

"Is this typical weather for this time of year?" I asked.

A conversation about the weather that was even more stilted and boring than most conversations about the weather was in its final death throes when Cornelia returned, bearing a tray of mugs and trailed by Zaria.

"We're all here now!" exclaimed Cornelia. "How lovely!"

Zaria nodded to me without speaking. She seemed to like me even less in person than over Skype. Up close she was striking in a Slavic harvest-maiden kind of way. There was no hint of Caucasian features that I could see. I wondered how she was related to the Daghestani family that Dima might be about to marry into.

"Well, why don't we all have a seat!" said Cornelia briskly. She directed us into the classroom, and had us arrange the uncomfortable plastic chairs so that the others were seated in a semi-circle facing me. It was supposed to be relaxed and informal, but it made me feel like I was being grilled by a hostile interrogation committee. Which was kind of true.

"Well," said Harry, once we were all seated. "Why don't you tell us about your research."

I launched into my five-minute spiel about Marina Tsvetaeva and narrative transvestism. Everyone other than Zaria nodded along as if they understood, even though I knew they didn't. Zaria just sat there with her muscular arms folded.

"Interesting," said Harry when I was done. "But what's your philosophical or theoretical underpinning?"

I launched into another well-practiced spiel about narrative transvestism and the psychology behind it.

"And you don't consider it inappropriate to apply Western theoretical concepts to Russian literature?" demanded Harry. I knew he was from Philosophy and didn't appear to know anything about Russian literature. I assumed he just liked to argue.

I began my defense of my choice of theoretical foundation for my dissertation. Harry countered with something about Fichte and the Jena School. I wasn't sure if this was something that had some actual connection to my research, and I just didn't know about it, or if he was talking through his hat in order to show me up. I suspected the latter, but I was nervous enough about the former, and sufficiently afraid of coming off as argumentative and difficult, that I didn't want to challenge him on it. So I murmured something about how that was very interesting and I hadn't considered that angle but it might be worth pursuing in the future.

Harry sat back with a satisfied look on his face, like he'd bested me in single combat. Orna started asking me about my future plans. I described my current attempts to publish my dissertation, which she brushed aside as a given.

"What I'd *really* like to know about is your *next* research project," she said. "After all, if you're to have any chance of getting tenure, you'll need to have another one ready to go as soon as your first book gets published." She sat back, looking almost as pleased as Harry. As far as I could tell, she thought I was an amateur, a flake, and a loser, someone who'd never get a single book published, let along two.

"Well," I said. I thought about pointing out that this job was a visiting position, with no actual chance of tenure or requirements for research. Yes, they were saying there was the possibility of it becoming tenure-track, but that was just them saying that. You could *say* all kinds of things.

"I'm considering continuing in the general area of contemporary women's writing," I said, instead of all that.

"I thought you said this Maria Sevtoyeva was from the early 20th century," said Orna. "That's more *Modernist* than contemporary, wouldn't you say?"

"Well," I said, "yes. But I was thinking of the 20th and 21st centuries more generally. Anna Politkovskaya—the opposition Russian journalist—wrote her thesis on Marina Tsvetaeva, so it seems like that might be a good bridge..."

"Journalism seems like a big stretch from poetry," said Zaria. It was the first time she'd spoken. She looked pleased to have spotted a major methodological error in my work.

"Well, in a way," I said. "But that's what's so intriguing about it. And both Tsvetaeva and Politkovskaya could be said to have interesting similarities in their approach to the truth..."

"Did you ever meet Politkovskaya in person?" Zaria demanded before I could finish.

"Unfortunately not, but that hardly disqualifies me from..."

"*I* did," she told me. She gave me an expression that was probably supposed to be a smile, but was too full of smugness to contain any warmth or kindness. "She came and spoke to our class in Ottawa."

"That's great," I said. "So, anyway, I was thinking of doing a study of truth and its subversion vis-à-vis political opposition..."

"Hmmm," said Harry, interrupting me mid-speech. He glanced at his watch. "I'm afraid we're almost out of time, so we'll have to ask you to leave the room while we deliberate."

"Um," I said. "Okay." Asking people to leave the room during deliberation was standard operating procedure following oral comprehensive exams and dissertation defenses. Cruel, but standard operating procedure. Asking job candidates to leave so that the search committee could deliberate was a major breach of protocol, as far as I knew, during an interview.

"There's a bench you can wait on in the corridor," Harry told me.

"Bring your tea," Cornelia said, with a slightly anxious smile, like she felt bad about what was happening but was helpless to prevent it.

"Okay," I said again, and left the room.

56

MUG IN HAND, I WALKED slowly away from the room. A burst of raucous laughter followed me down the hallway. I picked up my pace, hoping to outdistance it, but I could still hear it when I came to a halt in front of a handworked ceramics display in a glass case at the far end of the corridor.

I made myself relax my grip on my mug. I wanted to scream. I wanted to run back up the corridor, burst into the room, and shake the committee members by the shoulders until they confessed what they were up to and what their plans for me were. I wanted to force these people who were deciding my fate so carelessly to decide in my favor. The only time this sensation of enraged, desperate helplessness had been worse had been when Dima had broken things off with me and sent me back to America. Although Alex's current snit was beginning to approach that in sheer aggravation.

In all three cases, though, something I desperately wanted, something without which my life would be poorer in some very concrete and material way, not to mention in a very deeply felt emotional way that touched on the core of what I valued, what my life goals were, and who I was as a person, was being decided for me by other people, and there was nothing I could do to control the outcome. Hence my intense, almost insane desire to shake some sense into these people and make them choose me instead of whatever other, incredibly stupid, choice they were contemplating.

I stared with unseeing eyes at the ceramics display, still hearing the laughter coming from the classroom. What were they finding so funny? What had I done that was so hilarious? Was it because I was in jeans and a jacket instead of more formal attire? They'd all slouched in wearing what looked like the Goodwill reject pile. A horrifying thought crossed my mind. I did a quick check to make sure my fly was zipped. It was.

Maybe it's not about you at all! A lot of the time, other people's behavior wasn't about you or anything you'd done, even if it felt like what they were doing was painfully personal. They were probably laughing about something that had nothing to do with me.

"That was my advanced class's final project."

I jumped. Zaria had come up on me without any warning. "It's nice," I said automatically. Actually, I thought it was hideous. A collection of lumpy jugs and unusable cups and saucers with rough pastel glazes that looked unpleasant to the touch were stacked higgledy-piggledy, or so it seemed to me, in the case.

"It's supposed to question the utility of everyday items," Zaria said. "And demonstrate the underlying nature of the clay."

"Oh. That's nice," I said again. I searched my brain for something more intelligent to say. In fact, like most modern visual art, it looked and sounded like bullshit to me. I was aware that I was an ignorant philistine in this matter. I also suspected that most of it was, in fact, bullshit. Most of what most people did most of the time, especially in the arts, was nonsense. But it was also the necessary condition to create the occasional piece of great art. It takes a lot of manure to grow good roses.

"What's he like?" Zaria asked abruptly.

"Who?"

"Kuznetsov. What's he like?"

"He's..." I searched for a concise summing-up of the man I had almost married. "Intense," I finished.

"Will he make a good husband?"

I searched for another concise summing-up of a complex topic with no certain answer. "He tries really hard to be a good man," I finally said.

Zaria sniffed. "'Tries' doesn't mean 'is.'"

"No," I agreed.

"Polya's head-over-heels in love with him," she said.

"Polya is your cousin?"

"Yeah. She and I are second cousins, and she and Rinat are first cousins, and Rinat and I are…some kind of cousins. I got all my mother's Slavic looks, and a Slavic name."

"Uh-huh," I said. "Zaria" meant "dawn" in Russian.

"It was still tough," she said. "For both Polya and me. The two little Soviet girls in Ottawa in the early '90s. Neither of us ever fit in. Polya always wanted to go back home. Only where's home? The Soviet Union doesn't exist anymore. Russia? They have no love for Daghestanis. Daghestan? Polya's family left there when she was six months old. She's spent the majority of her life in Canada. But she's never felt like a Canadian. So she had to go running off to Ukraine last year, even though she'd never been there in her life. And now she's determined to marry a real Russian hero."

"Not everyone would consider him a hero," I said.

"Would you?" Zaria demanded.

"Yes," I said after a while. "In his own way."

"But you didn't want to marry him."

"That's not…anyway…"

Zaria was looking at me, her muscular arms folded, like I was an idiot. I was extremely familiar with Insecure Russian Girl as a subset of Insecure Immigrant and Insecure Minority, not to mention Insecure Woman, and I was aware of how desperate all such insecure people were to make themselves feel good by making me feel bad. I reminded myself not to take it personally, and definitely not to give her a good swift kick in the pants. What was it with the people in my life begging for a good swift kick in the pants?

"He didn't want to marry me," I said. "He thought he would be a bad husband. And he was probably right. If Polya truly loves him, I wish her all the best, not to mention all the luck in the world, but he's a highly intelligent, deeply driven, incredibly honorable and well-meaning, fucked-up pain the ass. Anyone who invites him into their life might be inviting in a lot of joy—but they'll definitely invite in a lot of pain."

"Oh." Zaria curled her upper lip. "He doesn't sound like much of a prize, to be honest. He doesn't have a lot of money, does he?"

I laughed in spite of myself. "No," I said. "He doesn't have a lot of money."

"I think Polya could do a lot better," said Zaria.

"Mmmm," I said.

"But I also heard you hurt him badly and treated him like shit."

"Mmmmm," I said again.

Zaria looked over her shoulder. The laughter in the classroom had stopped, and the rest of the committee was trickling out.

"We never had this conversation," she said.

"My lips are sealed," I promised.

57

INSTEAD OF GIVING ME their verdict immediately, which I'd half-hoped, half-feared that they'd do, the rest of the committee thanked me for coming, told me it had been a real pleasure to meet me, and promised to get back to me soon with their decision. I thanked them for taking the time to speak with me, told them I'd enjoyed visiting the campus and talking to them, and was very interested in the position. Then I hightailed it out of there.

Once back in Alex's car, though, I drove slowly through downtown Carmel-by-the-Sea with its fairy-tale houses that should have looked fake but were somehow charming instead, trying to imagine living in a place like this. Of course I wouldn't be able to afford the downtown, or anything even vaguely nice, but the California coast still seemed like someplace much too nice for me to ever be able to make it my home. This was where people dreamed of ending up. It wasn't going to happen to me. Or maybe it would.

Without consciously deciding to do so, I turned onto Ocean Avenue, parked, and walked out onto the white sand of the beach. I'd never lived anywhere near a beach. I'd never particularly wanted to live anywhere near a beach. Maybe I was wrong about that. Living not near the beach hadn't done much for me.

I took off my shoes and waded out into the surf. Then I almost shrieked from the bitter cold. The Pacific was not warm and friendly like the Georgia coast.

Maybe this would be a fresh new start. Maybe this new ocean would wash away all that old bad luck, that old sorrow. Wash my life clean.

My phone *pinged*. I retreated back onto dry sand so I could take out my phone without risking it in the cold seawater. Maybe it was Alex, texting to say he was sorry for wasting my visit with his descent into self-absorbed depression and asking me to hurry back so that we could kiss and make up.

I checked my phone. There was a green WhatsApp notification on the screen.

Darling Inna, it said. *What are you doing right now?*

58

I'M AT THE BEACH, I texted.

At the beach? That's nice, if unexpected)))))

What about you? I asked.

You won't believe it, but I'm in Petersburg.

Petersburg?!? What are you doing in Petersburg???

Following a story. Or something like that. But that's not why I wrote.

Why did you write? I asked.

Can you talk? Video?

Sure.

Thirty seconds later Dima's face was trying to resolve into a grainy picture on my phone screen. From the blurry background I gathered he was in a cheap post-Soviet hotel bedroom.

"You really are on the beach," he said. "I can see the ocean. Where are you?"

"California."

"Oh. With *him*?"

"Yes," I said.

"Is he there with you at the beach?"

"No. He's at work. I'm in a different town right now. I had an interview for a job."

Some complex expression crossed Dima's face. "A job. In California?"

"Maybe."

"But you're going to marry him?"

"That," I said, "has not yet been decided."

"But everything's going well?"

"That," I said, "is a good question."

Dima frowned. "Why?"

"He told me some things about himself. Now he doesn't want to talk to me."

"What kind of things?"

"You know," I said. "Bad things that happened to him. Bad things he did. In Iraq."

Dima frowned again. "So...what do you Americans call it...post-traumatic stress syndrome?"

"Something like that," I said. "Along with some good old-fashioned guilt."

"Oh." Dima leaned back against the rickety headboard of the cheap bed. I knew the bed wouldn't be long enough for him. Even though ethnic Russians tended to be tall, cheap Russian beds tended to be short. Dima had spent his entire life living in a world that was too small for him.

"What's wrong with you, Inna?" he said. "Why do you attract damaged men?"

"Bad luck?"

He frowned again and shifted against the headboard, making it creak audibly. "No," he said. "Not bad luck. I knew, the moment I saw you I knew, there was something about you that drew me to you. That can't be good. And now you say this American has similar problems. There's something wrong with you, Inna."

"Thanks," I said.

"I'm saying this to help you, Inna."

"Wow, thanks for the help." Good thing Dima was all the way across two continents and an ocean, or my resolution might snap and

I might give him the swift kick up the pants that everyone in my life seemed determined to deserve right now.

The most irritating thing was that I had been wondering if Dima were right. I had not failed to notice that here I was *again*, involved with an only semi-available, badly damaged man. What *was* it about me? I didn't have any terrible damage of my own that might make me into a target. My early life had been unusual but in many ways much happier than most people's. As an adolescent and adult I had mainly avoided the sexual assault and physical and emotional abuse so many of my female friends had stumbled into. War and political turmoil had touched me, but no more than they had most people in the world, and much less than many. I didn't have a lot of money, but I wasn't eating garbage off the streets. My work situation was stressful and full of insecurity and bullying, but many other people had it much worse. But somehow I was the one who drew damaged people to me.

I thought of Dima chasing after me and then cutting things off with me—again. I thought of Alex and his intense passion for me, which had transformed into an intense desire not to be in the same room with me. I thought of Aishat, who'd come to me for help and then refused to let me help her. I drew them to me, and then pushed them away, and I didn't know how or why.

"Maybe I was born broken inside," I said. "Like a flawed gem."

"*No*, Inna." Dima's face twisted in pain. "Don't even think that!"

"You're the one who said there was something wrong with me."

"That was me being an idiot. Don't believe anything I say."

"But you're right," I said. "I attract damaged and broken people. There has to be a reason."

"Maybe it's because you're whole, Inna," said Dima.

"So why do they run away from me then?" My voice was higher and angrier than I'd meant it to be.

"Because they're broken, Inna. They want the wholeness, but healing hurts, Inna. So they run towards it, and then when they realize they might get it, they run away."

"Are you speaking for yourself?" I asked.

Dima was silent for long enough for me to feel how my bare feet were sinking into the soft, white, cold Pacific sand. Even though I was wearing a windbreaker over my blazer, the wind coming off the water was starting to make me shiver.

"Yes," said Dima softly. "I'm speaking for myself. I want to be made whole, but I'm afraid of healing. It will be very painful, and I won't be the same person I was afterwards."

"Yes, you will," I said. "You'll be the same person, only better."

Dima laughed. Bitterly. "You know a lot, Inna, but you don't understand guilt and self-loathing at all. Only by hearsay."

I had been softening, filling up with compassion. All that stopped. I ground my teeth. My toes clenched, wanting to administer that swift kick up the ass. I unclenched them. "I *hate* it when people say I can't understand," I said. "I understand enough. I understand that you're suffering. I understand that it's difficult to change your behavior. I'm having this conversation in a foreign language, remember? I know about struggling to change yourself."

"You see," said Dima. He was still speaking softly. "You offer what we need. You offer it freely. But most of us don't have the courage to take it."

"I'm not a thing. You can't 'take' me. If you tried, you'd fail, or you'd break me—and still fail."

"I know that, Inna. And that's the scariest thing of all."

"Is that why you called?" My voice was rising again, threatening to morph into a primal scream of rage and despair.

"No, Inna. Actually...you'll laugh, it's so ironic...I called to ask for your help."

"Oh." I took a deep breath. "With what?"

"I need help with mama. To convince her to leave Moscow. It's not safe for her there. And her health isn't great. I've been trying to convince her to move to Murmansk, to her brother. I thought it might be safer there. But now I think she needs specialists, Western specialists. She's been talking about going to Israel. I'm trying to convince her to go, but she doesn't want to leave Moscow. But maybe if you ask her...you're the closest thing to a daughter she has. Maybe she'll listen to you when she won't listen to anyone else."

"Oh," I said. "Of course. I'll write to her today."

"She'll probably want to talk to you. I've taught her how to use WhatsApp."

"Okay. Send me her number and I'll message her, talk to her if she wants."

"Thanks, Inna." Dima's phone *pinged*. He frowned at it. "I have to go now. My source finally came through. Thank you again, Inna."

"You're welcome," I said. But he'd already hung up.

59

I DROVE HOME WITH MY fingers white-knuckled on the steering wheel. Not because I was afraid. Because I was furious. With myself, with everyone else in my life, with the world. Until that conversation with Dima, I hadn't fully twigged to the fact that here I was, repeating the same old unhealthy patterns. I hadn't fully twigged to the fact that I *had* unhealthy patterns. But I did. The evidence was damning. If I were an experiment, I was pretty sure the results would be declared conclusive. Papers would be written about me, careers would be made off of me. Only for the subject herself, the experiment felt like a giant failure.

Unfortunately, all my rage didn't give me any answers about what to do. The one thing I was sure of was that confronting Alex and screaming and smashing dishes, which is what I wanted to do, was a bad idea. It wouldn't fix things between us, I would be ashamed of myself afterwards, and Alex only had two plates anyway. If I smashed them tonight, we'd have to eat breakfast off of paper towels.

When Alex came home that afternoon, though, he looked so haggard that pity and compassion overcame my desire to scream and smash plates.

"You look exhausted," I said. I went over and put my arms around him, pulling him close. For a moment he let me hold him. Then he stiffened and pulled away.

"You're the one who had the interview," he said. "You should be the one who's exhausted."

"Yeah, but you really look like you've been put through the wringer. What happened?"

He grimaced. "Just class. Oh, and we've been invited to have dinner with Frank and Erin tomorrow night."

"Oh," I said. "Okay. Do you want to go?"

"No, I don't fucking want to go, Rowena!"

"Well..." I began.

"I'm sorry. That was uncalled for. That was me being a shit to you again. I'm going out." Alex grabbed the car keys from the hook by the door.

"Where are you going?" I asked.

"I don't fucking know. Out."

"What about supper?"

He dug his wallet out of his pocket with angry, clumsy movements, pulled out a twenty, and threw it on the table. "Take yourself out," he said, and stormed out the door, slamming it behind him.

60

MORE BITTER LIFE EXPERIENCE had shown me that waiting up, crossing my arms and tapping my foot, for my man to come home after a stormy guilt-and-PTSD-induced exit, so that I could tell him exactly what I thought of such behavior, was counterproductive. The worry that he might get paralytically drunk and/or shoot up with horse-sized doses of street drugs, pick up a prostitute, drive off a bridge, flee the country, shoot himself, or a combo of any or all of the above, was well-founded, but my ability to do anything about it was limited.

Once Galina Ivanovna and I had seriously discussed drugging Dima and tying him to the bed, but in the end we'd recognized that he'd only free himself, run off, and never come back. And it would just be one more violation for someone who had already been violated many times over in body, mind, and spirit.

Now I was sorely tempted to run after Alex, tackle him, hogtie him, and drag him back to the apartment so that I could list all the ways he was being a self-destructive ass, but even if I could, I was acutely aware that it would break whatever trust there was between us. You can't actually force someone else to do what you want, not really. You certainly can't force someone else to feel what you want them to feel. Generations of well-intentioned parents, partners, and rapists could all attest to that. As I'd told Miranda, we're all our brothers' keepers, but sometimes that means letting them go free until they decide they're ready to come home themselves.

Reminding myself of that about once every thirty seconds, I went shopping—leaving that insulting twenty on the table because I was still pretty pissed, even though I really could have used it—made supper, texted with Fevronia's caretaker about her health and wellbeing, and tried to do some reading for next week's classes. But I couldn't focus on *fin de siècle* literature and the image of the *femme fatale*. Coming on the heels of *Anna Karenina* it was just too painful. I desperately wanted a love story with a happy ending. Maybe I should read a romance novel.

Most of my friends would rather die than read romance novels. I myself was more agnostic about them, since in theory I approved of them as a genre written by, for, and about women. But since I only read them when I was in a particularly deep funk, and didn't have anyone to talk to about them, I didn't have a lot of good recommendations. Luckily there was now such a thing as a recommendation algorithm.

I went onto Amazon and it recommended something about a Russian professor. Feeling guilty about spending the $2.99, I downloaded it and started reading. The Russian professor was a hunky man with bulging biceps and six-pack abs who held his students spellbound with his piercing blue eyes. There was no mention of unbrushed hair, a beard that was the result of forgetting to shave, or shirts missing their buttons. Not once did he lock himself out of his own office and then have an emotional meltdown about it. He never once spent forty-five minutes of a fifty-minute class trying to get the projector to work, only to discover that he'd forgotten his flash drive with the PowerPoint he was planning to show. And he had a nice car and a sleek bachelor pad.

The heroine was a student who fantasized about him pinning her up against his desk during office hours and demanding that she do something to raise her midterm grade. Rather than hiding under the desk in terror once she confessed her fantasies, he raised a masculine brow over his perfectly chiseled cheekbones and said he'd be happy to oblige.

After a few chapters of that I was feeling even sicker than before. I shut the book and looked to see what else Amazon was recommending. They thought I might like multicultural/multiracial and African-American romance. That sounded promising.

Unfortunately, all the multicultural/multiracial and African-American romances had titles like *Claimed by the Savage*, and showed incredibly shredded black men in leopard skin loincloths dragging women of various races off into the savannah. That seemed less promising than I had initially hoped.

Next Amazon recommended a "wounded hero" romance, which apparently was a big genre now. I had to hand it to the ladies writing romance: at least they were at the forefront of social issues. "Wounded hero" did sound a little too close to home, but maybe it would be like my real life, only with the sure and certain promise of a happy ending. I downloaded one—wincing at the $2.99 I could ill afford, but driven by a sick and frankly rather prurient curiosity—and started reading.

The hero was scarred, but sexily, with no loss of function to limbs, cognitive processes, or the ability to get and maintain erections. The healing process of love seemed to involve him ordering the heroine to get down on her knees and suck his dick on command, and then tying her up, spanking her, and making her beg him to fuck her. Apparently she found it nurturing and relaxing, like she could really trust the man she was with. Many women claimed to find this kind of thing empowering. It made them feel desired while allowing them to embrace their own deepest desires.

Hmmmm. I believed people when they said that. But the thing that I found empowering was having power. I preferred to take charge of my own destiny, in and out of the bedroom, rather than depending on someone else to take charge of it for me. Even if he were as trusty and true as every glorious fantasy could make him, carrying all of my needs and problems as well as his own seemed like too big of a burden to put on anyone. I'd rather stand up for myself than kneel for someone else and hope he could read my mind and act accordingly.

As usual in these situations, I had the acute awareness that I was profoundly different than the audience these books were aimed at. In fact, the impression that a lifetime of books, TV, and movies had given me was that in most people's preferred narratives, I would be the dangerous, predatory *femme fatale* who had to be destroyed in order to keep society safe. Anything with romance in it, especially your straight-up romance novel, always portrayed a vision of heterosexual relations that was anathema to me.

But since I still wanted to feel desired and nurtured too, and I was still desperate for romance and a happy ending, I occasionally indulged, like a starving woman digging through trash, hoping to find a few edible scraps. Where were the love stories for women like me? Where were the love stories that would provide only wholesome nourishment, with no trace of trash or poison?

I gave up on literature. Cinema was better, because it had less sex and therefore the relationships depicted were less obviously about male dominance and female submission. I watched a romantic comedy in which everything worked out in the end, and went to bed. Alone. Alex was still gone.

I woke up at 1:17am to the sound of him stumbling in through the door.

"Don't even fucking start," he said when I came out of the bedroom.

"I'm not going to start," I said. "I'm going to tell you to brush your teeth and go to bed."

"On the fucking couch, right?"

"No." I really, really wanted to point out to him that sleeping on the couch had been entirely his decision, made over my explicit protests. I didn't.

"Why don't you go get in bed," I told him. "I'll sleep on the couch if you want. You look like hell. You need to sleep."

"The only thing that would make this fucking fiasco even worse would be if I made you sleep on the couch," said Alex.

"Okay then. We'll sleep together on the bed. I've already promised your honor is safe with me. If you like, we can place a naked blade between us for your protection."

Alex looked like he wanted to shout something. Then his mouth twitched into a smile in spite of himself.

"I'm going to go pee," I told him. "Then the bathroom's yours. You should brush your teeth before you get into bed. Alcohol and tobacco tar are terrible for oral hygiene."

Alex almost smiled again. But he did as I said. Not that it helped that much. He really needed to be pressure-washed to get rid of the cigarette smoke that I could almost see hanging over him.

He still reeked of cigarette smoke the next morning, but he looked calmer and more rested than he had all week. He was even semi-civil to me over breakfast, and we had an almost-rational conversation about what to bring to the dinner at Erin's house that evening.

Buoyed by that, I went for a careful run/walk on the waterfront before returning to the apartment and settling for what I hoped was a quick check of email before a productive session working on my article.

I opened my Crimsonmail. The top email in my inbox was from Aishat.

61

ESTEEMED PROFESSOR *Halley!*

Please accept my apologies for disturbing you during spring break. I beg your forgiveness for not answering you sooner. Things have been very difficult for me this semester.

I am writing to you to ask if you would still be able to come speak with my family. Perhaps next week? If you cannot, I understand; I have not listened to your excellent advice when I should have. I have no excuses; I can only beg for forgiveness once again. But I will be very grateful if you can overlook my behavior and help me, if not for me, then for my family. As you can imagine, things are very difficult for them here. But I think we are ready to act as you have advised.

Thank you for your attention.

With respect,

Aishat

Well, finally. Maybe. Who knows how this would actually turn out. I wrote back:

Hello, Aishat!

Thank you for your response. I will be happy to meet with you and your family at any time convenient for all of us. Would next Tuesday or Wednesday suit you? If not, please tell me when would be better.

With warmest wishes,

RH

Another round of emails, and we had arranged for me to pick her up on campus Tuesday evening after a meeting of the Muslim Students' Union and drive with her over to her house.

After what I hoped was an auspicious start, the day got less auspicious. The next time I checked my email, it was to find a rejection from the latest publisher I had submitted my book proposal to. I entered it into my spreadsheet, and contemplated immediately submitting a proposal to the next publisher on my list. Then I shut down my computer and went to Del Monte beach.

Del Monte beach was a state park tucked away behind a housing community. I slipped off my shoes and walked out onto the sand, towards the surf.

It was another cool, damp day, more like Seattle than the popular conception of California. Two figures, their age and sex obscured by their heavy wetsuits, were surfing off in the distance. An elderly man was walking a Boston terrier. No one paid any attention to me at all.

The water was frigidly cold when I stepped into it, turning my feet instantly white. I waded out until the waves were lapping at my calves, and began walking along it, parallel to the tide line.

This could be my life, I thought. *If Alex doesn't ruin everything*. But of course, he seemed determined to do so. I wanted to say, like Tatyana Larina in *Eugene Onegin*, "Happiness was so possible! So near!"

Maybe he hasn't ruined everything. Maybe this is just something we have to go through, to prove to each other that it's worth it. That we're worth it.

The water was getting deeper. The tide must be coming in. I thought about what Alex had told me, the night I had arrived: that I was like a ritual bath. And Dima had said I drew broken people to me because I myself was whole, and offered a vision of healing.

Part of me rejected both of those statements. They made me a thing that existed for the sake of others. I'd never been able to tolerate even a little bit of that. Love and marriage as generally practiced the world over, where the woman was a self-sacrificing, sexually submissive, second-class citizen willing to put up with financial dependence, emotional contempt, and even physical abuse as long as it meant she had a family, had always been inimical to the very core of who I was as a person.

But I still needed love, so I chased after men who only sort of wanted me, and read romance novels like a starving woman choking down dirt, aware that it was poison to someone like me, but it was the closest thing to sustenance I could find. Perhaps, like I'd told Dima, I was like a flawed gem, with a crack in the core that made it impossible for me to be what the world expected I be. Maybe that was why I had ended up with badly damaged, only semi-available men. They were willing to give me my independence, and look up to me instead of looking down. But maybe they were still seeing me as a means to an end rather than a person. They saw me as their ritual bath, their magical healing potion, not someone with her own problems and desires, just like them.

And even if I embraced that identity they wanted to impose on me, it wasn't possible to heal others anyway. Not if they didn't want to be healed, and were willing to do most of the work themselves. A physician was only as good as her patients, and if her patients tended to run screaming in terror at the critical moment, she wasn't much good at all.

But it was also true that sometimes people needed help to heal, and that I might be able to provide that help. Being that healing hand for others could make me a victim if I let it. But it could also be a source of strength for both of us. This was something I could give that could result in both of us having more, not less. If the other person would receive that gift, and accept it for what it was.

My phone *pinged*.

About to leave work, Alex texted. *Are you about ready to go?*

The cold seawater was lapping at the bottom of my rolled-up jeans. A bone-deep cold was seeping up my legs into the rest of my body. *Just about*, I texted back. *I'll meet you there.*

62

"YOU'RE SHIVERING." Alex had gotten back before I had, and appeared to have been waiting impatiently for my return. He looked me up and down. "What happened to you? Your pants are a mess, and you're shaking all over."

"I went to the beach and went out into the water."

"Jesus! To swim?"

"No, just to wade. But the tide came in while I was thinking. I got kind of wet."

"Those must have been some thoughts."

"Mainly I was thinking about how I might be like a flawed gem. You know, with a crack right in the center."

Alex swallowed. Lots of thoughts chased across his face. "I think Leonard Cohen might have something to say about that," he said eventually. "Something about cracks being what lets the light in."

"Yeah," I said. "Maybe."

"You should go take a shower," he told me. "We've got plenty of time before we have to leave."

Showering and changing my clothes warmed me up. When I came out into the kitchen, Alex was pulling together the bread, salad, and dessert that we'd agreed to bring.

"Frank will probably give you shit about not eating meat," Alex warned me.

"Along with everyone else in my life. If you ever want people to hate you, just tell them you don't eat meat."

"You have to make things hard for yourself, don't you, Rowena?" Alex was steadfastly looking at the salad as he said that, as if he were performing some incredibly complex task, not putting pre-packaged food items into a grocery bag.

"Yep," I said. "Let me just check my email, and then I'll be ready to go."

There was nothing interesting in my email. Except...oh jeez. An email from the Monterey Summer Intensive Language Program.

Heart beating too fast, not sure what answer I wanted to find, I opened it. It was an offer of a position teaching a section of Intermediate Russian here in Monterey.

Oh God! It was what I'd been sure I wanted a week ago. But if things continued to go downhill between me and Alex, spending a summer here would be awkward as hell.

I checked the terms of the offer. They wanted an answer by Monday. They'd sent it at 4:00pm on Friday afternoon. That was a legitimate reason not to reply right away. Maybe there would be a little clarity to the situation by tomorrow or Sunday.

"You ready?" Alex called.

I closed my laptop without answering the email. "Let's go."

Erin had a house in Salinas, half an hour away from Monterey. She'd inherited it from her great-aunt, Alex told me on the drive over, and decided to keep it rather than sell it and get something less nice in Monterey.

"The commute sucks, but housing prices in Monterey are fucking outrageous," he said. He was looking at the road without so much as glancing at me, but he was talking almost like normal. "I mean, Erin's house is valued at a cool half million, but that'll hardly get you a one-bedroom condo in Monterey."

"Yeah," I said. "It's pretty intimidating, to be honest."

"Yeah," said Alex, and lapsed back into silence. I tried not to dwell on the fact that he knew the way without even a glance at his phone.

Erin's place was a simple ranch-style house with an attached garage and a tiny patch of lawn out front as its only landscaping. It was fancier than anywhere I'd ever even considered living, but I could also recognize that it was basically a small, cheap house that was in no way worth half a million dollars. If everything worked out like I had thought it was going to, but was now having serious doubts about, would Alex and I end up scrimping and saving for years in order to buy a place that made me feel vaguely depressed just looking at it?

Erin met us at the door, and, awkwardly, as if she had been about to give Alex a hug and a kiss on the cheek, and then thought better of it at the last minute, let us in. The interior of the house was nicer than the outside, with laminate floors that looked like hardwood, and plenty of windows to let the light in. I still felt a faint headache as soon as I stepped inside. Maybe it was just the presence of Erin.

"There you are! Come in, come in!" Frank came in from the back patio, waving grilling tongs. My headache deepened a notch.

"Oh, you brought salad? Great! Something for the girls to eat." Frank winked at me. "I hear you're a *vegetarian*, Rowena."

"Mmmm-hmmm," I said.

"Erin was for a while, till I talked her out of it." He made a winky-smirky kind of face at Alex. "I convinced her to *eat meat* again pretty quick, didn't I, babe?"

"You sure did," said Erin, with a smile that had very little that was happy in it. "But I'm glad you brought the salad, even if Frank won't eat it, and we got some veggie burgers for you, Rowena."

"Thanks," I said, and followed her into the kitchen with the bag of food. Then I realized we were alone together. Ugh. Now what?

"Nice place," I said.

"Thanks. Alex probably told you: I inherited it from my great-aunt."

"Yeah," I said.

That was the height of our witty repartee as we set the table. I was tall enough to look down on the back of Erin's neck as she got out plates and silverware and napkins for me to bring out to the table. Unpleasantly, the main thing that sight inspired in me was pity. She really did look like a smaller, more fragile, less happy version of me.

"Frank seems nice," I eventually said, in order to say something. "How long have you two been together?"

"Oh...about six months, I guess...of course we'd known each other before...but we ran into each other last fall, and well, he swept me off my feet, I guess you'd say."

"That sounds romantic," I said.

"Yeah." Erin showed zero signs of being the recipient of romance and wild passion. She looked like someone who was trying to convince herself she should be feeling all those things, but was failing utterly to feel them.

"Although it must be difficult—doesn't he work in San Francisco?"

"Yeah," she said. "Although it's nothing compared to the commute you and Alex have."

"Well," I said. "That's true."

"Alex said you're wanting to find a job out here? Frank really might be able to help you with that." Erin busied herself with a platter of crudités and ranch dip, carefully not looking at me.

"Yeah," I said. "I mean, I am looking at ways to move out here. I just had an interview for a job, but if that doesn't work out, then I'd certainly be interested in other opportunities."

"Other opportunities? Sounds like a woman after my own heart!" Frank had come inside, bearing a platter of grilled things.

Alex came in after him, looking like he, too, was getting a nasty headache.

"Um," I said. "Yeah."

"So tell me about yourself, Rowena. I've heard a bit from Erin, and Alex here has just been filling me in, but I like to get my info straight from the horse's mouth."

For the next half hour the conversation was carried entirely by me and Frank. Not that we were natural friends—not at all. But Erin and Alex had sunk into oppressed silence, while Frank was more than happy to talk, and I felt that I had to do something to make this dinner party seem less like the more miserable class of wake.

We covered my childhood, my time in Russia—at least bits of it—my education, and my current job.

"NGO experience is good—*if* you can get a security clearance," Frank told me. He winked at me. "What do you think, Rowena: can you get a security clearance? Or do you have some dark secrets in your past?"

"I have dark secrets," I said. "I'm just not sure that they're the kind of dark secrets the government will care about."

Frank laughed loudly. Alex gave a pained smile. Erin shrank down a little more in her seat. I reminded myself that she had tortured people. Where had she found the backbone? Maybe she'd tortured people because she had no backbone. How had she made Alex fall in love with her? There must be depths to her that I wasn't seeing.

"We like to pry pretty deep," Frank told me. Like everything else he said, it sounded vaguely obscene, and also like it hinted at things even more unsavory than a little soulless sex. "But if you'll let us pry around in you a little, Rowena, and come up clean, you could have a real future with the Bureau. What do you think? Could you give up the ivory tower for a life of solving mysteries and fighting crime?"

"Um," I said. "Sure. I mean, it's all talking to people and doing research, right? It's all the same basic skillset."

Frank's face sharpened. A lot of the genial exterior dropped away, and someone much more intelligent than I had originally taken him to be peered out. The hair on the back of my neck prickled.

"She's a bright one, isn't she?" he said to Alex. "She's more than just a pretty face."

"Yes," said Alex.

"Send me your résumé, Rowena," said Frank. "Even if we don't have anything open right away, I'm sure we could find something for a smart cookie like you."

"Oh, okay," I said. "That'd be great."

63

WE LEFT ERIN'S HOUSE mercifully early. Alex pleaded tiredness and the fact that I would be leaving Sunday morning as reasons to get out of there before 9:00pm. Complicated expressions crossed Erin's face as he said all that. I told myself I didn't care and didn't feel sorry for her. That was a lie.

Alex navigated his way through the residential streets back towards the Cabrillo Highway as if he'd done it dozens of times before. I told myself that didn't worry me. That was also a lie. I told myself I wasn't going to pick a fight with him over it. That, at least, was the truth.

"Why don't you put on some music," said Alex once we were on the highway and heading down the coast, breaking the silence that had reigned since we'd gotten in the car. "Put on that album you were playing on the way up. That was nice."

I hit play on the music app on my phone. There was still silence between us, but now it was silence filled with the sound of Gary Lightbody from Snow Patrol asking what would happen if the storm ended, and begging to be overwhelmed.

I looked out onto the bay. The moon was rising. The water looked clean and pure. I knew that wasn't true. But it made me feel like it was.

"Erin doesn't seem very happy," Alex said abruptly.

"No," I said. "She doesn't."

"She's had a hard time."

"I know," I said.

"And now she's taken up with Frank, which is about the worst thing she could do."

"Uh-huh," I said.

"She always had a fucking self-destructive streak. She seems like she has it together on the outside, and then you start to get inside, and you see she's completely fucked up. And not just because of the war. She was fucked up way before that."

"Uh-huh," I said again.

"She was so fucking smart. The first woman I'd ever met who made me feel dumb. So of course I had to prove to her that I was as smart as she was. And that wounded, damaged shit...it was irresistible, you know what I mean?"

"Uh-huh," I said for a third time, but this time with more force.

"But she never could get her shit together. Every time it seemed like she was about to do it and we could have a proper future, she'd go and fuck it up. Go on a drinking binge, pick up some stranger for a one-night stand, disappear for a couple of weeks so that I'd be wondering if she'd died—or all of the above. It drove me crazy. I'd lie awake at night wondering what I'd done this time to set her off and thinking about how I was a terrible boyfriend and an all-around worthless human being who couldn't even keep the person I loved most in the world from running away from me. I'd go over every word, every gesture of our last day together with a fine-tooth comb, trying to come up with a better approach for next time, if I could only get her to come back to me. And I'd bargain with God to send her back to me so that I could have one more try—and I'm a fucking atheist."

"Believe me, I know," I said.

"Yeah. And then one day I realized the problem wasn't me, it was her. I tried to get her do something about it, but that only made her crazier. So eventually her refusal to get fixed meant she broke us apart. Only now that she can't have me, she's, like..."

"Now that she can't have you and there's no real danger of you solving her problems and making her happy, she wants you back," I said.

"Yeah, I guess. And this thing with Frank..."

"Feeds her self-loathing while allowing her to torment all three of you," I said.

"This really isn't your first goat rodeo," said Alex.

"Nope. Only I never had any of that 'other-woman' crap from Dima. A lot of the drinking binges and disappearing and risky behavior, but if he slept around, I never knew about it. And I think I would have known."

"Oh. So you do know. It made me crazy when Erin pulled shit like that. Like, wanting to scream and shoot stuff crazy. And now I'm pulling it with you."

"These things happen," I said.

My phone was sitting warmly on my leg. Low and quiet, so that it was barely audible, Gary Lightbody was singing about things being bound to go right sometime, and feeling his worth in the middle of the flood.

"I'm really sorry," said Alex. "Really, really sorry. I didn't mean to take my pain out on you, and treat you in the same shitty way I've been treated. But I did anyway."

"I know," I said. "That you didn't mean to. And like I said, sometimes these things happen. You're in a lot of pain."

"And I completely fucked up your spring break, after you spent all that time and money coming out to see me. I hurt you. I caused you pain, when all I wanted to do was run away from my own."

"Life isn't just about having fun," I said. "Yeah, it would have been more pleasant if you'd been cheerful and happy and we'd spent the week going to the beach together and making love three times a day. But that wouldn't have gotten us anywhere in the long term. Going through the hard stuff is more important than any of that. Deciding you're not going to quit when the going gets tough is more important than going surfing or trying out some new sex position you read about in *Cosmo*. Sometimes beautiful things are built on foundations of great pain."

"So..." The album had finished, making Alex's words loud in the closed car. "You don't want to quit, then?"

"No," I said.

"Oh." Alex was silent as we turned off the highway and made our way through the side streets to his little apartment. He was silent as we got out of the car and went into the apartment. He waited until we'd taken off our jackets and put the leftover food away to put his arms around me and bury his face in my hair.

"I don't want to quit either," he said.

"Come to bed," I said.

64

WE SPENT SATURDAY ACCORDING to the playbook I had laid out of visiting the beach—briefly—between other, sexier activities. I even showed Alex some *Cosmo* articles I found online after he expressed an interest. He said he wasn't sure he was up for anything quite that wild yet, but he was glad to know that the information was out there.

"Erin was into some really crazy shit," he said. "Handcuffs and whips and shit. I never could make myself go there with her. And then I'd beat myself up over letting her down. When I told her that, she told me I should beat *her* up. Which made me feel really fucking great, I tell you what."

"I'm sorry," I said. "We can talk about it if you want to, but if you don't, then let's not. But I can assure you that I will *never* ask you to tie me up or hit me. That is a hard, hard no for me. I'm willing to dish it out—in a consensual, sexy way—if that's what you want, but I will never, never take it."

"I think," said Alex, "that what I want is something sweet and gentle and wholesome. Something completely different than all this shit I've had going around in my head."

"Sweet and gentle and wholesome can be arranged," I said.

We also agreed that I should accept the summer job at the Monterey SILP. Feeling like a huge weight had lifted from my shoulders, I emailed them back with an acceptance Saturday afternoon, and got an acknowledgement Saturday evening and a contract to print off, sign, and send back.

"Do it right now," Alex urged. "Don't wait to get back to Georgia. I've got a scanner right here. Or I can put it in the mail or, fuck, hand deliver it, Monday morning."

I printed it off, signed it, scanned it, and returned it in time to go out for one last dinner Saturday evening, and return home for an early night, which Alex said he intended to put to good use.

My flight home left San Francisco at 11:50 Sunday morning. Which meant leaving Monterey at 8:00am. I reminded myself that that was 11:00am in Georgia, so not early at all.

Alex held my hand whenever he could on the drive up to the airport. Then he pulled me to him so hard when we stopped at the curb for departures that I ended up halfway on the gearstick, and it went up my shirt and we had to do some creative maneuvering to free me. At least it kept us both from crying when I got out of the car.

On the flight from San Francisco to Dallas-Fort Worth I was between two people who both had the nasty cough that was going around. Since I hadn't gotten it on the way over, I assumed I was going to pick it up this time around. Then on the flight from Dallas-Fort Worth to Atlanta I was sitting next to a woman with a fussy baby who was probably sick too. I hoped it was just the same crud everyone else in the plane had, and not measles or whooping cough or whatever the unvaccinated masses were currently spreading around.

It was after midnight when I got back to my apartment. Midnight Georgia time, so it didn't feel that late, but I was going to have to teach a 9:00am class the next morning, which was going to feel like 6:00am. And I was almost certainly going to get sick. I told myself it was probably worth it. I remembered the way Alex had held me after we'd made up, and how he'd said that touching me made him feel healed. Definitely worth it. But it didn't mean the next morning wasn't going to suck.

I set an alarm for myself for Monday morning, in case I didn't wake up automatically on Georgia time. Fortunately, Fevronia made sure I didn't sleep in. She had come running out when I'd arrived the night before, purring loudly. When I'd reached down to scratch her head, she'd swiped at me with her claws and disappeared under the bed. Then at about three in the morning she'd come out and sat on the pillow next to mine, purring loudly again. By six she'd decided I'd slept enough, and climbed onto my chest and stared at me meaningfully until I jerked awake, convinced a demon was suffocating me.

"Just you," I said to Fevronia. "I'm glad you're glad I'm back." I reached up to scratch her head. She took a swipe at me and scuttled off under the bed.

I checked my phone. A text from Alex saying he missed me, followed by a string of heart emojis. And a text from Dima.

65

WHERE ARE YOU? he asked.

Georgia, I wrote back. *I got back late last night. What about you?*

Moscow. I got back yesterday morning.

From Petersburg? I asked.

The very one.

How was it? I asked.

It was...interesting.

Interesting—meaning dangerous? I asked.

Maybe a little)))))) But don't worry: I was like Blok's Jesus, floating unseen through the snow and unharmed through the bullets. I made it back to Moscow whole and unharmed. What about you?

The same, I wrote. *So far. There were no bullets, only germs. I'm expecting to come down with something unpleasant this week.*

Drink some hot tea with lemon and honey)))))) You always were healthy: I'll bet you'll remain whole and unharmed.

I hope so, I wrote.

Anyway, I promised you I'd send you mama's new number so you could text her, so I'm sending it to you. I won't hide it, Inna: I'm concerned about her. She seemed a little off before I left for Petersburg. Now she seems obviously sick.

Kidneys? I asked.

Uh-huh. She says there's nothing that can be done about it. She's had diabetes for fifty years, she says, and this is the result.

Surely there are things that can be tried, I wrote.

I want her to go to more specialists. But she doesn't want to. So please, Inna, write to her and ask her. Maybe she'll listen to you.

I'll write to her today, I promised.

Instead of paying off my life debt to you, I'm adding to it.

That's okay, I wrote.

I know that you think so. And I really need your help with this, so...thank you, Inna. I bow down to the earth before you, beat my brow, kiss your feet, etc. etc.

Of course, I wrote. After a while, when there was no reply—Dima liked to cut off conversations abruptly, sometimes for weeks at a time—I texted a quick note to Galina Ivanovna, and got up.

That was the high point of my day. I felt, not surprisingly, jet-lagged and exhausted, with a low-grade migraine that started up as soon as I stepped into Bedford Hall. Since all my students were in the same condition, though, no one cared.

I ran into Chloe in the hallway outside our classrooms between our first and second classes. She was massaging the scars on her temples.

"Panic attack?" I asked.

"What?" She started. "Oh, hi, Rowena. No, not a panic attack, although I keep getting scared I'm going to get one. That'll probably trigger one, huh? Being anxious you're going to have an anxiety attack is a sure way to get one. But no. They've kind of died down recently. Maybe all the counseling and stuff is working. Instead I keep getting these headaches." She hugged herself. "And I feel like I'm coming down with something."

"There's certainly a ton of crud going around," I said. "How was your spring break?"

She made a face. "Meh. I got the reader comments back on my book, which was pretty quick, and the publisher wants to go ahead with it, which is great, but of course they want a bunch of changes.

Some of them make sense, but some of them would mean making it into a completely different, or two completely different, books, since they went off in completely different directions. And it really hurts, you know, reading that stuff. And I haven't been able to even draw up a reading plan of the suggested sources, because I spent most of break going to doctor's appointments."

"Ugh," I said. "I hope it was helpful."

She shrugged. "Apparently I don't have diabetes—yet. They muttered some scary stuff about pre-diabetes and how I need to lose weight. I just don't know if I can go on any stricter a diet. I'm already having hypoglycemia crashes or something like that all the time as it is."

"A stricter diet might not be a good idea then," I said. Chloe had said she'd struggled with her weight since adolescence, and was certainly on the "pleasantly plump" side of things. But she was far from grossly obese, and to my eyes had lost weight over the spring. Starving herself hardly seemed like a positive step.

"I guess I could try exercise," she said, with the enthusiasm of a woman contemplating electroshock therapy.

"If you want to try taking up jogging, I'm happy to go jogging with you," I offered.

"Oh. Ugh." She made a face, and then made herself stop. "That's really nice of you. I'm just being silly about it. I told I you have kind of a Tourette's thing, where I say stuff I shouldn't, right?"

"No worries," I said. "I know it's not your cup of tea. And there's no pressure. But if you want, the offer's there. Or we could just try walking. We could go out after class together or something and walk around campus. If you wanted to get away from everyone else and get some fresh air, we could walk over to The Hollow and do some 'forest bathing' or something."

She shuddered. "The Hollow freaks me out. I tried to do just what you're talking about, get out in the fresh air and do some forest bathing, and I went out there once last semester when the leaves were changing. But I was all creeped out by it. It felt sort of...feral. I guess I'm a city girl."

"No worries," I said. "We don't have to do that. Anything you want to do, I'm up for."

"That's really kind of you." She hugged herself, shivering slightly. "Maybe once I get over whatever it is I'm coming down with. I guess this'll be a great weight loss opportunity, huh?"

"Maybe not a very healthy one," I said.

"Yeah. And then there's all the worrying about my performance review. Have you gotten yours yet?"

"Karen observed me the Friday before spring break. I haven't gotten the official review back yet."

"Yeah, me neither. And I'm absolutely dreading it. I don't think I'm cut out for this."

"I don't think anyone is," I said.

66

GALINA IVANOVNA TEXTED me back that afternoon.

Innochka, my darling! I'm so glad to hear from you. I've missed you terribly. Dima was very wrong to tell you not to write to me—and you were very wrong to listen to him)))) Well, I listened too, which was my mistake. I should know better than to listen to a man))))) Even my own son.

It was a grave mistake, I wrote back. *But we can still recover from it))))) Dima says you're having some problems with your health?*

Oh, you know how it is)))) Old age is not a pleasure))))

I know. But maybe something can be done. Have you been to a specialist?

My colleague Arkady Stepanovich in the nephrology department says nothing can be done. Except a transplant, and I don't want that yet. Well, he says maybe some other specialist might know something. But no other specialist will see me.

Why not? I asked.

They say it's a hopeless case. I think it's really because of Dima.

Because they're afraid there will be trouble from helping out his mother?

Yes. Don't tell him!

I won't, I promised. *Maybe you should consider moving to your brother in Murmansk, though. It might be less stress for you. Or you could see an American specialist,* I added. *They won't care who your* son is. *None of them know that such a person as Dima Kuznetsov even exists.*

True))))) *It's a long journey to America, though. And it's hard to get a visa. And it would be very expensive.*

True, I agreed. *But your life is worth all that.*

Sweetheart! That's very kind on your part. But I still have a few friends here in Moscow who might be able to help me.

That's good, I wrote. *But you know you have a friend in America, too, if it comes to that. And it might be safer for Dima, as well.*

I've thought of that, darling. Many times. Especially with this business in Petersburg—has he told you about it?

Just that he was in Petersburg last week, I wrote.

That's all he told me, too. But I think it was something serious. He came back "unseen and unharmed," though, thank God. And now he's trying to decide whether to stay here or go back to Ukraine. I don't know which one is more dangerous. He's got a lot of enemies here, but he was in an actual war zone there. And the authorities in Kiev aren't happy with him now. They liked him as long as he only criticized Moscow, but once he started to tell the truth about them, they named him a Russian provocateur and a hired killer, there to wage war on the Ukrainian people. I told him to go to Israel, I told him to go to America, but he wouldn't listen. Maybe if I tell him he has to escort me there for medical reasons, he'll listen. I'll keep it as my ace in the hole, agreed?

Agreed, I wrote.

I didn't feel like I'd accomplished much, other than to reconnect with Galina Ivanovna, but I texted Dima to let him know that I'd written to her and urged her to come to America to see specialists here, and she'd said she'd consider it.

I was hoping to hear back from Dima, both because I always wanted to hear from him, and because I wanted reassurance that he was alive, but he must have been going through one of his "don't touch me" phases, because by Tuesday morning he was still maintaining complete radio silence. I thought some hard thoughts about thoughtless, inconsiderate men, but fortunately I didn't have too much mental energy to spare on it. Tuesday was my meeting with Aishat, and I was expecting it to be difficult.

67

I SENT A QUICK PRAYER to St. Fevronia and whomever else was listening Tuesday morning for nothing to interfere with my meeting with Aishat that evening. The only thing I hated more than when other people stood me up and let me down was when I did it to them.

Mel and I had agreed to carpool over to campus in my car. I asked about her spring break.

"Nothing to tell," she said. "I went and spent it arguing about politics and shit with my family. Damn near joined my uncle's militia just to get him off my back."

"Oh," I said.

"I'm shitting you, of course. I'd never actually join a crazy paramilitary militia."

"I know," I said.

"'Cause they'd never let me in. 'Specially not with my face all fucked up."

"I think you're talking a little better," I said.

"Yeah. My face is still all weird, but I've kind of gotten used to it and figured out some work-arounds. Still really hoping it gets better soon, though."

"Yeah," I said. "Did you ever talk to Jase?"

"Yeah. Didn't fill me with a lot of hope, actually. He said it took him months to find a doctor who'd deal with him. The first five doctors he went to all told him that we don't have Lyme disease in Georgia and wouldn't even test him for it. And then when he found someone, it cost an arm and a leg. He gave me the name of the clinic he went to, and I checked 'em out. Not sure if they're legit or complete peddlers of snake oil. Plus insurance isn't going to cover a lot of what they do."

"That sucks," I said. "But if they can help you, it might be worth it."

"Yeah. Jase sent me some articles and some links to some movies and stuff, so I watched them and they scared the absolute crap out of me. Turns out what I'm dealing with is just the tip of the iceberg if it really is Lyme. Or maybe it's MS or some shit like that. Maybe it's MS caused by Lyme disease."

"Maybe you should see someone who knows something about it sooner rather than later," I said.

"Yeah. Meanwhile, Karen's insisting we do the teaching observation *this week*"—Mel did an uncannily good impression of Karen's Debbie Downer voice, but with a South Carolina accent—"so I guess I better gird my loins for that. She already observe you?"

"The Friday before spring break. It was...well, you know."

"Oh boy," said Mel. "I can hardly fuckin' wait."

My own delightful interaction with Karen came even sooner than hers, however. Karen came bustling up to me as I was reassuring Jessica after my second class that her 9.5 out of 10 on the latest vocab quiz was A) correct, and B) unlikely to tank her semester grade.

"But I conjugated the verb передавать correctly!" Jessica was protesting.

"But I was looking for the perfective form передать," I told her.

Jessica looked like she had more she wanted to say on that topic, but Karen interrupted us before Jessica could explain why she should be given full credit for using the wrong aspect. Normally I hated having these kinds of discussions with students. But compared with a chat with Karen, they seemed like wonderful love-fests.

"Oh *there* you are, Rowena," said Karen. "I've been *looking* for you."

"Well, here I am," I said.

Jessica looked back and forth between us, and then, deciding to take the better part of valor, even when half a point on a vocab quiz was at stake, retreated.

"*What* was *she* so unhappy about?" Karen demanded.

"She thought she should have gotten a perfect grade on her vocab quiz," I said.

"So I *heard*. Really, Rowena, you *need* to make your assessment instructions clearer, if even your *good* students can't understand them."

"Uh-huh." In truth, writing clear assessment instructions was a bugaboo for all instructors. I couldn't say that I always hit the mark, especially with something as tricky as verbal aspect. But I'd looked the quiz over carefully when I'd seen that Jessica had, most unusually, gotten something wrong, and I'd decided that my instructions were as clear as they could be. She just hadn't understood the difference between perfective and imperfective verbal aspect. Well, maybe in ten or fifteen years she'd start to get the hang of it.

"So anyway, Rowena, we *need* to go over your performance evaluation for the semester."

"Okay," I said.

"Right *now*, if you can."

"Sure," I said.

Karen broke into three separate coughing fits as we walked the few dozen yards from my classroom to her office. I entertained the notion that she was doing it to garner sympathy. But the obvious aggravation and embarrassment she felt when she broke into another coughing fit once we got into her office that left her speechless for several minutes made me decide that she really was sick. Still. Maybe that would make her hurry up and get this over with.

"*Well*," she said when she could speak again. "This is *most* inconvenient. I take it *you* haven't gotten sick yet?"

I shook my head. I was still waiting for it to happen, but so far I was showing no signs of sickness—other than the ever-present low-level migraine symptoms that were nudging at my consciousness even as we spoke—despite being jammed together with sick people everywhere on campus and both plane rides to and from California.

Karen pursed her saggy mouth. "You have *all* the luck, don't you, Rowena?"

"Well..." I said.

"*Anyway*, I have your performance review...where is it..." She shuffled through the ever-present and ever-growing pile of random paper on her desk, knocking a bunch of old quizzes and an honors thesis from 2009 onto the floor. Then we both fell into an intense sneezing fit from all the dust that raised.

Karen pulled a cough drop out from a bag in her desk and put the empty wrapper on her keyboard. The heating kicked on, making the cough drop wrapper lift off the keyboard and flutter gently to the floor. Another sneezing fit threatened to overtake me. I stifled it by clamping my fingers over my nose, but when I took them away, the beginnings of a migraine scotoma swam blobbily in front of me.

"Oh, *here* it is," Karen was saying. "Yes, well..." She held it out at arm's length, as if she were having trouble reading it. "Yes, so, as you'll see here, Rowena, although I *have*—after some deliberation—recommended that your contract be extended for another semester, I *do* have a *list* of changes I want implemented."

She looked at me meaningfully.

"Okay," I said.

"This is *particularly* important, since—I have decided you should be informed—the department has applied for permission to do a search for a tenure-track position in Russian."

She looked at me meaningfully again.

"Wow," I said. In truth, I was so stunned I was having a hard time coming up with anything more.

"And *of course* you would be *welcome* to apply, although we will *of course* be conducting a national search—we'd want to see what we can get."

She licked her saggy lips. It was probably because they were dry from all the coughing and the canned air. But it looked lascivious, almost obscene.

"Wow," I said again. "When will the call for applications go out, do you think?"

"Next fall, *if* we get permission to conduct the search. But in the meantime, Rowena, if you want to have *any* chance of being a strong candidate for it, you *must* raise your teaching to the level we expect at Crimson, which means paying *close* attention to these improvements I have laid out for you."

"Um," I said. "Okay."

The improvements were, of course, bullshit. She criticized me for not having a dynamic and engaging seating layout, even though the classroom was too crowded to have any kind of a seating layout, and if there had been one, she would have disturbed it by kicking students out of their seats. Then she complained that there was a lack of content to the class, even though it had been intended as a discussion of out-of-class viewings. She said I should have shown snippets of the films in class. Then she said I'd spent too much time on "info-dumping," and I should have had the students master the material out of class. Then she complained that the material hadn't been engaging, even though she hadn't actually watched any of it. Then she said the class hadn't fostered critical thinking, focusing too much instead on rote memorization of facts, and also that I should have content quizzes at the beginning of each class to make sure the students had gone over the assigned materials ahead of time. She finished up with a remark that I must not be a very engaging instructor overall, since only half the class had shown up.

"It was the Friday afternoon before spring break," I pointed out.

"*My* class had 100% attendance!" she snapped.

I opened my mouth. I was sure I'd heard her saying that she'd canceled her class that day and given them a take-home assignment instead. So if they'd all turned in the assignment, then technically yes, she could have counted it as 100% attendance. But students were much more likely to turn in a take-home assignment than to show up to an in-person class on the Friday afternoon before spring break.

The heat clicked on again. Karen broke into another coughing fit. I shut my mouth. Then I kept it clenched shut as a stabbing pain lanced through my left eye.

"That's nice," I said, once the pain had eased. "I'll, um, take everything you've said under advisement."

"You need to do more than take it under *advisement*, Rowena," said Karen, but another coughing fit stopped her from saying more, so I was able to sign off on the performance review and flee before things got any worse.

68

I FILLED MEL IN ON what had happened during the ride home. We agreed that her observation tomorrow was likely to be a shit show. Then I tried to prepare myself for whatever was going to happen during my meeting with Aishat's family.

Not that there was much I could do to ready myself. It was entirely possible that her family had already declared, or was preparing to declare, a blood feud against Jamal or Owen or both. If they were planning to carry out an honor killing of Aishat, I doubted they would inform me of it. Either way, I didn't see what I could do about it. But I wasn't going to refuse to talk to them, even though I wanted to. Much as it shamed me to admit it, I was afraid of them. Not from anything I knew about them in particular, but because I had developed an instinctive fear of North Caucasians.

Some of it had, no doubt, been exposure to the deep anti-Caucasian sentiment currently running wild in Russia. Some of it had been from my own experiences. The kindness and decency the vast majority of my Caucasian acquaintances had shown me, against all odds, wasn't enough to overcome the bone-deep fear caused by being trapped in the Moscow metro during the suicide bombings in 2004, the interactions I'd had with the boys who'd committed honor killings of their sisters, or the man who'd held a gun to my head in Gorky Park and threatened to rape and kill me if Dima didn't do as he wanted. Not to mention the Boston Marathon bombing and the assassinations of Anna Politkovskaya and Boris Nemtsov. A few bad people had tainted an entire nation for me, a nation for whom I felt deep compassion and genuinely wanted to help. Even so, every time I saw North Caucasian features or heard a North Caucasian accent, the hairs on the back of my neck rose, and I thought I might be sick. But none of that was Aishat's fault. Aishat was even more of a victim here than I was.

When I arrived to pick Aishat up at six, campus had already transitioned from its daytime lively bustle to its evening self, which was darker and much wilder. Even a cozy small-town liberal arts college like Crimson always held that edge of an orgy at night, when faculty and staff left and the campus was taken over by thousands of people in late adolescence, mostly wanting to do the right thing, but too reckless and self-centered to avoid doing bad things half the time.

Aishat met me at the loading zone behind Bedford Hall.

"Thanks for this, Professor Halley," she said as she got into the car. She fiddled nervously with her headscarf.

"No problem. Glad to help. How was the Muslim Students' Union meeting?"

She made a face. "There were only four of us. As usual. We want to do something for the Spring Fling Student Engagement Fair that will happen at the same time as the Lamb Chop Trot. Well, Jibril, the president, is offended that it will be part of the Easter celebration. But it's the only chance we'll have. And I really want to do at least *something*. Jibril has had awful things written on his dormitory door. Like 'Go home, sand nigger.' Only, he was born in Atlanta. And people have shouted at me to take off my headscarf, and told me to go home too."

"That's awful," I said. And I meant it. I thought that headscarves, hijabs, burkas, and most other items of apparel required by Middle Eastern monotheism to be clear and open signs of the subjugation of women, and women who wore them were objectifying themselves and flaunting their subjugation for the world to see. No wonder the liberal left was so in love with them—it was another excellent chance to express misogyny while patting yourself on the back for your enlightened feminism. But most of the women actually wearing these signs of patriarchal authority on their heads didn't have a lot of good choices, and I was against shouting hateful things at random people on the street in any case.

"We want to do something to teach people about Islam," Aishat told me. "Something about the Five Pillars. Most Americans don't know what they are at all. Maybe if they did, they wouldn't hate Islam so much. Only—I'm afraid it might make them hate us more. My father has been accused of raising money for ISIS or al-Qaeda when he gives money to charity. We raise money for orphans!" Aishat gave me an anxious sideways glance. "We don't have anything to do with ISIS at all! I swear it!"

"I know," I said soothingly. I actually knew no such thing, and Aishat's vehemence was starting to make me worry, but I figured it was very unlikely that a major recruiter for ISIS was operating out of Greenfields, Georgia, and in any case, Aishat really did need help, and I was the only one she would accept it from.

She directed me to a neighborhood on the outskirts of town, past Peachtree Estates and on the far side of the drug-dealing neighborhood, where it transitioned into empty countryside. The house we pulled up to was a cheap two-bedroom, one-bathroom ranch-style house with a short gravel drive and raggedy lawn out front. Everything about it told a very familiar tale of low-grade poverty in the South. Most of my friends growing up had lived in houses like this, when they hadn't lived in doublewides and house trailers. I'd lived in a house like this for a while too. I could already envision the plywood veneer cabinets, peeling linoleum flooring, cheap fixtures, and faint smell of mold and mildew before I even set foot inside.

The people who greeted me at the door were definitely North Caucasian, though, not rednecks. Along with Aishat's parents and grandparents, her two older brothers were also there. I told the hairs on the back of my neck to stay calm as we all crowded into the cramped living room and sat down on the shabby furniture.

"We thank you for coming," Dzhambek, Aishat's father, said formally, once we were all settled. "We have a serious problem, and we are turning to you for help." His Chechen accent was even stronger than Aishat's, to the point that I struggled to understand him. He was about 5'8", with sharp dark eyes, thick graying hair that had once been dark auburn, and a full beard that emphasized the distinctive triangular facial shape and broad cheekbones of the Caucasus. "Khalimat"—he pointed his chin at Aishat's mother—"is in despair, and my sons have threatened to take matters into their own hands to avenge the family's honor. I have told them not to. I fear people will think they are terrorists or rebels. We have nothing to do with terrorists or rebels! Do we, Dzhokhar? Shamil?"

"Of course not," I murmured. Dzhokhar and Shamil were popular men's names in Chechnya. They also happened to be the names of the president who had declared independence from Russia, and a field commander who had led a series of high-impact, high-casualty terrorist operations, including holding a hospital and a school hostage. Maybe those names were an innocent coincidence. Maybe they weren't. Either way, they could have gotten their bearers killed during the worst years of the wars.

Dzhokhar and Shamil agreed that they had nothing to do with terrorists or rebels. I couldn't tell whether they were telling the truth or not. They both looked like younger versions of their father. They also both looked royally pissed, like they might do something unwise at any moment.

"Aishat has told you about her...trouble?" Dzhambek asked. "At the party?" He shook his head irritably, like a horse ridding itself of flies.

"Yes," I said. "But I really think the police..."

"If we go to the police, they will say we are terrorists! They will do nothing. And they will not understand our anger. But you might. You will listen to us, and they might listen to you. You must be our go-between."

"Okay," I said.

"We never should have let her go...but her Muslim student circle wanted to attend college functions, and we all wanted to show everyone that we are regular people, good people, normal Americans. You see what becomes of trying to be a normal American! My only daughter dishonored by jackals!"

"It's very unfortunate," I said. "If she gave a statement..."

"She already tried to give a statement! And was threatened! First my daughter was dishonored, then threatened when she tried to seek justice! And now this Ow-en, this *foreigner*, is trying to blackmail her!"

Khalimat emitted a wail of distress. I turned to Aishat. "Is it true?" I asked. "Owen's blackmailing you again?"

She nodded miserably. "This time he has actually posted a video."

"Really?!? Then we have to tell the police! Does it have any useful evidence on it?"

"It shows Jamal," she said. "It shows Jamal...he...he's kind of...undressing me and Brittany. Then it cuts off. But we know what happened next. And now Owen is blackmailing me to do all his work for him, *and* give him a thousand dollars a month, or he'll show the rest of the video. The first part is already up on YouTube."

"One thousand views!" barked Dzhokhar. "One thousand people have already seen my sister dishonored by that disgusting beast! I should kill him and be done with it!"

"We don't kill people!" Dzhambek shouted. "Not even for blood vengeance! Not anymore!"

A heated argument broke out in Chechen between the men. I wished they weren't being such stereotypes of hotheaded Caucasians and purity-obsessed Muslims. The problem with stereotypes is that they tend to be true.

I turned back to Aishat. "Can you forward me Owen's email? And send me the link to the video? It could prove everything you said—and what Brittany said, too. But we need the video, and we *need* a statement from you."

Aishat hunched her shoulders.

"Do it," said Khalimat. She stroked Aishat's head. "I know it is frightening. I'm frightened too. I wish we could resolve this issue ourselves. But we can't. Not without causing your brothers more trouble than they already have. We must do it American-style."

"There's no justice in America!" Aishat burst out. "No honor! When I tried to tell my story to the dean, she *laughed* at me! She *laughed* in my face! Then she told me that I was lying, and I would be expelled if I didn't stop!"

"I know," I said. "That was wrong. But justice can still be done."

"I'll never get my honor back," said Aishat.

I didn't know what to say. It was true that she would never be able to undo what had been done to her. I tried to come up with a comforting and culturally appropriate platitude in Russian that would make sense to a Chechen.

"Some drunken beast can't take away your honor," her mother said, stroking her head again. "Your honor is still intact in all the ways that count. And we will *make him pay* for what he did to you." She looked up at me. "Won't we, Professor Khalli?"

"Um," I said. "Sure. Can you send me the link to that video?"

69

AISHAT FORWARDED ME the email she had gotten from Owen, which contained the link to the YouTube video. I forwarded it immediately to Brian Michaels. Then I turned down, I hoped politely, an invitation to stay for some lamb stew, and went home.

Brian Michaels emailed me back after dinner.

Thanks Rowena, this might be the smoking gun we need! Have you seen the video? You should watch it, let me know if you recognize anyone.

I wrote back that I would. My desire to watch the video was strongly negative, but if it would help identify any of the perpetrators, I could overcome my aversion.

I clicked on the link. It brought me to a YouTube video with 1,012 views and 36 "likes." Could be worse. Could be better. I'd hate for something like that to be circulated about me, and for Aishat it was probably ten times worse.

The video was jerky and slightly out of focus, like it was being shot by a drunk college kid holding a phone, which was no doubt the case. It panned across two girls sitting up but obviously passed out on a ratty-looking couch. I recognized the girl on the right side of the couch as Aishat, even though she was slumped forward with her headscarf falling over half her face. The girl on the left, who was leaning back against the corner of the couch, was short and athletic, with dark Latina features and dyed blonde hair pulled up in a high ponytail. I was pretty sure this was Brittany Gutierrez.

Adolescent male giggling came from behind the camera. My skin prickled.

"You filming this, Owen dude?" a drunk male voice said. American, white and upper-class, with a hint of southern drawl. It could have been familiar, or it could have belonged to any one of the male students at Crimson.

"I'm filming this." Another male voice, this one with a distinct Chinese accent. It could have been Owen, or it could have been one of the other Chinese students. The sound quality was poor, and the voices were partially obscured by the sound of dance music coming from a different room.

"Jamal! My man!"

It was the first speaker. Or maybe a different speaker with a similar voice. The background giggling made me think there were at least ten boys in the room.

"What the fuck's goin' on?" The sound was still poor quality, but that speaker was undeniably a working-class black male from the South. Which at Crimson narrowed it down to a field of one.

"Jamal, my man, we got you a present."

"What kinda present?" Jamal's voice sounded wary.

"You remember you told us at initiation you'd never been with a girl before? And we said we'd have to do something about that? We only take real men into Pi Chi."

Heavy silence. Then Jamal burst out, "I'll find my own girl when the time's right, man."

"You haven't done anything about it yet, my man. Except you're not a man, are you? Still a little boy."

"What the fuck's wrong with you, man? I got trainin', Coach is watchin' me like a hawk, I got Academic Advisin' on my ass 'bout keepin' my grades up—when you think I got time to go chasin' girls?

'Sides, all these fancy white girls turn their noses up at me. They like lookin' at me, but they don't wanna listen to anythin' I got to say. They don't know shit 'bout my life, and they don't wanna know shit 'bout it. They jus' wanna piss off they daddies an' think they walkin' on the wild side by goin' out with a black football player."

"Well, my man, here's your big chance. Two of those fancy white girls, just waiting for you."

"Ain't that Brittany?" demanded Jamal. "Brittany ain't white. An' that other girl don't look too white either. An' they both look like they passed out to me. I don't go messin' with girls that's passed out. 'Specially when they be my friends. Brittany ain't never done nothin' 'cept be nice to me."

"And she wants to be nice to you now. She knows this is what you need if you're going to be accepted as a real Pi Chi man, so she said she wanted to do this for you."

"An' the other girl?" demanded Jamal.

"She did too," said the other voice. "Come on man, you know you gotta do this. This is how you become a real Pi Chi. Right, men?"

There was a chorus of cheering and bellowing in the background.

"This is some bullshit," said Jamal.

"Come on man, you gotta do this. You'll be glad you did. Think of all the doors it'll open for you."

"I think football's gonna open doors for me," said Jamal.

"Come on, man. You may be the star quarterback here at Crimson, but who the fuck cares about Crimson? This isn't Notre Dame or Texas or some shit like that. You're not going to get recruited for a sweet gig with the Cowboys or the Panthers out of Crimson. They're just going to play you till you blow out both your knees and dislocate your shoulder and get one too many concussions, and then they're going to let you flunk all your classes and go be a used car salesman. Only in your case it'll probably be a drug dealer, right?"

"Fuck you, man," said Jamal flatly.

"But *we*, my man, can open doors for you. We can get you in with investment bankers and financial managers and any kind of Fortune 500 company you want—can't we, fellas?"

There was another chorus of drunken cheering and bellowing.

"All you have to do is, well...prove your manhood. Come on, man," the voice said persuasively. "They both said this is what they wanted. They *want* to help you. They were just shy, so they asked for a drink or two beforehand. This way it'll be easier for everyone. Come on. At least take a look at them."

Jamal edged into the frame. He reached out and tentatively pushed back Aishat's headscarf, revealing her face and her smooth dark hair. I felt sick. I thought that Aishat's headscarf was bad and she should take it off. I also thought she should be the one to take it off. Having some strange man take it off in front of a gang of other strange men was a terrible violation. She twitched and made a helpless movement, like she was trying to wake up and fend him off, but couldn't.

"Aw, man, you gotta show us more. Show us Brittany's panties," urged the voice.

"Panties! Panties!" cheered the others.

Jamal reached over and, squeamishly, like he was handling week-old dead fish, started raising the hem of Brittany's miniskirt. She jerked and her eyes flew open. She stared at Jamal in half-conscious horror and tried to squirm away, before collapsing and slithering halfway off the couch, making her skirt ride the rest of the way up to her waist.

Jamal stared down at her. "This is some bullshit," he repeated. Then the screen went black.

70

MULTIPLE EMAILS TUESDAY night and Wednesday morning confirmed that Aishat would go in Wednesday afternoon to give a statement to campus police. First she wanted me to accompany her. Then she said she wanted her mother to accompany her. Finally it was arranged that both of us would accompany her.

I could understand her hesitance, difficult as it made things. Reporting sexual assault is always a dicey business, and when she'd come forward before, she'd been threatened. And her family had genuine reason to be suspicious of the authorities. I was reasonably confident that they weren't criminals or terrorists—right now. I was sure that they had been treated as criminals and terrorists their entire lives, first in Russia, now in the US.

For them, the police were the people who came and dragged you away and held you without trial, probably beat you, maybe tortured you, before dumping you somewhere. If you were lucky, you were still alive when you were thrown out of the moving car into a muddy ditch. If you were really lucky, someone would find you and help you before you died. Voluntarily going to the police probably seemed like lunacy to them.

I had a moment of acute awareness that, much as I might not like it, I was on the side of the torturers and oppressors, not the tortured and oppressed. I thought of Alex and Erin, who were good people—well, Alex was, at least—who had helped run a state-sponsored torture program; and John, who had helped lead invasions of two impoverished countries full of innocent civilians; and Dima, who had been an instrument of violent oppression of his own people. And now I was friends with the chief of campus police. I hoped I wasn't leading Aishat and her family horribly astray. I trusted Brian Michaels as much as I trusted anyone in authority. But his powers were limited. If other people took over the situation, it could spin out of control and all our worst fears could come true.

I was supposed to meet with Aishat and her mother at 2:00pm to go give her statement. I was mainly focused on that instead of my classes, which I semi-sleepwalked through. Fortunately it was all stuff I could teach in my sleep, so I was hoping no harm was done.

Miranda had seemed anxious and on edge throughout the class. Afterwards, she came over to me and asked if she could talk to me during my office hours.

"Sure," I said.

"It's about Jamal," she said, fidgeting with her bookbag strap and not looking at me.

"Um, okay." I resisted the urge to fidget with my own bookbag strap and look away. I debated what to say. Tell her that Jamal was probably about to get arrested, if he hadn't been already? Warn her that he might be a rapist? I knew she'd been spending time with him. Had he assaulted her and that's what she wanted to tell me about? Oh God.

"Let's meet at 11:00," I said.

"Thanks, Professor." She gave me a wan smile and hurried off.

When I came out of my second class at 10:52, Miranda was already waiting outside my office door. As I started in that direction, Jamal appeared around the corner and headed towards my office. A trace of that almost childlike purity, innocence, and joy he'd shown crossing the finish line at the race flashed across his face when he saw Miranda. Her face lit up with an answering joy.

Oh God. I did my best to wipe the dread of what was about to be revealed off my face, and went over to them.

"Wow," said Jamal when I let them into my office. "I thought professors had, like, nice offices."

"Some of them do," I said. "There isn't a lot of office space in Bedford. I think they gave me an old broom closet."

"Yeah. You don't even got a window. Hope you ain't claustrophobic."

"Unfortunately, I am." I rubbed my eyes, which were already starting to hurt. Strange, otherworldly shimmers hung over everything when I pulled my fingers away.

Miranda and Jamal sat down, Jamal easing himself carefully into the rickety chair. He was only about six feet tall, but incredibly fit. He'd probably gone through life being too strong and fast for his surroundings, and had learned to be cautious, in case he accidentally broke everything around him. And maybe he had accidentally broken Brittany and Aishat. The impression of a young Count Vronsky was still strong. Count Vronsky had destroyed all the females, equine and human, he'd loved, without meaning for an instant to do any harm.

"So what's going on?" I asked.

Miranda and Jamal shared a quick glance.

"We're hoping you can help us, Professor," said Miranda. "See, it's about that Chechen girl, I think her name is Aishat?"

I suppressed a groan. "What about her?" I asked.

"See"—Miranda and Jamal shared another quick glance—"her family's been bothering Jamal."

"I heard something about that before spring break," I said.

"Yeah," said Jamal. "Anthony said he'd said somethin' 'bout it to you."

"Yes," I said. "Well, I did just speak with Aishat and her family, as it happens..."

"An' now a video's come out, an' I'm gettin' blackmailed about it!" Jamal burst out.

"Um," I said. "A video of what? By whom?"

Jamal and Miranda shared another glance. "See, the thing is, Professor," said Miranda. "It doesn't look good for Jamal. I mean, he's innocent, but it doesn't look good for him. And everyone else involved is related to the Russian program in some way, so we were hoping maybe you could...smooth things over."

"If it's the video I'm thinking of, I don't think things can be 'smoothed over,'" I said.

"How'd you find out about it?" Jamal demanded.

"Aishat sent me a link." I debated for a moment and then added, "And I forwarded it to campus police."

"Oh fuck." Jamal slumped back in his chair, making it creak alarmingly.

"You should go talk to them," I said. "Make a statement. It will look better if you come forward voluntarily and confess."

"I ain't got nothin' to confess!"

"The video I saw," I said quietly, "showed you molesting Aishat and Brittany."

"I never molested 'em!"

I waited in silence.

"Okay," said Jamal after a moment. "I kinda...messed with their clothes a little. But then I thought better of it an' I...I ran off," he finished in a small voice.

"Is there any proof of that?" I asked.

He shook his head. His jaunty twists bounced with an energy entirely at odds with the rest of him.

"Tell her about it," Miranda urged him. "Tell her what happened. She'll understand, won't you, Professor Halley?" She looked at me anxiously.

"Yes," I said. In truth, I wasn't sure I would. I had heard a lot of bad things in my time, and I could find compassion in my heart for a lot of people. But rapists triggered a "kill them now" response that most others didn't. I thought of Jamal pulling off Aishat's headscarf and lifting the hem of Brittany's skirt. Memories of the frat boy who'd come up behind me and grabbed both my breasts on a dare my sophomore year of college, the boys who'd staged a panty raid in my dorm and displayed my dirty underwear like trophies, the man sitting next to me on my first flight to Moscow who'd grabbed my crotch at 36,000 feet somewhere over Iceland, the man who'd grabbed my arm and pinned me against the wall in Sheremetyevo Airport when I'd been waiting for the flight back, the man who'd stared into my bathroom stall last year at UNC-Matthews, all the men who'd shouted at me and chased me down the street, who'd pinched me and rubbed their crotches against me at parties, rose up in me.

And I was one of the lucky ones. Nothing like what had happened to Aishat or Brittany had ever happened to me—that I knew of. I'd always been careful to avoid insensibility in public places, but who knows what had happened to me when I hadn't been able to hold out any longer and had dozed off on all the plane rides, train rides, and bus rides I'd taken? I wanted to scream at Jamal, punch his face, do something to him that would bring home what a violation he'd committed and how his victims felt.

"I'll understand," I said. "You can tell me anything."

Miranda relaxed. Jamal jumped to his feet, eliciting another creak in protest from the chair.

"See," he said. He had his back to us. I let him stand like that. In my experience, men tended to talk more openly when they had plenty of physical space and little eye contact. "This was supposed to be my big chance."

"Uh-huh," I said.

"I mean, I know Crimson ain't a big football school. Or a big anythin' school. But they offered me a full ride scholarship an' a guaranteed startin' position on the team, freshman year."

"Mmm-hmmm," I said.

"My momma was so thrilled. It's just me an' her: she ain't got no one else. We're one of those 'impoverished inner-city single-parent families'"—his voice rose and took on faux posh tones—"white folks like to read about an' shake their heads over an' thank God it ain't them."

"Uh-huh," I said. My side of the conversation was decidedly lacking in wit. But it seemed to be working, so I kept at it.

"So this was s'pposed to be it for me. I knew it was gonna be tough. I ain't never been good at school."

"Jamal's smart," Miranda interjected anxiously. "Really smart. But, you know, he didn't have the, um, preparation that a lot of the kids have here."

"Uh-huh," I said again. I was sure just from the few minutes I'd spent in Jamal's company that he was intelligent. I was also willing to bet that the schools he'd gone to as a child had been so bad he'd probably have been better off being raised by wolves.

"And then I got here an' it was even crazier 'n I thought it was gonna be. But then I got encouraged to rush for a frat. I was like, 'No way! No way they gonna take me!' But they did. I was in Pi Chi with all those rich white boys, an' they was promisin' they'd make me just like 'em."

"Mmmmm," I said.

"An' then...an' then...that fuckin' party...they brought me into that room...it was a fuckin' costume party. The team'd been told to wear they uniforms, so you can see my face and my name and everythin', but everyone else was all dressed up in fuckin' ghost an' devil costumes, shit like that, so you couldn't tell who they was...they brought me in an' they told me...well...if you saw the video you know..."

"But you left!" Miranda said quickly. "Once you realized what was going on, you left!"

"Yeah." Jamal was calming back down. "Yeah, that's right. I left. Right after what the video shows, I left. I got the hell outta there, an' I didn't come back. Thought I was gonna get kicked out, an' my big chance'd be all gone, but nothin' like that happened. They just told me to keep my mouth shut, so I did. Even when Brittany...said what she did...such shit...I shoulda said somethin'...but 'stead I said she was lyin'...well, she was, kinda...it wasn't me that did it...now my life's 'bout to be ruined by somethin' I didn't do..."

"That makes it even more important for you to come forward and make a statement," I said. "If you know who the real rapists are, you can see that justice is done for Brittany and Aishat, and clear your name at the same time."

Jamal turned around and gave me a scathing look. "That ain't how it's gonna be," he said. "I'll tell you how it's gonna be. Them rich white boys who did the actual rapin' are gonna go free, and I'll lose everythin' an' spend the rest of my life in prison."

That was an all too accurate depiction of the likely outcome of this event. "The video's already out there," I said gently. "Thousands of people have already seen it by now. The police have already seen it by now. The truth is already out."

"That video ain't the truth!"

"Then you need to get your truth out there," I said. "And I know you don't have a lot of reason to trust the police, but hiding from them isn't going to help. I'm supposed to go to them this afternoon. If you like you can come with me."

I regretted the invitation as soon as I'd uttered it. Aishat and Khalimat were not going to appreciate Jamal appearing at what was already a very difficult time. But I wanted to make sure he had a chance to tell his story on his own terms, as much as possible. If he could help bring the real culprits to justice, then it was essential.

"Professor Halley is friends with the chief of police, aren't you, Professor Halley?" said Miranda.

"That's true," I said. "It might go best with you if we go together. And...I know a lawyer. Maybe she can help us out."

"Yeah...I guess...it's just such shit!" he burst out. "This was s'pposed to be my chance...I was gonna build a better life for myself, for my momma, she's done so much for me...but seems like the only way you can get ahead as a black man in America is if you do all the dirty work for the rich white folks. Rap about wearin' bling an' slappin' hoes, clown aroun' an' let 'em laugh at you, let 'em watch you while you bust your body to pieces for their entertainment. They'll give you money quick enough for that. But if you stand up for somethin' you know is right, they'll turn on you quick as shit."

"I'm afraid your assessment is probably correct," I said. "But the video is already out there. And Brittany and Aishat deserve justice."

"Yeah," said Jamal. "You know, I didn't do nothin' to 'em—well, nothin' that the video didn't show—but I ran off an' left 'em. I coulda stood up for 'em, tried to get 'em outta there, but I didn't. I turned an' ran like a bitch, an' then I lied when they tried to tell the truth. My momma raised me better 'n that." He swallowed. "She's gonna be so disappointed in me."

"You can still make things right," I said.

"Yeah, right," said Jamal, but he agreed to go with me to Brian Michaels at 2:00pm.

71

MIRANDA HUNG BACK AFTER Jamal left.

"You must think I'm stupid," she said.

"Why?"

"Because..." She pulled at the hem of her sleeve, looking down at her hands rather than at me. Her hair was almost completely grown out into a normal, attractive dark brown bob, with no trace of the punk/goth style she'd had last semester. "I mean, I'm just another girl saying some boy didn't do all the bad things everyone's saying he did. You must think I'm just another sucker, getting conned by some guy."

"Do *you* think you're a sucker getting conned by some guy?" I asked.

She pulled some more at her sleeves and then wrapped her arms around her body, like she wanted to hide away from me. "No," she said. "I mean, I wouldn't go out with Jamal if I thought he was, like, a sex predator."

"Good," I said.

"I believe what he told me."

"What did he tell you?" I asked.

"That...that he was that party, the one where...and they tried to get him to...but he said he wouldn't, and left. And then afterwards...when he heard what Brittany was saying...he feels awful about it, he really does. He said he never did anything to her, but he just left her there. He thought she'd be safe there, that they just wanted him to...but if she really was, you know...then he just left her there...and then he didn't stand up for her later, either...and now it's just killing him inside..."

"Good," I said. "I mean, I'm sorry for the pain he's going through. But that means he's a good person at heart. And I don't think you're stupid or a sucker."

"Really?" She looked up.

"Really," I said. "Standing by a friend when they're in need isn't stupid. It's strong. You obviously think Jamal is worth standing by, and for what it's worth, I agree."

"You do?"

"I do," I said. "I think at heart he's a good kid, and he could be a good man. But this is going to be really tough for him. What he said is true. Chances are good that he's going to be made the scapegoat in this while all the rich white boys walk free, even though his role in it was minor. And it's going to hurt him a lot. He's probably going to feel like it's one more terrible injustice in a life full of them. He's probably going to be bitter and angry, and for good reason."

"You don't think..." She went back to fidgeting with her sleeves. "You don't think I shouldn't have anything to do with him, after what he did? I mean...I saw the video...he did, like...mess with their clothes a little...that was, like, kinda like...assault, I guess you could say..."

"It wasn't good," I said. "But he also did speak out against it on the video, and if what he says is true, then he thought better of it and left. He didn't protect them, but he did speak out against what happened to them, and refused to participate in it, and maybe that's the best he could have done. And everyone deserves a shot at redemption. This is his. And I'm sure he could use a friend to stand by him while he seeks it."

"Okay. Thanks. That, um...that makes me feel a lot better. I just feel like, you know, with the thing with Chris and everything, and now this...I feel, like, cursed or something when it comes to guys."

I stood up. "You're not cursed. You just have, um, interesting friends. But seriously, everyone has problems. Everyone goes through hard times. The same is going to be true for any guy you end up with. That doesn't mean you should put up with losers and abusers, but you can't expect things to be picture-perfect all the time. And, to use a cliché, sometimes you really do have to stand by your man. Now, if you'll excuse me, I have to call that lawyer I mentioned and then get to class."

"Oh. Okay. Thanks, Professor. And...I guess I'll go find Jamal. See if he wants me to walk over to the police with him."

"That sounds like a good idea," I said, and got out my phone.

Irene answered on the first ring.

"Rowena, honey, is that you?"

"It is. And I'm, um, calling for a favor."

She laughed. "Well, don't sound so shy about it, hon, spit it out! I'm sitting here bored to death, wondering if I should change my living room drapes. You know I'm desperate when I start thinking about interior decorating. What is it?"

I outlined the Jamal situation.

"And now I'm wondering if he should have, you know, legal counsel present when he speaks with the police."

"You're damn right he should, hon. What time did you say? 2:00pm? At Lee Hall? I'll be there."

"Thanks," I said.

"Any time, hon. I'm spoiling for a fight, so your call came at just the right time. See you at two."

Feeling relieved, I hung up and set off to RUS/HUM 150.

The class was supposed to turn in proposals for their final research project. Alicia came up to me after class and asked if she could talk to me about her idea.

"Sure," I said.

"So, I was, like, thinking about, like, doing a project on, like, comparing Russian serfdom with the African slave trade."

"Sure," I said. "That sounds interesting."

"Yeah, so I've, like, already been researching it. It's pretty interesting. You'd think they were the same, but they were, like, pretty different. Like, you know, Russian serfs were like, treated like members of the family and, like, cared for and stuff. Like, they were really valued and cared for and stuff like family members."

I opened my mouth to respond to that, but the only thing that came out was "Um."

"Yeah, it was, like, kind of sweet, actually." She gave me a beatific smile.

"Well," I said. "That, um, happened sometimes, it's true. But, um, that's not exactly the *whole* picture..." I was struggling with how to explain, in a sensitive and thoughtful way that would not get me fired, to a black student with a keen sense of justice that she had just recreated one of the main arguments in favor of slavery and cheerfully applied it to another culture, just like American slavery apologists she found so abhorrent.

"I can some suggest some useful readings," was what I finally came up with.

"Oh, thanks, Professor!" She gave me another beatific smile and pushed her pink cotton-candy hair back from her eyes. "Oh, hey, Anthony!"

Anthony came up behind her and stood so close they were almost touching. "You ready, babe?" he asked. "We'd better get going. We've got a function tonight," he told me. "The first function we'll be going to as a couple."

"That's nice," I said.

"I'm excited!" said Alicia. "Although...it's with Security Solutions...I just don't get a good feeling from them..."

"I know, babe. But I already explained it to you," he told her earnestly. "What they do isn't something we like to think about, but it's necessary for society to function."

She made a kittenish face of distaste. "I know, it's just...well, you know the statistics...so many black men end up in jail..."

"Yeah, but that's not Security Solution's fault," Anthony said. "And they provide good, legitimate, well-paying employment for a lot of black men. *You* know. You've met some of them on campus. And you know if you want to make change the best way is to do it from the inside."

"That's true," said Alicia. "Well...anyway...I guess we'd better go so we can make ourselves pretty for the event..."

"You're already pretty," said Anthony. I repressed a gag. I disliked watching other people flirt. I particularly disliked watching students flirt.

Alicia giggled. "You're so sweet," she said. "Well, anyway, so you think my project sounds good, Professor?"

"Let me send you some readings," I told her. Then I gathered up my things and set off to meet with Aishat and Jamal.

72

I MET UP WITH AISHAT and Khalimat outside of Lee Hall at 2:00 on the dot. There was no sign of Irene yet. "Thank you for coming," Aishat told me solemnly. She stiffened. "What is *he* doing here?"

I looked over. Jamal was walking slowly in our direction, accompanied by Miranda.

"He's giving a statement too," I said.

Now Khalimat stiffened even more than Aishat. "That is...*him*?" she demanded.

"Yes," said Aishat, at the same time as I said, "No."

"It is!" insisted Aishat. "I remember him! And he is in the video."

"Yes, but he left," I explained. "He didn't actually, um, participate. So he's here now to give a statement so that the police can find the actual perpetrators."

"Oh." Aishat and Khalimat both contemplated that as Jamal slowly drew closer.

"I don't feel so good," said Aishat. She fanned herself. "I know you say he did not do it," she told me. "But simply looking at him makes me feel sick. My organism knows that he is connected to something bad."

"Why don't we get you inside," I said.

I tried to convey what was going on to Miranda and Jamal with body language and expressive looks as I hustled Aishat and Khalimat inside. Then we were in Lee Hall and I couldn't see if Miranda and Jamal had followed or turned tail and run.

We went through the big doors of the main entrance, and headed down the long corridor with its high ceiling. It should have felt airy and spacious, but I was having a hard time drawing a full breath. The air seemed to shimmer in front of me, and when we stepped into the stairwell, the light from the fluorescent bulbs hit me square in the eyes, causing the gray-green-orange blob that heralded a migraine to fill the center of my vision.

"I don't feel very good," Aishat repeated, fanning herself some more.

"It's nerves, darling," Khalimat told her. "Be strong!"

Brian was waiting for us when we reached the two rooms tucked away in the basement of Lee Hall that was the police station. "Aishat Aslanbekova?" he asked when he saw us. "Thanks so much for coming."

"You are welcome," said Aishat. She continued to fan herself, and was plucking and pulling at the hem of her headscarf with her other hand. I could heartily sympathize. It was the middle of March and already starting to heat up outside, but not enough for the AC to come on inside the buildings. The basement felt clammy and close. No doubt her headscarf was stifling. But she certainly wasn't going to take it off.

"Why don't we go to my office," said Brian Michaels. "I understand you want to have Doctor Halley accompany you at the interview?"

"Well..." said Aishat. She looked at me uncertainly. "I don't know...I don't want to be by myself...but now my mother is here...I don't want to...I...I think my English is good enough...and I don't want to tell my story to many people..."

"I can leave," I said. "I need to go check on Jamal anyway. Jamal Warner is also supposed to come," I told Brian. "I saw him walking this way as we came in. If Aishat would prefer being by herself, I'll go look for him."

"Okay," said Brian. "Is Jamal planning to give a statement?"

"That is the plan," I confirmed.

"Okay. That makes things a little more complicated. Go get him and tell O'Hare to take his statement, and keep him until I can talk to him myself."

I fled the basement gratefully. Once I stepped outside my lungs suddenly started working again. The migraine scotoma expanded and turned into a shimmering, jagged semi-circle on the left side of my vision, though.

Jamal and Miranda were standing outside the main entrance to Lee Hall, arguing.

"She went an' left us!" Jamal was saying heatedly when I came up to them.

"Yeah," I said. "Sorry about that. Aishat...she wanted to go in by herself."

Jamal looked ashamed. "She hate me?" he asked.

"She's afraid of you," I said.

He kicked at the ground with the toe of his boot. "My momma's gonna be so ashamed of me," he said. "Mad as hell, but that's okay. It's the shame that's gonna kill her. She raised me better 'n that."

"I don't see any of those other boys here," I said. "So she must have done something right with you, since you're the only one who's acting like a man."

Jamal ran his hand over his face, maybe to suppress a smile, maybe to suppress tears. He swallowed. "C'mon," he said. "Let's do this thing."

"Hang on a minute," I said. Irene was hurrying towards us. "I got you some legal counsel."

Jamal looked at me like I'd grown a second head. "What?"

"Legal counsel," I said. "A lawyer."

"I can't afford no lawyer."

"Let me worry about that," I said.

Jamal was still staring at me like I'd grown a second head. "Why you doin' this?" he demanded suspiciously.

"Because someone needs to," I said.

Irene came up to us. I made the introductions.

"I ain't got no money," Jamal told her bluntly. "I can't afford no lawyer."

"This is pro bono," Irene told him.

"You mean, like, for free?"

"That's right."

Jamal eyed her with even more suspicion than he'd shown me. "You hopin' to make a name for yourself or somethin'?"

"Darling, I've already made a name for myself," Irene told him. "Mostly I'm looking for a reason to get out of the house. And I'm just spoiling for a fight, and it sounds like this might give me one."

That did make Jamal smile. "You a real pit bull, huh?"

"Honey, you have no idea. Now, are you ready?"

We trooped into Lee Hall. I was hoping that the return to the indoor darkness would soothe my migraine. It was a vain hope. Stabbing pain lanced through my left eye as soon as I stepped back into the building, and my chest grew tight. I took deep slow breaths through my nose and told myself there was plenty of oxygen and I wasn't in any danger.

Dustin O'Hare, Brian's second-in-command—of two—met us at the entrance to the police station. Jamal swallowed again, and stopped. Miranda put her hand on his arm.

"Jamal Warner?" Dustin said. "Thanks for coming down, son. We appreciate it."

Jamal's shoulders relaxed a tiny bit. He took a step forward, then stopped again.

"Reckon I should do this myself," he told Miranda. "See you afterwards, okay?"

"Okay," said Miranda. He and Irene followed Dustin into the police station, and Miranda and I turned around and walked away.

73

MY CHEST TIGHTNESS eased as soon as we were back out in the fresh air. My migraine did not. Once one got started, it had to run its course, and there wasn't a lot I could do about it.

"I think I'll wait here," said Miranda. Her face was looking pinched and anxious. "They're not going to do anything to him, right?"

"I hope not," I said.

"I mean, they're nice, right? They're not going to, like, beat him up or anything, right?"

"That seems very unlikely," I said. And it did. As long as he remained with the campus police. They seemed safe enough. But if he did get arrested, and transferred to the town jail...

"Waiting here is probably a good idea," I said. "But try not to worry. Irene knows what she's doing."

"Yeah, my mom knows her," Miranda said. "I feel a lot better with her with him. But it's still scary, you know what I mean?"

"Yeah, I know what you mean."

"You ever had a friend in trouble with the police?"

"My former fiancé got arrested several times, and even did several short stints in jail."

Miranda goggled at me. "He did?! What for?!?!"

"Political protest," I said. "It's a high-contact sport in Russia."

"Oh my God! That must have been so scary! I'm freaking out as it is. I don't know how you stood it!"

"It wasn't pleasant," I said. "But you get used to it. Are you going to be okay here, or would you like me to stay with you?"

"I'll probably be okay."

"Great," I said. "You've got my number, right? Text me or give me a call if you need anything."

I made my way across the back quad to Bedford Hall, rubbing my temples and trying to avoid anything resembling direct sunlight. I felt sweaty and nauseous, and also shivery and exhausted. Maybe I was finally coming down with the plane crud.

I gathered up my things from my office, and headed out. There was nothing more I could do on campus—I hoped.

Chloe's office door was open. I peeked in as I walked by. She was sitting at her desk with her head in her hands, also rubbing her temples.

"Hey," I said. "You okay?"

She looked up. She was visibly trembling. "Wh-wh-what? Oh, yeah. J-j-just an-n-nother p-p-panic at-t-tack."

"Ugh," I said. "I thought you stopped having them.

"G-g-guess not."

"Come on," I said. "Let's get out of here."

"I'm-m-m-m t-t-trying t-to ac-c-climate m-m-myself t-t-to m-m-my of-f-fice. It-t-t-t's s-s-s-something m-m-my th-th-therapist w-w-wants m-me t-to w-w-work on."

"Oh," I said. "Well...I'm having a migraine. I need someone to walk me to my car."

"R-r-really? And-d-d-d y-y-you w-w-want m-m-my h-h-help?"

"Yep."

Chloe stood up. "P-p-people d-d-don't n-n-normally ask-k-k m-me f-f-f-for h-help."

"I'm sure you'll do great," I said. "I'm just having some trouble seeing right now."

"Oh my God! Do you need to go to the doctor?!!?"

"Nah," I said. "I'll be fine. I just need some help getting home."

Chloe walked me out the front entrance of Bedford. By the time we were halfway across the quad, her panic attack had calmed down to the point that she could talk normally again.

"Maybe I should drive you home," she said. "If you can't see."

"That might be a good idea," I said. "Normally I carpool with Mel, but today I had some stuff going on, so I drove myself. But I'm sure I can get a ride with her tomorrow or Friday to come pick up my car."

"Great. And wow, I'm already feeling a lot better. Bedford Hall really freaks me out, I guess."

"Understandable," I said.

"Yeah, I know. My therapist is trying to get me to do some exposure therapy. She wants me to come in on weekends and just sit there when there isn't anything else going on, and get used to being there when there's no reason to be stressed out."

"Sounds sensible," I said.

"Yeah, only...I haven't done it yet. I keep freaking out and not doing it."

"Would you like some company?" I asked.

"Really? You'd do that?"

"Sure," I said.

"Yeah, that'd be great, then. I'm sure if I have some help, some accountability, I'll get it under control in no time."

I rubbed my temple. "I hope so," I said.

74

IRENE CALLED ME THAT evening to tell me that she'd shepherded Jamal safely through his statement, and he had not been arrested.

"Thank God," I said.

"I know, honey. Although that video is not helping him."

"I know. But he's trying to make amends, and arresting him won't help us find the real rapists."

"Too true. I think the police are taking it seriously for once, and they're going to try to find more videos and see if they can find anything that points to the identity of the perpetrators. But it was a costume party. Jamal insists he doesn't know who else was in the room."

"I can't believe that," I said.

"I know...but he'd just joined the fraternity. He probably didn't know half the boys in it yet."

"You'd think he would have recognized them since then."

"Maybe he's trying not to," said Irene. "That way he can say he doesn't know anything about it, and tell himself his conscience is clear."

"Maybe," I said. "What's next?"

"The police do their thing. Try to find that video that's being used to blackmail Jamal and that girl, interview potential suspects, try to put together a case."

"Meanwhile, the college and Pi Chi will stonewall them," I said.

"I'm sure they'll say they'll do everything in their power to help see justice done, honey, but we both know what they'll really do is everything in their power to make themselves look good, and cast all the blame on Jamal and the girls."

"There's probably not a lot we can do about that," I said.

"I'll see what I can do, honey, but even my power is limited. And there's probably not a lot you can do about it at all."

"Well, if there is, let me know," I said.

"Will do, hon, and thanks again for giving an old woman something to keep her busy."

"Any time," I said.

75

I WANTED TO WORRY FRUITLESSLY about Jamal and Aishat's situation, but fortunately, I had other things on my mind. Mel and I had both been volunteered to run in the Lamb Chop Trot, the faculty race on the Saturday the weekend before Easter, just as we'd been press-ganged into running in the Pre-Turkey Trot in the fall. Due to a series of events beyond our control, we'd ended up coming in first and second in the Pre-Turkey Trot. The word on the street was that we were the hot favorites for the Lamb Chop Trot as well. I hoped no one had a lot of money riding on us. Neither of us had been well enough to train properly for months.

We drove over together in Mel's Jeep Saturday morning.

"You ready for this?" I asked.

"As ready as I'm ever gonna be. So no. Good news is, I think my face is getting better."

I gave it a keen once-over. "Yeah, I think you're right." The right side of her face was still weirdly droopy, but less so than it had been a month ago, and her speech was clearer.

"What about you?" she asked.

"I've tried to get in shape a little bit. But my knee's still bothering me on and off, and every time I run more than a couple of miles, it flares up again for days. I'm going to have to baby it in order to get through a 5k."

"Ugh. I'll be babying my knees right along with you. They still hurt like a motherfucker sometimes, and I think the right one's kind of swollen all the time now. Fuck! I really don't feel like doing this."

"No, me neither," I said. "Besides, I find it morally offensive to celebrate the slaughter of innocent beings with cutesy costumes and saccharine sentiments about how happy they are."

"Yeah, I guess so," said Mel. "But hey, I guess you could say it's a metaphor or whatever for how senior faculty treat us."

"Gosh," I said. "You better watch out, or one of these days you'll end up a hardened cynic."

Mel flashed me a lopsided grin. "Yeah, wouldn't want that, would we?"

We parked in the faculty parking lot behind the football stadium and started making our way around it to the track, where the start and finish lines were.

"Wonder what they're going to do with it when the new football stadium is finished," Mel said, nodding at the stadium.

"Have two football stadiums," I said. "You never know when you might need a spare."

"Yeah...is that girl trying to talk to you?"

I looked up. Sticking out in her black headscarf and beige below-the-knee skirt amongst all the people frolicking about in lamb, bunny, and chick costumes, Aishat was motioning to me. Frantically.

I jogged over to her. "What is it?"

"My father! My brothers! They have decided to take matters into their own hands!"

I looked around instinctively. No sign of them. "Here?" I asked. "Now?"

Aishat nodded vigorously. "They say they are going to go after Jamal and Owen."

"Jamal isn't even guilty," I said.

"He is guilty enough!"

"Well...okay." From their perspective, he probably was. And he was the only one we knew for certain had been involved. "Where are they?" I asked.

"Waiting outside Jamal's dormitory."

"Let's go." I turned back to Mel. "You go ahead," I told her. "I'm going to go with Aishat. There's a...situation developing."

"You want backup?"

"I don't want you to miss the race."

"Believe me, I'd be happy to miss this fuckin' race. Besides." She smiled lopsidedly. "If there's a 'situation' developing, maybe I can use my Halloween freak face to scare folks into behaving."

"Okay. Let's go."

We followed Aishat at a brisk walk that soon broke into a jog around the football stadium and the athletic center that was filling up with frolicking bunnies and lambs, past the copse that held The Hollow, through the beach volleyball courts that were already lined with eager spectators bearing homemade signs, and over to the dorm at the far end of the residential area.

"I followed Jamal for several weeks," Aishat told me, panting slightly, as we jogged along. "To find out where he lived. I was very frightened, but I wanted justice more. So I made myself follow him until I learned where he lived. I even followed him inside his dormitory to find out which room he lived in."

"Did you ever follow Anthony or Alicia?" I asked.

She made an uneasy motion. "Anthony...he was always with Jamal. So I guess you could say I followed him a little. Alicia...I went looking for her a few times...I wanted to talk to her about some stuff, ask her about Anthony and Jamal...but I didn't want to hurt her. She was my friend. She never did me any harm."

"Someone has been leaving hateful messages on her door. She thought it might be you."

Aishat shrugged. "Definitely not. I have never even been in her dormitory. She was mistaken. Oh, there they are!" She picked up her pace.

"I'm gonna go talk to the front desk," declared Mel, and peeled off from us. I followed Aishat.

We ran up to where Dzhambek, Dzhokhar, and Shamil were standing by the back entrance to the old brick dormitory. Students were trickling out, giving the three men sideways looks and then moving quickly on to the racecourse.

"Aishat!" said Dzhambek when he saw us. He said something to her in Chechen, and then demanded in Russian, "What are *you* doing here, Professor Khalli?"

"Aishat was worried," I said.

"Aishat should not have told you."

"Aishat is afraid you will cause more trouble for yourself and your family," I said.

"We have had enough trouble!" said Dzhambek. "And the American police are doing *nothing* to solve it! As we always knew they would. They are worse than useless in a matter such as this. So we must take matters into our own hands."

"What are you intending to do?" I asked.

Dzhambek, Dzhokhar, and Shamil shared a glance. "What must be done," said Dzhambek.

"Please," I said. "Why don't we go talk. I know the police chief. He has a life debt before my brother. He will listen to me."

Dzhambek relaxed slightly. "A life debt before your brother? Why did he not listen to you before?"

"He did," I said. "There just wasn't much the law could do. But we can go talk to him again. Perhaps he has news, good news, about the progress of the case. These things take time. But you don't want to spoil your chance at justice against the real culprits by attacking Jamal. He was only slightly involved."

"He knows who did it," Dzhambek said grimly. "I am certain of it. He is simply afraid to tell the truth. His scholarship and his football is more important to him than my daughter's honor."

"Then let us speak with him," I said. "But quietly, peacefully..."

"There he is!" cried Dzhokhar.

Jamal stepped out of the dorm. He was looking back over his shoulder, arguing with someone, and didn't notice the cluster of men waiting for him outside the door until Dzhokhar sprang forward.

"Watch out!" I shouted. Mel, who was the person arguing with Jamal, sprang forward too, past Jamal and straight into Dzhokhar. They collided with a heavy thud and hit the ground, both looking stunned.

Jamal froze. Dzhambek took a step forward.

"Run!" I shouted.

Jamal took in the scene at a glance. Understanding dawned, and he took off towards the volleyball courts.

Dzhambek and Shamil took off after him.

"Stop!" I shouted.

Dzhokhar punched Mel hard in the face and took off after Jamal, limping. I took off after them. Jamal was almost to the volleyball courts. Shamil was showing a fair turn of speed and was only a couple of lengths behind him. Dzhambek was already lagging. Dzhokhar was far behind and unlikely to catch up with any of them. I passed him and accelerated. Jamal was way out of my league, but I might be able to stop Shamil from doing something unwise.

Cheers of "Jamal, Jamal!" were spreading out across the racecourse. I was right behind Shamil. He had something in his hand. Something metallic. Like a knife. I needed to take him down before he got himself into the kind of trouble he couldn't get out of.

We hit the sand of the volleyball courts. Now would be a good time to stop him. There was a group of students in two-part lamb costumes on the other side of the court we were crossing. They showed no signs of moving, and Shamil showed no signs of going around them.

I launched myself at him just as the giant lambs realized this wasn't some kind of funny stunt. The closest lamb screamed, and the students inside tried to run in opposite directions. An enormous woolly rump knocked into me.

I stumbled, stepped hard on my left foot, and twisted around. Something inside my knee snapped. It buckled, making me crumple onto the sand.

Shamil glanced back, then leapt over a lamb that had gotten tangled up in itself and fallen to the ground, and kept running.

I staggered back up. I tried to follow him. Every time I tried to put my left foot down, my left knee buckled. I was never going to catch them. Cunning was called for, or at least backup.

I pulled out my phone, which was still intact, and called Brian.

"Rowena?" he shouted into my ear. "You calling about the men I got running through the middle of the racecourse?"

"Yes," I said.

"O'Hare tried to take 'em down, but they knocked him over and took off again."

I suppressed a groan, as well as a hearty curse. "That's probably assaulting an officer, isn't it?" I asked.

"You're damn right it is. You know who they are?"

Aishat was running over, with Mel, looking confused and dizzy, jogging slowly after her.

"Is that the police?" asked Aishat.

I nodded. She made a resigned shrugging motion.

"Yes," I said. "It's the Aslanbekovs. Aishat's family. They wanted to talk to Jamal. Only...things got out of hand."

"Good news is it looks like Jamal's gonna outrun 'em," said Brian. "Bad news is I'm pissed as hell at all of 'em. Gotta go." He hung up.

"Well," I said. "That didn't go very well."

"No fucking shit," said Mel. She rubbed the back of her neck. "Damn, I feel like I'm gonna pass out or something."

"If you give me your keys, I'll go get the Jeep. There's an unloading zone right over there."

She looked me over. "You able to walk?"

"Not very fast."

"Not at all, looks like," said Mel. "I'll go get the Jeep. You stay here." She set off, weaving slightly and walking like her feet were trapped in molasses.

"I'm really sorry," said Aishat in a small voice. "This is all my fault."

"No, it's not," I said. "It's their fault." I nodded in the direction of where Dzhambek, Dzhokhar, and Shamil were trudging back towards the volleyball courts. Brian and Dustin were walking right behind them. They hadn't cuffed them, but they looked like they really, really wanted to.

"They did it for me!"

My knee was really starting to hurt. "They did it for themselves," I said. "None of this was your fault, Aishat. Don't let them drag you into something you'll regret."

"I regret all of it already," said Aishat. "I wish I had never come to college."

I tried to think of something comforting and wise. But my knee was really hurting now, with a pain that suggested there was something badly wrong with it, and I was feeling more and more irritated with honor-obsessed men who knocked over women in order to get their way, and women who let them do it. Comforting and wise was out of my reach.

"It'll get better," was the best I could come up with.

76

MEL LOOKED A LITTLE better when she came back for me with the Jeep. I was distinctly worse.

Brian collected Aishat and herded all the Aslanbekovs off to the police station. While I was waiting for Mel he said that he wanted to take a statement from all of us. I told him Mel and I were injured and should probably go to Urgent Care. He offered to call an ambulance.

"Hell no," I said. "Ambulances are for rich people. We'll drive ourselves."

"You sure?"

"Damn sure," said Mel, who had come back and was listening to the conversation. "Come on, Rowena. Let's go before your knee gets any worse."

I was wearing running shorts, which showed off my rapidly swelling knee to its best advantage. Mel helped me hop over to the Jeep and climb in, and we took off.

"Whaddya think?" she asked. "Local Urgent Care good enough, or do we need to head to the ER in Macon?"

"I'm sure Urgent Care is good enough for me," I said. "But what about you? Are you still feeling bad?"

"Yeah, but like I said, this is a thing that happens to me. I get too stressed and I go all lightheaded and weird."

"You should still get it checked out. You got punched in the face. You could have a concussion. Speaking of which, should I drive?"

"Nah," said Mel. "I'll be fine to get to Urgent Care."

"Yeah," I said. "Oh shit! The race. We're supposed to be running in the race!"

"No one's going to notice we're not there," said Mel.

"We're the favorites! Karen has told me three times she expects us to win again!"

"Yeah, and I told her four times it ain't happening."

"I doubt she heard you. We need to tell someone. "

"Yeah. Like who?"

We contemplated this problem. I didn't know who was officially in charge of organizing the race, and I certainly didn't have their phone number. I didn't have the phone number of any of the admin-type people I did know.

"I'll call Chloe," I finally said. "Maybe she's there and she can tell someone."

Chloe answered on the first ring. "Where *are* you? The race is about to start! People are talking!"

"Yeah," I said. "We're on our way to Urgent Care. There was an, um, incident before the race."

"An incident!" Suspicion crept into her voice. "This didn't have anything to do with that Jamal boy streaking across campus with a couple of guys running after him like they wanted to kill him?"

"Maybe," I said. "And Mel and I kind of got caught up in it, and now we're kind of messed up and we need to go to Urgent Care."

"Oh. Okay."

"So can you tell someone?"

"I guess...Oh. Here comes Karen."

There was a muffled conversation. Then Karen said, "Give me the phone!"

"Rowena!" she shouted into my ear. "Rowena, are you there?"

I held the phone away from me. "Yes."

"Rowena, *what* are you doing! You and Melissa are the favorites! You're the only representatives from Modern Languages! We *need* you to represent us!"

"Sorry," I said. "We both got pretty badly injured."

"Badly inj...I can't believe you're *that* badly injured."

"I'm afraid so," I said.

"And I hear it has something to do with Jamal Warner running through the racecourse! The rumor is that he was *streaking*."

"Um," I said. "I'm sure he was running very fast. But if you mean streaking in the sense of running naked, he had all his clothes on the last time I saw him."

Karen made a huffing noise. "Well, I have to say, this is *very* disappointing."

"Yeah," I said. "For me too, since I'm currently unable to walk. Oh, here we are at Urgent Care. Gotta go."

Karen made some more huffing noises. I hung up without responding.

77

GREENFIELDS' ONLY URGENT Care clinic, which was in the same strip mall as the radiology clinic I'd taken Mel to last semester, was in a state of Saturday morning somnolence when we arrived. This meant we were able to get seen right away. Hurray for small towns.

Forty-five minutes later I came hobbling out on crutches. Mel was waiting for me in the lobby.

"Oh hey," she said. "Nice look you've got going there. Very badass Olympic-skier-after-a-fall chic."

"Thanks," I said. "They think it's a torn ACL. I'm going to be sporting these babies for a while. You ready to go?"

She grimaced. "They want me to have another CAT scan. Just in case it's a hairline fracture or something."

"Makes sense." I tried to say it cheerfully, although I didn't like the sound of Mel having to have another CAT scan. So far no signs of brain damage had been detected, but her recurring neurological problems on top of a history of head injuries was worrisome. Especially if she was going to be driving me around.

Getting the CAT scan was equally fast. Half an hour later we were ready to head home.

"You want me to drive?" I offered.

"You can't bend your knee. How are you gonna drive?"

"It's my left knee," I pointed out. "The Jeep is an automatic."

"Good point. Sounds like you're gonna be Jeepin' it for a while, since your car's stick. But it's fine. I can drive."

"You sure? Are you still feeling lightheaded?"

"A bit, but it's getting better. I'm probably just hungry or something."

I stopped myself from pointing out that low blood sugar could also be a major driving hazard, and let Mel help me into the Jeep.

"Dang," she said, once we were heading back to Peachtree Estates. "Some Saturday, huh? Bet you weren't expecting anything like this when you got up this morning."

"I think I should be saying that to you," I said. "It was my problem. I just dragged you into it."

"Yeah, no worries," she said. "Besides, getting punched in the face beats running in that race any day."

"There is that," I agreed.

"Plus, we got the shitty stuff over with already. The rest of the day is bound to go great."

"Yeah," I said.

I repeated that to myself as Mel helped me up to my apartment on the third floor. I had always taken my ability to climb stairs and generally move around for granted. Now, with my left knee throbbing painfully and my entire left leg in a brace, I was discovering that even simple operations I would normally do without thinking were excruciatingly difficult, if not impossible.

"You stay there," Mel told me, once I was inside. "Keep your leg propped up, and don't move 'less you have to. If you need anything, give me a call and I'll get it for you."

"You sure you're up for that?" I asked.

"Sure. And helping you out will keep my mind off my own troubles."

"There is that."

"Yeah...this day was already shitty...I got a rejection yesterday from the LA job."

"I'm sorry."

"Thanks. It was a shit job, but it woulda made me feel better to get the offer, you know? Then this morning, outta the blue, I got an email from Jewel."

"Wow," I said. "How come?"

She shrugged. "Psychic vibes? She knew I wasn't coming back to LA, so she decided to reach out and torment me a little? She sent me this email saying she was sorry about how things had ended between us, and she hoped I was okay."

"Gosh," I said. "Did you answer it?"

"Damn right I did. I hit 'Reply' straight away and said I was fine, thanks for asking, and how was she doing. Then I wanted to kick myself from here to Charleston for being like that, but it was too late to take it back."

"Did she write back?" I asked.

"It was six in the morning, LA time, when I left, so no. But now I'm itching to go check my email and see."

"You go do that," I said.

Once Mel was gone, I went to check my own email. Maybe there would be something great in it, that would balance out what I suspected was a life-changing injury to my knee.

As soon as I opened my inbox, my eyes fell on an email from Carmel. An electric shock shot through my stomach. I opened it.

Dear Candidate,

We regret to inform you..

I told myself I wasn't going to cry. I had known it was a long shot all along, hadn't I? And most of the faculty I'd met seemed like real pills. But it had also been my best chance at moving out to California and building a life with Alex. Also, I was pissed that they'd sent me a generic "Dear Candidate" email after I'd made it to the final round of interviews and met with them in person.

I texted Alex with the news. He texted back immediately.

Dammit. That sucks. I'm really sorry, Rowena.

Thanks.

But it sounds like they were assholes to you.

They were, I wrote.

And hey, speaking of assholes, Frank says he really might have a position for you. And I think he doesn't just mean a sexual one, although knowing him he might have something like that in mind too.

Yeah, I got that impression off of him too. But seriously? He might have a job for me?

He sent me a link. I'll forward it to you.

Thanks.

How was the rest of your day? Wasn't today the day of that race? How did that go?

I filled him in on the incident with Aishat's family and our trip to Urgent Care. Instead of texting, Alex called.

"Jesus," he said, when I turned on my video and showed him the brace and the crutches. "That looks bad."

"It's not great."

"No shit. How long are you supposed to wear that thing?"

"Four to six weeks."

Alex winced.

"Minimum," I added.

He winced again.

"So I might still be wearing it when I come back out to Monterey to start teaching."

"Damn."

"Yeah," I said.

"I think you need to go lie down," he said.

"It's the middle of the day."

"The middle of the day on a Saturday where you got knocked down and ended up on crutches."

"I should really look at this job Frank sent me. Maybe this is my big chance."

"I'd love to think so. I'd love to have you out in California with me, especially working a job where you get paid something closer to what you deserve. And I won't lie: the thought of you as an FBI agent is sexy as hell. But right now I think you should take the day off."

"I can try," I said.

78

DESPITE MY PROMISE to Alex to take it easy, the first thing I did after hanging up was look at the job posting.

I had been expecting a search for Russian speakers, but it was for a special agent with a background in education. Well, I had that too, in spades. 50+hour work week, willingness to travel and work evenings and weekends. I didn't have a problem with working evenings and weekends—I did that already. Spending 50+ hours trapped in an office was more of an issue. But the starting salary was a minimum of $62,000. Holy crap. That sounded like a fortune. I remembered the housing prices around Monterey and the Bay Area. $62,000 was barely enough to keep from being a street person. But if Alex and I were living together, it wouldn't be too bad. Provided we didn't do anything irresponsible like have kids. Oh God! How would we survive if we had kids?

I'd never discussed having kids with him. Dima and I had talked about frequently, but never actually taken that all-important next step, since Dima yoyo-ed back and forth between desperately wanting them ("at least two, maybe three or four") and declaring he could never be a father. Alex had never expressed any thoughts on the subject either way. I hoped that meant I could persuade him when the time was right. But moving out to live with him might make having kids with him out of my reach, financially.

I tabled that difficult problem for a later date, and read more about the position. Training and probationary period at Quantico—dammit. I mean, it would probably be a cool experience. But it would mean spending several more months on the opposite coast from Alex. But if I stayed here, that could mean several more years on the opposite coast from Alex.

I was still young enough to apply—barely. I was pretty sure I could pass the physical fitness test. If I recovered from this current setback, that is. The actual documentation required for the first round of the procedure was laughably skimpy. I knew there would be a background check if I made it that far. Hmmm. Well, I'd cross that bridge when I came to it. It wasn't like I'd ever done drugs or run up gambling debts or provided aid and comfort to the enemy. Unless you counted Russians as the enemy, which a lot of Americans did. Was being the former fiancée of someone on the Kremlin's shit list an asset or an obstacle? I guessed I'd find that out too.

My knee was really, really starting to hurt. I wanted to get a jump on the application process, but I was afraid I would be confused by the pain and not know it, and make a stupid mistake. The application was ridiculously short and easy, but I had learned to take even ridiculously easy applications seriously. I shut down my laptop and staggered over to my bed. I would spend the afternoon napping and doing light reading.

Since my bookshopping spree over spring break, Amazon had been overflowing with reading suggestions for me. I scrolled through a few of them, curious. It sent me one about an American woman who gets caught up in a relationship with a troubled Russian man on the run after taking vengeance on the Chechens who murdered his family. I was pretty sure it was going to be terrible, but I downloaded it anyway. Maybe it was better than it looked.

Fifteen minutes later I was staggering into the shower, desperate to cleanse myself physically and spiritually. The relationship dynamics had been offensive, but it had been the prose style that had triggered my gag reflex.

Showering with only one good leg was a cumbersome process that gave me plenty of time to wonder what was wrong with me. Judging by the reviews, thousands of people had loved that book. Why couldn't I? Why was I at cross-purposes with the world?

Although it must be said that the fictional versions of those kinds of relationships made them seem a lot more fun than they actually were. Having actually experienced relationships with men tormented by guilt and PTSD, I had to say that there was a lot less hot sex than the books showed, and a lot more trying to keep him from doing something stupid and listening while he ranted on and on about why he didn't deserve sex and couldn't stand to be touched. But that was the case with most things.

"Maybe the FBI will be different," I said out loud.

Fevronia, who had hidden in the vanity, poked her head out, gave me a sideways glare, and retreated back behind the plumbing, the vanity door slamming shut behind her.

"Thanks for being honest with me," I told her. "I knew I could count on you."

79

I HEARD FROM AISHAT and Brian separately that Brian had let the Aslanbekovs off with a warning. When I asked Aishat if she thought they would heed the warning, she didn't answer. When I asked Brian if he was any closer to finding out who the actual culprits were at the party, he said that the frat's lawyers were doing such a fine job of stonewalling that he doubted he'd ever get permission to investigate the case.

I hated that Aishat was getting punished for doing the right thing, and I especially hated that she had done so on my urging. But I couldn't think of anything I could do about it.

The good news over the next few weeks was that Jamal didn't get arrested. The bad news was that no one else did, either.

Irene, who had retained herself as Jamal's legal counsel pro bono, kept me abreast of developments. Jamal had insisted that he had left immediately after the end of the video up on YouTube. There was reason to suppose that there was a second video, one that showed what had happened afterwards, since Owen had threatened Aishat with it. But when the police finally got a warrant and searched Owen's computer and phone, they weren't able to find either that second video, or the original one, which had since been taken down from YouTube.

The police had saved that first video, but had succeeded only in tracing the account that had posted it back to an anonymous Gmail account, which was different from the anonymous Gmail account that had sent the emails to Jamal and Aishat. Owen was steadfastly denying any involvement in the matter, insisting that the "Owen Wu" who had signed both emails wasn't him, and that Aishat was lying when she said he'd approached her about it in person. Requests had been put in motion to trace the accounts associated with both the emails and the YouTube video, but so far nothing had come of it.

The police had tried to question all the members of Pi Chi. The ones they had spoken to before they got shut down insisted they knew nothing about the video or anything that had happened that night. The fraternity's very expensive law firm was making noise about the video being a setup designed to make the fraternity look bad. Some articles came out in which Brittany Gutierrez was described as a troubled young woman with a history of drug use and questionable immigration status (she had once smoked pot in high school, and her parents had come over from Mexico before she was born to work the local tobacco fields). Aishat was treated slightly more sympathetically—my suspicion that a woman wearing a sign of patriarchal authority on her head would be treated better was correct—but connections between Aishat's family and ISIS were hinted at.

I was afraid that Aishat's family would blame me for this unfortunate, if predictable, outcome, but if they were angry with me, they said nothing about it. And after numerous nights lying awake worrying about it, I still didn't know what else I could have done. I wasn't about to get involved in some scheme of vigilante justice. I didn't have much faith in the judicial system, but taking matters into my own hands, no matter how tempting, was unlikely to turn out any better. Besides, it might get me fired. So I just had to hope that the truth would come out someday.

Since I had no control over the situation, I tried to focus on other things. For instance, congratulating my former student Shaniqua on getting into the Ukrainian program she'd applied to, sending out more job applications, submitting another book proposal when the previous one was rejected, and helping Chloe with her plan to desensitize herself to Bedford Hall by going in on weekends and practicing deep breathing exercises.

We went three times during the end of March and beginning of April. The first time we went and sat on one of the benches in the hallway outside our classrooms. It was the bench Nathan had hidden behind during the shooting last semester. I didn't point this out to Chloe, who had chosen the bench, in case she didn't know.

Maybe she still sensed some kind of psychic vibe from it, because she started getting anxious within seconds of sitting down. We did some deep breathing exercises, which ended up with me coughing until I thought I was going to choke.

"Okay, that didn't go so well," Chloe said. "Let's try in my classroom."

The next weekend we went and sat in her classroom. She spent the entire time alternating between fanning herself and shivering.

"Maybe I'm coming down with something," she said. "That's how I feel."

"Yeah, me too," I said. "I keep thinking I'm going to come down with the crud that's been going around since before spring break, but I never quite do. Although I've been having these weird coughing spells and asthma-y symptoms, so maybe that's what that is."

"Yeah. I don't think this is working today. Maybe we should go. But I want to come back next week. I *cannot* let this beat me."

"Sure thing," I said.

When we came back the next weekend, though, Chloe had a full-blown panic attack that left her sweating and shaking.

"I don't think this is working," I told her as I led her out of the building. I had one hand on her arm and the other shielding my eyes from the April sun. A migraine had started lurking as soon as I'd walked into Bedford, and I didn't want to give it any reason to jump out and get me.

"Oh my God." Chloe stumbled over to a bench by the walkway through the back quad and collapsed onto it, her head hanging. "What am I going to *do*? I can't even go into my own classroom without having a panic attack. I've tried half a dozen anti-anxiety meds, but they all make me so out of it I can't function. What good's a professor who can't think?"

"What does your doctor say?" I asked. "Your therapist?"

"My doctors all say I'm perfectly healthy. Not even diabetes, which runs in my family. My dad keeps talking about hypoglycemia and pre-diabetes, but I monitored my blood sugar for a while and it was normal. My dad says sometimes people get the symptoms of hypoglycemia when their blood sugar levels are technically in the normal range, and maybe that's what's happening to me. My therapist says I'm too caught up in my career and putting too much pressure on myself."

"Well," I said. That was a given for a young tenure-track scholar, and doubly so for Chloe. "Is the therapy helping overall?" I asked.

"No! Now I've started having panic attacks whenever I go to my therapy sessions."

"Maybe you should stop," I suggested. "Maybe they're causing more problems than they're solving."

"But what else am I going to do? I've got to do *something*."

"Maybe you should look into this blood sugar thing some more," I said. "Maybe that's your problem."

"I don't have the time to go traipsing around to doctors again! It's almost the end of the semester, and the deadline for my manuscript revisions is coming right up! Besides, they'll probably just tell me I'm fat and I need to lay off the watermelon and fried chicken again."

"Maybe your dad can find you some decent doctors," I said.

"I just don't want to bother him about it more! He's got enough to deal with already, and I was always the one in the family who didn't cause trouble. I've always been the one he could count on to behave and do well and come through. He doesn't need to be dealing with my panic attacks."

"I'm sure he doesn't want you to suffer when there's something he can do about it," I said. "Meanwhile, can I respectfully suggest that this exposure thing is a bust. Also, I hope you're feeling better, because I'm definitely getting a migraine."

"Oh God. Have you been to the doctor about that?"

"No. Maybe I should."

"I'd tell you that you should," said Chloe, "except I don't have a lot of faith in them anymore. I don't have a lot of faith in *anyone* anymore."

"You can have faith in yourself," I said. I stood up. "But meanwhile, why don't we take a break from this? Maybe we should just try to hang in there until finals are over, and then we can try the exposure thing again if you want."

"Okay." Chloe stood up too. "I'm sure it'll go a lot better once finals are over."

"Oh, definitely," I said.

80

FINALS COULDN'T COME soon enough as far as I was concerned. Teaching in a full leg brace and crutches was even more of a pain than I had thought it would be.

Over the course of three weeks my knee went from hurting like the dickens and keeping me up at night—when my worry about the Aishat situation wasn't keeping me up already, that is—to a dull ache that only bothered me if I jarred it. But I could feel that there was something seriously wrong with it, and that it would be all too easy to wreck it forever. When I really wanted to freak myself out, I Googled "torn ACL," and promptly fell into a pit of despair that helped nothing.

Meanwhile, I was discovering that limping along on crutches caused every other part of my body to hurt, and made carrying two bags full of textbooks, files, and computer equipment somewhere between difficult and impossible. My classrooms were so crowded that I couldn't actually make it to the board with my crutches, and once I got there, I couldn't write and use my crutches at the same time. I ended up leaving my crutches at the door, and then peglegging it around the classroom like an old pirate, holding onto the wall with one hand for balance.

That was the worst, but every action of every day was fraught with danger and difficulty. Going to the bathroom involved doing a one-legged squat on my right leg while holding my left leg out at a 45-degree angle. This maneuver made me develop a deep appreciation for Belarusian gymnast Meletina Staniuta's signature Cossack turns. It also made me develop a deep appreciation for how small most bathroom stalls were. When I was on campus I had to hobble, followed by stricken stares, into the handicap stall in order to be able to spread myself, so to speak, properly. There was probably some kind of excellent life lesson in all of this, but at the moment I was too aggravated to appreciate it.

On the Monday of the penultimate week of class, Karen pulled me into her office. I braced myself. What was she going to do now?

"You're *still* wearing that thing?" were her opening words.

"What? Oh, my brace. Yes. I might be in it for a good part of the summer, actually."

She sniffed, and then broke out into a coughing fit. "I hope you'll be *fit* to return in the fall, Rowena. I've already had to talk to Melissa about it. She's *still* having trouble talking, which is a *major* problem for a language instructor, as I'm *sure* you'll agree. And after both of you stood us *up*, I mean the department, at the Lamb Chop Trot..."

"We were in Urgent Care," I said. "I'm in a full leg brace with a torn ACL. Mel had to have a CAT scan of her head because they were worried she might have a hairline skull fracture."

Karen sniffed again, demonstrating her disdain for trivialities like torn ACLs and skull fractures.

"Anyway," she said. "I need you to sign this." She pushed a piece of paper at me.

I took it and read it. It was a contract for the next academic year. One year, $45,000 plus insurance. Hallelujah.

"In some cases we give a 1% raise," said Karen. "But in your case, since you're still on probation..." She made a motion with her shoulders to suggest that my performance had been so poor that I didn't deserve a raise that was less than a cost of living increase. With my salary staying the same, I would actually have less buying power next year.

"Okay," I said. Feeling a lot more violated than I had two minutes earlier, I signed the contract and handed it back to her. She perused it slowly, as if suspecting I might be trying to pull a fast one on her.

"Everything seems to be in order," she said eventually. "I'll pass this on to the Dean's Office for approval this week. You should get an official letter from them sometime this summer. You're going to be in Greenfields this summer, aren't you?"

"Actually, I'll be teaching at Monterey most of the summer," I said.

"*Monterey*? Monterey, *California*?!? Whatever for?"

"Because I need the money." I said nothing about Alex. I didn't want to mention his name around here, in case it gave her ammunition against me. Also, it felt like it would dirty him in some way to have her know about him.

"You really *should* have asked my permission before accepting another contract, Rowena!"

"When I accepted that contract, the contract I was under with Crimson ended in May," I pointed out. "And the Monterey contract doesn't overlap with the Crimson teaching schedule, and there's no exclusivity clause in the Crimson contract."

Her gray cheeks were going an unpleasant blotchy purple. "I *need* to know the availability of my instructors at *all* times, Rowena!"

"Okay," I said.

That seemed to take the wind out of her sails. She sat there in silence for a moment, her mouth moving as if she were about to say something but couldn't quite get the words out, and then told me I could go.

When I got back to my office, Alicia was waiting for me.

"Oh, hi, Alicia," I said. "Sorry I was out. I had to talk to my department chair. What's up?"

She fidgeted and twisted back and forth for a moment before blurting out, "I need to talk to you, professor."

"Sure." I unlocked my office door. "Come on in."

She followed me inside and sat down in the slightly less stained and rickety of the two chairs for students. She held her backpack in both arms, hugging it like a security toy and twisting the straps with both hands.

"What's up?" I asked again. "You look pretty stressed out, to be honest."

She gave a nervous giggle that threatened to morph into hysterical laughter. "Yeah...I'm having a really hard time...I'm wondering...maybe I need to drop your course."

"You're doing fine in the course. Besides, you can't drop. It's only two weeks until the end of the semester. The withdrawal period ended weeks ago."

"Oh...I didn't know that...I just don't know what to do..."

"So far your grades have been excellent in my class," I told her. I didn't add that I had grave doubts about her final paper, which I was afraid was going to come up with some very questionable and problematic conclusions. That seemed like a conversation for another time. Right now I wanted to prevent her from having a nervous breakdown before my eyes.

"Yeah...I just don't know if I can finish all my projects...finish out the semester...I just...you remember what I told you, about people writing funny stuff, mean stuff, on my dorm door?"

"Of course. Is it still happening?"

"Yeah...and it's getting worse..." She swallowed back tears. "This morning when I got back from my first class, someone had written 'I hope you get lynched' on my little whiteboard."

"Did you report it?" I asked.

She shook her head convulsively, making her cotton-candy pink cloud of hair bounce joyfully around her face.

"Did you take a picture of it?"

"I just...I just wanted it gone!"

"So you erased it," I guessed.

She nodded.

"That's very understandable," I said. "But we can't figure out what's going on if there's no evidence. You need to document it and report it."

"If I do that, I'll be the whiny black girl who turned in her friends for silly microaggressions!"

"I can see why you would be worried about that," I told her. "But 'I hope you get lynched' is a death threat."

"The police probably aren't going to do anything about it!"

"Well...maybe not." They hadn't done much about the death threats I'd gotten last semester, that was for sure. Death threats occupied a gray, liminal legal space, and threats against women and minorities tended to get taken even less seriously than they would otherwise. "But it's still good to document it," I said.

"I don't know how much more of this I can take! I don't think I can take one more horrible thing on my whiteboard!"

"Maybe you should take the whiteboard down," I said.

She looked at me like I'd gone crazy.

"They can't leave threats on your whiteboard if there's no whiteboard for them to leave threats on," I said. "And defacing school property by spray-painting your door might give them pause."

"I'm not going to give in to them!"

"You're not giving in to them," I told her. "You're outwitting them."

That almost made her smile, but only for a moment. "I just don't know how I can focus on my coursework!" she said. "Not with all this going on!"

I wanted to tell her that focusing on her coursework might help her take her mind off her other problems. In my experience, that lecture rarely went down well.

"You can't drop your courses," I repeated. "At this point, your best bet is to tough it out. But perhaps we could arrange an extension on the due date for your final paper, if that would help."

"Yeah...I guess..."

"What if we pushed it back to the end of finals week," I suggested.

"I guess that would help..."

"Let's do it, then," I said. "And as I've told you before, I really think you should report the hateful messages on your whiteboard. Even if the police can't or won't do anything, at least you'll have a paper trail. And you could try to set up a surveillance system. Maybe your RA can set up some cameras, or your neighbors can watch out for you."

"They said they would," she told me, sniffing and wiping her eyes. "They're all my sorority sisters, and Hannah, who's next door to me, said she'd watch out for me. But they haven't seen anything!"

"Is there a specific time when the messages are left?" I asked. "Is it always the same handwriting?"

"It's always when I'm in class. I don't know about the handwriting. Sometimes it's in big block capitals, sometimes it's in cursive. But it could be the same person."

"Documenting it could help," I said. "You could leave your whiteboard up, like bait, and photograph every hateful message, and compare it with the handwriting of the other people in your dorm. How often do you get the messages?"

She sniffled again. "It was about once a week. Lately it's been more like every 2-3 days."

"So, a pattern of escalation," I said.

"Yeah, I guess."

"When did it start to escalate?"

"I don't know...I guess around Easter. I went home for Easter, and when I came back, my board was covered with awful messages. And I've been getting them every couple of days since then."

"Any days in particular?" I asked. "Like, is it a Monday-Wednesday-Friday thing, or a Tuesday-Thursday thing?"

She frowned. "A Monday-Wednesday-Friday thing," she said, after thinking for a moment. "I think it's always happened during my 9:00am MWF class."

"So you know it's someone who doesn't have class then," I said. "That should narrow down the list of suspects."

That earned me a watery smile. "It's like a crime story, huh, Professor Halley?"

"It is a crime story," I told her. "And you get to be the plucky, intrepid girl detective."

"Yeah, I guess. It always seems more fun in books and on TV."

"That is often the way," I said.

"Yeah, I guess so. I still think it must be Aishat, though."

"I asked Aishat about it, and she told me didn't do it," I said. "And I think she has a 9:00am class, anyway."

"She could cut class," Alicia pointed out. "And if she's doing it, she's not going to tell anyone, is she?"

"Good point. Did the handwriting look...foreign? Aishat's handwriting would probably look foreign. And her grammar and punctuation might be a little off. Were there any misplaced commas in the messages? Did the last message say, 'I hope comma you get lynched'?"

Alicia shook her head. "Why would there be a comma there?"

"Because a Russian-speaker would put a comma after 'I hope,'" I said. "Did all the messages look like they'd been written by an American?"

Alicia shrugged. "I guess so. There was nothing foreign about them."

"Foreigners are unlikely to know the vernacular of American racism, too," I pointed out.

"Yeah, I guess. So what should I do?"

"If it were me," I said, "I'd leave the whiteboard out, and then I'd photograph all the messages and track the dates and times they were left. Of course, the best thing would be secret video surveillance of the hall, but that might not be possible. So—if you wanted to really let your inner sleuth loose—you could, I don't know, do something like arrange some kind of an event where everyone on your floor or in the dorm wrote some kind of a message. Like a 'Good luck on your finals!' or 'Congratulations, Seniors!' poster. Then you could compare all the handwriting samples with the messages on the board. Maybe you'd catch your culprit that way."

Alicia was starting to smile. "That'd be pretty lulzy, Professor Halley. I'd love to be a badass sleuth, wouldn't you?"

"Yeah," I said. "And it might not work, but at least it'd give you something to do, and make you feel like you were in control of the situation. Of course, the semester's almost over. You might not have time to carry out your plan."

"Yeah...Oh, hey, Anthony."

Anthony stuck his head in the door. "*There* you are. I've been looking all over for you!"

Alicia smiled. Beatifically, of course. "Thank goodness for Anthony," she told me. "He's been *so* supportive during this whole ordeal, and he's been watching out for me as best he can."

"That's nice," I said. I wondered if I'd ever gazed at a man as soppily as Alicia was currently gazing at Anthony. I hoped not. Maybe one of the reasons I was drawn to damaged, semi-available men was because there was less expectation to stare at them with an adoration more suited, in my opinion, to the better class of deities. I was willing to sleep with the important men in my life, bind my fate to theirs, and hopefully bear their children, but that kind of worship was a hard, hard "no." Which maybe explained why only damaged, semi-available men wanted to have anything to do with me. Men with more normal egos expected women to worship the ground they walked on. Only men filled with guilt and self-loathing could accept a woman who treated them like a fellow human being.

"Somebody needs to take care of you, baby," Anthony was saying. He picked up Alicia's hand and kissed it. "And like I keep telling you, you're my princess."

She giggled. I repressed a gag.

"We should probably get to class," I said, interrupting the scene before it got any mushier. "Thanks for filling me in on what's going on, Alicia, and please let me know if you need any more help, or anything comes up."

"Will do, Professor!" she said. She followed Anthony out of the office, her hand tucked in his arm, letting him pull her along.

81

I WAS AFRAID THAT ALICIA was going to have a meltdown and disappear from class forever, thus turning her grade from an A to an F. It wouldn't be the first time a promising student snatched defeat from the jaws of victory and sabotaged their own success in the final weeks of class. But she came bouncing into every class session over the next week, apparently in high spirits.

My own spirits were pretty high as well. My torn ACL was mending with annoying slowness, but on other fronts, things were looking up. On the Monday of the last week of class, I got an email from the latest publisher I had submitted my book proposal to, requesting the full manuscript.

"Oh my gosh!" Chloe said when I told her. "We could both have books out within the next year!"

"Yeah," I said. "A request for the full manuscript isn't the same as a contract, but it's a good sign."

"I can't *wait* to hold my book in my hands," said Chloe. "Everything has been so tough since I started here, and sometimes it feels like my life is falling apart, but my own book...it feels like if I can just get my book out, my life will have meaning, you know what I mean? Like I've done something worthwhile with my life."

"I know," I said. "Although you can't hang your whole life's worth on something so dependent on other people, especially people as fickle as reviewers and publishers."

"I know. But that's part of the gauntlet, isn't it? It's like being some ancient hero upon whom the gods smile with favor. You're the one who makes it through the maze, or whatever, and gets the prize at the end."

"Yeah," I said. "But statistically, most of us aren't going to make it through the maze. We're going to get eaten by the Minotaur."

She shivered. "Don't say that! We're both going to get our books out, I can feel it. We're going to be heroes."

"Hopefully," I said.

Then on Tuesday I got an email inviting me for an interview and language test with the FBI. They wanted me to come to their offices in Atlanta, so we arranged for it to happen after finals. That meant another two weeks to wait until I could even have the interview and test, followed by weeks or months before I heard back about the results. But it was a good first step. A step down a path I wasn't sure I wanted to take. But finding out more seemed better than running away and avoiding any possibility of it working out.

On Wednesday, the last day of class, Alicia was absent. Anthony volunteered the information that she wasn't feeling well and had decided to stay in her room in case she was coming down with something.

"Poor thing," I said. "Have her email me if she has any questions."

But when I came back to my office after class, Alicia was waiting for me.

"Can I talk to you, Professor?" she asked. She looked furtively over her shoulder, like she was afraid someone might see us together.

"Um, okay. Come on in." I ushered her into my office. I tried to look her over without making it too obvious that's what I was doing. So far I had miraculously escaped all the plagues going around this semester, but it would be all too easy to come down with something during finals week. And I was supposed to set off for California as soon as finals and my interview with the FBI were over.

She slipped quickly into my office and perched on the edge of the chair in the corner, out of the line of sight of anyone walking down the hall. I closed the door. She visibly relaxed.

"Thanks," she said. "I just...I'm so freaked out...and upset...and I don't know who else to go to!"

"What happened?" I asked.

She twisted her hands in her lap, made herself stop, started gnawing on a hangnail, and made herself stop that too. "I did what you suggested," she said. "I left my little whiteboard up, and I took pictures of the messages on it. There were three more mean messages, and I took pictures of all of those, and I also took pictures of all the other messages people left on it, and I compared the handwriting."

She started to sniffle.

"Did you find anything?" I asked.

"No...there weren't any matches, exactly...the mean messages were different each time...but they looked like they were trying to be different, you know what I mean? Like sometimes they'd be in block capitals, sometimes in italics, sometimes in cursive...but they were always kind of similar. My mom's always been interested in handwriting analysis, and when I told her what I was doing, she told me some things to look out for, so I did. And it seemed to me like it was the same person writing them each time. Like, the lines always sloped up, and the Os always had a little curlicue on top, and the upper-case Is always had little, what do you call them, serifs. The letters always looked like they were in italic calligraphy, even when they weren't. So I thought it must be the same person."

I nodded encouragingly.

"So I did like you suggested. I put out a big poster for everyone to leave supportive messages for finals, and I got everyone on my hall to sign it. Then I took pictures of it, including close-ups of the messages, and I uploaded them onto my computer and enlarged them and compared them with the pictures of the mean messages."

I nodded encouragingly some more.

"And then...it's too awful..."

Her shoulders started to shake.

"You figured out who it was?" I guessed.

She nodded.

"It was someone you thought was a friend?" I guessed again.

She nodded and sniffled some more. I waited while she pulled out a packet of tissues, blew her nose, and composed herself a little.

"It was...it was my next-door neighbor," she said in a small voice. "Hannah. She was my Big Sister when I got initiated into Rho Beta Delta! She was the one who was supposed to be watching out for me! And she's Jewish, so she knows what it's like not to fit in here, and to get hate speech and stuff! She *told* me that! She *told* me that sometimes people make Holocaust jokes around her! But she was writing stuff like 'I hope you get lynched' on my door!"

"I'm sorry," I said. "That's awful. Have you reported it yet?"

"What am I going to do? The police will laugh at me if I come to them with my pictures and tell them I've cracked the case with graphomancy! No one takes my mom seriously, and she's good at it! No one's going to believe a word I say about it!"

"This might not be a matter for the police anyway," I said. "But maybe you should bring it up with your sorority and your RA. Have you asked Hannah about it?"

She shook her head. "I want to. I want to ask her why she did it. But I'm afraid of what she'll say. I'm so mad at her...but I'm also afraid people'll laugh at me and tell me I'm crazy. Even if I convince them I'm right, what's my life going to be like then? Hannah's, like, the queen of our sorority, as well as our vice president, and we're all expecting her to be made president next year. At every meeting it's like 'Hannah Reiser this' and 'Hannah Reiser that.' If I accuse her of hate speech, I'll be the one who gets ostracized, even if I'm right."

"Yeah," I said. "I can see how that would be a tough situation. But I still think you need to do something. Do you think you can go to the president for help?"

Alicia hunched her shoulders. "I'd like to think so. But after finding out about Hannah, I'm afraid to trust anyone."

"That's very understandable," I said. "And you might be right not to trust them. I guess the question is whether you'd rather stay in the sorority and put up with this, or leave the sorority and move to a different dorm."

"I can't do that!"

"It might solve your problem," I pointed out.

"It's not fair! I shouldn't have to leave the sorority because Hannah's racist!"

"It's not fair," I agreed. "But you need to think about all your options, and what's most important to you. Have you considered reporting it to the Office of Student Wellbeing? They might have some options for you."

"I guess," said Alicia. Her voice let me know what she thought of that idea. About the same as what I thought of it, which was that it was unlikely to do any good. If she reported it, the most likely outcome would be that nothing would change and she would continue getting hateful messages left on her door. If her sorority sisters discovered what she'd done, she would be, just as she said, outcast, even if she was the victim. Or if the university or the Pan-Hellenic Council decided to use her case to send a message, then she could be responsible for some kind of draconian punishment that shut down the sorority and made her a campus-wide pariah. There were no good options.

"I know it would be a super-awkward conversation," I said. "But maybe you should start by talking with Hannah about it. Give her a chance to explain what's going on, and to apologize. Maybe there's some explanation, like it's a stupid initiation prank or something someone else's making her do. In any case, maybe if you're honest with her about how much it's hurting you, she'll apologize and stop."

Alicia made a face at that idea, but then agreed that it might work better than anything else, and left.

82

I WENT HOME WITH ALICIA'S conversation niggling at me. Not just because I felt sorry for her, which I did. Because there was something she'd said that was bothering me. I just couldn't figure out what it was.

When I got home, there was a message from Galina Ivanovna on my phone.

Darling Innochka! How are you? I suppose you're heard that Dima has gone back to the front?

He told me, I wrote back. Dima had, as usual, been incommunicado for a couple of weeks, before suddenly texting to say he was back in the Donbass.

He can't stay home! And...darling Innochka, forgive me if I'm bringing up something hurtful, but he mentioned something about a woman in Ukraine. Have you heard anything about this?

I've heard. The cousin of a friend. A Canadian citizen. He said—my hands shook as I typed the words—*they might get married. Then he could bring you to Canada.*

He should have asked *me* about bringing me to Canada! But darling Innochka, doesn't it bother you?

Yes. I looked at the word after I'd sent it, sitting there so bold and alone in the message string. Finally, an honest admission of how I felt. I knew it shouldn't bother me. But it did. And I needed to confront that before I agreed to any kind of a long-term future with Alex.

It's his business, I wrote. *His decision. And he'll do what's best for you.*

Hahaha! You know Dimochka! He'll do whatever he wants, and then tell me it's what's best for me.

Well...yes, I agreed.

I'll see if I can't talk some sense into him! He can't bring home a bride without my approval anyway. I need to vet any prospective daughter-in-law very carefully. I put all that effort into making sure you were okay, Innochka, and then he had to...I really should speak to him about it. I'll let him know he can't be running around with strange brides! Especially with a mother in delicate health. Old age is not a pleasure, Innochka.

How is your health? I asked.

You know how it goes. There is talk of this specialist and that specialist, but meanwhile my kidneys are continuing to fail.

Maybe you need to see a specialist in America, I wrote.

If I could get Dimochka to come with me...

Forgot Dima, I wrote. *Come on your own if you have to. I'll help you any way I can.*

Thank you, Innochka. You're a good girl. I'll tell you if there are any developments. But enough about that! Have you been following the season? What do you think of our Olympic prospects?

I've been following a little, I wrote. *They don't show it much in America, so I have to wait for the Russian broadcast to be put up on YouTube.*

Galina Ivanovna was a keen fan of rhythmic gymnastics, which in Russia was a very big deal. She had converted me when I'd been living with them, and we both followed the season and Russia's chances (always excellent) at the major world competitions closely.

But even if I had a TV, which I didn't, American TV rarely showed rhythmic gymnastics, so I was behind.

That's too bad, she wrote. *The World Cup in Pesaro was wonderful. Our Yanochka—do you know the results yet?*

No. But go ahead and tell me. I probably won't be able to watch it for another couple of months anyway.

Well, our Yanochka got the all-around gold. And our Ritochka got the all-around silver. Gannochka got the bronze, and a gold in ball and ribbon as well. I won't hide that I'm worried, Innochka. What if she wins at the Olympics?

The Russian team is very strong, I wrote back. Yana Kudryavtseva and Margarita Mamun were the two strongest Russian gymnasts, and both favored for the all-around title at the Olympics. Meletina Staniuta and the Ukrainian Ganna Rizatdinova were also contenders.

Galina Ivanovna agreed that the Russian team's chances were excellent, and signed off. I stared down at the text string. Whatever had been niggling at me earlier was niggling at me again. But I couldn't figure out what it was.

I made myself start going through the pile of final papers that the 150 class had turned in. The fun of that palled very quickly. I went over my final exam for RUS 102. Everything seemed to be in order.

With my knee still out of commission, I couldn't go for a run or a walk, or do any yoga asanas or hapkido forms. Going through the papers and reviewing the exam had given me the beginnings of a migraine. I could still see okay, but my vision was blurry and shimmery, with flashing lights when I turned my head abruptly. Maybe I needed to just lie down for a while or something.

I went and lay down in bed. I tried to read, but that was even harder on my eyes than working at the computer. Maybe if I just rested my eyes for a few minutes, I could get back to work.

My eyes closed. Then they flew back open. This was intolerably boring. I pulled out my phone and did a search for the Pesaro 2016 World Cup. A bootleg video of Ganna Rizatdinova's ribbon routine came up.

I watched it. She did look like she might give the Russians a run for their money at the Olympics. Her coaches came out, clapping and looking delighted (the younger one), or at least slightly less dour (the older one), at the end of the routine. The commentator, speaking in an East Asian language I couldn't identify, was saying something in an approving tone of voice.

"Oh my God!" I dropped the phone in my excitement, nearly cracking my nose in the process. I sat up. Wouldn't want to hurt myself in my investigatory zeal. I just needed to check... "I am such an idiot!"

83

I JUMPED OUT OF BED, rushed over to my laptop, and started an email to Brian.

Hi Brian,

Did you ever talk to Hannah Reiser about Owen Wu's video? She's Owen's girlfriend, or at least she was last semester. Now Alicia McTighe thinks that Hannah is the one leaving racist hate messages on her (Alicia's) dorm door.

I know it's tenuous. But it struck me as odd. At the very least, Hannah has a close connection with Owen.

Best,

Rowena

I was hoping for a quick reply confirming...something. But the only response I got was a *Thanks for the tip* the next morning, and then silence.

I spent Thursday grading and working on that article I'd promised myself I'd submit before the end of the semester. Now I was promising myself I'd submit it before the end of the summer. I'd fit it in between interviewing with the FBI, moving to California and back, teaching an intensive program, and prepping for my fall classes. Absolutely.

Friday afternoon I held pre-finals review sessions for both my 102 classes. Friday evening I got a call from Irene.

"Rowena honey, how are you doing? Edith tells me your knee is still busted up six ways to Sunday."

"Pretty much," I said.

"I'm so sorry, hon. I've got all my fingers and toes crossed that it heals up real soon. Anyway, sweetheart, I wanted to call and thank you. I hear we've got you to thank for the raid on Hannah Reiser's computer."

"So they went ahead and did it?"

"They sure did, hon. And guess what? They found the video. Not just the bit that was posted on YouTube. They found the whole thing." Irene's voice dropped. "I hear it was pretty bad. Brittany and Aishat...it's good they don't remember it well. The boys took turns...But"—her voice grew stronger—"it proves Jamal is innocent, just as he's been maintaining all along. It shows him leaving right after the YouTube video cut off, and he never comes back."

"That's great," I said. "Have they arrested the people who actually did it?"

"Now, that's the thing, hon. They've arrested Hannah and Owen, but none of the boys in the video took off those dang masks they were wearing. Between that and the poor video and sound quality, it's going to be hard to get a positive ID on any of them. But none of them was Jamal."

"I'm glad to hear it," I said. "Although I'm sorry they haven't found the actual perpetrators. Brittany and Aishat deserve justice."

"You're damn right they do. And I'm going to raise Cain about it, you can be sure. I'm sure there are some who need to be reminded that we've got yet another heinous gang rape getting hushed up, and yet another black man who was almost charged with a crime he hadn't committed. Crimson doesn't need that kind of stink. *Georgia* doesn't need that kind of stink."

"So of course you're going to raise a big ruckus about it," I said.

"You bet your sweet heinie I will.

"Well," I said. "All power to you."

On Saturday I got an email from Miranda.

Hi Professor Halley!

Jamal told me Irene Collins told him you were the one who tipped off the police about Hannah Reiser's connection with Owen Wu and led to them finding the video on her computer and Jamal getting cleared. Thanks so much! Jamal wants to meet with you. Can we meet sometime? What about Monday? Neither of us has any exams on Monday.

Best,

Miranda

I wrote back that I didn't have any exams on Monday either—my exams were Tuesday, Wednesday, and Thursday—and I'd be happy to meet with him.

84

JAMAL AND MIRANDA SHOWED up together at my office at 10:00am on Monday morning.

"Thanks for seein' me, Professor," said Jamal, taking a seat on the slightly less rickety of the two rickety chairs. It still creaked alarmingly under his weight. "I wanted to come an' thank you in person for what you done."

"I'm glad it helped," I said.

"Yeah. An'..." He shifted uncomfortably in his seat. It creaked alarmingly again. He looked more relaxed than he'd been during our previous meeting, but beaten down, like he had things weighing on him. "I wanted to ask if you'd, like, send a message from me to what's-her-name. That other girl who was...the one in the hijab."

"Aishat," I said.

"Yeah, her. I already tried to write to Brittany. Ain't heard nothin' back from her yet, but even if she got my message, I can't blame her for not wantin' to speak with me. An' I wanted to do the same for that other girl. I wanted to tell her I ain't got nothin' 'gainst her family for comin' after me. I'da done the same if it'd been my little cousin who got...you know. An' I wanted to say...sorry. Wait." He held up his hand to forestall any objections Miranda and I had been about to make. "I know I ain't the one who...you know. But I was there. I was part o' that group, you know what I'm sayin'? I was part o' that, I guess you'd call it...I don't know...atmosphere or

374

somethin'. I was one o' the ones makin' jokes about girls and treatin' 'em like they didn't matter an' they wasn't people an' shit like that. I was just goin' along with what all those frat boys was doin'—but the boys on the team talk shit like that all the time too. I used to think it was funny. Now it makes me sick to my stomach. An' I know if I go pro it ain't gonna be any better."

"Probably not," I agreed. "But it's good that you're realizing this now. And I'd be happy to pass on a message from you to Aishat and her family."

"Yeah. Thanks." He shifted again. The chair threatened to collapse, but held firm. "I guess maybe I better write it down." He smiled briefly. "You might not think it to listen to me, but I can write pretty good."

Miranda nodded eagerly. "It's true. Jamal's an excellent writer."

"I'd be happy to forward your message to her," I said. "And I'll pass on my own message that you were genuinely sorry about what's happened to her."

"Thanks. 'Cause...I didn't do it, but I fuckin' walked away, didn't I? I was part o' that crowd. In my eyes, that makes me guilty."

"Contrition for genuine sins is important," I said. "But don't let it destroy you. You did pretty well under the circumstances. A lot of people go against everything they think they stand for when they get their first little taste of power, get their first introduction to the in crowd. But you walked away."

"Yeah. I know. But I been thinking...maybe I need to become a spokesman or somethin'. Speak out against the culture of sexual assault in sports or somethin'."

"That would be noble of you," I said. "It would take this bad thing and turn it into something good. But it would be a very tough row for you to hoe."

Another ghost of a smile flickered across his face. "Yeah. An' maybe while I'm at it, I'll start speakin' out against police harassment o' black folks. Then everyone'll really hate me. 'Cause like I said, if you're a black man in America, they love you as long as you're all about wearin' bling an' sellin' coke an' slappin' hoes. Speak out against it, an' that love'll turn to hate quick as that." He snapped his fingers.

"I know," I said. "But someone's still got to speak out."

"Yeah. An' it might as well be me." He stood up. "Thanks, Professor. I'll send you that email tonight or tomorrow, okay? An' you tell that Aishat girl that if she ever wants to talk to me, I'm here. I ain't gonna run away again."

"Will do," I said.

85

ASIDE FROM THE BLINDING headache that hit me during Wednesday's exam (RUS 102-001) and left me still groggy and out of it for Thursday's exam (RUS 102-002), my finals went smoothly. Everyone showed up more or less on time and turned in their exams in a more-or-less completed state.

Jamal emailed me his message to Aishat, which was indeed both eloquent and heartfelt, on Tuesday morning during the 150 exam. I promptly forwarded it to her, but got no response. Well, maybe she didn't feel like dealing with it right now. I found people who didn't at least have the decency to tell you they were sick/busy/suffering from crippling depression/etc. and would get back to you soon to be profoundly irritating, but there wasn't a lot I could do about it.

Mel and I carpooled in together for our Thursday exams, which were in the 12:00-3:00 slot. I was holding a regular pencil-and-paper exam, but Mel was having the students present their final projects. This meant I was out of there by 1:30, but Mel expected it to take the full three hours, if not more.

If the weather had been nicer and I had been more mobile, I might have skived off and gone for a run or something. But I was still in a full leg brace, and there was a major storm warning for the afternoon. Inside was better. I was planning to use that time to get some grading done. It wouldn't be fun to spend an hour and a half grading exams in that stuffy office, but it would concentrate the mind. Or so I told myself.

My mind might have been concentrated, but my students' minds were not. Half the RUS 102 students had written "I piss Russian-style" instead of "I can write in Russian." And that was only the start of their troubles.

More or less repressing the moans of agony and despair that kept threatening to burst forth from my lips at every fresh outrage against the Russian language, I worked away at the RUS 102 finals. Since I'd gotten a lot of them done while proctoring the actual exam, I was finished with them by 2:40. No sign of Mel. I reached for the pile of RUS 150 finals.

I was just settling into an essay on "Sonay Mamerladovna, the heroine of Chekhov's great post-modernist novel *Anna Karenina*," when there was a knock at the door.

"Come on in," I called.

I was expecting it to be Miranda, or possibly Jamal, or perhaps Jessica, who was all in a state to know her final grade, even though—as I'd explained to her on at least three occasions—she could be in a coma for the final exam and still pull a B for the class. But it was Anthony who appeared in my door.

"Oh, hey, Anthony," I said. "What's up?

"Oh hi, Professor Halley," he said. He continued standing in the doorway, his back to the light, instead of coming inside. I was struck once again by how tall he was.

"I'm still in the process of grading, I'm afraid," I said. "I probably won't have final grades for anyone until tomorrow at the earliest."

"That's okay. I'm not here about that, anyway."

"Okay," I said. "What are you here for, then?"

He shifted from foot to foot. "It's about Alicia," he said eventually.

"What about Alicia?" She'd come to the Tuesday final, and turned in her final paper, even though her extension had been until Friday. As far as I could tell, she was upset about what Hannah had done, but knowing the truth had allowed her to pull herself together and focus on her schoolwork again.

"She's...um...I think she might...hurt herself."

"Have you called anyone? Where is she?"

"I don't want to get her in trouble."

"More trouble than suicide?" I said. Maybe it was just undergraduates being overdramatic. But suicide was common enough amongst college students that I was going to take it seriously. "Where is she?" I repeated.

"She's...uh...you know The Hollow?"

"Uh-huh."

"Yeah...so...I think she's there. She was talking about...like...going out there and maybe taking a bunch of pills or something. She's on anti-anxiety meds and she said she's been saving 'em up. That's dangerous, right? You can kill yourself with Ativan, right?"

I stood up, knocking a stack of ungraded exams onto the floor. "If you really think she's in danger of hurting herself, you need to call 911," I said. "Right now."

He gave me a pleading look. "If she's just out there to, like, think or something, she'll never forgive me."

"And that's worse than killing herself?" I said.

He gave me another pleading look. Probably death seemed abstract to him, while a breakup was the worst pain he could imagine.

"You're her favorite professor," he said. "Can't you come out and talk to her? It'll be faster anyway."

I peglegged over to my crutches. "It might not be faster," I said. "But I'll go anyway. Come on."

Anthony led the way out of Bedford at a pace I was hard pressed to keep up with. I crutched along after him, panting, across a corner of the back quad. We dodged the crowds of players in the beach volleyball courts, crossed the road, and went into the copse.

We picked up a narrow trail through the woods. It was early May and everything was already lush and jungley. Within a very few paces we were out of sight of the rest of campus. It was hard to remember that the little patch of woods we were in was only a couple of acres at most, surrounded by a semi-urban setting. It felt like we had fallen back in time to some primeval, dinosaur-age forest.

The path split. Anthony took the right fork. It split again. This time he took the left fork. It seemed like we should have passed through the copse already and come out the other side, but there was no sign of the edge of the woods. The air was damp and dark and heavy, with the promise of summer's first real thunderstorm hanging over our heads. I was panting hard now, trying to keep up with Anthony on the rough terrain with my crutches, and my chest felt tight, like I was about to go into a panic or have an asthma attack.

Abruptly, we came out into a small clearing. I looked around. No sign of Alicia.

"She's not here," I said. I looked around again. "I thought The Hollow had benches," I added. "And a firepit."

Anthony turned around, faster than I was expecting. "We must have gotten lost," he said. "Can you loan me your phone so I can try to call her? I think I left mine in my dorm."

I stepped closer to him, holding out my phone. "What's that in your hand..." I jerked back. Anthony was holding a syringe full of clear liquid in his right hand.

"What are you doing?" I demanded. Stupidly. But I felt so slow and stupid. I was still having trouble breathing, and I couldn't make sense of what was happening. "Is that an EpiPen?" I asked, my brain jumping to the first semi-logical conclusion it could. "I don't need it. I don't actually have asthma."

"It's not an EpiPen," said Anthony. He smiled. All my hair rose up all over my body. "You can kill yourself with Ativan, right?" he said, with the same anxious intonation he'd used earlier. He smiled again. This time his eyes were full of eager anticipation for something terrible.

My brain clicked back on. I was leaning on my crutches and holding my phone in my left hand. I one-thumbed it onto the login screen and hit "Emergency."

"Stop it!" Anthony took a step towards me. I jabbed at him with my right crutch. He jumped back. I hit "911."

Anthony lunged at me, trying to grab the phone. I cracked him across the shin with my right crutch, making him howl in pain. I hit "Call."

"911, what's your emergency?" said a crackly voice.

"Crimson College Campus, The Hollow!" I shouted. "He's trying to kill me!"

Anthony lunged at my phone again. I knocked his hand aside and overhand-threw the phone as hard as I could into a luxuriant patch of poison ivy.

For a moment he froze. I could see him thinking. Go after the phone, which would mean turning his back on me and diving into the poison ivy? Or take me out now, even if the phone was still potentially on, with 911 recording everything?

"Where's Alicia?" I shouted. My chest still felt tight, but I had lots of practice with voice projection. Surely if the phone was still on, it was picking up everything loud and clear. "Is she here in the woods with us? Did you lure her back here and inject her with Ativan too? Your 'princess,' isn't that what you called her?"

"She's still my princess," said Anthony. "She just has to stop asking so many questions."

"Questions about what?"

Anthony lunged at my left, syringe raised. I whacked at him again with my crutches. He was a good six inches taller than me and under other circumstances would have better reach. But the crutches gave the advantage back to me. Until they tripped me up.

As if the thought had conjured up bad luck, my left crutch got caught on an exposed root. I stumbled and almost went down. My right leg was already weak and shaky from the fast walk over here, and my left leg was still close to useless.

Anthony jumped towards me. I dropped the left crutch. He got tangled up in it, cursing and almost dropping the syringe.

Now! I scythed my right crutch across his body with every ounce of vicious strength I could summon. It connected with his left upper arm with a solid *thwack*, followed by the *crack* of breaking bone. Anthony yelled in shock and pain and went down completely.

I took off down the path in a sideways half-gallop, vaulting myself along with my remaining crutch. Vines and underbrush reached out like living things, threatening to trip me up in their snares. I leapt over them with the agility of an Olympic hurdler and kept going. The back quad was only a few hundred yards away. If I could just reach it, I would be safe. The back quad would be filled with hundreds of people. Anthony would never dare attack me there.

The air changed. All the leaves turned inside out, like the sky had taken a sudden sharp breath. Lightning flashed, so bright it left blinding afterimages, followed immediately by a crack of thunder so loud it made my ears ring. Rain poured down like Thor's own spigot had been opened wide just above my head.

Keep going! I continued down the path in my lurching sideways half-gallop. The thin layer of forest loam had worn through on the path, revealing slippery red clay. I was slithering as much as running.

I came to the first fork. Thank God. My hair was plastered to my face and getting in my eyes, but I didn't have time to push it back.

Through it and the pouring rain, I could just make out the second fork in the path. I picked up speed.

"AAAARGH!" Anthony came charging out of the woods and barreled straight into me, knocking us both to the ground. Lightning flashed again, glinting wickedly off the syringe in his right hand.

86

I WENT DOWN ON THE wet ground with a juicy *splat*. Anthony was on top of me, his right hand raised up high to come down and plunge the syringe into me at full force.

I bucked underneath him, throwing him off-balance and causing him to miss when he jabbed the syringe down at me. He raised his arm again.

Try to catch it? In any kind of a straight-up wrestling match, Anthony was sure to win. He was six inches taller than me, and on top. But his broken left arm was hanging down limply in front of my face. I heaved myself up just enough to sink my teeth into his left forearm.

He screamed and tried to jerk his arm away from me. What he succeeded in doing was pulling me up as he fell half onto his side. I shoved him the rest of the way over and jumped to my feet.

Keep running or stay and fight? I knew I had to be only a few dozen yards from the edge of the copse. My crutch was underneath Anthony. I couldn't run or fight without it.

Anthony hauled himself to his knees without using his hands. His left arm was nonfunctional from the blow I'd given him earlier and the bite I'd given him now. He still had the syringe clutched in his right hand. His right hand looked fine.

"HEEEEEELLLLP!" I screamed. Thunder cracked, drowning out my voice. I tried again. "HEEEELLLLLLLP!"

Anthony froze. Excellent. People often underestimate the value of a good loud scream in self-defense. With any luck, my voice had carried to the dorms and the beach volleyball courts, and people were already heading our way to investigate. I turned to start hobbling off as fast as I could.

"Anthony? What's happening?"

I stopped. Alicia stepped out of the trees. She was soaked with rain and streaked with mud, and she wavered as she walked. Her voice was slurred and confused.

"Get back, baby!" he shouted.

Alicia's eyes tried to focus on me. "Professor Halley?" she said. "What are you doing here? What's going on?"

"She attacked me!" Anthony said. He pushed himself to his feet. Lightning flashed. I could feel the crack of thunder that followed as a shock wave on my skin.

"Alicia, get out of here!" I yelled. "Get out and get help!"

"Anthony?" she said in a little-girl voice.

"Just get back, baby," he said. His voice was low and soothing. "I know you don't feel great right now. Go lie down for a bit and everything'll be better."

"Was I...drugged?" she asked.

"You did it yourself, baby. Don't you remember? You said you were so upset about everything that you just wanted to end the pain."

"No." Alicia shook her head, almost making herself fall down. She caught onto a tree trunk and held herself upright. "I wouldn't have done something like that."

"You were hurting real bad after what you found out about what Hannah did, baby."

"Hannah," Alicia repeated slowly. "Hannah...I talked to her..."

"And then you were real upset, baby, and you came out here to...end the pain."

"No," said Alicia. She was steadier on her feet now, and her voice was growing stronger. "No. I came out here because I wanted to talk to you, and I didn't want anyone to overhear what I had to say. Because I wanted to ask you about what Hannah said."

"I know, baby. She hurt you real bad. I get that."

"She did hurt me real bad. But she did so because you told her to."

"What? No, baby, no. You're confused. Or she's lying. You're my princess. I'd never do anything to hurt you."

"She told me you made her leave those messages on my door. It was all your idea. She told me you blackmailed her. You had a video of, you know, you having *sex* with her"—Alicia's voice rose until it cracked in a painful shriek—"you made her have sex with you on video as part of the initiation process. And she kept talking about another video you made her keep on her computer. Something about Owen Wu and Brittany Gutierrez. Anthony, what did you have to do with Brittany Gutierrez?"

"Nothing, baby, nothing. Brittany Gutierrez was nothing to me."

"Brittany was a Rho Beta Delta, just like me and Hannah. You made her have sex with you, didn't you? That's what you do to all the RBD girls you like! That's what you were going to do to *me*. You were going to force me to have sex with you on video, weren't you? Or were you going to *drug* me first, like you did Brittany? Is that...oh my God...is that...is that what you were going to do *here*? Oh my God, Anthony! Were you planning to drug me and rape me in The Hollow, and then post the video for everyone to see?"

"No, baby, no! Never. I'd *never* do anything like that to you. You're not like those other girls."

Alicia's face softened for a moment. Then it filled up again with stark thoughts.

"You made Hannah write those messages," she said. "She cried when she told me about it. She told me she wants to die after what you did to her, and what you made her do."

"Baby." Anthony took a step closer to Alicia. She didn't move. He took another step towards her. "All I ever wanted was to be with you. Everything I did was to be with you."

He took another step towards her. Thunder cracked again, a little farther off but still loud enough to cover up the sound of me hopping forward and grabbing my crutch.

"All I ever wanted was to be with you," Alicia said. She gave him an imploring look. "I just don't understand. And then you brought me out here, and you..." She looked at the syringe in his hand. "Anthony, did you *inject* me with something?"

"No, baby, no..."

I took a step in his direction. Even hopping and dragging myself along as I was, the sound was masked by the rain. I took another step.

"You did," she insisted. "I'm remembering it now. You brought me out to The Hollow, and then you *injected* me with something. You *were* planning to drug me and rape me. Oh my God, Anthony! I trusted you! I *loved* you!"

"And I love you, baby." Anthony's voice was breaking up, sounding like he was about to cry. "You were getting hysterical, baby. I had to calm you down."

"What did you give me, Anthony?"

He glanced down at the syringe in his hand. "Just a little lorazepam, sweety. Just enough to calm you down."

"You *drugged* me! Get *away* from me!"

Anthony was now within arm's reach of Alicia. He lunged at her with the syringe. She slapped his hand away. He lunged at her again. She screamed, the sound full of terror and primal rage, and gave him a hard shove on the chest, knocking him off-balance. I whipped my crutch into the air and smashed it into the back of his head.

87

ANTHONY COLLAPSED TO the ground like a polled ox. Had I killed him?

"Run to campus and get help," I told Alicia. "I'll stay here with him."

She was staring down at him with eyes that filled half her face. "I can't believe I did that," she said. "I can't believe *you* did that. But he was so scary...like he'd become a monster."

"He had. And real monsters need real heroes to slay them. Now run and get help!"

"Oh. Yeah." She set of towards campus, weaving slightly but heading in the right direction.

Anthony groaned. Looked like I hadn't killed him. Relief washed over me. Then I felt guilty for feeling relief. I shouldn't feel bad about protecting myself and Alicia from a serial rapist who had wanted to kill me. But I still didn't want to be a killer.

Anthony groaned again and made aimless motions. Had I shattered his spine when I'd hit the back of his head?

"Stay still," I told him.

He muttered something incoherent and tried to sit up. Guess his spine was still okay. I pushed him back down with the tip of my crutch and held him there until Alicia came back with EMTs and all three members of campus police.

Anthony was cuffed to a stretcher and carried away, still muttering incoherently. When they lifted him up, they found the syringe. He'd fallen on it and appeared to have injected part of it into his arm before breaking the needle. That should keep him nice and calm for a while.

Dustin O'Hare went and found my phone. It was still on, with 911 still on the line. He thanked them, hung up, and gave the phone back to me. I texted Mel to tell her what had happened and why I wasn't there to meet her.

"We'd already gotten a call from 911 that somethin' was happening in The Hollow," Brian told me. "So we were ready when Miss Alicia here came lookin' for us."

Alicia smiled. Wanly, not beatifically. She looked bedraggled and extremely miserable. When one of the EMTs draped a blanket over her shoulders, she burst into tears.

"I think she was drugged," I told them. "Maybe with lorazepam."

"Why don't we go get you checked out, hon," the EMT told her, and started leading her out of the woods.

"What about you?" Brian asked me.

"He wanted to inject me with lorazepam," I said. "But I don't think he ever actually got me with it. He just knocked me down."

"You gonna be able to walk back?" he asked. "Or we need to get another stretcher out here for you?"

"I can walk back if you give me my crutches," I said.

By the time I hobbled out of the woods, the storm was over and watery, post-storm sunlight was coming through the clouds. Brian insisted on both me and Alicia getting full physical exams, including drug testing. In Macon, since they had a proper hospital. Dustin would take us.

Mel found us and insisted on following us to Macon so that she could drive us back. Dustin and I both said she didn't need to, but when I finally got out of the exam room in Macon Presbyterian three hours later, after being examined all over and having various fluids taken away for analysis, I was glad she was there to drive me home.

"'Course," she said when I told her. "You drove me here. Seems like driving you back is the least I could do. How're you feeling?"

"Very sore." My knee had been re-injured and was worse than before. The rest of me was pretty banged up as well. I was wet, dirty, exhausted, and starving. And I'd hit a student on the head hard enough to knock him out. Granted, he deserved it. I didn't know which made me feel worse: that I'd hurt a student, or that I'd been teaching someone who was probably a serial rapist.

"You knew it was the case," Mel told me when I said all this to her. "We all know that some of our students are creepy little rapists. It's just that most of the time we can shut our eyes to it 'cause we don't know which ones they are."

"Yeah. But from what I got from what he said, he'd forced Hannah Reiser to have sex with him and then blackmailed her with the video, he was probably one of boys who attacked Brittany and Aishat, and who knows what else he's done. And he drugged Alicia. Who knows what he was planning to do to her. And the creepiest thing of all is that I think he really did love her, in his own sick way. I think he was totally sincere when he told her she was his princess. And he was willing to drug her and maybe kill me in order to keep her from leaving him."

"Men are sick as shit," said Mel. "You should really consider taking up the Sapphic lifestyle."

"It's sounding pretty good right about now," I said.

She glanced over at me. The right side of her face was towards me so it couldn't emote much, but I was pretty sure a flicker of a smile made her lips twitch. "You ever want to act on that, you just let me know."

"Will do," I said.

88

MY DRUG TESTS CAME back clean. Anthony had never gotten me with his syringe, just as I'd thought, and my life of impeccable virtue meant that everything else was clean as well. I hadn't had so much as a poppyseed bagel in the previous week.

From what I gathered from the news, cryptic hints Brian dropped, and Irene's energetic efforts to gather information on Jamal's behalf, some of which she shared with me, Anthony and some of the other boys at Pi Chi had indeed been running a "rape club." Sometimes they'd forced girls from Rho Beta Delta, their sister sorority, to have sex with them as part of their initiation, as had happened with Hannah Reiser. Sometimes they'd drugged girls at parties and raped them, as had happened with Brittany and Aishat.

Owen Wu had broken his silence once Anthony had been arrested. According to Owen, he'd been lonely and out of place until Anthony approached him about joining Pi Chi. Then one thing had led to another, and Owen had found himself acting as cinematographer for increasingly violent sexual assaults. He was now giving the names of all the boys involved in the hopes of leniency when the case went to trial.

By Monday *The Washington Post* had published an in-depth article about it, with references to sources who claimed that Anthony was procuring the drugs via Security Solutions, who kept a large collection of sedatives on hand to use as chemical restraints on difficult or inconvenient prisoners. Anthony had just expanded that into using them on his targets.

But being a rapist doesn't preclude falling in love, it just means that you'll do it in a rape-y way. Anthony had decided that Alicia was his "precious princess," and in order to keep her he'd blackmailed Hannah into leaving hate messages on her door so that Alicia would be afraid of everyone else on campus and rely more on him.

Then when she'd found out about it, he'd fallen back on his regular MO and drugged her when she'd confronted him. What he was planning to do then—other than silence me—was unclear. Maybe he hadn't known either. Thinking that the love of your life is about to leave you can make you do some pretty crazy things.

"Promise me you'll never treat me like a precious princess," I told Alex, when we were hashing it out one evening over the phone. "And absolutely no mushy, lovey-dovey stuff! Men who do that can't be trusted."

He laughed. "I hope you know me well enough to know I don't do mushy, lovey-dovey stuff. It's always been a major weak spot of mine."

"And thank God for that."

"Yeah. How's your knee? Are you going to be able to make the drive out to California?"

"I hope so. I can shift gears—sort of."

"Maybe you need to trade that car in for an automatic. And while you're at it, get something a little newer and more reliable."

"You got an extra $15,000 lying around for a new car?" I asked.

"Good point. Well, do the best you can. I'm sure Fevronia can help."

"I'm sure." I tried to pet Fevronia, who was lying next to me on the bed. She hissed and swiped at me with her claws. "She's always watching my back."

"I can tell. What's going on with that Jamal kid?"

"He's already given two press conferences, apologizing for his part in what happened, pledging to dedicate himself to raising awareness of sexual assault in sports, and expressing dissatisfaction with the fact that the best way for a black man to do well in America is by acting as a shill for materialist consumption and an enforcer of patriarchal oppression. Although he didn't put it in quite such PhD-y words."

"Well, it is a dissatisfactory state of affairs. How's the university responding?"

I groaned a little. "Officially, they're 100% behind him and expressing support for his initiative. Unofficially, his days might be numbered. Can't have athletes going around speaking out against sexual assault and racial injustice left, right, and center."

"Fuck no. Although I hope we're wrong in this case. And what do you think: was Anthony just using him for his own sick purposes? Or was he sincere about trying to help him and address injustice?"

"If you ask me, a bit of both," I said. "My take on Anthony is that he's a needy narcissist. He wanted other people's love and adoration, and he preyed on people in difficult circumstances in order to get it. I didn't fail to notice that the girls he went after were Hannah Reiser, who's Jewish, Brittany Gutierrez, who's Hispanic, and Alicia McTighe, who's black. None of them fit in very well on Crimson's super-WASP-y campus. He was able to manipulate them, as well as Owen and Jamal, into thinking he was their friend by saying the things they really needed to hear when they were feeling like outsiders. And I think he really did care about them, in a way. After all, they gave him what he needed too."

"Ugh. Criminals and psychos. Speaking of which, when's your interview with the FBI? Tuesday?"

"Tuesday," I confirmed.

"You gonna be able to make it to Atlanta?"

"I think so," I said. "It'll be a good dress rehearsal for the drive out to California next week."

"I'd tell you to break a leg, but you've already done that, or near enough, so I'll just wish you good luck."

"Thanks," I told him.

The drive out to Atlanta was tiring, as was navigating the giant office building on crutches. Even a minor, temporary disability was turning out to be a giant pain in the ass. Still, I thought both the interview and the multi-hour language test went well. I was told they'd get back to me, maybe in a few weeks, maybe in a few months, with the results, and if they were favorable, we could move on with a second language test and a polygraph.

Wednesday morning I submitted all my final grades. Wednesday afternoon, as I was basking in the glow of having finished everything for the semester, I got an email. From the publisher who had requested the full manuscript. They were interested in offering me a contract.

I wrote back to say I was very interested in a contract too, and could they please send me the terms. Then, since hobbling down from the third floor to go outside was an ordeal, I sat by the window and looked out onto the sunny world below me. For the first time in a long time I felt optimism rising up within me. I would publish my book, and it would be good. Opportunities would come my way, maybe in academia now that I was going to be a published author, maybe with the FBI. I would make my peace with the situation between me and Dima, free myself from all that painful history that was holding me in its grip, and Alex and I would build a future together. I could feel it all just on the horizon, promising that at long last, something was bound to go right.

My phone *pinged*. I checked it. A text from Alex had come in. *Frank just shot Erin.*

THE END

*What will happen next? Get **Total Immersion**, the next book in the series, to find out! Just scan the QR code below:*

*And if you'd like to know what Dima's been up to, you can get the free novella **Spring Break** about his adventures in St. Petersburg and sign up for my newsletter (but only if you want to! by scanning the QR code below:*

From the Author

LIKE IN ALL THE BOOKS in the Doctor Rowena Halley series, much of what takes place in *Honor Court*, while fiction, was inspired by things in the "real" world. Many people have contributed to this story, some directly, many indirectly.

I should start by extending my sincere thanks to Marnie, Natasha, and Paul for sharing their knowledge of the area around Monterey, and their suggestions for what Rowena and Alex should see and do there. More sincere thanks are due to Rod for giving me tips on Jamal's hairstyle. And finally, I must credit my student Clint with the phrase (and the insight) "The problem with stereotypes is that they're true!"

When thinking about this series as a whole, and this book in particular, one of the driving forces I identified behind it was a desire to figure out "what happened?!?" that would cause the results of the 2016 US presidential election. I realize that's a political statement and many of my fellow authors would advise me to steer far, far away from politics, but in case you hadn't noticed, these stories are all about politics.

Or rather, it would be more accurate to say that they're about today's America and this wild moment in history in which we find ourselves, and politics play a huge part in that. So the characters in *Honor Court* contemplate the cultural and political milieu surrounding them, and respond to it in their different ways.

Although *Honor Court* is entirely fictional, it is, like all the novels in this series, flavored by my personal experiences. In this case, alongside personal experiences, a lot of reading and research went into this book. For insight into the lives and experiences of modern Chechen women, Paul J. Murphy's *Allah's Angel's: Chechen Women in War* was a very valuable text, as was Åsne Seierstad's *The Angel of Grozny: Orphans of a Forgotten War*, and of course Anna Politkovskaya's works, especially the two collections of her articles on the Second Chechen War, *A Dirty War* and *A Small Corner of Hell*.

Insight into the US's program of torture was gleaned from Eric Fair's excellent *Consequence: A Memoir*, in which he describes how he went from an idealistic young man who wanted to serve and protect, to operating an interrogation booth at Abu Ghraib and other black sites. Another enlightening, if spine-chilling, book on the topic is *Enhanced Interrogation*, by James Mitchell, who helped develop the CIA's "enhanced interrogation" program and who personally "interrogated" a number of people.

I should also give a shoutout to the WRITERSDETECTIVE: Q&A Facebook group, whose knowledgeable members patiently answered my questions about the law surrounding evidence and warrants.

All of these people and works have been extremely useful to me, and I am immeasurably grateful to them for their help. All inaccuracies and errors are, of course, my own.

Sid Stark

About the Author

SID STARK LIVES A LIFE very similar to her characters', only with more grading and fewer exciting chase scenes. She did once get held up in Heathrow on suspicion of being a Russian criminal traveling on an American passport, though, which was fun. She loves to hear from her readers, and can be reached by email at **sidstark@sidstarkauthor.com**, at her website at **https://sidstarkauthor.com/**, on Facebook at **https://www.facebook.com/SidStarkAuthor/**, and Twitter at **@SidStarkAuthor**.

Don't miss out!

Visit the website below and you can sign up to receive emails whenever Sid Stark publishes a new book. There's no charge and no obligation.

https://books2read.com/r/B-A-NVEK-UUQHB

BOOKS 2 READ

Connecting independent readers to independent writers.

Also by Sid Stark

Doctor Rowena Halley
Campus Confidential: An Academic Thriller
Permanent Position: An Academic Thriller
Summer Session: An Academic Thriller
Trigger Warning: An Academic Thriller
Honor Court: An Academic Thriller
Total Immersion: An Academic Thriller
Under Review: An Academic Thriller

Doctor Rowena Halley Boxed Sets
The Doctor Rowena Halley Series Books 1-4: Four Dark Comedy
Mysteries